KILLERS FROM A DISTANCE

KOREA-FALL 1951: COMBAT WHILE TRUCE TALKS STUTTERED

James F. Walsh

KILLERS FROM A DISTANCE

DEDICATED TO ALL WHO SERVED IN KOREA,

GI OR ROK

ESPECIALLY THOSE FROM THE 35TH, 27TH, 24TH AND 14TH REGIMENTS OF THE 25TH INFANTRY DIVISION WHO SERVED IN THE EIGHT ARMY UNDER THE UNITED NATIONS' BANNER AND FOUGHT AT KUMHWA, NORTH KOREA, FALL 1951

AND

TO ALL MILITARY MEN AND WOMEN

WHO SERVED ON BEHALF OF THE UNITED NATIONS AND THE EIGHT ARMY DURING THE KOREAN WAR,1950 To 1953

IN PRAYERFUL MEMORY OF ALL

KILLED IN ACTION (KIA)

WOUNDED IN ACTION (WIA)

MISSING IN ACTION (MIA)

Contents

KUMHWA

WHEN DAWN PUSHED THE NIGHT'S BLANKET TO THE WEST, COMBAT INFANTRYMEN AT KUMHWA SAW A RUGGED TERRAIN OF TWISTED AND CONTORTED HILLS, SOME WITH SLOPES OF NEARLY PERPENDICULAR WALLS CUPPING VALLEYS; TERRACES THAT STEPPED UP THE SIDES OF SOME HILLS LIKE A GIANT'S STAIRCASE; RIDGE LINES THAT HAD FINGERS AS IF FROM UNSEEN HANDS RUNNING DOWNSLOPE TO VALLEYS TO BRAID WITH OTHER FINGERS FROM OPPOSITE HANDS.

HILL 1062- A MOUNTAIN TO THE NORTH ROSE UP FROM GROUND LEVEL LIKE AN ENORMOUS WART.

CHARACTERS

25TH INFANTRY DIVISION, 35TH REGIMENTAL COMBAT TEAM, 1ST BATTALION

DOG COMPANY HEAVY MACHINE GUN (HMG) PLATOON

DOG CP

CAPTAIN BUSIN, LT. BREEZEDALE, MASTER SERGEANT O'HARA, CPL. MINER

3RD SECTION DOG'S HMG

SGT. SINGLETARY

MEDIC DOC BLOCK

DOG 1ST GUN SQUAD: SGT. VAN METER, SQUAD LEADER, FENTON, GUNNER, BRANNAGH, GUNNER. JOE ROK (IM TA SONG), DREAMER, HARVILLE, SWINFORD, LA VIE, DAVIS, BLACZYK, GLORIO, HARRISON, STAG, BROWNLEE,

DOG 2ND GUN SQUAD

SGT. CERVERA, SQUAD LEADER, BAITER, GUNNER, TROUT, REVELS, BILL ROK, JOHN ROK, WATT, STEIN, JONES, PERKINS

CHARLEY COMPANY

THIRD PLATOON, 3RD SQUAD RIFLEMEN

SGT. GRANT, SQUAD LEADER, CRANE, POCASKI, DEMOS, GIBBARD, PAISLEY, AQUILA, CORNEY WICKSTRAND, ODEGARD

CHAPTER ONE
KUMHWA

Brannagh's aggrieved imagination conjured his Dad's face on each simmering roadside idol. The Koreans called them "changsuns." They were being illuminated by baths of troop truck headlights. Was each changsun curling its tense, violent lips around cutting teeth and hissing Dad's scoffs that his son wasn't cut from the basalt of Ireland's Antrim mountains as were the men of the Irish Republican Army; that his son's temper was a maddening disorder that would betray him in Korea's sanguinary atrocities? Was it so? The war Brannagh sought to test these theses was winding down to a dim out tie. He had quit the seminary too late. His crusade against atheistic communism was ending before it started. He'd be a sit down troop under a United Nations' white flag of truce on bleak hills with Dad's aspersions falling like perpetual night shadows over him.

The restless billows of the ghostly mist felt like warm cotton switches as surly against his face as the truck's wood seat against his bottom riding over the corrugated war road to Dog's machine-guns. The chasis of the two and a half ton truck was having a nervous fit as its wheels probed the thick dingy mud and its life pulse of pistons hushed. Brannagh saw, under the glow of distant search lights, long black hills on either side of a wide flat velvet ribbon of river close to clusters of raven dark figures. Was there an entire battalion present to welcome him to North Korea, 20 miles above the 38th parallel?

Something was out of whack! Brannagh could educe that the clusters of soldiers were organized, the men readying weapons and field gear, drawing combat rations and filling canteens. Were they going into battle? They couldn't be! The truce talks were on, at least a week now! Hadn't the clerks in the 35th Replacement Company told him the war would end this August 1951? The Chinese had come to Kaesong to talk. They had been butchered since they intervened in November 1950!

Coming toward the truck he saw a form that looked to be a hunk of log sawed out of a tree trunk, maybe close to a six footer with shoulders two arms stretched might not span. This soldier's night black hair curled about his forehead beneath his helmet's lip, as if to contradict a weathered, puffy, homely down country face.

"Staff Sergeant Van Meter," the robust troop boomed. "Are you Brannagh," he asked?

"Yes, Private Dan Brannagh."

"You got here just in time. We're moving out on the last attack against the Chinese."

In all of Brannagh's six months in the army, he had hurried, then waited. Nothing went off on time back stateside. He was always hurried so he could wait hours for the allegedly scheduled exercise. In Korea damned if the replacement company didn't see fit to rewrite that dictum. He was hurried onto the troop truck to make a jumpoff. Glory to the rear echelon!

"Attack," Brannagh echoed incredulously?

"Attack it is, Brannagh," growled a baritone in reply.

Brannagh gave thanks his sergeant remembered his name, but he wanted Van Meter to remmember his face, too.

"Sergeant," Brannagh adjured, "look at me. I've

got freckles all over my face. Here," he pointed to the right side of his neck, "see this enormous freckle; it's my birthmark. Take a look at my hair." He lifted his helmet. "It's red, see? If I had gotten any sleep this morning on this truck, these eyes would have been blue, not red. I'm six foot two. Remember me, won't you," he pleaded?

If he were to be the last casualty in August's battle, he wanted someone to identify his body on sight, not by dog tags, to the graves registration unit. Brannagh sensed his own trepidation. Was Dad right, Brannagh's inquisitional conscience inquired? He began to pray for courage.

Van Meter was moved. He, too, had felt invisible last April when he carried ammo for Dog Company's third section of heavy machine guns. He had trembled, too, at the thought of being an unknown soldier.

"Even in this light, I'd know you anywhere, Red," he assured the ammo bearer. "You'll get to know the guys in the squad real fast as we climb those hills and dig in, and they'll get to know you. Hop off that truck, and follow Joe ROK, there," he said as he faded from view.

The Sergeant's finger had pointed to a helmet atop a hairlike stalk in fatigues standing on inky ground by the truck's tail gate. The truck lurched as Brannagh squatted to jump. He saw looming below him that tiny Korean soldier, and a mire of mud. Brannagh's helmet obeyed gravity, crowning the oriental, but Brannagh's body obeyed the acrobat in him and coiled to a sommersault, his right arm holding out a newly issued M1 carbine as if it were the seminary rector's shepherd staff. Brannagh's back, butt and boots circumnavigated the muck as he lept to his feet, his hind side plastered a skunk's streak.

"Nikola shibola," shrieked the slumping Korean.

Brannagh reasoned the Korean's litany wasn't to any saints; most likely to his ancestry, raising aspersions thereon.

"You some kind of asshole, Recruit," asked a corporal?

Brannagh saw eyes manhole big, a mouth a dime in circumference. Skier's could traverse the slopes of this corporal's cheeks. Neither his helmet nor poncho was effective against the wind, nor was his heavy machine gun protected from precipitation that changed angles as often as did a politician his ethics.

Brannagh surmised the corporal's question was rhetorical, not for information, but to produce an effect. He realized the better part of an answer was not to define the meaning of the principal term, as in small or big, but to remain silent, turn away and move on.

"Yo, Recruit," called the corporal. "Take your yellow streak and follow the gook to Van Meter's squad. You'll fit in with those back slope dregs."

Those were fighting words. Brannagh turned to face their utterer. He saw the corporal grin as he framed a female form with expressive hands, punctuated by a lower body thrust.

"Nikola shibola, Corplee' Baiter," the Korean illiterated.

"Fresh meat, hey Revels, Trout," Baiter declared! "I get first on the new mujerado. As for you, Gook, I'll nickle-shinola you when we come back off this hill."

"Come," Joe ROK said to Brannagh. "No fightee."

The tug by the Korean pulled Brannagh back a

step, but not before he viewed the disgusting Baiter
double clutching a simulated erection, and heard the
laughter of two others, with guffaws as wet as the air
and as penetrating. Brannagh felt his stomach heaving
again. He was inclined to inquire further into the
corporal's need to demean so unmercifully Joe ROK,
and himself, with a yellow streak. Obviously, calling
someone a gook or yellow wasn't granting honors, but
what was a mujerado anyway? His was a hell of a
welcome to the 35th Infantry Regiment's first battalion.
Then, this regiment was the 'cacti', and for sure, that
corporal had more spines than a shark had teeth. He
belonged among bizarre looking plants.

"Come," said the doleful Korean again and
Brannagh followed.

"Hey, Red," called someone from behing a fag.

"What about him," Brannagh sighed?

He put his words out cautiously, to avoid
another mouthy corporal.

"I was on the troop ship with you, Red. I'm
Crane," the glow worm exclaimed. "Hey Colgan, Allen,"
he hollered to other forms, "here's Red from the boat.
You guys remember how Red fought Stag back on the
ship. Red never quit."

"He sure didn't quit," another agreed. "Red, you
got to take off some of that corned-beef sausage you
wear around your belly, even if it is your source of
strength."

"More like his concrete head," coughed Crane.

Brannagh immediately began to feel at home.
This good natured teasing was more like it; he knew
where he stood with these guys.

"Yea, I lost money on Stag," a third soldier
bitched. "Rumor was Stag would take Red in two, or his

cornerman Lieutenant Breezedale would throw in the towel."

"I heard that, too," answered a GI, "so I took a big piece of Master Sergeant O'Hara's action. I lost my ass."

"Where's Breezedale and O'Hara going to be assigned, anyone know," inquired Brannagh of the bobbing nicotine lamp?

"Yea," answered Crane. "Breezedale got shipped to the deuce-four. His balls'll get barbequed by Stag when he gets that doublecrossing officer straddled over a charcoal pit." Crane waited for his laughs. "Dog Company got O'Hara. Who got you, Red," Crane inquired?

"I'm in Dog, too," Brannagh answered. "Where are you headed?"

"I'm to Charley," said Crane, "these guys go to Able."

"Good luck," Brannagh said.

"You'll need it more with O'Hara," Crane warned.

Brannagh sensed another twinge in his transfusion of emotions; this twist, one of dismay. O'Hara was downstream of a river yet to be crossed. Upstream there was a germ of a Korean, a homophile of a corporal, and Brannagh, a puppy in Dog Company's kennel who wasn't to bark, but who was to bear the whip while being fed to the enemy.

Joe ROK pulled Brannagh away, leading him to stacked ammo boxes.

"Grabee two cans' ammo. Checkee carbine. When movee out, follow me. Stay five yards close," Joe ROK instructed the last ammo bearer.

As dawn pushed the night's blanket to the west,

Brannagh saw to his north a rugged terrain of twisted and contorted hills, some with slopes of nearly perpendicular walls cupping valleys. He looked at terraces that stepped up the sides of some hills like a giant's staircase. He saw the ridgelines in the distance had fingers, as if from an unseen hand, running quickly down to the valley to braid with other fingers from opposite hands. His eyes widened to encompass a high mountain further north that came right up from ground level like an enormous wart. Yet, the vista wasn't all forbidding. He viewed a landscape of scattered flowers: roses of sharon, peonies with red petals, and an orange lily or two with black spots. Some fir and spruce trees stood on higher elevations; smatterings of elms, beech, poplars and maples were midway; while scrub oaks and pines dotted fingers and foothills.

"What's that stink, Joe ROK," asked Brannagh? His olfactory senses detected what must be a sewage treatment cess pool upstream that had been flushed out by the heavy rain into the valley, its excrement roiling in the flooding river.

"Hav' a no stink," wheezed the Korean!

"Be shit, Recruit," a soldier said.

Brannagh saw a troop who wore no poncho, whose pack dragged. It looked as if it were a lump of mud. His pack suspenders pulled his cartridge belt up near his chest. Beneath his helmet was a face blackened as if by cohabitation with charcoal.

"Korea's covered by shit. Gooks farm with shit," said the soldier. Each of his pronunciations of 'shit' were slid to elongate emphasis.

"Dreamer be shit," Joe ROK execrated!

"Be not," came Private Dreamer's retort!

Brannagh wished he hadn't flushed this toilet. He looked for an out.

"Cut it out," Van Meter ordered. "Joe ROK don't take kindly to Dreamer," he said. "I got to watch them like the prices of feed and hogs."

"Where are we Sergeant?" Brannagh asked to change the topic, but he had a purpose in his question, none the less. Rear echelon war stories had stressed the importance to the Chinese of the Iron Triangle, particularly its eastern corner at Kumhwa, as the key avenue of attack down its valley southeast through Uijongbu into Seoul. He had been told the twenty-fifth Infantry Division held the line from just east of Chorwon to Kumhwa with the 9th Republic of Korea, or ROK, Division on its left flank and the 2d ROK Division on its right. Chinese were notorious for hitting ROK Divisions first in hope of a breakout, causing the Yanks to run a gauntlet while withdrawing.

"At Kumhwa," Van Meter said. "We're going out on that north high ground, about four thousand meters south of Pyonggang, looking for Chinks. There's no concealment near the top of the hills. Not much on the lower slopes either. Chinks may be watching us all the way up hills 717 and 682, maybe not."

Brannagh heard an emphasis placed on the words 'maybe not'. He couldn't see any village near by, but the north high ground fell abruptly into the wide and level valley of the Hantan River. He could see its waters were high, its murky fury bathing large stones with a wrathful vigor.

"Hear the word," sounded an earthquake visage in olive drab.

Atop a stone stood the source of this stern voice, its awful stare plunging two squads of machine gun soldiers to silence. It spoke again. "I Corps gave our division its objective. The 35th has to carry it out. Charley Company of the 89th tank battalion, a platoon from the 21st AAA, and Charley of the 65th engineers are going out with us."

"Who's that, Joe," Brannagh asked.

"Sargee Sing," whispered the Korean, "third section machine gun sargee."

Brannagh marvelled at the broadchested, large nostrilled horse of a soldier, hard-bodied with fierce eyes and with the name of 'sing'. Was this first sergeant Chinese-American? If so, he was the tallest Chinaman in the states.

"You got something important to say, Recruit?" crashed the storm heaved words of the Sergeant at Brannagh.

"His butts mine, Singletary," a hoarse voice said. Baiter whistled his admiration, as if for his girl!

"No," answered Brannagh. The quiet 'no' was intended as an apology to the section sergeant. It also gave the signal of a murderous intent toward the perverted Corporal Baiter.

"We cross the Hantan in ducks," Singletary continued, "then move up to take two hills. We hope the Chinks think this is another routine recon to establish an advance patrol base. Chinks have seen it before." He paused. "We stay out a few days." He turned away so as to ignore the groans from his rain-washed section of heavy machine guns. "Be quick," he hollered over his shoulder, "or ya' gonna' be dead!"

Brannagh wished he hadn't heard the admonition. He felt out of place in any event. He could see that most everyone in the large assemblage of troops across the valley seemed to know what they were doing. Only moments ago, he was riding carefree in a jousting troop truck worried about his lost pride over never going into combat. Now he was about to pee in his own pants because he was going up into the hills where the enemy lived!

He watched soldiers check their packs for combat rations, towels, personal gear. Some put their mess gear in their packs; others hung it from cartridge belts. He saw soldiers, some under ponchos and other not, hang an entrenching tool onto the pack, then attach their packs to webbed suspenders. Canteens and first aid packets were attached to cartridge belts. A shelter half, enclosing a blanket, was horseshoed about each pack and lashed to place. The whole burden was lifted high onto shoulders and secured when the cartridge belt was clicked closed.

Brannagh observed riflemen shoulder M1s upside down, but a few, to keep them dry inside, placed a prophalatic over several inches of phallic barrel. Then most riflemen crossed themselves with bandoleers of ammo in clips, hanging one from each shoulder. Grenades were carefully hung high from loops on webbed suspenders, ominous fragmentation tits. Brannagh did likewise, imitating the green sea of fatigue clad, helmeted combat infantrymen.

Brannagh had expected to go into action. He joined for that very purpose, but he sensed the smell permeating the humid air might be emerging from the trunk of his own fatigues. He felt he stood out as if alone among the thousand soldiers, and a tenseness was riding up and down his spine. He tried to ignore his own constricted breathing. "Which way is the enemy," he inquired?

"In a hurry to get your ass blown off,"
questioned a face?

Brannagh saw one of Caesare Lombroso's
criminal profiles: a sloping forehead and puffed
eyebrows above bulging orbs that were the epitomy of
evil eyes framed by deep set sockets. Brannagh had
seen the like in the movies; an ugly, puffy faced James
Cagney, perhaps! At least Joe ROK had a sunshine face,
round as the blistering orb with as vivid a glow.
Brannagh understood he wasn't viewing a beauty
contest, but there was no end to the eyesores in his
squad. Next to Joe stood Dreamer, a frowzy devil with
the nefarious smell of sulphur, and beyond James
Cagney stood an elegant perpendicular pillar rising
from the mud.

"Listen to les coqs mort," the pillar uttered.

Brannagh hadn't expected so much attention, or
anticipated derision, but it was a stupid question, at
variance with the immediate prospects. He wished he
had kept his mouth shut, but doing so wasn't among his
accomplishments, he conceded. What did 'les coqs
mort' mean? Brannagh's French translated morts as
death, and coqs as birds. He was being called a buzzard
by the linear looney.

"Saddle up" came out as if a tuba's throat was
cleared. Brannagh's peek at its origins again revealed
Sergeant First Class Singletary, his carbine shouldered
at right arms, standing broad as a hundred year old
cottonwood tree. His helmet was pulled low on a
gnarled knot, with a nose the size of a horseapple. The
Sergeant's poncho wasn't much avail against the rain,
but he didn't appear to notice. The sergeant obviously
expected his section of heavy thirty machine guns to get
their gear shoulder mounted, and a box of ammunition

in each hand, and each of his men rapidly did as told. When he appeared satisfied, he turned to the north, raising his right arm high above his helmet with its pointed finger tall as the statue of Liberty's torch, then dropped the arm and its pointer as if a spear to indicate where they were headed.

"Move out," came Singletary's command. "Be quick or you're gonna be dead," he said!

Brannagh couldn't swallow the lump in his throat which grew as if it were a vigorous tumor. It cut back on air traffic through his esophagus. When he swallowed wrong, he choked, coughing! "Lord," he beseeched, "remember me."

"That new mujerado's choked up, hey Trout," laughed Baiter! "I could give him something to swallow!"

"Stick it in your ear," Brannagh challenged.

"Up yours, Recruit," Baiter retorted. "See to your butt, buddy!"

Was this jerk a pervert, or did he just talk like this to get the new men's goat? Surely, if he were really homosexual, he would be out of the army on a Section 8. Whether he was or wasn't, Brannagh had had more than enough of his guff, and he figured the time and place was as good as any other, as only the Lord knew whether he'd get back to have the opportunity to put a few fists into Baiter's face.

"Put down your machine gun, foul mouth, and I'll give your teeth more space to whistle," Brannagh threatened.

"Don't do it, Baiter," Singletary hollered. "As for you, tough recruit, when I tell you to do something, you do it," he thundered.

Brannagh nodded assent, chagrined that his

quick temper had taken its usual control over him, the same temper that placed him nearly weekly before the Seminary's Dean of Discipline and the basic training company commander where accusations of insolence were on parade.

Brannagh didn't walk long in the mud and muck before the swollen Hantan River rumbled across his line of movement.

"What rifle company is that crossing ahead of us, Joe," asked Brannagh?

"Charwee companee."

Brannagh recalled an infantry fable that trucks and ducks were always available to move fighting men to battle, but foot power was the transport back. An unceremonious debarkation on the north side of the torrent caused him to amend the adage, thusly: trucks and ducks were always available to move the fighting man as far as the last safe traffic circle. Thereon, only infantry men trod!

He couldn't see a visible sun to blame for the morning's heat and humidity. Yet a cup of the warm rain mixed with the powdered milk in his C-rations could be used as a sleep inducer. He might try it this night. Was he sweating? Every aspect of the weather seemed angry. He felt as hot as an Advent candle but dripping vapor, not wax.

Whenever had he got so badly out of shape? The constant rise of the terrain was already collecting a toll in the form of his energy. How could the earth's crust have been bent and broken into the form of Korea he was climbing? Some of the hills were rugged with rock, others smooth as babys' butts. Then there were peaks that jutted like Lincoln's chin. Geologists may have called them mere wrinkles on the earth's crust, but they weren't climbing hills with a full field pack, weapon and two boxes each with two hundred and fifty rounds of thirty caliber bullets in web belts. Brannagh remembered the geological process that operated on Korea's surface throughout the ages generated these ridges, mounds, mountains, hills, cliffs and valleys by the steady action of rain, frost, wind, ice and other forces unceasingly at work. His own bootmarks impressed in the slippery soil were but fresh detritus that would gradually vanish under other inwashings. He concluded combat troops left no more than that over the course of time.

Where were the Chinese? Why didn't they start shooting and stop this excruciating agony of hill climbing?

"Take ten," Singletary conceded.

Brannagh couldn't draw breath enough even to talk. He assumed talking would waste the little wind he had left in his lungs, like decompressing a vacuum. He couldn't make it further on one lung. He had doubts he could make it up any more hills on two lungs. He watched stragglers as strewn across the hills as were rocks, then worried he too might turn to stone after sitting down. Could he move again on the big Sergeant's order? He gazed down the wet hillside pocked with scrubs and saw the dark shadow of Dreamer fold like a black handled jack knife.

"He's been hit," Brannagh deplored.

"No shotee," answered Joe. "He fall out."

"Watch my ammo, Joe. I'm going down there," Brannagh pronounced. He moved quickly toward the second gun squad.

"Bugging out, butt-buddy," exclaimed Baiter!

Brannagh paused when his temper flashed. He

crooked his middle finger high, and informed the corporal of obvious disdain. It wasn't a usual seminarian's response to stupidity; more along the lines of his beer buddies back at Camp Breckinridge's PX. When in the army, one did it the army's way. He retracted his gear and continued down the wild gloomy finger.

"I'll take your ammo. Hold on to my cartridge belt," Brannagh directed.

He pulled Dreamer the long traverse toward the silent section of heavy machine gun squads waiting in the day's purple pall. Baiter appeared to Brannagh to be in burning thought, with vengeance in his raging soul. He no doubt had catalogued the insult in his library of retribution.

"Couldn't keep up," Dreamer told his squad leader.

Van Meter was pleased that Brannagh had thrown Dreamer a life preserver. The squad leader admitted to himself he was nearly at his wit's end to figure a way to keep the farm hand Dreamer up with the members of his squad, what with his lack of incentive and intelligence. Probably, as Van thought on it, the best farm hands were those reared on farms by parents who liked their kids as well as their crops. It was my upbringing, Van reflected, then corrected himself. He couldn't count Grandpa as his parent. Dreamer was raised in an orphanage by hard-nosed adults, like Grandpa, but as Van had smelled the barn yard with his first breath, Dreamer was dumped on manure. He started too late in life and really didn't learn farming, nor was he up to the military. What would become of him after the war? Van toyed with the idea of using Dreamer on his own farm, but the mind boggled at the chaos that would follow.

"Couldn't keep up," Dreamer told his squad leader!

Singletary was on his feet. "Van Meter, Cervera, come forward."

Brannagh watched as both soldiers hopped to it. Sergeant Cervera looked like a short shot of tequila built along the lines of a stunted balsam fir tree, wide at the butt and tapering upward. Van Meter, Brannagh imagined, was a hard rock maple in contrast to Cervera. He must be the 2d gun's squad leader, Brannagh concluded. He was taking everything on presumption, anyhow. He presumed the officers in the division, regiment, battalion and company knew what they were about leaving the sergeants alone in the field. What were the sergeants discussing, Brannagh wondered?

Singletary wanted opinions. He had watched riflemen on the ridgeline, silhouetted, their concern for Chinese absent. Exhaustion would do it every time to a replacement troop. So many new recruits were filling the ranks since May, Sing hardly knew his own section anymore. He hadn't really talked to the new tough guy that morning. What was his name? Sing couldn't recall it. No matter! Van Meter always knew one eight ball from another in his squad. Sing rued his choice of Van Meter over Baiter as leader of the 1st gun squad. It was a mistake figuring Van's nice guy approach, rather than Baiter's bullying would shape up the dregs of Dog Company.

"Damn rifles are on the ridgeline. There ain't no concealment up there, probably no chinks either. Should we take the high road to hill 717," Sing asked his leaders?

"Ain't no shrubs on these slopes either, Sing," said the Californian Cervera.

"No," the Iowan muttered.

He shook a negative, his helmet repeating it. He had sewn on his stripes by following military manuals. Now wasn't the time to throw away the book.

"No flat trajectory gun can hit us on the reverse slope," Van stated his case.

It was a characteristic of the corn-fed squad leader - Sing reflected, conservative like Herbert Hoover. He must be as conservative, too, back in Lake Mills, environmentally rotating crops.

"No matter the lack of chink fire, or the rain, or slippery slopes, Sing," amplified the Van Meter, "stay down on the reverse side!"

Singletary acknowledged he would have stayed there anyhow. He pretended he needed advice. Officers had said to him a good leader sought other opinions. Sing figured doing it didn't hurt. He had aspirations for his master sergeant rocker before he rotated, and if Captain Busin took notice of these frequent consultations, he might move this section sergeant back to the CP as top kick to fill its vacancy. Hadn't Sing been in the thick of it since March? With the truce coming up, other sergeants could lead the sections. He had done his time on line. A little peace and quiet in the reverse slope company command post was deserved; that and the last rocker before his happy ass rotated back to the zone of the interior.

Sing looked at Cervera a moment contemplating why he didn't get in the motor pool. He drove a fruit truck back near Los Angeles, and was a mechanic, but he was as placid as his gunner, Baiter, was ornery. Cervera the grinning Hispanic, was forever sign-of-crossing himself, and Baiter was too mean to go back to Dallas without a medal under his big belt buckle. Baiter had said a few war stories would be the ultimate erotic weapon in his strategy of conquest of voluptuous road house women waiting for his big libido!

Singletary felt he was as much a professional soldier as the Army regulars, though he answered an early draft call! Hadn't he too set aside experience in his hardware store back in Dayton so he could avoid the quartermaster corps to go infantry? Recalling April and May attacks by the Chinese, Sing remembered even S-4, the battalion Supply Staff, had rifles in their holes, so going with supply wouldn't have made much difference then. He liked the hardware business, but it needed new marketing methods. Sing gave thought to Baiter's tactic. If Sing put in a line of household goods, like washers, dryers, even refrigerators, his store would attack women galore who'd want home delivery. Why should he let Baiter be the only one to dabble his paint brush in others' buckets?

"We'll stick to the reverse slope," Singletary told his squad leaders, ignoring Cervera's circular eyes.

Sing had the third section hug whatever brush it found for footing the long elongated climb towards the crest of hill 717. He followed the deployed skirmishers of Charley Company. He found no opposition to delay him.

"Van Meter, place the 1st gun squad to the right. Cervera, put your squad over there on the left knoll. Dig in," Sing ordered it.

He had his guns cover a long running finger to the northwest, the most likely approach on hill 717 for a counter attack.

When he saw Van's men dilly-dallying with their entrenching tools he was pissed off, particularly at Dreamer, sitting on a wide stone as visible as a mountain guide looking over the distant hills to blaze a trail.

"Dig, Dreamer! Dig deep or I'll bury you in a shallow grave when them gooks hit tonight," Sing shouted.

Dreamer had no desire for a shallow fighting hole if Chinese did pay him a night's visitation, for a shallow gun hole was tantamount to a shallow grave.

Brannagh was hunting for his wind again, when the rugged oxygen of the section sergeant revived his lungs. He dug like a steam shovel into the wet earth, undressing rocks and stones which delayed his progress towards the center of the globe. He loosened stones with his hands; once freed, he hurled them down a brown burly finger. Had trees ever grown around these stones, their roots lingering in the hoary soil? He looked to the north where the Chinese must be, as dismal and wet, planning mischief that might fall on him this very night! He felt the cold finger of terror on his spine as the wind showed its breath.

"Smart GI," Joe ROK sputtered to Brannagh in a liquid English! "Rocks chipee, when bullee hit," he warned.

Brannagh quickly digested the lesson.

"Two hour guard, I do. You sleep. I wakee. You guard two hour. I sleep. You wakee me," Joe ROK wheezed. "All night, if no chinkee."

Brannagh understood. Night guard was two hours on guard, two to sleep, all through the night. If there were Chinese it would be a 100% alert. He nodded, wondering why Joe ROK added 'ee' to his words.

"No can see," Joe ROK castigated. He was six inches less tall than Brannagh's six foot two.

"I'll cut a firing step," Brannagh stated.

He stabbed the foxhole's northward epidermis to open a niche for his Korean vase. He etched its crevice up to the lip of the gun hole and down again, prying mounds of dirt and stone out of the recess. Separating stone from loosened earth Brannagh placed the clay around the forward gun slots, and flipped the stones a distance north. He sized up his endeavor. Joe ROK not only could see over the rim, but might sit in the niche, poncho-covered and dry. Knowing a good thing, Brannagh did the same for himself. The pangs of exhaustion were as nothing to his will to survive.

"What a day at the office," Brannagh said as the black evening descended; the blue day retired. "I commuted by open truck from the replacement company to a combat company, crossed a swift river, walked seven hours up the cousin of the Himalaya mountains, dug a well sized hole for seven more hours to look out for Chinese that want to kill me, and a buddy that wants me to stay awake. Is this the army, Joe?"

"Im Ta Song," Joe ROK said softly. "Name Im Ta Song. Not Joe ROK. Americee soldiers call Joe ROK, Bill ROK, John ROK! Not so! Namee Im Ta Song!"

Brannagh detected emphasis, not vehemence, in the words. He studied the cake plate face with its eyes of a cat, alive, despite dim and gray. Im Ta Song! Im, Brannagh surmised was Joe's last name, or was it the first? Better to call him Im Ta Song. Brannagh spoke it.

"Im Ta Song! Did I get it right?"

Im's vigorous affirmation bobbed his huge

helmet.

"Im Ta Song," repeated Brannagh, "I can't sleep. If you want, I'll take first guard. I'm too scared to sleep."

"Brannee scared," inquired the puzzled Korean?

It wasn't that he didn't know or hadn't seen Yankee soldiers as frightened as was he, it was that none had ever said it out loud before.

"Yea, to the soles of my boots," Brannagh declared.

Not a shot had he heard fired from the north, nor had there been a single outgoing round, still there was fright in him. Were the battle wise afraid? They were a few thousand meters in front of the 25th Infantry Division's 27th and 24th RCTs, regimental combat teams, and only the Lord knew the unestimable distance between the 35th RCT's positions on hills 717 and 682 and the rear echelon. He knew he was scared, but not a coward; a hell of a distinction!

Im Ta Song was thinking. He remembered that Yankee officers not only ignored the names of KATUSAs, Koreans augmenting the United States Army, but also ignored release from their units to go to religious services at a temple, to be taught the holy Buddist text, the Diamond Sutra; nor find the spirit of Buddha in the sound of a wooden chanting block, or in the fragrance of sandalwood incense, or in the halo surrounding the Buddha's head. Yet GI's went often. There were no non believers in combat companies, only a recognition that Yankees were worthy to praise God. Must all twelve thousand KATUSAs serve until wounded, killed, or the war ends, meditated the Korean?

"Joe ROK," whispered Van Meter as if his voice

were a sheriff's. "Go to Sing," he ordered. Van crawled in Army manner across the forward slope back toward his foxhole.

"Nikola shibola." Joe ROK expected a rotten assignment.

Brannagh watched the bamboo thin soldier with a grasshopper's head and popped eyes crawl out of their foxhole, but then stand tall, striding as if on parade.

If there were a truce, Im Ta Song questioned, would the Americans leave Korea? Would they put him in a ROK division? He reflected a moment on life with an American infantry division as opposed to a division of the Republic of Korea. Soldiering with well-fed barbarians wasn't the worst way to serve Korea. Im walked up the slope to its ridgeline, to walk the crest. He slung his M-1 carbine on his right shoulder. He watched apathetically as GIs ran from their foxholes on the forward slope up over the ridgeline to pinch off one in hurried frenzies.

"Joe ROK," came Sing's stage whisper, "get your gook ass off the skyline. Get down here."

Im Ta Song quickly hauled his butt toward the section sergeant's bunker. The two new KATUSA troopers, To Kae Tae and Ung Chon - Bill ROK and John ROK - would have dug Sing's foxhole and fortified it with logs and sandbags before digging in for themselves Im concluded, despite Singletary treating them as boysans. Im Ta Song wanted to be a soldier in a soldiers' army and treated as one, but Sing wouldn't give equality to an oriental.

Im felt like a chopstick among railroad ties. Singletary had his binoculars aiming northeast, scanning the black billowing lumps across the curfew shade. Cervera and Van Meter crowded his dug out.

"Joe ROK, which hill is hill 472," Singletary barked?

"Sargee," Joe ROK pointed northeast from the bunkers gun slot," over there, separatee by low pass from this hill." His high pitched voice was soft. "Behind, high ground fall into valley of Hantan River."

Singletary set his binoculars to follow Joe ROK's aim.

Im Ta Song embellished his scouting report. "Pass called Walmi. Hill 717 called Sobong-San. Hill 682 called Turyu Bong."

"You gooks got names for everything," snarled Sing. "Stupid gooks, naming hills and passes."

Im Ta Song rolled his pie-eyes at the GI slang for a Korean, north or south - gook! It was a word Sing and Baiter pronounced with the same gutturals they used in their word for fornicating. "Nikola shibola, hav a not Yankee's a Mountee Rushmore? Hav a not sargee?" Im Ta Song spit back, imitating Sing's snarl. The Korean's mind quickly gave thought that the morning might find him on Walmi pass on a one man outpost.

"Get back to your hole, ROK," Singletary directed, subconsciously elevating the Korean from gook to ROK.

Brannagh listened to the illiterative phraseology of the returning Im Ta Song as he hissed nouns, verbs and an adverb or two, crowned by an exaggerated "yipe" at the sound of a swoosh from an air footed shell aimed at the skyline's forager. Strong but unequal motions, joined with a horrible roar, filled the air above Brannagh's foxhole. Its slope writhed with a dreadful convulsion. Out of the grit, Brannagh saw Im Ta Song dive headlong into their foxhole's deep recesses, then wrap his pliable body like that of a coiled reptile.

Another flat trajectory round detonated with fury and vehemence throwing huge stones high into the smell of sulphur. The earth erupted, debris falling like fiery rain in atomized particles into Brannagh's fighting hole. The bitten mountain was tossing chunks of its vegatative physique at him.

Brannagh worried the Chinese were demonstrating their displeasure at the 35th RCT's intrusion into no man's land so soon after the initiation of the truce talks. Might not the Chinese believe this was an American double cross - talking truce while attacking? Was it, he pondered? Brannagh gave thought to his anger of the morning when he felt the truce talks deprived him of his opportunity to go into battle. Why should that have bothered him? It was Dad's words that had jolted him so, a verbal electric chair.

A glare flashed from an upwelling plume, its violent blowout cascading more of Korea's minerals on to Brannagh's helmet. His mind raced at the thought the next shell would drop into his hole, that he and Im Ta Song might be consumed in its thermal activity. More incoming blazed grit. A cone of dirt hissed stones above him. To a murky mind, the crude Baiter was a blessing in contrast to this Chinese curse. A geyser of destruction sizzled the hole's air. Brannagh regretted joining the army. The next round shook the earth around his fox hole and rumbled its throat. One broke the sky with a low pitched reverberation, followed by raining stone. Brannagh rolled his tongue and gurgled to avoid choking. Was the ground ripping into shreds? Were the Chinese playing a grizzly game of free throws with him and Im Ta Song sitting in the basketball net?

He heard awful crashes go down the line like an assembly line of volcanoes migrating to the west. Amazement flooded his mind that the Chinese hadn't hit him while ladling out hot lead. Absent a deep fox hole, he comprehended an animate infantryman wasn't the equal of inanimate artillery and mortar fire.

Brannagh felt embarrassed. It wasn't anger that gripped him, but terror. He was terrorized. He wished his fox hole were a cave, and he need never come out of annual hibernation. He wanted to crawl and claw on the bottom of that hole whether or not the Chinese launched an attack. He prayed for courage.

The silence, its suddenness as terrifying as the series of tremendous shocks, fell on the mountain's bruised shoulder. The ground might have ceased reverberating, but not Brannagh's ears. Were the Chinese attacking? He worried about looking out of his foxhole, perhaps timing his helmet's protrusion with the arrival of incoming. He listened for the staccato of his squad's heavy machine gun, the popping of M-1s, sounds he heard during stateside training. There were no sounds of a fire fight. He slowly poked his head into the night's dingy shroud, his eyes looking over the dark wastes of the slope, into the deep dark abyss of a valley from where came wind gusts that brushed the hill like a dirge.

He heard so many sounds. Which were friendly, or enemy? Im could tell him if the Korean ever unwound himself again. If the swoosh was the sound of an incoming Chinese 76 millimeter, it was deadly close! There was hardly time to react, but react Im Ta Song had, Brannagh noted. There were so many sounds he must yet learn. Was the word 'learn' the right word, or would the right word be 'experiencing'? He concluded it would be experiencing for it denoted a sensory reaction, not a mental abstraction. Hear a 'swoosh' and hit the ground, preferably a hole in the ground. If he were to react to the sounds of incoming by trajectory sounds, it meant he would have survived each inundation. From his senses to his intellect, he would know. Brannagh worried on night guard. Had someone stolen away with the distant mountains after the setting of whatever sun there was? Were Chinese hidden by the dense fast moving and turbulent rain clouds? It seemed he was in a lousy location in a colorless country to scan for signs of Chinese. What were the sounds of tennis shoes in the mud? Surely, if he saw a Chinese in front of him, there would be more frog than man present. Brannagh felt the hairs on the back of his neck turn to toothbrush bristles. If a Chinese had crept seven hundred meters over stones and through slime to get at him, it was to surprise him, and not to attack up the field of fire Van Meter had each fighting hole lay out. Brannagh's tension mounted.

Im Ta Song's relief signalled Brannagh's escape from peering into the bog of darkness with its ghostly moaning. Suspended in the murky recesses of his mental fire alarm went night guard's cautionary trepidations, and his being was embalmed by exhaustion.

The earth vibrated Brannagh awake. For terrifying seconds a cascade of flashing eruptions lit up the line of foxholes.

"Chinkee com," whispered Im Ta Song.

Brannagh felt coldly calm and slid his carbine into its gun slot. He could see no one in his field of fire, but rotated off the weapon's safety.

"Chinkee down slope, on finger" Im whispered,

"two three hundred meters down." He stared intently. "No com now," he said, as coldly calm as Brannagh.

"How come," the surprised Brannagh asked?

"Chinkee no good, plant mines. Know we come there morning," came Im's nonchalant analysis. "Chinkee 76 kept us pinned while Chinkee plant mines."

Brannagh sat down on his firing step. He heard a deep rumbling in his stomach unlike any he had heard before. He had forgotten to eat. He began to shake when a BAR let loose a torrent of hot lead at a distant Chinese probe.

"Sleepee," warned Im. "Soon we jump off."

When the sobs of the rain mingled with voices in the predawn wail of the mountain wind, Brannagh woke up.

"Saddle up," quietly spoke Van Meter to the foxhole of Im Ta Song and Brannagh. He saw the squad leader was hunched as if a humpback biped. He had been scooting from hole to hole to alert his men of the morning's movement.

"Baker Company will stay on the outpost. We move out on Singletary's order."

As quietly as he arrived, Van faded back into the black heavens' tears.

Brannagh laid prone in a shell hole. He heard the surging sounds of outgoing artillery above him. They were mighty sounds, as if distant trains dashing on rails to a terminal. A torrent of shells like thunderstorm hail were leaping great distances with deadly stings. Their shattering blows were smashing hills and men on the front and flank of the recon patrols, like Chinese 76 millimeter shells had lashed his last foxhole. How many were slain across the ridgeline's red swell?

"Saddle up," hollered Sergeant Singletary from the reverse slope.

His sound was steely. Brannagh saw as much steel in the sergeant's backbone as in his voice, a man of prowess and mettle and might, at home on the hills with the dead at his feet. Such a man was one to follow, Brannagh reasoned, into the burning fray. If he had to advance further across the brown hills this day he was glad he would be led by the fierce Singletary.

"Move out," Singletary commanded, pivoting to the south. He led them toward a dark hollow, and down the hill, away from the bloody hot steel still greeting the Chinese to the north.

"We're going back to blocking position and a truce." His smile exhulted.

The howling cheers from Sing's men sent shivers into the soggy ground. Brannagh listened as the men talked of hell raising, of hot food, of movies, when back in blocking until the war ended. He smiled along with them, but felt out of it. Although the shelling he endured last night might have qualified him for the Combat Infantryman's Badge, he'd not fired a single round at an enemy. The others had served with distinction, while he was distinguished for cowering from incoming. Annoyed at himself, he hid it and acted as enraptured as his buddies.

"Take ten," Singletary ordered.

He sought out a chair-like stone to cradle his weary body. He was happily tired. He sensed the exhaustion of his sleepless squads, despite the exhileration of pulling back and not being in the second section of heavy machine guns left out on the new outpost with Baker Company. It was a stroke of

momentary luck, he sensed, that Red Six chose
Charley, then Able to lead assaults on hill 717 and 472,
but found no enemy resistance! That left Baker! Sing
felt it had evened out over time. Then a premonition of
a battle where he sat made him shudder in the gray
gloom. The Chinese were still out there, truce talks or
no truce talks.

Van Meter listened to the interrogation of the
Chinese prisoner brought back by Able's patrol. He saw
a little man in padded cotton pants and a shirt, both
dyed a dirty brown nearly the color of the man's skin. If
Chinamen were of yellow skin, then the same humid
sun and wild wind were tanning their hides too, Van
reflected. He matched the squat of the the enemy.

"What's his name, rank and serial number,
Lieutenant Wong," asked Able Company's patrol
leader?

"Tzow Kwan Tzoa, private, age 20, a farmer,"
came the reply of the much taller American officer.
"Tzow was in a nine man infantry squad, 4th Platoon,
6th Company, 2d battalion of the 133rd infantry
regiment. He says he's in the CCF's, Chinese
Communist Forces, 78th division, 26th Army." He
paused when he focused on Van Meter. "The CCF 26th
Army is the outfit we are facing in the Iron Triangle,"
Wong said.

Van Meter wondered about Tzow's life. How did
he farm? What did he farm? Van knew nothing about
life in China, or its farmers, but he remembered seeing
pictures of farming by ox drawn plows. His own
grandpa insisted on keeping his two horse gang plow to
turn two furrows at a time. Grandpa wouldn't get up his
money to buy one of those new fangled gasoline
traction engines that could pull larger gang plows. Too

poor they were, Tzow, too, thought Van; farmers wanting nothing more than producing rice or corn, chickens, pigs, or cattle. They would have children too, if their governments hadn't pulled them from out behind their plows to dig trenches around Korea and shoot to kill one another, he reflected. Was that the way their different and distant societies wanted it? Was Tzow the last prisoner of war now that the truce talks were on? What if governments left the young farmers like Tzow and him alone and they had met at the county fair. Would we have talked crops, weather, yields, about our families? Would he have asked Tzow home? Would Tzow have brought rice wine? Would he have opened home brew? If we got drunk together, we wouldn't have warred. Van thought, we would have held a corn shucking contest. If there were only a truce!

Van Meter rose and approached the squatting China soldier, offering him a full pack of American cigarettes.

Tzow rose to accept, and Van saw a smile working the worried corners of his mouth. He glanced fearfully at the muted Lieutenant Wong.

Van Meter extended his right hand his left releasing the gift to Tzow. Van shook the private soldier's hand. They didn't speak, but Tzow seemed to know a fellow farmer's hand.

Brannagh was surprised. What ever happened to the Army's dictum: hate the enemy?

Singletary felt disgusted. His own squad leader was consorting with the enemy, so to speak. It was the same squad leader that couldn't get his own men to act as combat infantrymen should. Wasn't Van's squad the droppings of Dog Company, a place for the turds of the world? Things would have to change back in reserve or

Sing would see to Van's transfer to another outfit. Van might be a hell of a nice guy, but crap as a leader. Well, there was always the fart-mouthed Baiter to head up a squad, if it came down to that level.

Singletary studied the dish shaped knoll with rock lips he had just left behind. He was sick of a country with nothing but mountains running six hundred miles from north to south, and one hundred and fifty from east to west. Had he trod every twisting valley covered with stultifying, smelly rice paddies from Seoul to north of the 38th parallel? If only every inch didn't have to be climbed or descended. What happened to flat land? He had pulled through the cold of March to the hot humid August. It wasn't at all like Ohio weather, even when he worked his forge. Could there ever again be times as good as those he had in forging? He could put out a chain grabhook in no time, or make a tool on order to the customer's full satisfaction.

"Saddle up," Singletary ordered.

He stepped out smartly. He looked forward to blocking, it was gravy, the right way to do military time training recruits, until the truce - maybe never back on the front line!

CHAPTER TWO
BLOCKING POSITION

Master Sergeant Seamus O'Hara didn't expect much of a reception at Dog Company's CP, the Command Point. After all, its fighting men just returned from the field. Yet, he was a top kick of long standing in this man's army and someone other than a bespectacled arrow head of a corporal should have met him. At least a fat mess sergeant should have known who would eat his chow from here on.

Corporal Miner saw a soldier statuesque as Andy Jackson on horseback in front of the county court house back home. The top kick's fatigue pants' creases ran a clean demarcation line from belt to boots, and dared not melt in the torrid tent. He saw an older man, his age belied by his magnificent physique, his face lighted as if in a lantern's glow. Atop his elongated frame was a roof of gray.

Miner realized he had better do something. If he were to remain the company clerk he had to jump in this Sergeant's CP just as high as he jumped back home when a potential client walked into his casualty insurance office. He knew he had hot coffee on the burner.

"Cup'a coffee, Master Sergeant," Miner inquired while smiling and shimmying to display his obeisence? He poured lava, thick as the mud on the back slope, into an opaque canteen cup. "I'm Jim Miner, Corporal; Dog Company Clerk. Welcome to Kumhwa, Master Sergeant."

O'Hara could have his pick of the men for clerk, but this toothy Miner was after his well being like an old maid after a man to marry. Didn't O'Hara know the type, for he married one of them. He learned from it that if he had known as much before as after, the old maid population would have stayed up one. "O'Hara," he said.

That was all any clerk needed to know. As the sergeant spoke, he saw Miner listen with his eyes cast down, face as pale as linen, hair as black as any angus bull's hide. Miner was humble, as he should be, O'Hara acknowledged.

No little finger pointer was this muscular old timer, Miner observed, as the Master Sergeant sipped the inky ooze.

"Its good stuff, Master Sergeant," Miner bragged. "Made the way Captain Busin likes it."

"I know. He 'naded' less water and more coffee than any soldier through the campaign in France," said O'Hara emphasizing his unmistakable, but remantory Irish brogue.

"Captain Busin served in World War One?"

What other deduction was there, thought Miner, seeing a soldier as old as a doughboy standing right there in front of him, and the captain with ash on his head, too!

O'Hara rolled his eyes in as much wonderment over the questionable gullibility of the awe struck, and extremely nervous clerk. The Sergeant would stoke this fire.

"We got gassed during Black Jack's Meuse-Argonne offensive, lad," O'Hara said. "Then we fought Nazis in the campaign for France." He whispered, "I took a sniper's bullet at Hombressen meant for Busin." O'Hara's face flushed in anger. "Busin took my field commission. Busin owes me," the top kick mumbled. "I've not seen the uncivil Jimmy

Busin since Hombressen to this day."

As the top kick sat down on an ammo box, Miner acted as if he hadn't heard the tone of disparagement in O'Hara's words toward the little officer. Captain Busin was as much a mite as O'Hara was mighty big, but no less petulant and peevish. What might happen to Dog Company when they meet up? Ruin, Miner contemplated? He reflected on being the captain's fair haired boy. Busin had brought Miner off the hill to the CP instead of Fenton, although it was assistant gunner Fenton who knocked Miner into the hole and saved his life when an 82mm mortar round crumpled their machine gun. A scalpel sharp sliver of shrapnel somehow streaked Miner's scalp giving him a permanent zipper, while Fenton was bounced like a handball off four walls. Miner felt lucky the stiches in his scalp made him noticeable - like a baseball - so Busin had made him his clerk! Unlucky Fenton was made Sergeant Van Meter's gunner, and Fenton hadn't been right in his head since. So went the luck of infantrymen. As an afterthought, Miner worried on lady luck, and how to deal his cards to a top kick out to get their company commander.

Miner feared his mind might be read. He sensed his right hand, palm up, had been twirling. He knew he did that when he worried. He quickly proceeded to drop his eyes and arms towards the tent floor, that O'Hara might not notice.

O'Hara had noticed Miner's physical movements. He sensed they were the clerk's way of concealing something, probably an eagerness to snitch to the company commander. O'Hara was more than certain the clerk would be after looking out for his own butt, and make the hairs of Busin 'shtand' up like a mad cat's tail. O'Hara wanted it no other way.

O'Hara could feel the heat from glowing red eyes in the soaking wet diminutive officer at the tent's entrance. The first sergeant knew what to do about it.

"Corporal," O'Hara said, "Cover Captain Busin with that blanket, over there."

Miner hopped to it, his wide arms spreading the dun colored cloth like brown bat wings over Dog Six.

"Good to see you again, Jimmy," O'Hara said.

He got up and saluted casually. He watched the blood tranfuse from Busin's eyeballs to his cheeks.

Busin stared as if he were seeing an apparition. O'Hara had caught the last act at Hombressen, hadn't he? Busin recalled it as if on film. Platoon Sergeant O'Hara was marching ten Krauts and their officer into the house when the sniping erupted. O'Hara was hit, but he pushed Busin out of the line of fire. It was the sergeant's moaning that Busin still heard. He remembered he didn't make a move for O'Hara. He died, didn't he? Then someone later saw fit to write the paper for Busin as the man that captured eleven Krauts during the hailstorm of slugs. Busin rode this silver star to a field commission. He thought it wouldn't have done any good buried with O'Hara.

"I didn't know," Busin gasped.

"Sure as I'm alive, Jimmy, I'll remind you to the end of your tour," O'Hara said.

Minor stood deep in the sarcasm, as still as a telephone pole, deadly afraid to tell Busin or O'Hara that a private soldier was visible outside the headquarters tent.

Busin' eyes pivoted looking for an escape. He seized the opportunity of the arrival of the soldier to turn his back on O'Hara.

Brannagh entered the quiet headquarters tent. He stepped toward a tall soldier and saluted the corporal, the lowest ranking man in the tent, smartly. "Private Brannagh reporting as ordered, sir."

Miner was confused. He was loath to return the salute and forever more, until the day of rotation, should it ever come, carry the damnable heavy thirty machine gun to the battle of hill 1062. He stood still instead, and cast eyes and arms down.

Brannagh realized he had done a dumb thing. The short barrel chested, squinty eyed soldier with the prominent teeth was the commanding officer. So Brannagh figured he should act as if that one was as worthy, and snapped off another salute.

Busin answered in kind. "At ease," he ordered, glad for the diversion. He motioned the soldier to follow him to the back of the tent, away from O'Hara.

Brannagh followed the moving blanket but noticed the CO's, the Company Commander's, desk was obviously framed to fit his canvas chair so his legs didn't dangle.

"I've read your file, Brannagh. Your training company CO wrote you had a sloppy attitude. Is that right," Busin inquired?

"He must have thought so, Sir," Brannagh responded to a voice as piercing as a spear.

"Why in hell would he think that?"

Busin, his pitch up scale, folded his hands behind his neck. If he couldn't challenge O'Hara, sure and hell he might ride a lowly private's ass. Dog Six liked to raise his voice and arms to make up for what he lacked in size.

"It was because I declined to go to leadership school, Sir," Brannagh replied.

Captain Busin was surprised. "Why did you do that?"

"I doubted I could lead men into battle. I wasn't sure I could lead myself into battle," came the explanation.

Dog Six sensed O'Hara saw the parallel of the private's answer to their situation in Germany. Things had changed since Hombressen, but O'Hara wouldn't know that Busin had become a fighting man, and leader of men. Busin needed to show O'Hara this officer didn't cotton to a soldier, a big one yet, who was afraid to overcome a problem. He would show O'Hara this CO wouldn't tolerate a soldier who kept doubting himself and didn't try - a quitter!

"I'll tell you one time, Private Brannagh, if you ever quit on Dog Company you would sooner have the gooks drive a sliver up your nose than have to face me."

Busin deliberately pitched his voice into a colossal savageness, then looked to see if O'Hara had heard.

"Yes, Sir," Brannagh politely replied.

He feigned inflection that reflected an iota of fear. He realized all brass seemed to crave power and inspire fear, perhaps prerequisites to a commission. No further explanation was warranted. Neither this captain nor the one at leadership school would have believed an ex-seminarian resigned from the school and its sequel, Officer's Candidate, simply because attendance would delay his assignment to Korean combat. Hadn't he joined the Army Infantry to fight atheistic communists, to be a martial missionary, a combat prelate? "Vir si militaverit manet in patris potestate," he muttered as he felt Busin's chiding was as unfounded and fierce as was Dad Brannagh's.

"What was that," roared Busin?

Brannagh instantly regretted that he again let his temper unhinge his lips.

Brannagh hesitated, then answered, "that I understand what you are saying, Sir!"

"Like hell," Busin cursed!" It was Latin," he said. "I'm Italian. I know when Latin is used. Translate it."

Brannagh was relieved he hadn't been snide. Perhaps the little officer did understand a word or two for something had settled his seething emotions down as quickly as they had been roasted red. It was as if some huge dark hand had wrathfully roused a sea of passion, then bestowed serenity.

I would translate it in these words, Sir," Brannagh said. "A man, though he becomes a soldier, remains in the power of his father."

Dog Six templed his fingers in front of his mouth, reflecting on the tall top kick who in Germany had taken so kindly to the assignment of a jockey to his platoon, who overlooked the obvious result of genetic adversity or other freakish cross breeding, and never let this particle of a being forget he was a man with as much power as if he were the putative son of O'Hara. Busin remembered who his martial father truly was, that he was, then and now, in O'Hara's power.

"I better see you bring some good to Van Meter's men. Dismissed."

Sergeant O'Hara nugged the wind whipped private. "Come to attention, lad. Salute! Then about face, and out," he directed.

Brannagh's helmet almost stayed in place as his head rotated to his right to once again see his troop-ship duplicitous boxing manager.

"Sergeant O'Hara," came the exclamation!

"Salute, lad, and leave."

He felt uncomfortable with Busin. What Busin didn't know about the O'Hara of 1951, Busin shouldn't get to know. Better he remember the great man of 1945!

Brannagh did as he was told. He again came to attention, saluted smartly; as sharply about faced, and marched away. He bemoaned his basic training personnel file, his fate in Busin's outfit. Busin had given umbrage over an alleged sloppy attitude of a trainee toward leadership and wouldn't soon forget one he had labeled a quitter. Brannagh gave his gray matter to reflecting on why the desire to be a combat infantryman rather than a student at leadership school was tantamount to quitting? Whatever the meaning given to 'quitting', Brannagh admitted to himself that if the spit and polish endemic to attendees at leadership school were elements of the definition, he was indeed a quitter. He rued the day that Dad Brannagh's letter convinced the son to submit his application to OCS, Officer's Candidate School. Damned if he wasn't graded higher by the interviewing officers than any other applicant, even in light of the besmirching of the training company's commander. Hadn't Dog Six read those other opinions, Brannagh questioned? Nor would O'Hara become Brannagh's CP medic. Any more needles, since the troop ship boxing match, administered by the top kick wouldn't be inserted into a life sustaining vein, but in the back, Brannagh concluded. He was crushed gravel over which Busin and O'Hara would walk. Although the soon to come truce might mitigate the direct threats to life, Brannagh foresaw a miserable existence ahead as a troop undergoing constant training.

Singletary glanced up briefly from his poker game as Brannagh entered the squad tent. "What did the old man want," he asked?

"A review of my stateside file," was the only detail offered.

"Play poker," Singletary asked, unconcerned about the CP?

"No," Brannagh replied. "Never have."

"Poker's a man's game, Sing," smirked Baiter, "where stallions gather after a battle, not rockless geldings."

Brannagh, concluded he was among pirahna, and himself but a lowly carp. The future wasn't much more heavenly as an occupational soldier in the dungheap named Korea.

"This here's your cot, Brannagh," Van said pointing to the distant rear, "between Joe ROK and Dreamer. Got to keep them fenced apart."

Brannagh took a look at Dreamer. He was a soiled, sour soldier with wild, bright eyes and the smile of a gaseous infant. Brannagh did a double take. His eyes saw a repeat, someone about to burp, someone whose fatigue shirt had stains running down its front like a baby's bib.

Van Meter said he had gone the line of least resistance with Dreamer. It was impossible for him to keep himself and his equipment even half-clean at the same time, so Joe ROK had the despised assignment of tending to the handling and cleaning of Dreamer's weapon and equipment while the lettuce cutter from California concentrated on personal hygiene. Van related that even that instant of time when Joe ROK handed Dreamer his rust free carbine before the squad was called to attention for inspection, a dirt spot would spout, Dreamer would go on detail, and the first gun squad on report.

Van likened Dreamer to fertilizer, turning tooled steel by mere touch to corrosion, and clean fatigue to rags. Van indicated he had Dreamer washed, even scrubbed like a champion hog before a judging, with changed fatigues as often as Van could get clean clothes from the rear, but Dreamer's cleanliness was less lasting than the light speed it took for him to break wind after his first bite of chow at any meal. Van said to see to it that Dreamer was always downwind.

"Harville," said a soldier with an earnest, square, stolid face of a lean whip of a corporal, "Nathan Harville, assistant gunner to Fenton. Didn't get to talk to you up the hill. Glad to have you in the squad, Brannagh."

Harville sat himself down beside Brannagh as if he were a precinct captain welcoming a new voter, extending a hand, to shake the other in friendship.

"Ain't that nice," mocked a woozy Baiter at the card table. "Glad to have you in the squad," he imitated.

Baiter skewed a smile on his face to not betray his simmering anger at losing once again to Singletary.

"Damn Sing can always draw two to a flush," Baiter slurred. "He suckers Cervera's squad to Van Meter's tent and cleans us out."

Baiter pointed toward the smoke ring around a half dozen fuming troops whose contorted mouths were blowing smoke, engulfing everything in the tent with cigarette soot.

"Singletary will clean all those clods' fatigues, even Cervera's. Damn spick can't play for shit," Baiter said of his squad leader. "Neither can Revels, plump little ass that he is." Baiter acted serious. "Damn good assistant gunner for a guy out of a Kansas wheatfield, though. The tall shoestring is Trout. He looks like a fishhook for a whale, and beauty boy Watt, here, you'd think he was the regimental standard bearer, instead of being Sing's banker, with the heart of a loan shark."

Brannagh saw Baiter focus on Dreamer's giddy grin; his hair at attention, as if on parade. Was Dreamer laughing at him?

Baiter felt an urge to sass Dreamer, a Californian like the quiet Mexican bull sticker Cervera! Those weren't men from California, just fruit feeders, Baiter determined. They weren't like Texan meat eaters with red blood cells in every vein who knocked the Mexicans out of the Republic of Texas. Californians pussy footed on film like faries at a nudist convention, all twitter and twat.

"What ya' looking at Dreamer," raved the 2d gun's gunner?

Dreamer didn't know at what he was supposed to be looking. All he saw were Baiter's lips pursed to suck a goat's tit. It was that orifice that had been exuding whiskey scented spittal.

Van Meter quickly came off his cot to sit beside his ammo bearer, who was grinning vacantly at nothing. Van had an urge to do this when Baiter placed any of the 1st gun's men at contest, which was often. Van Meter knew his own reputation for brute strength, a farmer's strength matured in the fields, was usually enough to put a halt to any physical undertaking on the part of Baiter. Yet Van knew he didn't know how to fight.

"Nutthin," Dreamer said.

Baiter didn't respond to Dreamer. Sing's liquor that had lit Baiter's lantern's wick was beginning to flicker. Before it went out, he hurried to get out a few words of horror on Van's squad. "Davis won't play poker either," Baiter lisped quietly. "He's one of them Mormons who smile at sinners."

No one said anything.

Brannagh looked at the studious Mormon who, prone on his cot with head lifted, was smiling benevolently.

"Van Meter's got a squad of buffalo chips," Baiter rhapsodized as if in song. "Baldy Swinford's a lunatic, La Vie's a frog from the bayou and Harville here knocked up two back in Pennsylvania's bogs. He had to split his GI insurance."

Brannagh was dismayed at the display of belittlement of the soldiers in his squad, more so at their silence. Some words must be fighting words. Was Van Meter's squad really a misfit outfit? Sure enough, the fellow called Baldy had a maniacal face, a face of a tomfool. His head gleamed beneath the lantern like a reflecting mirror. Then there was swarthy La Vie with brooding features that had the appearance of a Frenchman before a Nazi firing squad. Brannagh heard a loud inhalation when Baiter blew up his depleted lungs to balloons, apparently so that he might continue his insensate, uninhibited drunken snobbery.

"Fenton lost his mind up on hill 717. That's the last straw for a gunner. Look out, Fenton," Baiter shouted suddenly!

Brannagh saw the soldier jump from his cot as if surprised at the sudden sound, then cringe as if an Indian had him by his head hair to scalp it, tight muscular ribbons fanning out from his jaw to his shoulder at either side of his throat.

"I just can't take it any more," Fenton sobbed,

falling to his knees, head drooping, hands on his knees, tears watering the sod.

He looked to Brannagh as oddly babyish in his steel rimmed glasses, with blond hair falling over them.

Van Meter left Dreamer's side for Fenton's, the squad leader's sinewy cantilevered arm a comforting contractible mass of musculature that embraced Fenton's shoulders in sympathy. His squad tent was momentarily hushed, until the poker players anteed up for five card stud as if unconcerned.

Brannagh surmised the 1st gun's soldiers, but for the soon to come truce, were having misgivings that they could do the months as had Fenton in a combat outfit and still have nerves left.

Brannagh had been told that the longer an infantryman was in combat, the more anxious he was liable to become. At first, each felt he could take on alone an entire Chinese company, but when he discovered his buddies were getting hit, then he sensed it was only a matter of time until he took shrapnel or a slug. He wasn't so invulnerable anymore. There must be an understanding of Fenton's crying. He had done too much time. He didn't know when he might be rotated home. He was a gunner in the regiment's most mongrelized squad, serving in a latrine pit.

"He's our gunner, Brannagh," Van Meter's proud words boasted. "Fenton has seen a lot of action. He expected he would have been killed or rotated, but there's no word on rotation."

Baiter blasted back in. "The men in my gun squad, ain't none of them crying!" Baiter raised his eyebrows as if looking to avoid surprise. "Some of them read books, like fat Stein," the gunner said as if reading were a variation on veneral disease, "but he's okay.

Moonshine Jones' most likely is cleaning machine-gun parts right now to smuggle back to Kentucky."

Baiter had his hands on hips towering over Van Meter and Fenton, but turned to look down on Dreamer, Brannagh and Im Ta Song.

"Wait till elevator Trout whips his big lips. You watch out recruit," Baiter lifted his right hand to point its index finger at Brannagh, "Me and Trout need a mujerado."

Brannagh's urge was to confront the sour mash corporal and find out what mujerado meant, but Baiter's eyelids looked to Brannagh as if they had closed, the bull whip of a tongue swallowed, senses faded, miniscule brain waves flattened, heartless muscle stopped, when hibernation struck and he passed out, crumbling. Not Brannagh nor any them, Dreamer, Harville, Im Ta Song, or Van Meter moved a muscle to stay the fall of the rotted timber onto the dirt aisle of the tent.

"Do we take his guff for the hell of it, Sergeant Van Meter?"

"You'll get used to it," Van said. "Words won't hurt. We're not here to fight one another. It's like back home. A line fence doesn't lock out your farming neighbor. We exchange work during peak load periods in threshing, silo filling, haying. In a line outfit, we're partners, too; our machine guns work together."

"Throw a blanket on Baiter," hollered Cervera from the poker table.

"Do it, Trout." ordered Cervera.

Brannagh saw a soldier whose body had the circumferance of a tall sapling, a scarecrow in GI clothes rise from the table in disgust. He made two strides down the aisle and pulled a blanket off Fenton's cot to cover most of Baiter's head.

Brannagh moved over to the center of his cot to let Trout sit down, then lean forward, folding his hands together, extending his index fingers to a point, lifting his thumbs so as to cock a gun pointed at the dozing drunk at Trout's feet. To Brannagh, it appeared as if Trout were ready to shoot, and wisely so, the psycopathic Baiter.

"Reminds me of a story," the nodding Trout related. "Back home when Zechiel passed out on his cabin porch after boozing the day away, he'd wake up in the morning like he'd been draped over a whorehouse clothesline and whipped all night, plus he would have a fresh cut on his arm." Trout held out his arms.

Brannagh saw several neat scars. He heard a voice crying out of the depths of the deep South's mountain passes.

"Zeckiel had near as many scars," Trout's vernacular neighed. "Now Zechiel wasn't a man to fool with. He would have his way, but he didn't know who was wearing him out."

Brannagh saw the poker players pause in their game.

"Zechiel bragged on how he had cut up two or three men who had made a play for his pretty wife, June Mae. Now Zechiel had this long head of hair on a frame that put two hundred pounds on the back of his mule. Zechiel's temper was as ornery as his mule's was stubborn. They went to cursing and hee hawing each other most of each day until the whiskey sipping started. Next morn old sobering Zechiel felt a peculiar-good, but had lost another slice outta' his arm."

Brannagh visualized uneven crags and deep

chasms where hillbilly Zechiel's dangling feet plowed the earth as his mule took him to a back acre still, deep in a wooded crevice between mountains.

"All them hunks out of Zechiel's hide like to made him swear off, but his good common sense come to the fore," Trout's bobbing head affirmed. "Old Zechiel had to catch him that butcher - that's when I came in," the rustic story teller emphasized. "Zechiel got himself drunk and I pretended to pass out."

Brannagh watched Trout shift his sitting position, his left arm with hand on his hip while his right arm and hand slowly whirled in emphasis.

"Old Zechiel struggled, but he noodled onto the mule and rode out of the hollow to his cabin, as I snuck up through the wood to see him pass out on his cabin porch."

Brannagh watched animation play about Trout's long narrow face, a replication of hill breeding that showed a continuity from pre revolutionary first cousins to today's kin. He had lowered his voice.

"Then I saw pretty June Mae coming on like to Sunday dinner;" Trout said, "spreading a tablecloth out, but on the porch floor. She rolled Zechiel onto it, then pulled a long blade outta' her apron. It was as long as a carbine bayonet," he measured, "and as sure as I never held four aces against Singletary, June Mae cut on Zechiel's arm, drawing blood."

Brannagh could see the minds of tired soldiers were put in a trance by Trout's diamond-bright tale. Eyes were wide open!

Trout rested a dramatic moment before he whispered the secret of the blood letting. "June Mae was a vampire!"

Even Van Meter and Davis sucked in horrified

breaths. The squad tent's canvas walls seemed to pucker inwardly.

"June Mae sucked Zechiel's wound to drink his blood!" Trout said. "Then June Mae got violent."

Brannagh could imagine the chopping of the cadaver to gruesome chunks as Trout's ghastly inflections emphasized the awfulness of the act.

June Mae got so violent, what she did to Zekiel no wild whorehouse orgy could match," Trout exclaimed!

Brannagh blushed at the imagery.

"What did she do," screamed Dreamer?

"Don't tell," an embarrassed Davis reprimanded!

Fenton rolled over on his cot, hands over his ears, assuming his womb posture.

"Let him tell," purred Harville.

Trout gave the flushed faced recruit a long look. Trout didn't figure the new guy was fish for future punking in the absence of a battalion mujerado, but one had to troll.

"I never did tell Zechiel about June Mae. He held his woman so lightly he might have killed her, a woman with the mound of Venus and ice cream cone tits of a goddess."

Then, arms spread as if in supplication, Trout stared at Dreamer. "Zechiel and me got drunk together most every night for a month of Sundays after, then we would fall asleep on his front porch before it busted down."

Trout made sure Dreamer and Brannagh could see the scars on his arms. Then he walked out of the squad tent without saying another word.

Brannagh saw the poker players shrug their

shoulders each time the section sergeant swept a pot of bullets, there being no chips, towards his upright stack. There wasn't talk of the truce, nor did Brannagh hear another word on Trout's vampire as table talk had given way to distilled tied tongues. It appeared the section sergeant was always at the ready to pour a finger or two when a loser flashed the instinct of aggression.

What kind of guys were these odd shaped U.S. Army infantrymen, Brannagh questioned? No super race were they. He laid back and adjusted to the malleable canvas stretched across the ancient cot. At his feet was the angriest, most hostile of soldiers, passed out. No other, sober or drunk, appeared to hate, to brow beat lesser ranks with unkind sarcasm. Baiter seemed a maniac, spending his rage in senselessly harmful taunts. The man was a bully, and aptly named. The rest of them were his victims.

What an outfit, meditated Brannagh.

CHAPTER THREE
STAND-STILL ARMY

There was Dad's letter to read. Lately, they're become more and more vexatious. Anger was written into every word.

"Dear Danny,

They say the Korean conflict soon will cease, that cease fire negotiations will probably be only a matter of a few weeks. Yet, when Rusia wanted a five power conference to include Red China, the British Foreign Secretary Morrison, who had supported a U.N. seat for Red China, now turned against it. You can't trust the British to help bring a quick end to the Korean War. Prolonging it is to their advantage."

Brannagh recalled the tales his father told on the Brits, how the ruins throughout Ireland, of crumbled churches and demolished abbeys, were effective evidence of their plunder and spoliation.

"Look at what the British did to end the Irish civil war in 1921-1922. Ireland was broken in two like my heart when my county Antrim and five other counties of the north of Ireland were continued in captivity. Yet, DeValera and the south of Ireland were almighty quiet about it in return for self government."

Didn't Dad tell how he fought with the Irish Republican Army against the Black and Tans, then against Michael Collins and the Nationalist Army of the south of Ireland? Didn't Dad tell that DeValera was all puff and no fury, words not deeds, when calling for an all Ireland republic? Let's see, thought Brannagh, in 1924, when Dad emigrated he would have been twenty years old. When Dad fought with the IRA in 1921, he

must have been as young as seventeen. Brannagh
marvelled at his father's bravery at such a tender age, at
his resoluteness in coming alone to America; he had
seen to it Danny had been educated in their faith at
Catholic schools, even through the tough financial
years of the great depression and despite noting Danny
had the seeds of disobedience when he had disobeyed
rotund Sister Rose.

She had forbidden her pupils crossing the
wasteland called a public school lest its pupils pummel
any Catholic trespasser to unholy water. Yet, Danny
had done so, a fly cast on a trout stream. Rising to the
bait, with belief of superiority inculcated in every
emotional pore, tough public schoolboys had been daily
licensed to rebuke this sacrilege and to keep holy the
revered doctrine of separation of state tax supported
schools from Catholic school children. Public
schoolboys drew a no-scum crossing along their
baseball diamond's right field chalked foul line. It had
been defied by a firehead that hurled a look of a
bayonet, fists of an embryo blacksmith and the
instincts of an Irish wolfhound at the throat of the Lord
Protector, Cromwell. Each public school boy
missionary thereafter had not been wanting to practice
a physical faith further.

Dad had not been able to punish the lad, despite
his disobedience to Sister Rose, for hadn't the boy
refused to let the public school call a coroner's inquest
on Catholic pupils? Dad had also done nothing to
hinder Holy Mother Church's mission of sanctifying the
ruthless through the fists of his fighting seminarian,
although boxing had appeared not too liturgical. It had
been the untarnished good name of Father Servus, the
protection of St. Scholastica's parish grounds and the

Archdiocese's seminarians that Danny's good right cross had defended. Hadn't the Gaelic-Celtic souls in Purgatory, few as there were, found momentary relief in their longing for the sweet sounds of celestial harps by watching the lad win the light heavy weight championship of the Catholic Youth Organization?

Dad had ruled Danny with a nimble spirit, with song, with a horse-hide strap across the backside several times, the last more forceful than the first. Dad had Danny read, for books turned attention towards matters intellectual and spiritual, weening from peer influence and worldly praise. Dad had worried Danny might have grown accustomed to make much of transitory athletic praise, that he might have grown ashamed of studiousness.

Dad had felt that vainglory was a despicable thing, to be spat upon. Nothing had more eloquence than a modest seminarian, or more sublimity than the study of Christ's teachings and the writings of the ancient church fathers, Irish and otherwise. Dad had taught Danny to live the life of an Irishman, no matter if in America, as if he had grown up in County Antrim, as a soul that looked forward to heaven. Dad had wanted his lad to see the Christ of the cross, the Christ resurrected, as the center of his world. Through hard work and study, frequent prayer and meditation, with mind and heart given to elevation through the frequenting of the sacraments, Danny was to have had completed his seminary studies and have been ordained a priest forever.

Dad held that Danny had wrongly girded on the machines of war, that he had set aside obedience to his Archbishop by following Truman's patriotic prattle. Hadn't Danny left behind his study of cosmology, epistomology, latin verbs and logic for theories of machine gun placement, covering fire and attack to a hill's high ground?

Dad had accused his lad of going from the theological library to a machine gun bunker, from prayers in the seminary's chapel to shell pocked ridges. Dad stated his ex-seminarian had put on a badge of khaki servitude in preference to black clerical cloth; that he had quit benefit of clergy one month before he was a score of years, while Chinese bugles echoed. Dad had asked why other young men still heard the Lord's trumpet and eagerly had answered the call to religious life while Danny had heard only taps? Danny's was theological as well as geneological treason!

He read again:

"Truman and Acheson must have made a sweetheart deal with the Brits, or the Brits with them. If the Korean war ended soon would the well equipped Red Chinese Army go after the Brit's colony of Hong Kong?"

Hadn't Dad lectured, Brannagh cogitated, that money and markets fueled power struggles?

"Why is Truman saying a peaceful settlement in Korea must be a real settlement, when on the other hand, Congress is already talking about not giving the military so much money to the exclusion of the civiliam economy?"

"If the cease fire negotiators are hung up on the witdrawal of foreign troops - the U.N. Army and Red China - our side saying no, but the Red Chinese saying yes, why are the Reds increasing troop strength, artillery support, and bringing steel bridging equipment forward, if there's to be a quick end to it? The Communists must be planning another all out offensive along the same invasion route used when the war started, from the Iron Triangle."

Brannagh knew that Kumhwa was the eastern corner of the Iron Triangle. If Dad had so much information on what the Chinese were up to, why hadn't anyone in the outfit talked about it? Maybe they had, he reflected, but as he was the new guy, they hadn't told him. Tomorrow might bring the facts along with some sunshine.

"I've read that the North Korean Army has been rebuilt, and the Red Chinese have brought in two more armies supported by massive artillery. If the Reds are pretending to talk while actually preparing for another attack, Danny, you will get your crusader wish. You'll be up against the hordes of Communist China."

"I still can't believe I read it, but Acheson's state department said the talks would last but four weeks. Yet, neither side has agreed to where a cease fire line should be - on the 38th parallel or along the present battle line. As I write, all that has been agreed to is an agenda, can you believe it? The first item is establishing a military demarcation line, then setting up someone to supervise a truce, and finally to exchange prisoners. If the Reds and U.N. negotiators took more than two weeks just to agree to an agenda, it stands to reason it might take a month or more to agree to where that damn line is to be drawn."

Brannagh agreed with Dad's assessment. In the interim, would there be a shooting war, or a stand still? The guys in the first gun squad figured on a quick truce. For certain, it seemed clear that Corporal Fenton, who was withdrawing from reality by feeling he was an object and not a person, had to get relief soon, or crack up!

"Besides, Truman and Acheson selling out to the British, their administration will avoid a big war with the Reds until November. Why? There's a congressional election. Truman can't afford to have the American Eighth Army running away from the Red Chinese again."

Thanks, Dad, Brannagh thought, for your support of American fighting men. Brannagh remembered again his dad's questioning of this son's courage. Dad wasn't any higher on the Eighth Army`s devotion to duty!

"Speaking of the devil, Truman himself came to Detroit's 250th birthday party. Someone said the 4H club slogan really meant 'Help Hurry Harry Home.” In Truman's speech, he said he didn't know if the Communists really desired peace in Korea, or were simply trying to gain by negotiations what they couldn't conquer. He admitted the Chinese and North Koreans were bringing up men and equipment to the front, but damned if Truman didn't seem to be more worried about Europe and Yugoslavia! It is those damnable British again. If they can keep Truman worrying more about Europe than Korea, more of our tax dollars will go to England."

Brannagh had heard the bull that the Chinese had Russian artillery.

"I know you like sports, Danny, but I must tell you American baseball is a sissy game. It's not like hurling where Irishmen are as likely to hit an opponent as the caman - ball - with his hurling stick that's bigger than a bat."

Brannagh knew Dad wouldn't come to his baseball games because he thought baseball was

English cricket!

"American boxers are rugged men. Old man Jersey Joe Walcott knocked out the heavyweight champion, Ezzard Charles in the seventh. Jake Lamotta's been nothing since he fought Tony Zale, so Jake went down to Bob Murphy. Now there's a good name!

"Your Detroit Tigers aren't of much account, but the Yankees and Boston Red Sox lead the American league now.

"Make your volleys quick and sure, as we IRA men did.

I am your obedient servant,
Dad"

Would that Dad had sent along news on Mom, thought his son, of church, of the seminary, anything but the British and Truman. Brannagh knew his father's body was in America, but his heart and soul longed to be back with the IRA.

****

Kumhwa's gaunt, dun colored hills looked to the north and south, their brows of rugged rock bending the winds whistling wavelets to the east and west. Kumhwa was a time worn and weathered place. Brannagh went through the day training with the section on platoon problems and miserable military chores.

Usually unemotional, Brannagh saw that Harville's hollow eyes flashed a blue brilliance. The edge on him since Corporal Baiter's revelation of two fertilized eggs left behind in separate homemade nests was burnished. He had suffered a comment or two on his homespun needlework. But then he was just an apprentice tailor in Lancaster who had stitched himself into two suits, neither having anything to do with cloth, just law courts. Then Harville parted his lips, as the sea might have parted for Moses, flashing a smile the opposite of distress.

"I got a 'Dear John'!"

Brannagh saw the assistant gunner's animated face had nostrils rising and dilating while an upper lip did a horizontal revealing a plate that was a picket fence of spotted denture.

"It's a Dear John, alright," Harville confirmed.

Davis felt puzzled by his friend's reaction to a Dear John. Hadn't Davis received the like from his sweet little Salt Lake lady who wouldn't wait while he was at war, preferring the presence of a Brigham Young University sophomore to the long absence of a soldier of the United States? First ammo bearer Davis translated Harville's chortling as a compensatory screen, a masking of emotional hurt.

"There, there," said the Mormon, "the pain of a love lost will fade for you, as it has for me."

Brannagh noted that geniality was so much a part of the personality makeup of Davis, that one could hear the Mormon Tabernacle choir in his tone, or was it the unction of an insurance salesman?

"Pain? What pain," asked Harville in upbeat voice? "Rachel is getting married! Not to me, but to Herman Hinkle."

Davis again felt puzzled. Was Harville's manic manner the opposite side of depression? Had Harville conjured imminent death from Chinese 76 millimeters as punishment for his fornications and out-of-wedlock fathering of two babies?

"Why are you pretending so," unguently inquired Davis. "You can let it out. It will free your guilt."

"Guilt? What guilt," the dismayed assistant gunner questioned?

Brannagh saw a soldier in whom neither guilt or pain or pretension was a part of his relieved predicament.

Harville shook a negative. "You dumb tithe thief," he said to Davis. "Rachel was a buttonhole! Once Hinkle sews her on his coat, that dumb waiter will be father to this tailor's ham!"

Brannagh watched Harville's joyously cheeky face with its half cup smile turn to a frown.

"Or is the baby Hinkle's?"

"Either way," Van Meter explained, "whose ever hybrid seed it was, Hinkle will get the output."

Harville nodded agreement. Didn't he still have Rebecca at home, even if in a court room. She wanted an admission to paternity or submission to marriage. As he figured it, paternity was for eighteen years, and the other a life sentence. He decided to think on it when he got closer to rotation.

"What does constructive mean," interrupted Fenton?

"I don't know, Bob," answered Van Meter.

Corporal Fenton wanted to sleep, but his eyes, raised to the lighted lantern on its wire from tent pole to tent pole, saw a pearl like star that glowed brightly and followed each turn of his head. He figured questions on rotation might put him at ease.

Sergeant Van Meter had worried about Fenton's exhaustion, his over reaction to minor things, his anger at nothing, his flare ups, his tears at Baiter's bite. Van figured rotation was the key to recovery. Then Fenton would know the war wasn't his alone anymore.

"Hey, Brannagh," called Van, "what does constructive mean? Fenton wants to know."

"Constructive usually means something creative, Corporal Fenton," Brannagh answered.

He included rank, so as not to trigger an outburst or tears. He noted the puzzled look on Fenton's haunted face.

"How did you hear the word used, Sergeant," the last ammo bearer inquired of the squad leader?

"I didn't, Fenton did."

Brannagh could see Fenton looked flushed, but distant. Still there was a hostility underneath. Hadn't Fenton flared up when Harville merely jiggled the gunner's cot? Brannagh thought he better wait.

Fenton didn't think the new guy should talk to him. Only Sergeants Singletary and Van Meter should do so. After all wasn't he, Fenton, an old timer, in Korea since last Christmas? He had time on the rest of the troops. At that, he had time on his section sergeant and squad leader, but he was comfortable only with Van. It wasn't always so, just since April and May. Those battles changed everything. Only he and Van Meter remained from the first gun's members, so only Van could be trusted.

Fenton looked to the new recruit, the big guy with big words. Fenton sensed the red head's low calm voice came from a brain of mad fire intending to drive the gunner out of Van's squad. Then Fenton sensed a chill of fear, an image that a priest was talking from a whirling lantern as if it had become the moon.

"Fenton told me he heard the word constructive used when the new top kick was talking to Dog Six. O'Hara said rotation had a point system now, based on constructive months served on line, rather than on how close a soldier was to combat." Van Meter related.

Brannagh decided not to look at, or to talk directly to Fenton, but to Van.

"Then O"Hara must mean four weeks equals a constructive month. So one week is one point, and 40 weeks is ten constructive months."

Van Meter saw the time frame in the number of days needed to mature crops. "Listen to me, Bob, my grandpa could use help to harvest the crop this October, if you get a mind to leave the city behind."

Van smiled his assurances, but saw Fenton was mute, although his lips appeared to mouth words but not sound. Van wished that Fenton would get some sleep.

The squad leader put his perspective to Brannagh on the gunner's personality decompensation. "Fenton's morale is as low as the bottom of our latrine pit. He didn't even enjoy the movie."

Davis had a perspective of his own on that picture show. "It was a waste of time seeing 'On the Riveria'."

"So you say," Baldy Swinford retorted. "Danny Kaye was funny! Dem women - what a bevy of bouncing boobies had dem women's."

Brannagh was startled at Baldy's open display of feeling his place of bifarcation between legs.

"Stop that you degenerate," muttered Davis. "Is nothing sacred to you."

"Not my gun," exclaimed Baldy!

Baldy raised his carbine in his left hand, his right grasping his cylindrically shaped pole raising high his spreading underpants.

"This is sacred," Swinford said, raising his carbine head high, the carbine's oil as greasy on its barrel as the hair tonic spread across his polished pate to induce follicles to emerge once more. "But not my gun," he intoned, his hand waggling the equilibrium of his elevated crotch cloth.

"You're disgusting, Swinford," the unnerved Davis lectured.

Van Meter elected not to waste time on this conversation. His mind was full of rotation, and low morale of short timers. If there was to be a truce, why not get some of the short timers off the hill? He had heard rumors that rotation quotas wouldn't be given to the first battalion for the rest of August. How much longer could he let his gunner fester with rotation blues before Fenton was totally disabled?

Van recalled hill 717, when he had to lead Fenton over the skyline to the reverse slope just to take a leak. Would it be much longer before Van would have to open Fenton's fly for him, too? Van was certain Harville wouldn't complain to Singletary about Fenton's shivering in shock in the gun hole up there, for Harville didn't want to take over as gunner, nor did Davis. So Van did it himself, wondering how much longer he could hide the extent of his gunner's shattered nerves. Van wished for Fenton to rotate with honor, not as a mental case!

Even war horse Singletary was demonstrating signs of fatigue, Van meditated, maybe because Sing knew what he was fighting for until the Eighth Army let the Chinese up off the floor because some Russian on the radio said there should be truce talks. Singletary believed the Eight Army had been the finest fighting army ever fielded by the United States, until its leaders gave up the attack for training. Anymore, no objective was important to the outcome of the war. If an objective had any meaning now, like hill 717, it was for training the new recruits in manning a perimeter on an outpost, as a patrol base for G2, Divisional Intelligence, or as a warning redoubt if the Chinese changed their minds about being a stand still army. Sure as hell was a hot place, Van figured, the Eighth Army had quit the offensive in July! Van Meter admired his section sergeant, and didn't want to see the unmaking of an old Sergeant of established bravery by loss of respect for his officer corps. Van vowed to rectify his own lack of forcefulness with the first gun squad that the old Sergeant's pride in his third section would have no boundaries.

"Pfc Jean La Vie," Claude said to Brannagh, "is with the Second Division up near the place called the punchbowl. He is my last brother. Theo was killed in action at Normandy; Albert, he was KIA at Brittany; and Pierre, he was KIA at Falais. Was it not an honor for descendants of Acadians to die for their adopted country but in the land where their ancestors were born?" Brannagh nodded his agreement. "Points must be connect' to line time, ahn? What they think, mon Dieu," La Vie exclaimed!

"I heard tell some guys get line points for sleeping with gook mamasans in Seoul! That's not fair," Blaczyk answered La Vie.

Brannagh looked and saw an automobile frame of a body, whose squared legs were under him, Buddha like. It was the same ammo bearer who bitched every step of the way up the hill, who looked like a Lombroso criminal, but who never griped about the lack of a fire fight.

Davis exhorted a different viewpoint. "They'll need to do months to our weeks. The Army will see that its fair," he said.

Brannagh heard a general hilarity within the squad tent!

"At least now, rotation is precise," Davis preached. "I know my exact time to rotate, fair or not."

"Give me months in a warm bed with hot poontang any time to weeks of line time," ejaculated Baldy Swinford.

Davis saw more than ejaculating. "You're disgusting, Swinford," he said. "You and Trout are both degenerates!"

"Thank yew!" Baldy nodded to the compliment. He figured a degenerate must be Trout's vampire victim.

"Back to Seoul," Blaczyk emphasized the first word, "there's only one way to go home - alive! Is it fair Bishop Joseph" - Blaczyk had heard Davis tell the squad that he expected to become a bishop as had his father - "that you have to pull weeks fearing you're balls might be blown off, when some rear echelon bastard in Seoul has only to worry about wearing them out?"

Blaczyk often wondered if Davis had balls at all; what with him telling he was a Mormon priest and expecting a bishopric. Weren't bishops dressed in black cassocks with red piping and dinky beanies, that showed up at your church once a year to slap your twelve year old face because you just started playing with yours!

"At least now we know the basics of rotation," Van Meter said. "Before, it was so vague how division's rear echelon decided from 100 miles behind the line when we rotated. We'll know how many points we have, and how many points it takes to rotate."

Van kept quiet his worry that the rear echelon

would snafu his squad's records for their own. Maybe that was the problem why GIs who were called up from the enlisted reserve, and the old timers from the regular army troops were still here. The rear might even snafu Fenton's records for his early rotation, or Singletary's for Christmas! Van elected to switch emotions from dismal to delight.

"There's a good show tonight, Fenton. They're showing 'Half Angel' with Loretta Young. It's a comedy! You come with me." Van said.

"Yea, ok," Fenton replied.

Van saw Fenton grinning, eyes darting suspiciously among squad members, probably checking out imaginary friend or foe. Van Meter realized a close watch on his gunner would be required from now on until his rotation. His meaningless smiles seemed to come from the cold, makeshift mouth of a snowman. His mind was lost to a dreary daydream. If only he could sleep!

Fenton didn't see Baiter around, but saw his friend and leader, Van Meter, still was. It would be safe at the movie with Van at his side, an obstacle against the taunts of the domineering Baiter. Fenton shuddered at the thought of Baiter's presence, for he brought ridicule.

Brannagh considered his assignment to a line outfit in Korea, but for hill 717, hadn't been much different than his sixteen weeks of infantry basic and heavy weapons training back at Breckenridge, Kentucky. Here he was digging trenches and latrines instead of ditches; running ammunition up right angled hills instead of gently rounded mounds; sleeping in a squad tent on a canvas cot and not in a two story wooden barrack on springs and mattress.

There was at least one difference. At any moment his outfit could be pulled from training and sent north, not into Indiana, but into North Korea, to shoot and be shot at.

The army took care to see to their comfort in reserve, didn't it, Brannagh asked himself? There were two movies a week for troops assigned to blocking positions, and a twice weekly beer ration totaling seven cans. A soldier could partially quell his thirst twice a week, or horde for a movie, or sip a beer suavely daily. To horde meant stashing the excess in one's own back pack and lugging cans everywhere. It wasn't that he distrusted a fellow squad member, it was that he distrusted the fellows who were members of other squads. It was rare for ammo bearers in the third section of Dog to get to know their counterparts in the first section. Even back in reserve the three sections trained with their rifle companies, and went with them to dig bunkers in their rifle company's zone of defense. Though the sections were tented as a Dog platoon down a neat row of squad tents, there was a vagueness in belonging to the unit of Captain Busin and his new top kick Master Sergeant O'Hara. Brannagh figured he should ferry his back pack burden of fermented grain on all of 3d Section's details.

He brought his mind back within the canvas walls. He was appreciative some of the squad's conversation included him. He had done hill 717 with them. Generally, the old timers had excluded recruits as a matter of convenience, not knowing their names, and not much interested in any of their inclinations anyhow. Time would change all that, Brannagh concluded. He didn't have much to say, so listening was the order of the day. Weren't Im Ta Song or Dreamer included, Brannagh questioned himself? Was it because of Im's poor comprehension of English, because of Dreamer's incompentency? Brannagh observed that Im's eyes betrayed him, as did his malleable facial expressions, but not Dreamer's, for he looked like a wooden mallard duck. Brannagh had his doubts that Dreamer could read or write. All along the recruitment processing and basic training line, every officer and noncom must have ignored Dreamer's debilities. His own quick passage through the replacement pipeline had convinced Brannagh that the division rear was staffed by experienced regulars and collegiate draftees, that regimental rear was for skilled regulars, that battalion was for articulate regulars and draftees, while line companies got the residue. Dreamer was residue. Infantry was residue. There seemed to be a great deal of residue in the Eighth Army. It had its class distinctions, agreed Brannagh. Dreamer by intellect, Im Ta Song by race, and himself. Time might change his ascription, but never Im's or Dreamer's, Brannagh concluded, as their class had been ordained.

Im Ta Song sensed the ruminations emanating from the next cot occupant, his fox hole buddy with hair as red as a shaman's costume and red stovepipe hat.

"Why you lookee so at me," Im asked Brannagh?

"I was wondering why you were still an ammo bearer," Brannagh answered.

He was embarrassed to be caught staring, but he avoided telling a lie.

"Havee no on machine-gunee," yipped the Korean.

Brannagh again took note of Im's use of the

vowel `e' as an ending to so many words.

"Why not," asked Brannagh?

"Fenton gunner, Havee no Koree gunner on Americee machine-gun." Im was succint.

"Why?" Brannagh wouldn't leave the quiet voice alone.

"Havee no," was Im's reply.

He didn't want to go into the why and why not of squad politics. Wasn't he assigned to Dog of the 35th regiment as a part of what the Generals called the buddy-system? Wasn't he to learn combat techniques and bravery from Americans? Americans weren't afraid of the Chinese, were they? American soldiers held their positions. They didn't bug out! Im Ta Song's pensiveness admitted it was brave for his section to be up front during the most deadly of times - when the winds of peace were blowing away the clouds of war. He wished for the best of them that they not be buried in spirit graves like Fenton. Im knew he would never be a machine-gunner or squad leader, not until the pigmentation of his skin paled and almond shaped eyes rounded. That day would be the day all American soldiers left Korea.

Brannagh was aware that prejudice played games in the military. Why should the Army be different than its political bosses back home? President Truman's Democratic party split during the last presidential election over civil rights for blacks, didn't it, with Dixiecrats nominating Strom Thurmond of South Carolina? Truman's Fair Deal fell victim, and even the Army took two years to issue regulations that its manpower should be utilized without regard to race. A year after that, some combat organizations integrated, but not the 25th Infantry division. It still had the black deuce-four and the white 27th and 35th regiments. He knew stateside and military prejudice was as much a part of America as were segregated swimming pools. He realized why Im wasn't a gunner!

Im appreciated the attention, even if Brannagh was on a topic from which refraining was wise. At least the talking didn't relate to the care and cleaning of Dreamer's weapon and gear. Im studied the full bodied ammo bearer, one with an openness in his heart as wide as the Hantan Valley, a laughing voice, a face white as mountain snow with playful deep water blue eyes, as intelligent perhaps as artist Kong Hui-an's Sage at Rest on a Rock, painted in the fifteenth century. Im's wit concluded Brannagh was a different sort of GI.

"Papasan write?" inquired Im.

"Yea, several times!" Brannagh emphasized his last two words. "I don't know what I would do if he didn't write. Then most times I don't know what to do with what he writes!"

It was Dad Brannagh's ongoing agony, realized Brannagh, to be a loving father sorely beset by an erring son, the tool of an incompetent President following British advice.

Hadn't Dad scribbled a rage of words damning Truman and Acheson for partitioning Korea as the British had partitioned Ireland? Hadn't Dad raged that Truman's policies didn't care that Korea fell to the Communists, only that the fall not look as though the Truman Administration had pushed it? Hadn't Dad swore that the notice behind the President's Anglophile, Dean Acheson, for supporting the war was to build up America's military to protect the British, not in Korea, but in Hong Kong? When last, Dad had written, had a Chinaman sailed an armed junk across the Pacific to attack America?

"Papasan say," questioned Im Ta Song?

Brannagh read.

"Unless I bring up the Korean conflict, no one at Sullivan's Twin Gables Bar is talking about it. They only talk about the miserable Tigers being 18 games behind the Yankees."

"Havee tiger there," a surprised Im asked?

"The name of a baseball team," Brannagh explained. "You've seen GIs playing baseball. All the GIs on one team were named Tigers. GIs on the other team were named Indians. Teams take names to tell one another apart."

Why was he reading Dad's letter to Im, Brannagh pondered. Surely, there was little comprehension; yet in as much as he started reading, he'd finish reading.

"A Senator named Joe McCarthy claims Truman's Administration is infiltrated by communists. Senator McCarthy should investigate the British ties! The Detroit Free Press reported a subcommittee was negotiating with the Reds about a truce line, even flipping a coin to decide if the Commies or the U.N. makes the first proposal on where the line should be. Maybe after thirty or more meetings a coin toss was better than all that haggling."

Brannagh looked to see if Im was showing signs of recognition of the meanings of the words.

Im nodded his head in understanding. Hadn't he put in months with an American outfit - a two hundred and thirty day seminar on GI verbiage? Long forgotten, in his personnel file back at regiment, was the fact that he, and his father before him, had been taught by educated men, albeit Japanese; perhaps he and his father weren't taught to led, only to follow, but his revered grandfather, a graduate of the Hansong Normal School, saw to his grandson's real education. Im Ta Song knew he was well read and educated. He understood filial piety and loyalty. His roots grew a virtue that he weigh his words carefully before addressing his elders. Though Grandfather hadn't lived to see his dutiful grandson take up arms with westerners of high noses and deep set eyes, Grandfather would have approved. He himself supported the 1919 Samil Independence Movement. Would that Im could be again with his revered progenitor. Im longed to face his elders, lean slightly forward with his hands cupped in front of him, to inquire solicitously about their health. It was not to be. His grandfather didn't survive the imperial Japanese, his father didn't survive the Imum Gun from the north; the son expected not to survive the Communist Chinese forces. Im had settled on being a Korean soldier fighting for home and country in an American infantry squad. He expected no letters from home.

"Papasan worried," Im asked the letter reader?

"Yea, he is," answered Brannagh. "Dad is ticked off that we are being forgotten in Korea. He believes our president thinks the Chinese can't beat us, so the president is concentrating on Europe in case the Russians act up over there. Dad calls Korea a coffinless grave."

*****

Trout was on the prowl for truce talk news out of the many letters the recruit Brannagh had gotten at mail call. Trout situated himself strategically. He sat down beside Im Ta Song so as to better see and talk to the recruit.

"What your Paw figgering on out of the talks," Trout asked?

He hadn't paid much mind to Brannagh's induction into the hall of torpidity after he had finished reading. He watched the distant gaze slowly disappear and refocus its red streaked blue pupils on the questioner.

"Oh," said Brannagh as in a cavern, "he's figgering on an American occupation in a few weeks."

Brannagh hadn't an itch to spill the details of Dad's home manufactured verbal bullets.

"Hot damn," Trout exploded. "Aiming on prancing around Seoul for some poontang, if good old Joe ROK here tells me where to prance."

"For Kisaeng," the surprised Im Ta Song gasped? "Havee no," he vibrated.

Brannagh saw that Trout had lost his interest in the letters. Trout's interest was the 1st gun's Korean now, and how to reduce the Korean's contrariness. The 2d gun's first ammo bearer leaned forward, every muscle tense, his head jerking, his curved mouth twisting in a skewed smile that must have worked the mountain women to putty, as he eyeballed the Korean. Even if Trout never could understand Korea's language, Joe ROK's words still had a right good sound to them.

"What's that there Kisaeng," Trout asked?

He hoped his pronunciation - kiss wang - carried the connotation of what the puji might do on him. He continued to stare into the peach pits of Joe ROK's eyes which were glinting brightly as a jeep's taillights in a blackout.

Im Ta Song's words gushed like water over Niagra Falls.

"What's he saying," Trout asked?

Brannagh had an idea. The three years of Attic Greek back in high school and six years of Latin attuned his ear, as much as his parents' brogues. Im Ta Song had months in the company of GI speak, so there was a sense to the Korean's military English.

"He said something like this. 'Kisaeng are pretty women.' He said, 'villages have Confucian shrine and house for local big shots and military. So people are taxed much Won for Kisaeng who serve big shots.'"

"Are the houses still there," Trout nearly shouted.

"Havee, yes," Im Ta Song replied softly before rambling on.

Brannagh filled in the words between Im's ee. "He said 'yes. Two times a month a local big shot puts on his ceremonial belt and silk hat and stands before a Chompae. Women employed by big shot come before him and bow, each hoping to be chosen a Kisaeng for local house. Prettiest sent to house in Seoul."

"Hot damn," hollered Trout, "where can I find that chompae?"

Brannagh heard a pronunciation of the first syllable that emerged as - chomp. It evoked Anglo-Saxon verbiage applicable to the imagined act.

Im Ta Song seemed unusually animated, Brannagh witnessed, completely unlike the ammo bearer he was coming to know well.

"He said," Brannagh continued, 'each village has Chompae made of wood with Chink characters for royal Palace in front of Kisaeng house.

Trout smiled, then laughed. He expected much of his occupational duty whould be spent hanging around a chompae twice a month when the county chief showed up in his ceremonial belt and silk hat and

did his picking of Korea's golden delicious apples.
Trout was of a mindset that relished licking of juice
from the apple.

Brannagh watched the delirious warrior depart
for his own squad tent to await the happy moment the
truce freed his butt from the MLR to pursue Korean
culture.

"Is that true," Brannagh asked? He recognized
his own naivete.

Im Ta Song was of a mind not to answer. It
wasn't wise to trust most GIs with secrets. Yet this one
was somehow different.

"Havee no Kisaeng," Im Ta Song said. "Gonee.
Troutee no find for prickee."
*****

"Ya gotta be quick or ya're gonna be dead,"
boomed the voice of Sergeant Singletary.

Brannagh watched Sing's neck muscles constrict
as his lips worked to a pucker, one lip over the other.
He hucked up a gob with the noise of a consumptive in
a wino hotel, forcibly ejecting an egg-sized oyster
through long bore lips towards a distant moving speck
of protoplasm. His spit splotched as it hit just beyond
Brannagh's M-1 carbine that laid across his knees. He
saw the splash had drowned a bug of the Imun Gun in
viscous Yankee crud. The insect wasn't quick!

Brannagh figured the sputum was Sing's
disclaimer of his first gun squad. The fully equipped
third section had been raced by its section sergeant up
every grim wrinkle of hill 450 to beat the first and
second sections of machine guns to the hill's time worn
crest. Sing's second gun had flexed strong right arms as
conquerors, but his first gun squad had mislaid its
efforts and brought up the rear. Brannagh remembered

that Sing grunted and spat as he passed money to O'Hara, before grunting and spitting at the 1st gun squad well worn from struggle and strain, despite losing!

"There will be crew drills," Sing snorted, "the quickest gun crew getting double cigarettes, compliments of Master Sergeant O'Hara. There will also be an ammo bearer gallop up this hill," Sing asserted. "Each ammo bearer must carry six belts of machine gun ammo any way he wants, from down there," he pointed towards hell, "to where I'm standing! The winner gets a week's double beer ration compliments of Sergeant O'Hara."

Sing took another look at the ex-pulpit pupil to reevaluate his odds. O'Hara had his money on Brannagh for the ammo bearer race, while Sing pushed Trout. Auld Trout was a mountainy man, the recruit but a prayer breather. Sing worried O'Hara had some dope no one else had.

A double hernia was more like it, reflected Brannagh. Six belts of ammo weighed one hundred and twenty pounds, not counting the weight of gear, spare parts in one's pack, and one weapon. An American Army carried quite a load of ammo into battle, but used chogie bearers to bring up the extra stuff. There must be five hundred chogie bearers in the 25th Infantry Division, each drawing down good wages of five hundred Won daily, plus a rice ration, Brannagh figured. So what that 500 Won was but twelve cents American, it was big money in Korea. He knew there wasn't an ammo bearer in Dog Company's machine gun platoon that wouldn't finance a chogie run instead of an ammo bearer gallop.

Sitting on a gray rock, the sun broadly flashing

hues of gold, the wind wildly dashing, Brannagh mused on O'Hara's generosity. Back an eternity ago, so seemed the assembly before the advance on hill 717, didn't Crane and other replacements complain about losing their hind ends to O'Hara's bets?

"So thats it," Brannagh mumbled. Insight flitted within his brain that O'Hara and Sing had money on the outcome. Brannagh hoped Sing wasn't a double crossing crud like Breezedale and O'Hara had been back at the troop ship's boxing ring.

Brannagh saw the bright faced O'Hara smiling at the semi circle of troops. He looked to be a warrior in weaponry, but one who never spared a man at a disadvantage; a soldier that ordered his men through clouds of blood.

Brannagh saw a soldier in Singletary, one who was combat ready; one who exuded an aura of invulnerability from pale blue eyes either side of a beak the size of a shoehorn.

The strangeness of the landscape was as much a sight for Brannagh to behold as were the mastiff sergeants. Hills loomed like molars. There were buck teeth with sore gums and lowly growing vegetation. Valleys ran like narrow gage railroad tracks between formidable inclines. Infantry were below in a wilderness of high grass where once bullocks ploughed the earth for fields of winter wheat. A free wind breathed humidity off the sauna like rocks as the winds over the lakes brought stickiness to Detroit in late August.

Brannagh began to feel in place. So far it was a post graduate course in digging bunkers, laying barbed wire and clearing fields of fire. Then followed classes on weapon usuage and firing problems. There weren't any book-only cadre atop the hills, but experienced infantrymen.

"Ya gotta be quick or ya're gonna be dead," Sing repeated.

Brannagh saw him huck up another gob of foamy mucus, spitting it the other side. Sing had him bracketed. He could fire for effect.

"Recruit," Sing roared, "ya got something to say?"

"No, Sergeant."

"I heard you, or was Baiter throwing his voice to a dummy?"

Singletary, like all sergeants, Brannagh thought, liked the use of humiliation as a tool of authority.

"He ain't got a brain in his fat head, Sarge." Baiter said. "Com' here Charley McCarthy, Edgar Baiter needs his mujerado."

Baiter's hip popping gestures conveyed his obscene intent at his prey.

Brannagh hadn't been in the outfit long and he was in dutch with the section sergeant, and ready to rend the nose of the second gun's corporal. Brannagh felt the eyes of the men dig into him like insect bites.

"Sorry Sergeant," he apologized, "I must of- - -!"

A sudden eruption blew foliage backwards. It's wrath and roar siezed his sensiblilities. Brannagh, whirling himself from his rock seat to the earth, bit dirt in reaction.

An eruption was heard in distant reply. Cautiously, Brannagh moved his hands off of his helmet to raise his nose and mouth out of the hill's epidermis. He saw, again, the eyes of the section gleaming like reflecting mirrors the mock of Baiter's grim lips and carious teeth. La Vie, Trout, Im Ta Song,

Van Meter, everyone else was still sitting. Brannagh saw Sing's hands on his hips as if he had metamorphed to Mussolini. Van Meter stood and offered him a hand.

"You should have seen them setting up the recoiless rifle, chicken shanker," hooted Baiter!

Van Meter had another viewpoint. "It's always smart to hit the dirt where there's incoming or outgoing."

"Smart," hooted Baiter! "That's a whole lot of cosmoline, Van; that sweet fairy ain't nothing but a chicken."

Brannagh clenched his fists.

Van saw the sharp focus in the eyes of his new man, his flushed face and stare. Van knew Sing would back Baiter, even if Baiter broke every bone in the private's body. Van was certain that Sing would go so far to back up Baiter that charges would be sent to the Judge Advocate for court martial even if Baiter beat up Brannagh.

"Take it calm, Private Brannagh. Corporal Baiter's got a sewer mouth. He ain't nothing but a floater in a septic tank," Van said.

He was as calm as he wanted his ammo bearer to be. Van directed Brannagh back to place.

Baiter ignored the pointed reference to his vocal aperture. He ignored most everything he could about Van Meter anyway. The gunner saw nothing deep in the Iowa dirt farmer, nor anything presently threatening. Baiter saw a sergeant that tried to do what he was told, but couldn't bring it off in his own gun squad like Cervera did with the second gun. Yet, Baiter worried, Van had time in grade over Cervera and most likely would get Sing's place. Then where would the gunner stand? Baiter took consolation in knowing that Fenton was cracking up, and Harville and Davis not worth a hot piss! So there was no one but Baiter able to take the first gun squad as leader, was there?

Baiter's thoughts fired his burning mind. He would need to cultivate Dog company's new top kick, the one with a strut, and kiss ass to get Cervera the section and himself the second gun squad! Baiter vowed to work havoc on Van like a plague cloud streaming down on an artillery destroyed tank.

"We've got crew drills to run Van Meter, if you can get the asses of the blundering bunch you lead off the latrine," Baiter bantered!

Brannagh saw that Baiter's bombastic words carried even less than his usual unsubtlety. His once again thrusting inguinal ligament couldn't hide his meaning.

Singletary let it cool. Maybe the recruit was a chicken and Van Meter a wasted shell casing. Then maybe the recruit and Baiter should be left to duke it out, Sing reflected, planting another seed in his gambling mind. Time for that, Sing reckoned. Now he had money to win on gun crew drills.

"You gotta be quick or I'll have your ass, you hear, Van? You, too, Cervera," Sing called to his squad leaders.

"Si," Cervera responded.

Cervera played his role as that of an alien Mexican bracero that upped and joined the U.S. Army. He felt he couldn't admit to having been a migrant labor crew chief, recruiting stoop laborers for growers. It was a lousy business. He took contracts at one price from growers and provided picking crews at a much lower price per peck. So what if living conditions were poor in the migrant camps hidden in the trees on the

back acres of the farms. They were out of sight! They
were also out of mind! Yet when he saw children with
masses of lumps from myriads of stinging mosquitoes,
many bites festering from scratching; families that
were lving on a diet of beans and tortillas, with fresh
meat or milk only after a weekly shopping trip because
they had no refrigeration or storage space safe from
vermin and rats; when he discovered he could not
stomach the stench that permeated every pore of the
camp from an outhouse long used and never treated;
when he stood in pools of stagnant water waiting in line
to fill his pail with water from the camp's rusted tap;
when he saw kids that slept eight abreast separated
from the rotted wood floor by newspaper; and after
being battered by bouncing truck springs and knocking
motors driving through hostile farm towns to have a
successul season and a winter of wine and women
while his crews went home with a few hundred dollars
to sustain family life through the winter until the wheel
of life took another turn and it was spring and the crops
were ripening somewhere - Cervera quit! He wanted
his death in Korea to be atonement to the children of
lost summers.

"The longer you mess with me, the meaner I get,
Sing," Fenton angrily interrupted.

He didn't want gun drill! He didn't want to stay
on this hill, but he sensed he would be miserable all
alone back in the squad tent.

Sing saw Fenton's wild eyes roll a loop as his
furtive glances studied the recoilless rifle. It's backblast
must have triggered Fenton's left field response, the
section sergeant concluded. This gunner might not yet
be totally delusional, but a spring or two were missing
from his clockworks! Surely, Fenton would crumble

during the crew drills, and with him would go the side bet to O'Hara!

Sing calculated he needed a first and fourth place just to tie, if one of the other section's two gun crews took both a second and third. Six points went to the winner, then five to second and so on down to no points to the last crew. O'Hara was the field judge.

"We'll run some practices," Singletary instructed. "Stick to procedure. Be precise," he said.

Van Meter and Cervera took their positions fifteen yards from their three man crews of gunners, assistant gunners and first ammo bearers. Each soldier assumed the prone position, five yards between them in a line, equipment beside them in place, examined and reported.

"Action," came the command from the two squad leaders, pointing to a position where their guns were to be mounted.

Cervera watched as Baiter sprung to his feet as if jumping from a rattlesnake. He grasped his mount, swung it to his right hip and dashed to the point like a shot arrow, his tripod's frontal legs flying out to position. Assistant gunner Revels carried the gun, and waddled like a great pumpkin scampering on a scooter. Baiter rammed tight the tripod's legs jaming handles; then aligned the gun over the cradle seating, fixing it to place.

Trout's ostrich legs reciprocated like twin jack hammers, moving him forward with the water can and ammo box. Baiter raised the rear sight; Revels inserted the tab of the ammo belt; and Trout afixed the water hose. The gun's bolt was cocked to half load.

Van Meter was dismayed at the sight of his gun crew. Fenton was arriving, all legs of the tripod swinging loosely like broken limbs dangling from an uprooted tree in a wind storm.

"Up," called Baiter. He sat in the up gunner's position.

"Ready," answered Revels, on the left side to feed the gun.

"Out of action," ordered Cervera.

Baiter pulled the gun's cover to the rear, then raised it with his right hand. Revels removed the belt of thirty caliber rounds from the gun's feedway. He replaced the belt in the ammo box. He removed the hose from the gun, closing its plug. Trout was there to run back with the water, ammo can and water hose. Revels, with the gun, followed Trout. Baiter, with the tripod, was on their butts. All three, Baiter, Revels and Trout resumed the prone position, rearranging equipment in military orderliness.

Van's view saw that Harville hadn't yet set the gun into Fenton's tripod cradle. The locking pin was still in the cradle. Placing the gun on his knee, Harville's free hand pulled the locking pin out and set the gun into the cradle, returning the pin to position.

"Up," mocked Baiter.

Sing held his anger the long while until the first gun hollered up. They were pathetic. Sing was convinced Fenton put the section in jeopardy because of his psychological immobilization, not to give a thought to the lost wager.

"Damn me for listening to Van Meter," grumbled the section sergeant. "Let Fenton go home with honor, Van had begged. Don't let it be a section eight he said to me," Sing remembered. "Shit on that!"

Sing might have upheld the plea if they were digging bunkers and slit trenches back in blocking, but not upon the hill where money was at risk.

"Van Meter," ordered Singletary, "give Fenton a break."

"Yes, Sergeant. I'll put someone else on the gun," answered Van.

Sing figured no better than a first and last place with Baiter and Fenton, or six points. Any section getting a second and fifth, or third and fourth would beat him. He might catch a fifth with someone else on the first gun.

O'Hara saw Sing's irritation, his repulsive smile. They were good signs, O'Hara felt. He had his cash on the 2nd section. So simulating the voice of a deity, vast and taciturn, he gave the six squad leaders his words of wisdom, then expectantly watched their proceeding commence.

"Out of action," called Van Meter.

"Up," responded Brannagh.

O'Hara was disturbed by the outcome. He was ticked over the unannounced substitution of Brannagh for Fenton. O'Hara figured Brannagh and Singletary had suckered him. Their conspiracy was a kaleidoscope which assumed a new form and color at every turn. O'Hara vowed to be as inventive in the future.

*****

O'Hara wanted no rigging of the ammo gallop. He sat down the squad's Koreans. He knew they were used to carrying loads up hills higher than hill 450. Only GIs were to be raced!

"Each ammo bearer is free to carry six belts any way he wants, by hand, strung onto ammo belts, however," O'Hara instructed loudly.

He saw Brannagh among the ammo bearers, a tall Irish-American lad as white of face as polished stone, wrapped with four belts about his shoulders, crossing two to each side; with a box in each hand, his carbine at right shoulder arms, his pack in place, ready to give his all!

It wasn't as O'Hara wanted him. The straight square boy who never did other than his best, who was a man of morals who turned his face on the real Irishman. O'Hara had seen that side of the Army before. Its elite were powerfully resistant to the encroachment of a mere Irish immigrant, and consciously had defended its position and wealth against the indignity of commissioning a foreigner from its ranks. Fight and die for old glory and citizenship, but not in the officer corps, was his hearsay. O'Hara had bet on Brannagh's efforts, but now saw only perfidy in a spoiled seminarian.

"All the sergeants have their money down," O'Hara asked?

"In Watt's pocket," Singletary assured! "Everything's ready."

"Go," O'Hara ordered!

He read Singletary's inflections as immutable testimony another fix was in. At half point, O'Hara turned his binoculars to see Trout of the third, Dorsey of the first, and Castner of the second section leading the pack with three or four others off to Trout's left. All looked like frigates with one gun deck ready to fight in a line of battle. O'Hara saw Brannagh winding off near Trout, then cutting back criss cross, with an unkempt soldier dogging the heels of Brannagh, as if he were tied behind. A dozen other ammo bearers were following their bliss, but one after another, they popped like popcorn in the humidity.

Brannagh saw the sky was flecked with clouds of

gray bottoms, with white tops, like baseball uniforms. He felt like a wilted spinach.

Dreamer could see the sky line. He could be first. He would be important! He plowed past Brannagh, through the grass, inching uphill.

Trout saw Dreamer's weary move, hand over hand kissing the crumbling earth. Trout maneuvered towards the outcropping of turrets where the top kick O'Hara had told Trout of a gentle path up the ridgeline to the crest. If he made the plumb line where mountain goats dared not, a path lay ahead, ovaled through the stone by centuries of wind and rain.

Dreamer heard a ghostly cry vibrating from the castle's keep where Trout had gone. Dreamer fixed his eyes on the spot, but buckled a knee as he misstepped.

Brannagh thought it was a tube of brass casings clutching a hot dog. He stayed the fall of the tumbling tumbleweed. Dreamer's bloody face within looked to be a tomato in a stuffed green pepper.

"I can't help you up," Brannagh explained, "or you'd be out. So get up, Dreamer, and follow me."

Dreamer wanted to be buried there, never to leave until his heart shrunk, his lungs enfolded, and his bruised body healed.

"Get up, Dreamer. You can still win," Brannagh encouraged.

Brannagh saw they had yards on their closest pursuers. He figured none other than he, Trout and Dreamer wanted the beers, or else, none of the others were as stupid as the three of them.

"Something happened to Trout," Brannagh guessed. "Trout went into those pinacle rocks and I haven't seen him since."

Trout was cursing himself for his own stupidity

for stepping onto a loose rock slide and skiing on his ass like a little kid on his first snow. Worse, it felt like pulling his prong out of a knothole extricating himself from a ton of nature's buckshot.

Dreamer ignored his dirt encrusted ammo with dented cartridges. He squared his shoulders, and leaned into the climb. He threw, first one can, then the other, walking his ammo upwards. He let their weight buck the rest of him forward.

Brannagh slowed, placed himself behind Dreamer, occasionally simulating a surge as if to outmuscle Dreamer to reach the top.

O'Hara could twist Brannagh's neck, if he might have reached it. His keen eye pierced to the lad's thoughts, and found there spite at the doings to Trout. How could Brannagh have figured the blighting of Trout's apparent victory by misdirection, the favor for the Celt?

Dreamer was first to the crest. When his hands let loose their anchors, he toppled over.

Brannagh again stayed the cylindrical Dreamer from another down hill roll, unwinding him from his ammo-belts as if stripping an armadillo. With Dreamer done, Brannagh unloaded his own ammo, folding their belts into boxes like tucks in drapery. He opened his pack and liberated two lonely cans of hot beer. Brannagh marvelled at his P-38 can opener's folding blade and handle of tooled steel. It could cut open not only a beer can and C-ration but an Easy Eight's tank turret, given leverage and a lifetime.

"Have a beer, top dog," Brannagh offered Dreamer. "Get as wet inside as out.

Dreamer had his head in the clouds, but his arms on the ground were too tired to leave the clay.

Brannagh lifted Dreamer's head from his helmet pillow and poured beer from its half moon lid crease into a crooked ditch of a mouth.

O'Hara looked at Singletary, then up hill at Brannagh. The top kick saw foes. "I will be the scourge of your iniquities," O'Hara said.

Singletary wondered if scourge was Irish for screw Brannagh.

CHAPTER FOUR
A TACTICAL WEAKNESS

Im Ta Song lit up a cigarette, drawing it to a sunset radiance in the shadowless squad tent. He had not lit Sing's poker table lantern or opened the front tent flap to catch the evening's cool breezes. He hadn't felt the need for chow either. He felt a need to lay down.

"Hav' a no truce," Im murmured.

"What say, Im," inquired Brannagh?

"Hav' a no truce," Im repeated, tripping on the `t'. "Nam Il lose face!"

"He ain't much to look at nohow, Joe," Baldy said, responding to Im's nervously loud words.

Brannagh noted that Swinford's usual splutter came with chewing tobacco sounds, their liquid counterpart separating from their gaseous forms to speckle the matted floor.

"Nam Il lose face to Chinese," Im repeated.

"How so," Brannagh asked?

"Chinese soldier giv' matches to Nam Il. Chinese matches nev' burn. Nam Il no can light cigarette. So Nam Il pull GI cigarette lighter out'a pocket, light up, Chinese see," Im exclaimed!

Van Meter's squad gathered near Joe ROK's cot. He knew something they didn't.

"Go on, Joe," Van Meter ordered.

"When Chinese see, then Nam Il throw the GI lighter out'a window. Nam Il walked out on truce talk. Havee no truce," Im groaned.

"Bull Shit," spackled Baldy Swinford!

"Hav' a no," responded Im!

Im's tossed his words high in wrath. He too had a life he wanted to live outside the American Army, if the Yangban's brutality would ever cease. Even the hated Japanese occupiers of Korea had proclaimed against the Yangban's infringing on another person's rights under the shelter of their superior class. Im recalled his grandfather's tale of a beating he received for smoking his pipe as he walked past a Yangban's house. It was a lashing of belly and back. Nam Il wasn't that kindly. He lashed hope.

Van Meter felt as if hell had returned. He and Fenton had come through the bitter fighting of April and May. They had opened the roads to Pyongyang again, when the talk on the demarcation line stopped their advance. Now if the North Koreans had walked out over a cigarette lighter, would the war resume? He dreaded that it would.

He looked again at his upset Korean ammo bearer. "What's Joe ROK mumbling about, Brannagh?" "Best I can tell," he answered, "he would have lit Nam Il's cigarette, even if it meant a beating of belly and back."

"Would'a lit the damn cigarette for Nam Il," Im Ta Song said, "and let Nam Il lash my back and belly."

The haunting tone of Im Ta Song reminded Brannagh he had his Dad's letter. He reopened it. He felt the need to soothe the owl moans of the squad, the dreary wind whistling as if a subdued scream had fallen over a tomb like shadowy tent.

"Nam Il did walk out on the negotiations, but came back the next day, so Dad writes," Brannagh informed.

"What else does he write," the hopeful Van inquired?

"Nam Il walked out over the demarcation line. He wanted a line on the 38th parallel, not north of it,"

Brannagh read.

"What be demarb - demark line," Dreamer asked?

"A boundary line, like between California and Arizona." Brannagh replied. "Nam Il doesn't want us up north."

"Be north," the surprised Dreamer questioned?

"We are," answered Van Meter. "We've been in North Korea since June. Sure doesn't look any different from the south."

"So why stay here then," hollered Davis!

The energized Davis, Brannagh detected, absent his usual sanctifying and animated smile, hadn't restrained his passion in his exclamation.

"Let's get the hell back behind the 38th parallel," Harville echoed in support. " Let Nam Il keep these colossal columns we call hills!"

Brannagh saw that Harville's eyes flashed contempt he might have wished were electrical bolts running through chairs of the pompous and proud negotiators.

"You men keep it down," urged Van Meter, "let Brannagh read his letter."

It was scarcely Brannagh's mission to Korea to be the bearer of strain and strife. He surmised that Dad couldn't be correct in writing that the last break up of the talks over the alleged napalming of Kaesong was the end of the negotiations. Hadn't there been optimism when they formed an informal committee to iron out a demarcation line? If Dad was right, then General Ridgway's words - that the communist charges were `malicious falsehoods', must have blown away the truce tent's favorable vaporings! Brannagh, daunted, elected to reconstruct his Dad's implication that his son's training for occupation duty was off; not so his test of fortitude in the face of the enemy.

"The talking has stopped, again, just as it did two or three times before, nothing more." Brannagh said. "The Chinks are only ticked off at the U.N. Generals for regarding its forces as victors."

Van Meter sensed Brannagh's trepidation. The squad leader saw his spidery gunner was spread arms and legs akimbo as if protecting a frail web from a wind.

Brannagh obtained a nod from Fenton to continue, despite the life shown from what had long appeared to be insensible clay scowling with a stormy gloom.

"Dad writes that 'General Van Fleet said if we GIs have to start fighting Chinks again we will have a new hatred for the enemy; we will be an eager army'," Brannagh read.

"About as eager an army as grandpa was to repay his loan to the Farm Security Administration," Van Meter concluded.

He heard Joe ROK say something. "What's Joe on about, Brannagh?"

"Near as I can tell, he said other Koreans are saying the enemy is bringing up big guns, more troops. That many, many soldiers came with the big guns."

Van knew his squad had heard the news that ROK divisions had been attacking to the east of the Iron Triangle on hill 983. Rumor said there had been ROK bug outs. The brass told it was a limited offensive to straighten the line and take the high ground around the punchbowl. Whatever the truth of it, Van knew the operation started before the truce talks broke off on August 27.

"Seems the Detroit Tigers weren't too eager either, Sergeant Van," Brannagh said, changing the subject. "The Tiger's Bob Cain had to pitch to a 3'7" midget. Cain walked him, but the Tigers beat the St. Louis Browns 6 to 2. Maybe they should play more midgets, then they might win a few," he mused.

Brannagh put the lid on reading aloud Dad's anti-Brit paragraph, that a captured MIG-15 was powered by a British made Rolls-Royce Nene engine. The British maintained the engine, one of a hundred, was sold to Russia in 1948. Since then, no other engines had been sold. A likely lie, Dad had it!

"I was in the big battle last April," Fenton declared.

To Van, Fenton sounded as if he were in high triumph, and his long distance stare had roots in his delusion filled memory. He was talking to Brannagh.

"Two hundred and fifty thousands of chinks swarmed out of the night under a full moon. Hundreds of chinks in padded cotton brown clothes came at us. I couldn't hear them in their tennis shoes, but saw they wore bandoliers and grenades. The chinks leading the skirmishes looked like Jap soldiers I saw in the movies. Their weapons' squads carried their guns on bamboo poles, slung between the shoulders of two men. When the Turks were hit hard, they pulled out south across the Hantan River, but the 35th Regiment was sent up on the double. We had the 27th regiment to our right. We had artillery support up the ass!"

Van saw it as a song of sunshine, Fenton's face shining. He could hear the roar of battle. He was a man of courage again.

"It was a machine-gunner's dream." Fenton continued. " What a field of fire! I played our song - ta dum, ta dum, ta dum, ta dum, ta dum, ta dum," Fenton simulated, "bursts of six, using belt after belt of ammo. I ran the fanny's off the squad's ammo bearers. My bullets fell on the chinks like hell's spit balls. Artillery fell like horse piss. I forget the rest," Fenton said. Van Meter noticed that Fenton's eyeballs were vexed and tired, his nerve drained.

"It was the Van Fleet load!" Van Meter said, as he picked up the story, "that beat back the Chink's frontal attacks. Pieces of Chinamen were everywhere, but they weren't stopped. We were hit again, flares everywhere. We were cut off but we fought our way out. Our quad fifties had to spit lead as thick as mosquitos at a summer picnic. But for the trucks on fire, it was pitch dark. Still, ambulances got hit, and the soldiers on stretchers were hit two or three times. We set up another defensive line. Then the chink's attacked again. Fenton's gun mowed them down like McCormick's original reaper, then we pulled back and did it all over again."

Van rotated his hands boldly, reaper-like. He rolled on.

"By April 28 we were occupying Line Golden near Seoul. We were hit that night. We must have killed another thousand of them. The chinks had to attack through coiled barbed-wire, mines, booby traps, napalm drums and white phosphorus under searchlights towards our sandbagged bunkers and interconnecting trenches with firing steps."

To the emboldened Van it seemed as if he were still there. Van Meter was witness to casualties he hadn't expected to see during the course of his full duty in Korea. The Chinese generals displayed a manifest arrogance. They underrated the quality of the

American's replacement troops. Yet what courage and discipline, as Van saw it, had the Chinese troops, to leave their lines and attack dug-in-forces, and against massive artillery and air support. What fortitude to attack into the massed, steady, levelled machine-guns and rifle barrels of Americans of calm purpose and cool nerves, with quick, accurate artillery!

"We ended the yo-yo war. I had hoped these cease fire talks would have brought an end to the carnage," Van Meter concluded.

"Korea soldiers say Chinese and Imun Gun bring up many big guns, many troops. Round eye soldiers come up with big guns," interjected Im Ta Song.

"Round eyed," exclaimed Brannagh!

Brannagh knew he acted startled. The string bean Korean with a flat face and a lollipop head had kept back the best tidbit. KATUSAS had access to the ROKs and Chogie bearers fresh out of the division's rear. Im Ta Song must be well informed.

"Ruskee!" Im Ta Song said.

Brannagh heard the alarm in Im's tone. A cold chill rippled Brannagh's spine. The hairs on the back of his neck seemed to lift his head. It was as if his prone body sprung centipede legs. How many newsreels had he seen at the picture shows of Russian artillery endlessly firing on the eastern front against the Nazis during World War II? Was the 35th regiment up against fortresses? Was it siegecraft they were coming to, he pondered?

Mastery of the highest hill was the key. Was that what was happening in the punchbowl? Massive Chinese artillery would compel GI's to dig as deep as their enemy, to fortify their field positions, to dig trench works, to lay mines and booby traps in multiples every foot in front of every position. The main line of resistance would hang on the dominant slopes and follow the contour of undulating folded mountains. Heavy machine-guns would be placed at each sharp cusp of local importance. The outpost on hill 717 would be the fingertips of the regiment's fist. Brannagh felt as disquieted as Im Ta Song appeared.

*****

Singletary organized his thoughts on the problems patrols were having by running off of hill 717. It might dominate north and west of the Hanton River, but the Chinese were atop hill 1062, and looking down. No doubt they had mapped out every goat path and trail with their own patrols, including the hill 432.

"If the chinks attack our patrol base, hill 432 is midway between 717 and the MLR, Sergeant O'Hara," Sing maintained.

Sing's notebook held his pencil drawing. He pointed to his illustrations. He wanted to deliver his observations with authority.

"So," said O'Hara?

"It's an ambush site, O'Hara," Sing claimed.

"An ambush site?"

O'Hara looked at the drawing, but he minded more Singletary's alleged generalship, just when regiment wanted ratings on its top three grades. O'Hara saw a first class scam. Bucking for a Master's rocker, was Singletary?

"Yea, Sing, your drawing makes it clear," O'Hara said.

Sing nodded in relief. The command staff hadn't seen it, but an experienced non-com could. A non com's duty was to bring back all his men, to send them stateside using their own arms and legs. Sing didn't demean officers but being trained to accept losses, they might put too much attention on the objective and too little on the men who were to hold it - like out on hill 717! Regiment had two companies out there, thousands of meters in front of the line, but nothing in between. It was as if the Chinese, even if they recognized an ambush site, wouldn't dare to place a unit in between the outpost and MLR. Wouldn't they? Singletary would. Since when did the Chinese care about casualties? It was GI losses that made the newspapers back home! It was GI corpses that fed the political bonfires with dead-wood! Sing believed the Chinese would expend whatever manpower it took to cut off and cut up two companies - Item and Love!

"Look at my drawing," Singletary said. He instructed O'Hara, as if the top kick were the section sergeant's junior.

"Here is hill 432," Sing pointed midway. "Here are hills 717 and 682." He pointed north. "They are the highest points of a twisted four-sided hill with the open end facing south, towards us. Major spurs of this complex extent to the northeast, northwest and south. I remember how steep these ridges were," Sing recalled. "Only a single trail traverses the center of the area from north to south. It crosses a shallow saddle that connects the two high points. Look at the south side! Two valleys approach the area from the main valley of the Hantan River. The high ground between the two valleys is a natural line of advance for troops attacking 717."

O'Hara heard a passionate edginess flooding Singletary's voice.

"The chinks could infiltrate south at night," Sing continued. "The hills of 717 and 682 might front up like a castle, but they have a hole in their backside. The chinks could give it a hell of a goose. If I see the ambush on hill 432, why won't they?"

"You mean the chinks, not our officers," inquired O'Hara? He'd noted Sing's seriousness, his negative head bobbing, the turn of his lips. O'Hara's time in grade, and ever scheming mind saw an opportunity to boost O'Hara's future to that of a warrant officer until retirement from this man's army. O'Hara figured he would hot tail it to battalion with the analysis as his own, volunteering Sing's third section of heavy thirties as security on hill 432! A twenty man section dug in, with two guns and supporting carbines, would be a formidable plug to the backside hole! If nothing came of it, so it went, soon forgotten. If something happened, with or without Singletary's guns on hill 432, a grand Irishman from the townland of Curry in County Sligo, Ireland, would, in Korea, be seen as a leader of men who could well guide a combat infantry's platoon's swords of war!

"I'll take it up with battalion," O'Hara said. He harnessed his lightning bolts of thought and stood tall, to show Sing this O'Hara was stalwart and stern.
*****

"Hear the word," shouted Singletary.

He stood between squad tents, cupping his hands around his mouth so his volume carried to his men. Seeing heads pop out of each tent, he signalled that the 2nd gun squad join him in the 1st gun's tent.

Sing quieted his internal queasiness about the outpost on hill 717. He worried over the time it was taking O'Hara, but everything in the army took time to get done, more so pointing out a tactical weakness to those who should know better. Yet the outpost companies had taken eighteen rounds of flat trajectory early in the morning. It's patrols were reporting all kinds of enemy movements, most with pack animals. When his troops had taken their places, he motioned them to be quiet.

"If anyone wants a steak, the chinks are buying," Singletary informed his men.

"What ya' mean," Baiter asked?

"Chink radio intercepts say the gooks been calling GIs to come over for steak, ever since the truce talks broke off. Chinks say they would stop fighting if we go back to the 38th parallel."

"Wher' dat," inquired the Dreamer?

"South." Brannagh pointed away from the MLR. "It's south of here. Remember, its the boundary between South and North Korea. We talked about it."

"Yea?"

Dreamer was trying to remember, but faltering, Brannagh figured. He saw Baiter had a look of acrimony that appeared to turn to spit and spittal verbiage at the crusted latrine digger Dreamer. Brannagh intended to forestall Baiter's dour words.

"If the American's went back to the south side of the boundary, and gave back the territory we hold north of it, the chinks would quit fighting," Brannagh said, "so would we quit fighting."

"Dat okay! I like my steak rare." Dreamer prattled.

His eyes appeared to Brannagh to be two fireplaces ablaze with ignorance.

"I have a tenderloin I'll give ya Dreamer, raw," Baiter belched!

He opened his fly to flag his limp cylinder.

He came by acrimony too easily, perhaps, honed

by retorts from drunken waitresses and bar keeps; perhaps too inclined to squelch an insect that should be kept away from the men!

Dreamer turned his eyes away to concentrate on what Singletary would say.

"Charley first platoon has been spotting flashes in the valley between their positions and the ROKs. Could be a code," Sing said.

"Chinks signalling," observed Van Meter?

"That's it," answered Sing. "There's more! Regimental rear has kicked out a bunch of shoeshine boys recently. Chinks flood the rear with spies before they attack. No way to know for sure if the shoe shine boys had a spy or two, but so many walking into regimental rear is more than suspicious."

Brannagh could see an attack played on Fenton's mind, if his quivering was a sympton of his debilitation as much as his depression and insomnia were symptoms. Psychic wounds had been inflicted on the gunner, none cutting more deeply than the current uncertainty of truce talk resumption. But for Van Meter's changing the bandages on those mental wounds, Fenton would be a wax figure in a hospital, a victim of the barbarous cruelties of fear of imminent physical injury inflicting irrational delusions on his psychological life. Has it been wise to chance mental outrage by keeping Fenton in a line outfit?

"Another thing," said Singletary, "the 3rd battalion's got flying ants all over the patrol base. The whole place is infested. They're gonna spray DDT tomorrow. Van Meter, make sure Dreamer catches the wind drift."

Brannagh glanced quickly at Dreamer, as if the glance could lessen the insensitivity of the cruel joke.

There was no sign of dismay on the dirt streaked face, only his usual abstraction. Perhaps Dreamer still had Chinese steak on his mind, ever since Baiter had retracted his gear. Brannagh turned his head to the sound of Baiter hucking a gob which he spat Dreamer's way, Singletary-style, less his accuracy. It splatted instead next to Im Ta Song.

"Nikola shibola," muttered the foreign legionnaire.

Im Ta Song conjured his assignment to an outfit with as lousy soldiers as Dreamer and Baiter was equivalent to deportation. He glared at Baiter who returned his usual lip pucker accompanied with a stabbing stare.

Brannagh's anger at Baiter's degeneracies soared. The impulse to hit him seethed the more. Brannagh heard Baiter laugh.

"Last thing, the good news!" Sing said. "Red battalion got a large quota for rotation - seventy-seven for enlisted reserves. Regular army that came in November, December are next."

Van imagined the heart palpitations and pains Fenton must be feeling. "You'll go with the next quota, Bob."

Van tried to assure his gunner; but silently prayed that quota came before the Red battalion went up on line. Van watched Fenton's face as it took on the scowl of a wolf. He heard Fenton growl threateningly, ferociously, but then he went to puppy whimpering.

Singletary directed his whole section go about other duties. He ordered his 2nd gun squad out of Van's tent and Van's men to clean weapons they had cleaned minutes before to hide their palpitations over Fenton.

Brannagh's emotions floated more than Fenton's boat. Dad had written that he had come to the belief that Truman was showing himself a man like Dad remembered about certain British Loyalists in County Antrim, Ireland. Back after partition, a Judge was set to render a death sentence on a Republican Irishman found guilty of murder by a Loyalist jury, when the man alleged to have been murdered walked into the courtroom. The Judge charged the jury to reconsider its verdict. The jury retired. After long deliberation it returned and again pronounced a verdict of guilty, telling the Judge that the Irishman was still Sinn Fein, so they would let the verdict stand. As the Judge should have taken the case from the jury and dismissed the charge, so, too, should Truman have had the political courage to take over the truce talks when they collapsed.

*****

Back at Regimental HQ O'Hara heard, though the 223 Chinese regiment was capable of launching an attack to drive in the 35th's outpost on hill 717, the whole of the infantry in every valley and on green mountains needed only to be alert for the new moon of the autumnal season, for only then would its pale light be a jewel of guidance to a Chinese attack.

O'Hara heard back at battalion HQ that they weren't unaware of a need to plug a penetration of the MLR in the event the high ground was taken by the Chinese. Operations Plan No. 9 was being readied. The 24th regiment would secure the east shoulder of any penetration; the Turks the west shoulder; the 27th regiment would block; while the 35th regiment would counterattack to restore line Wyoming. As a matter of fact, the second battalion of the 35th was being relocated for this very purpose.

"Why today," asked O'Hara?

He heard that the patrol base of the 5th cavalry regiment had been hit by two Chinese companies in a half circle around the base, supported by tanks. They had taken under fire a GI reinforcing patrol on the supply route up to the patrol base. Maybe a battalion or more of Chinese had moved up. That wasn't all. The outpost of the 7th infantry division had been hit and overrun, the 1st Cavalry regiment's outpost had been driven in, while the 3d infantry division's outpost had been brought under heavy attack.

"Move my third section of machine guns out to hill 432," O'Hara said.

"Hell," he heard Staff Intelligence exclaim! "Full moon's eight-nine day's away. It's only September 6th."
*****

Singletary pushed his third section to cleaning weapons and spare parts, checking ammo, drawing fresh water. He bedeviled his squad leaders' every move towards preparedness. He had his own intelligence system. It centered around his poker playing and plentiful gifts of stateside booze. He only needed to send a runner with his comforting distillant and confidential question, and have returned a reply. Some might have suspected a breach of military secrecy via Singletary's system, save for the sergeant's location: at the front!

He trod the dirt floors of CPs on the MLR, even the wooden floors of regiment's tents, in defense of his poker playing proficiency. He was a sought after soldier, in the know! He got the word from the War tent's top enlisted men.

Sing had the word that Plan Overwhelming, the

attack to Pyongyang and Wonsan had been shelved by Van Fleet's doubts on his own army, a replacement army, drained of its cream by rotation. General Van Fleet's Operation Talons went to the same shelf. It was to have been an advance ranging a mile in one place to fifteen miles in another to remove a sag in the line on the eastern front. Then, at September's end, an attack would have been launched in the west by the 25th division attacking northeast followed by an amphibious landing on the east coast by the Marines attacking southwest. Their link up might have trapped innumerable Chinese and North Koreans.

Elbowing north, tidying the right flank remained, but not the linkup. Why? Oddly, Singletary had heard it, success of Talons might have caused the commies to lose too much face and thus jeopardize the resumption of the truce talks! The facts were plainly opposite. The Chinese and North Koreans only came to the negotiating table because so many of their comrades had had their faces blown off in April and May.

Singletary was tired of war. No combat infantryman cared if he ever fired his weapon in a second fire fight, having survived his first. Yet, if war he must, an infantryman cared about the fire support he got after he crossed the LD - line of departure. He expected every weapon the Army and Air Force could fire would precede him, cover him, then follow up along with the men climbing the hill. An infantryman didn't want limitation. He wanted a choreography of shells, napalm and bullets dancing with him as his partner. It gave heart!

If there was to be a battle, make it a big one, the bold Sing reflected. Spread the Chinese and North

Koreans to their limits. Spread the Chinese so that a
BAR could pin down a squad, a light thirty machine
gun a platoon, and a Dog heavy thirty section a Chinese
company. Singletary didn't want his men funneled in
the sights of concentrated enemy fire and grenades. He
didn't want a limited war, freeing Chinese from some
tunnel to reassemble at a hot spot. Concentrated
commies were like mowed dandelions; they
regenerated by the hour.

The termination of Talons, Singletary reasoned,
had more to do with fear of the reaction of the people
back home to an increasing casualty count, than to a
Chinaman's face. All hell would hit the fan back home
where there was already a sense of futility about the
fighting. Some sweet citizenry, Sing reflected, would be
inconvienced by the noises of opposition politicians
sounding off about a high casualty count. Back home,
police actions were cleared by arrest; in Korea, they
weren't!

Whatever bullshit O'Hara spread about the
outpost's patrols coming in without enemy contact, or
about Operation Bump that directed the second
battalion into counterattack positions, still no outfit
had been placed on hill 432. The main supply route
from the line to the outpost was left open to an oriental
express; a dismayed Singletary affirmed.

"What's got into the chicken coop, Sing," Van
Meter asked?

"Battalion didn't fortify hill 432," Sing
responded. He drew a map. "This is the outpost, this is
the line, and the MSR runs from the line to the outpost
across hill 432." He pointed. "If the chinks hit the 3d
battalion again today from the north, and swing behind
the outpost to take hill 432; you can imagine the

results."

It was a wild thought, its wildness heightened by the preparations for Operation Bump in response to the activity of the Chinese against the outpost. Sing's worry was a false note, Van Meter contemplated, for the Chinese had gone over to defense in Kumhwa.

Singletary had an explanation. "O'Hara said the 1st cavalry, 7th and 3d divisions all had their outposts hit last night. Chinks think no less about ours. Those outposts are our eyes. Why not blind us before a full moon, then launch an offensive like last May's, or trap and capture GIs on the outpost."

"Love took thirty three rounds before 2012 hours, then it was quiet," Sing paused, "until 0005 hours. For twenty minutes the chinks shelled hills 717 and 682 before probing those positions for an hour. At 0115 hours they attacked. They opened fire with rifles and burp guns. They hurled grenades, shouted, and chanted; blowing bugles between the hills."

CHAPTER FIVE
ENCIRCLED

Sing told of scuttlebutt that the second battalion had moved out at 0510 hours and into blocking as a part of Operation Bump. Fox had been formed up around Leader Baker's platoon of tanks from the 89th tank battalion to cross the Hantan River by the concrete bridge and there, deploy for an attack.

In ways known only to Singletary, his sergeants were told that King Company had moved out over the main supply route to the outpost to reinforce the third battalion out there. King had to traverse slopes in inky blackness.

Atop hill 432, Sing had it on good authority, the Chinese had laid down a withering fire on the unsuspecting skirmish line; had called down heavy mortar rounds and poured on King intense fire from automatic and small arms. Hill 432 was infested with Chinese soldiers well dug in. The enemy were between King and the outpost!

"The 14th regiment is coming in to relieve us," Sing informed his squad leaders. "If the second battalion jumps off on the left flank of 717, sure as hope for a cease fire has disappeared, the first battalion will attack on the right flank."

"Van, where's Fenton?"

Sing had separated himself from Fenton's trouble. Maybe that was why Van Meter got so close to the looney. Fenton had been in all the battles since Christmas. The guy hadn't ducked his duty. His body escaped, his mind, however worried itself into a state of mental immobility, fearing for itself the more since truce talks started than when war was waged.

"Fenton's back in battalion's laundry pool, Sing."

"Harville or Davis can't find fingers in their own assholes," Sing cursed. "If King company doesn't break through to the outpost we'll be sent out."

"Who do you want from Cervera's squad," asked Sing, "Trout or Revels?"

"Neither," Van responded, surprised at his own volume. "I've my gunner!"

"Who," inquired Singletary?

"Brannagh," came the reply.

Van Meter saw that Singletary's smile twisted like the Burma road.

"You're choosing a monk for a machine gunner," came the incredulous question?

*****

While Singletary had his section gear up, he heard King Company had driven the Chinese off hill 432. To what avail? King was still catching lead up slope from hill 528. Too, like blows from a blacksmith's hammer, King's positions on 432 were shivered to splinters by incoming Chinese rounds. King company was zeroed in. Not an inch uphill would be surrendered by the Chinese without killing, wounding or taking prisoners of everyone, or the destruction of the third battalion.

Singletary worried for the men of Item, Love and Mike up on the outpost. They had taken fire all night. They expected reinforcements, but King was stymied by noon. The Chinese had slipped between the outpost and the front line, coming in by foot through the northeast valley between the Hantan River and the back end of the outpost to cut off resupply. It had been a silent envelopment. What King had intended - reinforcements - had become a relief force.

Sing defined the Chinese mission as one of destruction of an American battalion, not a general attack. The Chinese hadn't hit the MLR, but controlled the valleys through which the men of the third battalion on the patrol base might withdraw, as well as holding back a reinforcing company. It was a well planned carp shoot!

Singletary blamed the peace talks. Even if the talks were suspended, no one took it as final, just another stutter between inflamatory rhetoricians. Maybe the line officers were distracted, forgetting the mobility of the Chinese. A simple ounce of prevention - a patrol each night atop 432 - might well have prevented the Chinese infiltration. That's the way it went! Too many of the Army's officers were educated and trained beyond the obvious. They couldn't see straight on. They saw the grand, the great picture, not the single Chinese in tennis shoes holding a burp gun in a gun hole on 432.

"The Raider platoon and Turks secured the area by the concrete bridge. A forward aid station has been set up over there," Sing informed his squad leaders. "Windmills are already evacuating the wounded from Chongyon-ni. Fox company and the Northstar tanks jumped off at 1410 hours to backstop King on 432. King has moved out against 528. A platoon of George and a tank platoon moved into the valley to break through the chinks," Sing continued. "There's no doubt now that Item, Love and Mike are encircled."

Singletary would not be of mortal strain had he not felt the wrong done to the third battalion - the Blue battalion, their endangerment inflicted by friendly forces, their wounds inflicted by the enemy.
*****

Brannagh felt more than queasiness in his stomach at the thought that this time the battalion wasn't looking for Chinese, but for GIs trapped by the Chinese. He felt diarrhea, too! Bad water he heard was the cause, but he drank only GI water from the water bag. At that, he touched it up with a halizone tablet. Not a drop of the natural fluid in mountain streams had passed his lips, yet his innards were in convulsion.

If it wasn't the water, might it have been the c-ration of canned meat that looked like hamburgers cemented between some lubricant? Even heated over the cook stove it tasted like axle grease on a conestoga wagon wheel. How could he go into combat with fatigues full of effluvium? A smile crossed his face at the thought he might fill them anyway at the impact of the first incoming. Then maybe the new tiny medic Doc Block had the cure. Bowel plugger, he called it, a sip or two to be taken every few hours. It would bind whatever needed to be bound; loosen what needed to be loosened.

"Hear the word," called Singletary.

"Hear the word," Sing repeated.

The rotation of Sing's shoulders diverted Brannagh's attention to Sing's helmet's lip, fringed by his long blond bangs, self cut, like Moe of the three Stooges might have barbered it.

"O'Hara says the trucks will move our battalion at 1800 hours," Sing informed. "Red Lynx will relieve us."

"Who be Red Lynx," inquired Dreamer.

Dreamer's weapon was clean. His cartridge belt and pack straps were clean, his pack squared. He was as sharp as if a joint venture of janitorial firms had taken him under contract.

Im Ta Song's big brown eyes were lit like lanterns at the spectacle of Dreamer, a clean soldier since winning the ammo chase. Yet there was so much that made him different from the other Americans.

Im Ta Song remembered slavery had been abolished in Korea in 1894, yet Dreamer must have been sold to an American Yangban family. When in olden times Korean parents found they could no longer provide for their children they sold them to preserve their lives, and their parents'. Children of such slaves were also slaves and compelled to serve the same master as their parents had served. Slaves could never escape from their recorded social status. They were branded for life. They were, even in death, carried behind a red mourning banner inscribed with the words 'private servant's coffin'. Had Dreamer escaped his social status?

Singletary choked on his sudden swallow of tobacco. He saw a miraculous apparition. He patooied a wad through the open tent flaps.

"They be," Sing choked!

He paused, clearing his throat, seeking a more grammatical form, while putting his hands on his waist.

"Red Lynx is the first battalion, 14th regiment," he said.

Singletary was quizzical as to why Dreamer asked, or why Sing answered. Why in the hell was relief by the 14th as opposed to any other unit of the slightest interest to Dreamer. For that matter, why did Sing tell him as if an orderly Dreamer were more deserving than the gritty Dreamer. After all it was Red Leopard, the first battalion of the 35th that was moving up. It made a hell of a difference to an outfit on line whether it was the reliever, or the relieved, the resolute sergeant knew!

"Saddle up," ordered Singletary.

Brannagh swung the tripod to his shoulders, then clomped a hand onto a thrust out forward leg. He began to wish he were going again on a training mission. He had a sinking sensation in his stomach. His innards roiled. Was his courage fleeing. He hadn't even left for the assembly area. An uncomfortably moist sensation ran between his shoulder blades. He hoped it was sweat, and not the last of his beer. What would Dad have thought of his flinching lad?

"Move out!" Singletary ordered.

Brannagh followed Van Meter down the slow incline, with Harville, Davis and the ammo bearers of the first gun in file behind, followed by the second gun squad. They snaked downhill in a bold front. The new gunner felt a plaintive breeze that wafted parting sighs toward the son of Irish immigrants; toward men descended from immigrant Poles, Frenchmen, Germans, Englishmen, and western and central Europeans. Crafty Singletary, caring Van Meter, excitable La Vie, methodical Davis, argumentative Blaczyk, quiet Harville, slim witted Dreamer, hysteric Swinford and puzzling Im Ta Song - nine men, armed and dangerous, going to battle as told, but not before verbalizing on the blood lines coursing through the veins of military planners.

Fine dust off the road powdered the section. Some coughed. Brannagh swigged bowel plug and squirmed. He didn't complain. No one complained. It was a ride, not a march. It might have been over smoother roads, but Korea had no Outer Drive. Yet sudden stops and starts had backsides sliding. Fatigues were proving non splinter proof. Trepidation was

Brannagh's relative.

A jerky stop stacked the men like dominoes. It shook loose Brannagh's sphincter. He lept from the stalled convoy like a deer from a hunter, hitting the grounds with legs precipitating him into a bushy ravine. He soon ambled back as if returning to a ride in a hay wagon. Remounted, he slurped more gastrointestinal stopper.

"The runs be like on a rollercoaster, Brannagh," spoke Dreamer. "When you be rumbling all over, you know you ain't being done right. When its over you know you been somewhere."

The trucks turned wheels again, jolting, jerking, shifting the troops in all directions.

Brannagh's Irish tenor freed his secret fears in song. He sang:

"The Minstrel Boy to the war is gone,
In the ranks of 'Dog' you'll find him.
His Father's sword he had girded on
And his wild harp slung behind him."

Van heard the lilt of an Irish tenor, a clear moving voice. The words inspired Van Meter to pray for the section as it rode over the rocky road, that the Good Lord might hear his voice as a faithful harp praising him.

The truck convoy burped its way forward over trails bulldozed through skinned slopes still bleeding clots of stone. The wheeled snake expanded and contracted like an anaconda beneath ridge lines pointing mean fingers at each deuce and a half ton truck passing by benevolently. Singletary didn't listen to the truck cab's canvas roof flapping up and down like a quacking duck. He saw dull ridge lines with grotesque humpback and pimple peaks wounded by jagged trench lines still catching fading sunlight, with haze from cordite clouds swirling above moonscape heights. He saw there was little greenery left between rival armies. Soldiers hadn't been issued green thumbs. The tools of their trade turned verdure to sable, cooked by military volcanoes - napalm and white phosphorus. Sing's calculating eyes witnessed the soot of combat. Then he saw a racing GI flash the sprinting style of the hundred yard dash along the roadside beside the line of idling trucks.

"Look at that guy run," Sing exclaimed, "like a cheetah after prey."

"Can't be bugging out," responded the truck driver, "he's running toward the L.D."

Something about the sprinter was familiar, but Sing was at a loss to conjure who in the hell had a fever to run to the battle.

"Hey back there," the section sergeant yelled. "Who was that? You know?"

"Yea," Baiter hollered back. "It's that damned dumb Brannagh. He's off to squat again."

Hilarity rippled Baiter's watermelon cheeks, his laughter imitating a Chinese shepherd's flute. Baiter had been bitten by that same bug when he first came up. He had felt the bestial turns his innards took, as if six butchers twisted his guts to make sausage. It made him happy Brannagh's convulsions must be doubling the new gunner with bursts of pain.

Brannagh shivered despite the warm evening. His legs had cramped. He pushed up from his haunches to let blood course through his veins. He viewed the long line of idling trucks with the assembled companies of the first battalion. Brannagh felt an unearthly fire in his eyes, not unlike the flame in his bowels, when he recognized the unmistakeable shape of a mine field sign. He was within its boundaries!

"Calm, be calm," he whispered. "First thing, pull up my pants," he concluded.

Brannagh pulled his belt buckle closed. He felt for his cartridge belt and bayonet. He had left them on the truck. He had no tool to probe for mines.

"Stand still, Brannagh," Van yelled resolutely.

"I am," came the shaking response. "I need a probe. Would you toss me a bayonet," Brannagh answered.

Van clicked open his cartridge belt, slipping it and his shoulder harness and pack off. He took out his bayonet and lept over the truck's rail like a pirate.

"Catch it." Van instructed.

He tossed the bayonet the ten yard distance. Unmindful of its blade, Brannagh two handed the cutting edges. He dropped to his hands and knees slowly. His bayonet gently probed an arc of ground in front of him. He crawled an arc at a time toward Van Meter, obsessed he'd never crap again.

"Better get back towards the trucks, Van," Brannagh warned. "There's ten yards to cover."

"Just keep probing carefully," Van warned. "And shut up."

The metallic click rippled the air as loudly as a sentry's safety when released for a challenge to a foe.

"A mine," Brannagh quivered. "I'll probe left, then angle back again." He marked it with a stick.

"Another mine," Brannagh whispered.

He looked back at his first marking. There was no discernable order to the mine field. He would probe right this time, before angling back to the warning sign. He found soft clay to his liking an arc at a time. He summoned up his last iota of nerves.

Van Meter could tell Brannagh's pasty face harbored every fugitive freckle that was passed through from his Irish ancestry. A faraway look spooked his frightened face. He looked like a prehistoric snail creeping an inch a minute.

"It's not your time, Brannagh," Van welcomed.

Singletary's manner of speech couldn't be described as relief, Brannagh reflected, especially the suggested treatment for loosened bowels - a carbine up the rectum. Everytime Singletary hollered, the scar on his chin grew white at the edges, matching the color of his huge eyebrows. There was a tone of admiration in his words.

Brannagh's heart felt of lead, his veins of cold coffee. "Thank you, Sergeant Van," Brannagh said.

"You've courage, Gunner," Van complimented. "Cool under pressure. Now get back on the truck, and stay there."

CHAPTER SIX
HILL 432

Nothing, not even a rock looked the same as that Brannagh saw less than a month ago when they seized hills 717 and 682. As dim twilight faded, Brannagh clung closely to Van Meter, following him down a deep ravine where hills above surrounded soldiers. Brannagh could have done with a cup of coffee to offset the chill that was descending with the gloomy darkness. It was another misery of the day. He sweated; his bowels twisted him green; he would shiver the night in sweat soaked fatigues; clean dust out of the machine gun and ammo belts, while his innards churned bowel plugger to cement.

He sat down on a rock to listen to the order of attack Singletary was setting down to his squad leaders.

"Baker Company's point squad will move out in a diamond to hill 432 with a connecting file back to the advance platoon, then the rest of Baker," Sing asserted. "Charley, Dog and Able companies follow in a column of twos maintaining tactical unity. Each man holds to a distance of two paces between them in this dark."

Reflections of searchlights exposed hundreds of GIs in the valley to Brannagh. Some cleaned weapons. Others stood tall, leaning on rifles. A few sat Indian style, weapons across their knees. No one smoked. Few talked.

He heard someone give the order to saddle up from out of the dark, and up came the tide of troops, orderly, in no hurry. Baker soon formed up, then moved out. An exodus of men went into the inky recesses of ravines and slopes as wrinkled as Oliver Hardy's waistline. Boots trampled through the lowering dark.

"Hear the word," shouted Singletary. "We're done farting around waiting for truce talks. We've had enough of them gooks on the outpost. We're going up there and circumcise the lot of them. First we're going up to hill 432 and dig in. Then we're going to cross a valley and go up that ridge line as quick-like as Red running to take a crap. We're going to bust through them chinks!"

Sing clamored in his best cheer leader tone. He wanted his men fired up. He wanted spirit. They had climbed these torturously twisted uphill ridges a few weeks back, now bald as a baby's butt. Then it was humidity undulating out of the valley. Now it would be heat from Chinese mortars, yet Sing sensed the adrenaline rising in his troops. They were quiet before combat, but quiet is the fire in their hearts. They would not let the lives of the third battalion, or theirs, be idly thrown away. The long sit down was over! To hell with the fiction of a demarcation line and a cease fire, Singletary swore. "We'll take it to the gooks! You hear, Cervera? You hear, Van Meter?" Sing put ferocity into his words. "I want a conversation out there, gunners! I want your guns talking. I want the bursts so synchronized, the gooks will look for one gun," Sing declared.

He slipped a grenade onto each of his pack strap loops. His cartridge belt carried extra magazine pouches. He right shouldered his carbine.

"Saddle up," Sing called. "Move out!"

Brannagh marvelled as Singletary strode forth vigorously as if on a pilgrimage to Canterbury, his helmet pitched at brushy eyebrow height. Behind the broad tree trunk of the section sergeant stepped the thickset Iowan as if off to the back eighty acres to hand husk corn from the stalks; and the orange picker from California, as if going after a bonus for migrant labor recruitment.

Brannagh was on his guard. The enemy was alive and well and in these hills. It wasn't training. Brannagh realized he was no longer moving with impunity from hostile fire. A mortar round had smacked forward somewhere. Had he stripped down to essentials: a pencil, notebook, his camera and film, toothbrush, shaving brush, soap, a brush for his weapon, three cans of beer, extra beer, extra socks, considerable toilet paper? He carried enough toilet paper if the bowel plug slowed the propulsive waves within his intestinal tract! He shivered.

He moved carefully over the rock strewn ridge. He worried that there might not be fox holes on 432, that mortars might catch the first gun squad digging in. Brannagh's carbine rode Van Meter's left shoulder. Van's own M1 rifle was on his right shoulder. Brannagh's back pack carried his set of spare parts - a lock frame, bolt and barrel extension, plus extra packing for the muzzle gland and muzzle end. Three cans of combat rations were tucked inside clean socks to avoid rattling. A termite grenade rode the loop of his left pack harness! He had been instructed to use it on his machine gun if over run by chinks. It was an image his fantasy hadn't yet constructed. Carbine ammo clips hung on his cartridge belt with his canteen, first aid packet and entrenching tool. A fragmentary grenade rode the loop of his right pack harness.

Once in a while, somewhere in the vast darkness, a pocket of resistance erupted, the long column halted, and a squad was sent around the pocket to envelope the blockage. Suddenly the column moved again! Brannagh welcomed these respites. Tripods, BARs, machine guns, weapons might be lowered, a quick breath taken before the oft repeated orders to saddle up and move out came again.

The wreckage of past fire fights was strewn all along the ridges: ammo boxes, expended clips, canteens, a broken weapon, the brass from expended rounds. Salvage was the chore of others. Infantrymen, he reflected, were the makers of waste, human or manufactured. He kept on the move across this desolate debris, under hissing white flares falling from the heavens that threw momentary garish light. The gunner was awe struck.

******

"Take ten," Singletary directed. He was uneasy. He called his squad leaders to him and spoke the truth, as he knew it, of the situation facing them in the hazy distance, beyond the dim horizon on nature's fort of hill 717.

"The remnants of the third battalion plus Fox were dug in up there last night," Sing said.

He had to clear his throat before he pointed towards hill 432, a vague peak beneath the shades of night. His point lingered as if he were outlining the terrain features. "No friendly sharks could move because of the box mines, so Blue three and twelve GIs had to hole up over night at Tanwon-ni. They got back to the MLR, plus sixty eight more that came in today. I've been told both the 24th and 27th regiments have pulled in their outposts." His head went form side to side. "This may be the beginning of the chinks' seventh phase offensive." He felt uncomfortable.

"Why the hell are we moving up then," the

startled Cervera questioned?

"There's still a lot of GI's unaccounted for," Sing told him. "They may still be alive up there."

"Blue Six took a chance that few of his men were on hill 528. He cleared the order to fire across its crest and on its north side," Sing sighed.

"Damn," moaned Cervera.

Van perceived an agony in the decision. The crushing crescendo of the thundering shells, the angry shock waves that stirred the still air to a tempest, the trembling of the very earth as if the god of volcanoes had come home, was not lightly called in where friendly troops might have been.

"George Company ran recon patrols all night beyond the perimeter of 432 to pick up friendly wounded and stragglers," Sing told it. "Instead they took fire from gooks all over the place looking for prisoners."

"The gooks aren't pulling out. They're dug in on 528 and patrolling. They have the patrol base. Its still anyone's guess if they're going to hit the MLR," Singletory said as he felt an aching.

"The gooks have changed their strategy," Singletary said. "They are standing still and fighting for ground."

"The Blue boys fought all night at Tanwon-ni. Gook fire came in like a tropical rain. Damned if the gooks didn't shoot our own weapons," Sing related. "GI ammo was too low to answer round for round, but they told me our artillery built a wall around them."

"It even looked as if the gooks would pay any price to drive Fox Company off of 432 last night. Gooks crept up to within yards of the perimeter. Pay they did. Fox and King were set for all around defense - had a lot of ammo and grenades. They were buttoned up."

Sing continued. "In came a heavy volley of rifle and burp gun fire; gooks were walking straight in, firing as they came. Gook mortarmen came up too, belching 57 millimeter rounds into Fox."

Even though the Chinese's night cover had been penetrated by the eerie flickering of yellow gold flares, and searchlights beams bouncing off low passing clouds, Singletary had heard that scores of hunched enemy had flowed down from hill 528.

"Fox's men thickened the air with lead. Their mortarmen fed their tubes until they were red hot. Artillery danced shells from 432 up the ridgeline," Sing said.

His mind viewed the terrible scene as if it were on stage. GI grenades perforated quilted cotton pants like so many needles. Heavy machine guns crackled blue, white and red streams of flame across the Chinese skirmishers, tracers ricocheting perpendicularly, dueling the enemy's automatic weaponry. It hadn't been a long fire fight, but the never ceasing cannonading of the 89th artillery battalion made it seem forever. Their bone shattering shells had walked the ridges up to hill 528, chopping remnants of crimson commies like hated weeds.

*****

Someone bore the breath of a drunk into Dog company's CP. The ubiquity of the essence colonized the close log and sandbagged lodgement. O'Hara turned to discover the headwater of the distillery. He saw a rather pathetic figure with eyeglasses skewed and steel helmet hung up on the right ear.

"Corporal," O'Hara asked, "what can I do for you?"

"G-g-g-o up," stuttered Fenton.

O'Hara saw a combat ready troop. Fenton had on his cartridge belt, harness webbing and back pack. His carbine was on his shoulder, at slung arms. His helmet bore two freshly painted blue stripes. Yet the eyes of Fenton showed those of a soldier in a perpetual twilight of mind. The top kick had read Fenton's file. The sodden soldier before him was a shadow of the infantryman described in writing before reassignment to the laundry pool. Yet O'Hara felt an apprehension. Was it a period of sanity or excitation?

"We appreciate your offer, Corporal," oozed O'Hara.

"G-g-g-go up," repeated Fenton! "V-V-Van needs m-m-me. B-B-B-Brannagh will get V-V-Van k-k-killed."

O'Hara viewed a face emotionally charged, with a protruding tongue. O'Hara elected to play a confidence game.

"And didn't Dog Six, himself, just tell me of a mission to the zone of the interior," spoke the top kick to Fenton, "and you the very soldier to do it?" Not waiting for a response, top sergeant O'Hara lathered his tongue. "May the devil's tears put blisters on me face, Corporal, if you're not on today's rotation quota."

O'Hara knew that Fenton hadn't been on this quota, but several soldiers in the third battalion who had been, like Fenton, volunteered to return to their units to finish the battle for hill 717. Fenton might easily be substituted. He was next due.

The corporal was stunned. He wanted out of Korea so bad his ears hurt from the throbbing in his head. Yet he owed Van Meter!

"I-I-I; quota?"

It sounded to O'Hara as if a spoiled child had been granted his wish.

"I-I-I-I; mission?"

"Indeed ye hav' lad," O'Hara's infested his words with a brogue. "You are Dog Six's corporal to tell the folks back home the bad effect on morale these on again, off again truce talks cause," O'Hara said.

O'Hara clandestinely motioned company clerk Miner to a ready position, as if Miner's beaver teeth were a fence, or his water tower height an attack advantage, if an effort to subdue the laundryman was needed.

"Dog Six is counting on you, Corporal Fenton! You ship out on this quota. Tell them back home to crap or get out of the water closet. God be wid' ye," O'Hara intoned.

O'Hara saw a display of scarlet astonishment on the laundryman's face. Was Fenton listening? Was the red in his cheeks happy excitement or blood anger?

O'Hara heard no sound of acceptance. Then, O'Hara had only just become aware of Fenton. The sergeant figured Fenton, if he reasoned at all, did so from deep within the shadows of a creviced mind, thus wasn't able to converse.

A great sigh brought with it a debilitating weakness draping an invisible strait jacked around Fenton. He sloshed in his own sweat. Exhaustion overcame him. He was tremulous and deadly pale.

"Miner," ordered O'Hara, "take the jeep and move Fenton to regimental. Make sure he's on the truck. Tell them he wanted to get back to the line with his unit. Tell them O'Hara wouldn't let him go. Blame me for the substitution."

Miner would. Fenton was no longer a problem.

He needed a little help to keep his feet, but that must
have been the booze, the clerk concluded. The booze
must have been Fenton's courage, too. Miner wouldn't
touch the stuff in case he might do the same dumb
thing sometime. The front line was the last place to do
four point time.

Miner recalled the interest of O'Hara in the new
recruit in Singletary's section. A peek at Brannagh's file
had revealed a two year college man. That was threat
enough for any clerk's future equilibrium. By
abstemiousness, piety and diligence to the CP's work,
Miner had labored to curry Captain Busin's gracious
favor, four point time, and immunity from a fire fight.
If all went well, the clerk had it made until rotation.
*****

Singletary stretched the ten minute break on the
back slope to tell his squad leaders of Fox's fire fight to
take hill 528, as if the section sergeant had heard it
from a play by play baseball announcer. Sing wished it
had been a mere baseball game played for a winner's
share of spectator's money. He knew he would never
again enjoy the artificial suspense created by a pitcher
holding a one run lead and a runner on third with the
bases loaded, two outs in the bottom of the ninth of the
world series, and a two strike, three ball count on the
batter. Such was a mere psychological hysteria. Death
didn't ride on the outcome.

"Fox deployed a platoon. It moved forward on
hill 528, firing at targets of opportunity. A BAR-man
went down from a bullet. Kneeling beside him, his
ammo bearer exchanged his rifle for the BAR, called for
the medic, then stood to fire a burst in anger. His
churning mind must have driven him forward. He fired
as he marched into an incoming burst. Riflemen to the

left of the formation fell, their buddies hesitating only to drag the wounded behind rock cover, calling for the medic, before moving up the hill in the skirmish line. They moved up the ridgeline like a sickle towards the chinks. Their lieutenant's hollering was stilled by a bullet, but they were a well-trained rifle outfit. They rallied behind the voice of their platoon sergeant. He moved the remnants of his four squads forward a hundred feet, before falling to a slug. Then the senior squad leader took over. The fire was so fierce, he ordered his men to take cover."

Van Meter saw that Singletary crushed his fists into his eyes before he resumed the narrative.

"When Fox Six offered the senior squad leader a fresh platoon, the offer was rejected. His men would conquer the crest. It was their mission. They would complete it.

Bayonets were fixed. Fresh platoons were asked to deploy and lay down overhead cover. A strange new energy must have flowed into every muscle of those men," Sing said. "They told the covering platoons not to shift fire before they saw the attackers actually in the gook trenches. Then they lit out, up the hill like Civil War cavalry. Their bayonets swept the crest of hill 528, just like they did last February on hill 440."

*****

The fighting hole on hill 432 fitted Harville and him too tightly. Brannagh wished his helmet was as large as his mother's wash tub. Why had the metalurgists of this infantryman's head armor formed tooled steel not much larger than a coffee cup? Brannagh wanted a helmet along the lines of a cast iron bathtub. There might not be much sense in a brain that committed its body to combat in the Korean War, but

whatever the amount of gray matter that resided
between his occipital and parietal bones, Brannagh
didn't want scattered across the rock strewn earth of
the mountains north of Kumhwa.

"Never can get deep enough in a gun hole," said
Harville.

He lost little time in getting to work enlarging
the position. He dug as quietly as he could, keeping the
entrenching tool under control as if looking for a
gourmet's delight called truffles. Every minute he
expected a burp gun to open up. Cold shivers crawled
his back each time his new gunner raised a striking
noise off a rock. Under his breath, Harville cursed this
recklessness. He motioned for less forceful digging.
When a parachute flare sparkled its garishness, he
froze in place until the darkness returned. When the
hole reached an acceptable depth, he rolled up.

"Take two sand bags out of my pack, Red, will
you?"

Brannagh saw Harville's helmet fit his head like
a diver's bell over a body that was drawn up like a
catatonic's in a sit down fetal grip. The gunner began to
doubt the assertion that steel pots were all of the same
size, that the helmet liner inside the helmet might be
adjusted to any size head - fat or thin! How could one
soldier wear a helmet turtle-like, while another looked
to be wearing no more than a thimble around his
temples? It was a matter Brannagh would look into
back again at Company. In the meanwhile, he freed two
floppy sacks from Harville's pack.

"Why are you carrying sand bags," asked
Brannagh?

"For sand," moaned Harville!

Brannagh saw child like cheeks and razor thin

lips puckered in exasperation, as it to remonstrate the silly questioner.

"For sand," Harville repeated, "if there is any sand or dirt on this forsaken pile of rocks."

Harville's head slumped, the nape of his grimy neck between the break of his olive drab fatigue shirt and rear helmet lip being his only epidermis exposed to his fighting hole buddy.

"Fill 'em up. Put them either side of the gun," Harville directed, "so our heads' got cover if its a fire fight."

It was a veteran's trick of the trade, marvelled the new gunner. Fenton wouldn't have expected less. He would have known Korea might be a country fortified by nature, but an entrenching tool and sand bags were man's tools to fortify defensible space. If a gun crew was to come back off a hill they sure should dig in and lay sand bags against a flood of lead, high pitched bravado and the screech of bugles. Sand bags absorbed shredded lead like breakfast oats did milk.

Brannagh credited Harville as a soldier of purpose; too high strung, but then with two women twisting his cords, perhaps that was why he sat almost comatose in the gun hole. Brannagh left the slight fellow alone, knowing he would recoup his fortitude, if that was what he had left behind.

Brannagh lessened grains' fierce grip from the soil's thin veneer. There must have been vegetation once upon a time, he reflected, because weathering eroded rocks while organic materials grasped tenuous footholds. Over centuries, rock was transformed to soil, but not much; just enough for two sand bags full. They took places of honor either side of the bullet- spitting weapon, to shield eyes above gun hole ramparts left by

Fox and George companies.

Up beyond 528, Brannagh watched the explosive flashes of friendly artillery fire walk the ridge line north through the trench lines of the Chinese up to hill 717. It was answered in kind. Mortar fire walked the ridgelines of 528. He saw a fearsome place where infantry curled like worms and burrowed ever deeper into the trembling earth. Survival was in a deep narrow hole.

Fox and George had left more than their excavations. They left a fearsome place; cordite as thick as a milk shake; extinguished Chinese laying about the slopes in weird, contorted poses. Brannagh was shocked at what artillery could do to flesh and bones - mangling and slaughtering men who moments before were bearers of intellects. The scene was appalling.

Brannagh had been trained to hate the enemy. The decimation of a foe that sought to mangle and slaughter Anericans of the third battalion was a quid pro quo. Chinese were the enemy. It was kill and not be killed! The dismal darkness and the gloomy dead were evidence that war was extirpation of infantrymen by bits and pieces, with the soldiers of China littering hill 432.

His grim thoughts weren't heartless, merely professional. They had attacked during the truce talk lull, with scorn on their mind, fire in their weapons, to beat back the outposts of a quiet army! They had asked for it!

Had the Chinese only sought talks so as to reorganize their armed manhood for reconstituted combat tactics formulated on Russian theories of battle as Dad had written?

Brannagh prayed for the souls of the carcasses

spread over the hillside. They were frightful spectres, their wretched legs hanging from tissue. There were horrible clumps of dissected limbs; guillotined heads; separated hands more claws than the agile digits they had once been but hours before. Their stench hung over hill 432 like a sordid cloud, its fetid stink blending with cordite, an odor of diarrhea, gangrene, violent straining, clots of blood, vomit, mucus, and discharged blood blotches. Unmeaning vacant stares locked their last view within decomposing bodies. The odor was a sickly odor of decaying, putrefying flesh unable to be buried while the living yet fought deadly battles throughout ghostly nights and glum days.

Brannagh's blood chilled at the sight of rats on the hill, going from corpse to corpse, running over bodies, foraging for food, chewing at faces. A low moan gave testimony to the gunner one Chinese wasn't dead, or inured to pain. A rodent was eating on live meat!

Brannagh shuddered. He shook Harville awake.

"I need you to cover me. I'm going out," Brannagh whispered.

"Going out where," Harville petulantly inquired?

"To chase that rat from that live chink," the gunner said. Brannagh pointed to the moaning form that must be suffering agony at the sharp end of an eight inch coarse furred critter.

"You'll get killed," warned Harville. "That damned gook might be faking. He'll grenade you."

"He won't," Brannagh assured.

The gunner hedged his assurances. He took his bayonet out of its scabbard, and set it on a sand bag. He removed his cartridge belt and pack straps, lowering his gear to the gun hole bottom.

"I'm going out," Brannagh whispered. "Pass it

on."

Swinford and Blaczyk were in the foxhole to his right. Van Meter and Davis were to the left.

"Stay there," Van Meter ordered!

The squad leader sensed the dead might rise. It was a ruse known to both sides. A failed attack often left squatters behind. Usually though, they waited only until the hundred percent fire was lifted to inch the hell out of there at the first convenient dark moment. On the other hand, corpses on the inclines were invitations to more than scaly tailed rodents on four legs. Two legged creatures crept the slant to infiltrate and slaughter sleepers.

"There's a wounded chink out there being eaten by rats," Brannagh explained.

Before his squad leader could remonstrate, Brannagh simulated the sly, creeping movements of a large-eyed rat.

Van Meter seethed at the defiance. The impulse to crawl after the idiot was controlled. There was nothing Van could do out there but unneccessarily expose a second GI. He passed on the word through the first gun squad and to their flanks.

"A GI is out front. Hold fire. Pass it on."

The eyes of the Van Meter were fixed on Brannagh's prone body, flat as possible on the ground. His left cheek plowed stones aside. He was pulling himself forward with his arms, pushing with the forward leg, his bayonet handle held firmly in his right hand.

A sense of horror pervaded Van. A live human being was being eaten by rats. It made little difference to most of them that it was a Chinese, for he was a soldier too. Soldiers deserved better! Any one of the squad would have put a round into that rat's head to end the poor Chinaman's torment and misery, but the firing of even one bullet would mushroom the jittery perimeter into an all out fire fest! Weapons were to be kept silent save for defense.

Brannagh felt chagrined the destructive elongated black mammal appeared not to be frightened by the encroaching form. The damnable rat began to hiss, not squeak, a rattlesnake sound to the creeper, or was it the wounded Chinese? From where ever, it sounded dreadful.

Brannagh readied his bayonet. Suddenly the rat leapt at the crawler, snatching at his arm, seizing a sleeve, shivering to the core his blood pumping heart. In a burst of frightened frenzy, Brannagh rolled to his back, whipped his arm and cracked free the terrorist. As quickly as the flesh bloated black rat regained its feet, Brannagh twisted toward the ferocious creature and struck it with the bayonet's sharpened point.

The rat's belly erupted. Then Brannagh saw a horde of cannibals of its own kind enticed away from cadavers across the ridge line to come to the bloody guts. Soon, they were a slithering mass of four footed forms tasting a snack.

Brannagh sensed the torn Chinaman had fought death as long as he could. Gazing on the awful picture of ripped, grisly flesh, a partially eaten ear, Brannagh's humanity mandated an end to this hideous infliction of agony. He would not let the China-soldier die that way. Brannagh decided to drag the fading being back to the first gun squad where Doc Block would administer a shot of morphine to stay the pangs of this powerful pain, and death could come quietly.

Brannagh raised himself to hands and knees,

free of the ground. He inserted his bayonet into his belt. He crawled to the Chinese and straddled him, seeing a brow cowering with grief, eyes too tired for terror. Brannagh fitted his hands through the enemy's armpits to carry the wounded man towards safety. Amid applauding outgoing rounds, Brannagh tugged him towards the machine gun's dark burrow.

Suddenly, the darkness became more awful with a scream as if from the dead. Brannagh's heart again locked in horror at the black desolation charging upslope towards him. He dropped his cargo, bulled his neck, quickly squared his feet to a wide, solid base, while retrieving his bayonet in his right hand and taking to a three point stance. His back was straight and parallel to the ground, weight concentrated well forward. He was prepared to lunge with a maximum of power at the attacker.

It was a deadly goal line defense; Brannagh a defensive tackle, his assignment very exacting. A slight error and his enemy would change the outcome of life. Brannagh timed his charge. It was a side step, a pivot, an aggressive hard crashing attack. His helmeted head drove straight into the side of the rampaging fiend. Brannagh slid his helmet right of the enemy's body, but the left shoulder and upwardly lifted and bent left arm caught the charger with the full force of a two hundred pound thrust of recoiling muscle. He knocked the Chinese backward, his captured GI rifle and bayonet flying forward like a spear.

Brannagh drove the Chinese onto the hard earth the force of the drive catapulting the American head over heels. He surged to his feet. On the slope, he stood face to face with his enemy, who with another scream, dived down the hill, tumbling away, his grim sad eyes the only weapon he flashed. Brannagh gazed at the departure as he would a car that swerved to avoid an injury. He was a nervous wreck! He wanted out of there! He would get the hell away! Had he wet his pants? Brannagh tugged the rat bitten casualty past his gun hole to the reverse slope.

"Medic," he called.

"Up here," answered Doc Block. "I'm busy here. Harville's wounded," he informed.

Fog was floating over the first gun's positions, Brannagh saw, and in it those words of distress about Harville. There had been no firing, no incoming. How did the assistant gunner get hit. A quick sprint brought the gunner to his foxhole. He saw the medic holding a GI rifle with its bayonet.

"Must have cut into tendons and ligaments," the grimacing Harville explained. "Stateside for me." He grinned.

Brannagh was chagrinned.

Doc Block explained. "Seems an M1 with a bayonet came flying in from out where you were. It hit Harville."

Brannagh's dumbfoundment was compounded by disbelief. It quickly turned to sorrow. His rashness had led to Harville's wound.

"Its my fault," he said.

"It is," answered Van Meter. "There wasn't a reason for any of my men to get wounded tonight. You're a green troop, Brannagh. You do what you're ordered to do or I'll bust you, understood?"

"Can you walk out, Harville," asked Van?

"I can," he answered.

Van Meter gave a moments thought to the Chinese. There were chogie bearers coming and going.

They could carry the wounded to the forward aid station. There would be no loss of manpower. He figured it was right.

"Have Chogies carry the chink, Doc," Van ordered.

"Sure," came Doc's stolid reply.

"And give the chink morphine," Van added.

"Sure," the Doc repeated laconicly.

Brannagh witnessed Van Meter's puzzlement at the laconic replies of the minute medic. His monosyllabic responses carried the twang of a ridge runner sitting on his front porch watching burros chase dogs out of the sheep fields. Yet he went about his duty expertly.

"You need an assistant gunner, Red. Davis is happy where he is. Who'd you want," Van asked?

"Im Ta Song," Brannagh quickly replied.

"Who?"

"Joe ROK," was Brannagh's correction.

"Joe ROK it is," Van Meter said, nodding his agreement. "No reason a ROK can't feed the gun if the gunner wants him. Its Joe ROK's country, isn't it?"

The sergeant hadn't concluded his investigation. He had lost a man. An explanation was needed, satisfactory to Singletary, if Brannagh was to remain the 1st gun's gunner, and Van its squad leader afterwards.

"What happened out there," Van asked?

Brannagh told him, but the truth didn't relieve his guilt. He'd let his rashness dominate and did a wrong he couldn't rectify. He questioned whether he belonged among these disciplined soldiers.

The fog shrouded hill 432 and Im Ta Song's view of the finger. He didn't like the quiet. But for the honor of finally being elevated from ammo bearer to assistant gunner, he would have preferred not being in the gun hole on the point, but back down the ridgeline on a safer flank.

There wasn't the smell of pork on the flank. Why was he smelling pork? GIs had combat rations. It must be a lingering odor from Chinese cookfires, Im Ta Song concluded. Chinese, like Korean butchers, were foreigners that came to Korea. He had heard his grandfather relate it. Butchers were originally Tartars who lived in great oppression in groups apart from the villagers. When they had hard times, they let out their wives and daughters as prostitutes. Butchers had to ride to their wedding on the back of a cow instead of on horseback, as was the common people's custom. Butchers had to bow and jump as if they were running when they passed a village, or be hanged for the affront. Butchers dared not be insolent! Their mouths might be ripped while they slept. Butchers smelled like the odor of the fog. He saw shapes weaving shade in the puffy whiteness. He recognised it wasn't a porker that was about to be gutted. He pulled a grenade's pin.

"Chinkee! Chinkee! Chinkee come," Im Ta Song hollered as he threw his grenade! "Grenade," he warned!

The grenade thumped the perimeter to life. Other grenades joined in a partnership.

Brannagh saw the Chinese stand up and commenced firing, some running, others walking, pushing their attack at the top of their vocal cords while grenading in retaliation, with burp guns belching. Their mortars looped rounds in front of the attackers near to dug in GI defenders.

Brannagh's bursts of six traversed the attacker's

skirmish line. The second gun traversed from the opposite flank. Both guns crossed the beaten zone's targets with steady chatter.

The bark of a chink heavy machine gun strung its string of Christmas tree lights from its distant knob to hill 432, popping embers across the GI firing line.

"Cervera," hollered Singletary. "Put your gun on that gook thirty!"

Cervera had Baiter switch to searching fire. After each burst was delivered, he changed elevation. His gun dueled the distant enemy's, exchanging rainbows of lead.

Brannagh had a front seat view of a war dance. Burning bursts, clouds emblazoned by flares, search lights dancing across devilish puffs, firey stitches sewing the sheet of night lit the murkiness with a dazzling display of death dealing fireworks. Like speedway fire flies, his tracers sought the attacking monsters of hill 432. Violent quakes followed the eruptions of GI 81 millimeter mortar rounds, setting off avalanches of debris. Bodies were swept down slope. Chinese writhed under the torture of glowing hot lead. They broke off from the blood crest. He heard the voices of their wounded wailing as loudly as did GIs. The needs of the communist state hadn't replaced ties to family. As many of the Chinese as GIs died little boys longing for their mothers arms.

Brannagh raised his weapon's sight, then its cover, and had the belt removed from its feedway. He knocked down the extractor with his left hand, checking that the belt feed lever stud was to the left. He lowered and latched the cover with his right hand, then the sight leaf with his left. He pulled the bolt handle to the rear and released it. With his left forefinger, he raised the trigger. His weapon was cleared, the fire fight over.

Im Ta Song reinserted the metal tab of an ammo belt back into the machine gun feedway from the left. His gunner pulled the tab to his right until the first round was positioned by the belt holding paw, then pulled the bolt fully to the rear and released it from his right hand, palm down and thumb along his forefinger. Their gun was half loaded. A second pull, when needed, would cock the 1917 A1 Browning machine gun ready to fire at a rate of five hundred rounds per minute. They remained on alert! Brannagh had become a military mechanic on the water cooled, recoil operated and belt fed weapon. He still felt scared!

He would continue killing, yet 'thou shall not kill', the Lord said! Then why had he turned killer, and taken so readily to the task? He told himself it was a necessity to kill. He accepted this. He had volunteered for combat duty. He owed a duty to his squad and section, to the company and battalion. This duty required him to go on, to bear the brunt of battle, to kill the enemy in combat no matter any religious or psychological limitations. Brannagh had given his word. He swore to the oath upon enlistment. He would keep his word. He would not allow himself to bend to self solicitude, but depression lingered because he felt the weight of guilt.

There were still two hours of guard duty to pull before crossing the morning's line of departure. The pangs of a bodily craving roiled him. He was famished. It had been a blind grab of rations before mounting the trucks, and with his chow time curtailed by sprints to the latrines in response to the expulsive tendencies of his entrails, he hadn't eaten. He couldn't eat while captured by the dusty convoy. He couldn't eat while on the long slow climb from the initiating point to the crest of hill 432. The gloomy and gaunt desolation of night guard and night combat turned his monitor from amino acids to animal survival. But at last the time to chow down was here.

He freed a circular, inch and a half deep can from his pack, then took hold of his can opener on his dog tag chain to open the lid of the morsel. The light of a flickering flare revealed his ration to be cheese and bacon. It was what Doc Block would have prescribed as a sequel to the original treatment for loose bowels, even though Brannagh assumed his intestines must have already been coated to a chalky goo.

He rummaged through his pack for a substitute meal. All three combat rations were cheese and bacon! Might be an alternative in Harville's abandoned pack? No luck! There were just sand bags in there. Brannagh gave entertainment to waking Im Ta Song, but thought better of it.

A breakfast of cheese and bacon wasn't all bad. It would plug him, for a certainty! A surety for the swigging of Doc's denominated "bowel plugger."

A beer, of course, was called for. The tiny but sharp point of the can opener ate into both can tops with the force of a tooth twisting. The cheese was congealed into a miniature wheel. If the label hadn't defined the dark particles interspersed throughout the yellowish substance as bacon, he might have concluded the cheese packing plant had included high protein flies. The cheese wheel was too thick for his all purpose spoon. He wouldn't use his bayonet, stained as it must have been. So he nibbled its edges, oblivious to salivating rodents.

What would Dad think of his ex-seminarian son if Dad knew the lad had been in hand to hand combat, had beaten off an assault, was in no-man's land poised to attack and retake the outpost? Brannagh reflected on it. Dad and Mom would be in church, not praying for themselves, but for the safety of their son, praying for a truce in Korea. It was Sunday, wasn't it? Dad's men's choir, like a concert of harps and tubas, would sing four part harmony at the Latin high Mass. In silent delight, the distant son was listening to the music from St. Scholastica church.

CHAPTER SEVEN
THE VALLEY

"Saddle up," hollered Singletary.

Brannagh shook Im Ta Song awake. Brannagh cleared the steam tube and web belt from the machine gun.

"Davis," the gunner called to the first ammo bearer, "come get the water can and ammo."

Brannagh pulled the rear locking pin out, while Im Ta Song removed the front locking pin and lifted the gun from the mount rotating it to his left shouder, looking like a little boy with a toy cannon. Brannagh swung the tripod to his shoulders.

"First gun," whispered the hoarse Van Meter, "come to the reverse slope, here!"

Van motioned Dreamer to keep a low profile. The squad leader saw the squalid soldier walking as to a garbageman's picnic. Whatever had happened to the temporarily sanitized Dreamer was beyond Van's comprehension. At least the ammo cans Dreamer carried were latched closed, assumedly protecting the belt from Dreamer's taint.

Van remembered why Dreamer had enlisted. Dreamer was all alone in California's orange groves, an infant abandoned at one of those Okie camps. He was raised in an orphanage that couldn't educate him, but did let him loose as soon as no one would take notice. Apparently, no one did! Dreamer had said he took hired man jobs on farms: vegetable, fruit, pig or bovine, whatever fed him. Cleanliness wasn't called a virtue for slopping pigs. Bedding was found in backacre sheds. Dreamer had slept apart, bathed in the rain, wore castoffs, except on Sundays. To pass through presbytery doors with the faithful, his hard earned nickels had purchased store bought finery neat enough to visit his God. God was his silent friend, non critical, accepting, unlike the sadistic hired hands or the farmer's cruel wife. Dreamer had no good reason to stay in his shed when he heard his country wanted men for soldiering. He had no girl friend to plead with her ruby red lips that he not forsake her for the army.

Van Meter visualized the recruiting sergeant slinking around the corner after letting Dreamer sign his papers. So must have done the medical doctor who declared the rancid Dreamer fit; also his basic training company cadre that graduated the mold from sixteen weeks of basic and heavy weapons training.

Van Meter believed everyone back stateside must have thought it was better that Dreamer, instead of them, ship out to Korea. Van had seen sad eyes and black soil on his ammo bearer until the ammo chase. Then pride filled Dreamer's fatigues, and with it a dashing headlong drive towards purgation. Something on hill 432 pulled Dreamer's dignity plug. Van was mystified as to what it was.

"Squad column, move," Van ordered.

He watched his first gun squad form. Brannagh stood before him. Im Ta Song was five yards across, and three back. Five yards behing Brannagh knelt Davis, then at five yard intervals Blaczyk and Dreamer, both standing mast tall. Behind Im Ta Song knelt Baldy Swinford, then La Vie, squatting Korean style, simulating taking a dump.

"Second gun," sputtered Cervera's dried throat, "squad column, move!"

Cervera craved his morning coffee. The damnable day never started well for him without his cup of coffee, but the rear echelon cooks were afraid to bring it up. Didn't they know a real man was fueled by high octane caffeine? Just send a jug of java to the crew chief on hill 432 and he would contract with the Chinese for the outpost as easily as Sergeant Sing hucked a gob of crud. What the hell was the matter back at company rear that they couldn't brew a pot of the strained juice for a fighting man on an attack. Cervera couldn't answer it, so he gave no more present mind to it.

Cervera had Baiter in his face, and at five yard intervals behind Baiter followed Trout, Moonshine Jones, Perkins and John ROK. Across were assistant gunner Revels, then followed Watt, Stein and Bill ROK.

Van Meter made his squad take the lowest profile possible. If there was a hole, they got down into it until his order to move out was given. He had his way. If there were no holes, they knelt, stayed low and stood by their weapons and gear, on the ready to hit dirt!

"You got ta' be quick or you're gonna be dead," Sing lectured. "Most of you ain't been on a real attack," he said, 'but we've trained ya'. Do what I and your squad leaders tell ya' to do," he said.

He spat towards Dreamer's boots. Singletary studied his men a while. Few were old timers. His section had been filled out with replacements, most of whom had arrived after Operation Piledriver ended. The real infantrymen had gone home since June 14. Those guys had driven north thirty-seven miles in ten days from May 21 to the 31st. Then they jumped off on June 3 on Piledriver.

Sing recalled the Chinese fought like hell, their rear guards on every hill around the roads of Chorwon and Kumhwa. It was a cock fight to reach line Wyoming, but they did! What the aid stations and grave registration hadn't colected, rotation did!

Singletary had tried to stifle them, but his doubts returned like turtles in from the sea to lay eggs in the sand. His new men had more than a thousand meters to attack over. There were meters of crevices, ravines, slopes, ridgelines, peaks, crests, and cliffs to climb in hot muggy weather. There were meters zeroed in by Chinese mortars and artillery. There would be meters defended by automatic weapons and small arms.

"Hear the word," called Singletary.

Brannagh marvelled at the poise of his section sergeant who pushed up the peak of his helmet. The wide expanse of his creepy eyebrows wiggled in the light, his eyes sparkled as if a military offensive was sexually satisfying. His smiling mouth flashed a cord of teeth stacked above the pillow of his chin.

The veins of Brannagh's neck constricted. His section sergeant was smiling at combat. What tremendous will power he must have to not only open the gate of hell, but to lead his Dog heavies across it's blazing coals.

"Hear the word," Sing repeated. "Baker Company will cross the LD at 0600 hours," he checked his wrist watch, "in two minutes. Charley Company follows, then Able Company. When Baker takes check point sixteen, Charley leapfrogs through to take check point thirty-five, then in attack echelon, Charley third platoon moves out to take the outpost. We go up with them, attached to Sergeant Grant's third squad," Singletary concluded.

As if a deadly cloud flowed out of the gate of hell

opened by Sing, Brannagh swore he saw crimson in the misty distance. It was a wild vision.

"Move out," Singletary ordered.

His right arm swung forward; his index finger pointed north. He stepped out. His third section's first and second guns tied in to Charley Company's third platoon echeloned to the right. Charley's first, second and weapons platoon moved in platoon columns, a rifle squad on the point in a diamond formation that connected with Baker's reserve platoon!

Nothing was going easily. Winds sighed in the thick brush on the lower slopes. Brannagh saw weary clouds stray. He discovered these hillsides of the morning were as rough and uneven as were those of last night. Heaps of stones were loosened by his clomping combat boots. Freed stones careened down rain water washes cut over decades by torrents. He saw shell bursts had branded tree trunks where his outfit was yet to march. Branches were shivered, roots castrated. Brannagh calculated the rumblings of artillery behind him, the explosions ahead were targeted missiles, acting as sky borne sweepers clearing Chinese mine fields. At least he hoped so!
*****

Coming down from hill 432, a fertile green valley opened before Brannagh's eyes, the valley's distant head quite wide but terraced as if an immense amphitheater had been cut below frowning cliffs. The broad flat floor at the close end was two football lengths between knife like ridges. It had to be crossed! There was an abundance of cover on the lower slopes as opposed to the egg head baldness of the peaks, where battle might be fought for the high ground. Baker Company had crossed these lower lands between desolate tentacles curving down from the outpost. Charley was next.

The valleys which laid athwart or sloped away from their promontories had been little altered by the guns of war, the winds or the weather, as far as Brannagh could determine. Were they the opposite end of the globe from Country Antrim, Ireland? He remembered his Dad's description of Glenballyeamon, a valley that swept down towards the little town of Cushendall, and echoed to the bleating of many sheep on its hillsides. Dad told of the hazel nut copse, the wild raspberry bed, a red rowan tree, as if he were in God's garden.

Suddenly, he heard Chinese snipers, ensconced in rock wall crevices, let loose a harrassing fire, shooting down at the approaching men of Charley and Dog, taking Charley Company's point squad under fire cutting off Baker! The squad deployed to return fire in kind. Its BAR men sprayed the successive steps of the ascent through the hard wood and scrub forest that was dressed in green on the lower fingers up to the high side scarred ridgelines. Charley's light machine guns overrode the BAR across the low dips to their front. The company had scant cover of leafy vegetation against the flailing lead of undetected snipers, and the light machine guns weren't defrocking the enemy's cloak.

"Send Dog heavies up," called a Sergeant.

"We're on the way, Grant," answered Singletary.

Grant's third squad of riflemen was pinned down. He wondered where the wells of courage and duty were back in America of which so many of these soldiers coming forward had imbibed. Under the changing strain from an imminent truce to war, even old timers like him and Singletary were beginning to show rust. It bothered Grant that he was presiding over the dispatch of third squad's and third section's nearly green troops against Chinese veterans. However, tying into Baker was imperative. There was to be no more encirclement. Getting up the hill to the checkpoint was the key to the plan of attack. Side by side, attacking battalions would eliminate flanking fire and free the third battalion from the jaws of an entrapment.

Van Meter and Cervera went at it as if back at crew drill. They had confidence in their men. They watched as their gunners put their weapons into action with precision and speed. Exactness of squad teamwork in the rear was replicated on the grassy field. The gunners took up positions, silhouetted as if for portraits, gunners' heads erect, observing to the front. On command, tracers chewed paths through flora and fauna up suspect crevices, across fingers, into dark black holes.

Charley Company moved across the valley. Sergeant Grant deploying his squad. They fanned out in the foliage to suppress any sniper residue, to engage any remaining islands of resistance.

"Cease fire," ordered Singletary.

The echo of Dog thirties still played the distant amphitheater as Brannagh and Baiter took their guns out of action, when a sniper's round whumped earth behind Brannagh. In the instant it took the sniper to sight and squeeze off another round, Brannagh wallowed in beds of grass and weeds, indistinguishable from any other lump in the tall shoots of wild growth in the untended pasture.

"Are you hit, Brannagh," called his prone squad leader?

"No," answered the trembling target. "The shot

came from the direction my head is pointing," he said.

Brannagh had fallen as if his trunk had been sawn by lumberjacks. He had fallen forward. He became a mere hand on a compass, a direction finder, a pointer towards the bushwacker.

"Are you near your tripod, Brannagh," called Van?

"Six inches to my left," answered the gunner.

"Sing," called Van, "where are you?"

"To your left," Sing answered.

"I'm shooting tracers," Van said. "We'll cover Dreamer's run to Sergeant Grant's position to get his squad to cover us," Van suggested.

Singletary saw the sense of it. Dreamer didn't. He felt a despair that his fate was in the swiftness of his feet, and the accuracy of the hail of tracers. His spirit bled with wounds he expected his body might receive.

"All ready," asked Sing?

Singletary took over. He felt he had to act. He knew he hadn't a lock on combat efficiency. Although good plans had once emanated from his cerebellum, lately, his good plans were scarce, like now. So he was open to listening.

"Take off when Van fires," Sing ordered.

"Yes, Sergeant," answered Dreamer.

"Fire," Sing cried!

Dreamer was alarmed. He visualized he was the duck that bobbed across the county fair's shooting gallery. The Japanese zero crossing the simulated tail gunner's sight. Every organ in his body was mobilized, alert and vigilant. He was determined to make it despite the foul air that fluttered past his sphincter muscle's opposition. He remembered the army had taught him that movement under enemy observation was movement from one concealed location to another. There was no such thing as a straight line, no off tackle dash into the end zone. He was to run with his body bent low, drop to earth quickly, and immediately crawl or roll a few paces from the place where he dropped; then look for the next concealed spot, spring up and do it all over again. It was rushing from the prone position only to drop again to the prone position.

Dreamer planted both feet in place, dropped to his knees while sliding his right hand to the heel of his carbine. He fell forward, breaking his fall with the carbine's butt. He fell flat, then quickly crept several yards towards a concealment of high grass on his left. It fed the next need for daring.

Singletary was shocked at the sight of two enemy flushed like quail at Dreamer's point. Before the section sergeant could sight his weapon, Dreamer, a bayonet on his carbine, was stupidly chasing them directly towards Sing. He had gone mad, Singletary groaned, wishing the dumb turd had run the other way towards Sergeant Grant's position. Sing fixed his own bayonet, fearful a missed shot might hit Dreamer.

It was a wild meadow. Dreamer believed he was a bull chasing cows. When, all of a sudden, rough hewn Singletary jumped up, his carbine lifted head high. He threw it like a polished spear into the throat of the lead Chinaman, his death shriek shivering in Dreamer's spine. He stopped his chase. In reckless amazement, as Dreamer figured it, the other Chinese watched as Singletary drew out his reddened blade from the fearful wound. Why that meek soldier didn't fire on Singletary first would be an unknown forever lost in his brain blown out by the sergeant's bullet. Dreamer saw Sing smile!

Dreamer quickly resumed the prone. He crept again, like a colubrid, its carnivorous moments at an end. He sprang to his feet and ran an unswerving line to the finger, listening to Van's deep toned weapon crooning at the hidden Chinese.

"Be covering us," Dreamer gasped to Grant. "Be pinned."

Sergeant Grant organized his squad for a sweep of the lower slopes. The light machine guns were called for cover. During the concert of machine guns, Grant saw the Dog messenger take off, retracing his pilgrimage; traversing the evergreen vegetation, resembling the shape of an olive September cloud.

"Go," ordered Singletary upon receiving Grant's message of covering fire.

Singletary and Van Meter collared the collapsed Dreamer.

"Why in hell did you chase those chinks?" asked Sing.

"Don't know," the subdued Dreamer replied.

He told he recalled the earth under him was silent. Then, as if by magic, two shadowy faces leered at him from a camouflaged fox hole, like jacks in a box, that lept when frightened. He told he drew his bayonet to oppose their advance. They fled. Bayonet fixed, he set out to kill them before they escaped to give warning.

"Why didn't you shoot," Sing examined his client.

"Don't know," repeated the Dreamer.

Dreamer envisioned the haze that enveloped his thinking. He was a bluefish with razor sharp teeth darting through the blue green sea of grass chasing herrings to rescue his section from thick showered rounds. He didn't know why he didn't shoot rather than chase. Somehow he had the feeling that the Chinese's escape might turn the attack around.

Singletary didn't press for an explanation. A soldier lived in a constant state of fear. Surprise was as unpleasant an evil as incoming. Reaction to surprise was as uncertain as knowing where next lightning strokes might rifle tree trunks. The sluices of life were open, and in a frenzy, sprung leaks.

"Saddle up," Sing called. "Move out," he ordered.

*****

Moving up the steep incline towards the checkpoint, it was beyond the scope of Brannagh's imagination to conceive that other human beings would call mountain climbing a sport, and fun to boot. If the colonels had soldiers climb mountains, there was neither sport or fun intended.

On the shoulders of the peaks above him, Brannagh could see piles of naked rocks. The outpost filled the sky on the north, as a long ridge line filled the west sky. Faint white puffs stole along. Whether they were nature's or military's, the gunner didn't know. What he saw ahead, through the wild foliage of still leafy trees or the side slopes, looked to be an edge of a mighty precipice. It marked a cleft stone, and a sharp upward turn to climb. It was a tortuous journey that never would be taken by anyone who still possessed their faculties and had brains as well as eyes.

Nature's charms, if this part of Kumhwa had any, were being hideously despoiled by booted feet seeking footings. Brannagh saw that stragglers lagged far down the mountain side. There had been no path to follow, save the beaten trail crushed into the soil by the soldiers who had gone on before. So, exhausted men dispersed to seek easier ways, to blaze trails of their own. The mountains were testing the limitations of America's foot soldiers.

Breasting the long ascent were more savage peaks in a group than Brannagh could have dreamt were possible. Still ahead were two thousand yards to reach check point thirty five and beyond that the right flank of the outpost. Its solitude had been desecrated and shaken by perpetual incoming rounds, belching with the lives they had devoured.

Brannagh pulled himself to the check point position, then tumbled onto the reverse slope's inhospitable stones. Even the wind was weary. Downward on the deep lengthy slope, he saw steam escape from water cooled bodies, as the battalion's stragglers inched their way to join the four squads of riflemen, and his machine gun with one can of ammo on the crest. The fortunes of war luckily found an absence of the Chinese on the high ground of check point sixteen. His sharp climb was over. It had taken six morning hours to climb to a peak that pierced shadowy clouds. The men were using feet, knees, fingernails, even teeth to grab holds to get themselves and their equipment up hill one foot at a time. Troops were strung out like boxer's teeth. Radiomen, mortarmen, recoilless rifle squads, Cervera's second gun squad, the first and second sections of heavy machine guns, ammo and chogie bearers; even riflemen were slow to assemble on the check point. Tactical unity hung in the balance.

*****

Dreamer was Dog's last man up. He sauntered, a nicotine stick dangling from lips of coal, his fatigues an abstract olive drab congealed with tossed earth. The mud on his face was as thick as a beauty queen's facial. Dreamer's ammo cans were frosted beyond the crud that was endemic to Korea. He plopped down his cargo. Brannagh watched as Dreamer laid down. He looked like a block of granite imperfectly chisled by the hands of a novice sculptor.

Dreamer's stupifaction left him momentarily. He laughed at the crystals in his eyes. He felt for his canteen. It was gone. He laughed again at his own discomfort. He made the mountain, hadn't he? He daydreamed of the ammo chase, the past joy on top that hill that ended in gloom when the new gunner took a Korean rather than the California farm hand as his assistant. At that rebuke, life's pleasant days of brightness faded.

"Take a swig, Dreamer," Brannagh said.

He offered his own canteen uncapped to the ammo bearer. Water on a ridgeline was blood to a living body. Dreamer drew more than a drop or two.

CHAPTER EIGHT
BATTLE ON A RIDGELINE

"Move out," Singletary ordered.

Brannagh shivered. Had he but one more minute to live? His gut felt as if a horse had kicked them. He diagnosed it as gastrointestinal. It was all that bacon and cheese! It must be! He calculated his intestines had turned to granite with all those chunks of cheese.

His hands held the tripod in a death vise grip. He heard the big guns open up. Thunderous blasts snorted ahead. A chugging round rent the air above him; its bits of shrapnel spider webbing the sky. The uneven ridgeline hadn't yet been denuded by human or insect vegetary encroachment. What looked to be mountain pines climbed from the streams below, up over the thousand foot ridge. There were white pines, quite tall, and quite out of reach of any villagers who had lived in the valleys. Some trees reminded Brannagh of balsam firs, others of junipers of ancient years, still crouching and stubbornly clinging. They bore picturesque gnarled branches. Some were even beautiful with tufts of gray-green leaves. A patch of larches gave witness to past limitations on timbering. He remembered Dad telling tall larches had heavy, hard, strong, dense and durable wood that took a brillian polish. Yet Brannagh felt he wasn't walking in a slyvan botanical arboretum but under a pall that shadowed yesterday's casualties.

It was his first glimpse of dead GIs. The effect was more of surprise than sorrow. Brannagh knew GIs were as likely to die in battle as was the enemy, but he hadn't seen a dead GI. His cognitive processes had focused on the high death toll of Chinamen, not friendly casualties, as ironic a phrase as the army could invent. Here was a field of KIAs, killed in action. Did the abbreviation KIA glorify these faithfully military departed? Did KIA give a flow to the sudden end of eminent activity of a loving human being? Was their death more glorious as a KIA than death from riding in a rear echelon jeep, a non battle casualty - NBC? Being accidently killed might not have the same alleged luster as being twisted to sinew by a zeroed in 120 millimeter mortar round, but Brannagh knew one was no less final than the other. What in the name of all that these dead soldiers held dear in life was enhanced by their removal from life as a KIA rather than a NBC?

Brannagh saw little glory in the stillness of the GI corpses. Although their families were regretfully told of their demise, there still would be pain and despair back in the zone of the interior. The beauty in fall's leaves of orange and gold would be overshadowed by the bleakness of the military grave. Families would weep over their lost loves. Their faces and forms would reappear in the picture shows of their mother's and father's memories until recollection was but a last snapshot taken when they shipped out to Korea.

Why did the sight of dead GIs stir him so, Brannagh questioned! He knew. The vague horror he had of the terrible consequences of war had become manifest. There came a calm recognition that life lived in combat might be very brief. Brannagh felt mortal, but not helpless, and never hopeless, but fragile. It was an enervating sensation. He controlled it.

Grant respected his enemy and their cunning. He determined the movement of tree leaves was not from an upslope breeze of air from the valley, but from distant weapon's lead and sent his squad to cover. He would know the location of the small arms. He took scouting as his personal obligation and crept forward to reconnoiter. Charley's second platoon was deployed to the right of the stalled squad. Charley first platoon to the left. They laid ripening under the sun. Grant crept back past his men toward Singletary.

"Put a gun on my left flank, and the other to the right, Sing," requested Grant. "Chinks out there have a machine gun, maybe two or three Czek brens."

"Will do," answered Singletary. "Van, go to the left of Grant's squad. Cervera, to the right."

Grant had rubbed in the grunge of earth to hide his tanned skin. Earth in all its forms was natural to him, a footsoldier, who caressed its folds both day and night as shelter from the enemy and the elements. Earth was a friend, whether gritted in teeth or dug by an entrenching tool. As long as he could harbor his mortal coil within earth's skirts for safety, he needed no more clothes. Grant hugged and kissed mother earth his long way back to his point squad.

Singletary watched as Van Meter's and Cervera's sidewinders slipped forward over rugged terrain. They squeezed through heavy brush. The first gun squad writhed in s-shaped curves in imitation of their squad leader. Cervera's squad hitched and hunched on their chests, up butt, then forward.

Brannagh dashed to the place Van had pointed out for the machine gun's location. The tripod went quickly to ground, the gun was mounted.

"Too tallee," hissed Im Ta Song, "not crew drill," he warned.

Im Ta Song saw that his gunner was sitting upright, a model pose of a soldier with head erect observing to his front as if an army photographer had been there to capture it forever on film. Dirt erupted from little volcanoes beside Brannagh's gun, scattering grit and chips that fell on his helmet like hailstones.

"What was that," asked the gunner?

"Too tallee, Chinkee see," cried Im!

Van Meter was stunned to look and see his new man sitting up, manual perfect, but a volunteer for combat brevity.

"You're too big a target, Brannagh," Van screamed in astonishment. "Go prone. Shoot from the tracers."

"Chinkee zero you," Im explained. "Move gun."

"S-S-Shit," exclaimed the ex-seminarian!

His hands drove the tripod's jamming handles free, the gun and cradle dropping to a low profile. Brannagh jammed tight the handles once more, then pulled the gun and tripod to new cover. Brannagh sighted his gun, fired a burst to follow the tracer line. He adjusted by tracer. He took to the dirt, down in the soil like a mole.

Sergeant Grant moved his squad out again, steadily, past freshly dug foxholes considerably far in advance of check point 35. Grant realized the Chinese were fighting as they withdrew. Beyond these fighting spots he saw the ridge line dip into a shallow saddle. He didn't see any gun holes ahead; then again, he hadn't seen those in the valley or those he just passed. He realized if he rode the saddle without a heavy thirty, his squad would be bucked off.

"Runner, goose one Dog heavy forward," he ordered.

Singletary wasted no time in sending his first gun squad forward with the runner. The first gun had been in a more exposed position. The second gun was in place to cover Grant's squad as well as Van Meter's.

Cervera," called Sing.

"Yea," came the reply.

"Stack ammo. Send four ammo bearers back to check point 16 for more ammo," Sing directed.

"Yea, Sarge."

Cervera hied his two ROKs, Bill and John, Rabbi Stein and Moonshine Jones back to Baker company's perimeter. Cervera tended toward identification by trait. When he told Stein that Jewish services were held clear back at Division rear, Stein's sudden and deep devotion to religious observances rated a rabbi prefix. Moonshine Jones fermented his own mash back home.

Grant played his binoculars on the Chinese moving near the saddle's horn. If it was a machine gun those Chinese were carrying to fire from the rocky point, there were going to be casualties in the third squad. Grant knew he had to secure it. Any platoon that inched past might be rippled by flanking fire. He pointed out the saddle horn to Van Meter, who lined his squad behind rock outcroppings on high ground.

"Give Grant overhead support," Van instructed his gunner. "If a chink gun opens up from the saddle horn, shift fire. Take him on, one to one."

Brannagh and Im Ta Song were hurriedly filling Harville's bags, so faithfully toted up the slopes.

"Can't you two make less noise," the worried squad leader chastized?

The noise of entrenching tools against rocks sent sharp shivers down Van's spine.

"Fire," he ordered.

Brannagh let loose a heavy base of fire. He watched the third platoon dash across the saddle and take cover at the rock lip. Then the second platoon jumped the enbankment near by, and at five yard intervals ran just below the crest of the saddle hidden from Chinese guns opposite. All but one rifleman! Brannagh saw his helmet fly off, and after the GI reversed directions, saw blood on his forehead. The GI, grenade in hand, was attacking! Brannagh wouldn't shoot him!

"Grenade," yelled the gunner.

He watched the arc of the deadly baseball with a catcher's eye counting the seconds. It would land to the gun hole's right, between him and Van.

All ducked for cover as steel fragments catapulted in a wild circle!

Brannagh was alive. He saw Im lived, and Van Meter, too!

As if electricity coursed through the squad leader, Van broke from his fox hole and tackled the counterattacker. It was the screaming of the wounded rifleman that was the worst part of the ordeal. The soldier never let up until Van's Iowa wrestling techniques pinned the wild arms. Van assured the terrorized GI he hadn't been captured, to little avail. Perhaps it was the exposed brain tissue, the blood that gushed, or pain that invigorated the rifleman. Perhaps he wasn't afraid of anything. Van didn't guess! He forced the crazed guy to his feet, pushing him up the slow slope, despite a verbal upbraiding, and again forced the GI to be prone.

Brannagh sensed the barking laugh was the GIs response to panic. Perhaps the guy thought he was a prisoner of war about to be executed? Thoughts of POWs being executed by the enemy trickled like a shallow stream in the valley of every soldiers' subconscious. He saw medic Block inject morphine into the wounded rifleman.

Brannagh felt his heart racing a 440 dash. He had butterflies. He was sweating. He had stopped firing his weapon. Was it the grenade? It wasn't killing, it was being killed that turned his anxiety switch on.

"Why aren't you firing," Van Meter questioned?

Brannagh didn't answer. He commenced the beat in bursts of six. He traversed and searched the saddle horn's indentations for pests. He hated. It felt good!

Grant jumped off, the other squads of the third platoon echelonned to his right and left. He saw the lack of visible enemy was a worrisome omen to the high strung men of Charley on either side of his platoon's zone of action. Grant pushed his unit upward to seize the crest of the horn, but where on the narrow point were the Chinese? The life pulse of combat seemed to be hushed and each of his lone rifleman looked to be a stumbling drunk.

A dozen meters up, the pall of Brannagh's fire had shrouded Chinese, but his shift of fire, due to the safety margin rule, freed them to pop up and fight again. Grant cursed as he encountered heavy small arms fire from chink foxholes at a point where the horn rounded near its top. Aiming well and firing rapidly, his BAR team pushed toward the redoubt. His riflemen swept upward in a rush. There, small units struggled. The flashes of hell roared on the ridgeline. The grimaces of death dealing soldiers contorted youthful faces just off the basketball courts of Indiana. Grant took the horn, a geologic structure that owed its Norman tower replication to the different rates of resistance of rocks under centruies of the horrible

North Korean weather.

It was the key to Grant's next maneuver. He needed Dog heavy's suppressing fire. There was no purpose in a rifle squad holding freshly dug Chinese fighting holes, giving time for the bugging enemy to regroup on the next point.

"Send for that heavy," Grant told his runner.

"Here we are," answered Van Meter.

Van had moved on his own order. Distant muzzle flashes from a Chinese machine gun had been seen coming from a knob in front of the blackened outpost. He didn't wait to find out if his squad would be under its beaten zone.

Singletary had seen the flashes, too. The enemy's plunging rounds were falling across the saddle. He picked a point midway to the Chinese gun, measured it by football fields and doubled the result to determine the distance to the enemy's weapon.

"Cervera! Six hundred yards northeast," Sing called. "Shift fire," he ordered.

"Do it," Cervera ordered Baiter!

The Texan took pride in his gun fighting. He knew he could fire a heavy weapon for effect. He sent a burst of six rounds of M-2 armor piercing ammo on a projected path toward their point of impact, followed quickly by seven more bursts that searched a beaten zone of its own on the knob. His was a duel of plunging fire, either side's gunners traversing for the others gunhole.

A strange fierce energy permeated Grant. He leaned forward from the waist, his right knee on the rocky soil, his left knee raised, every muscle tense, his head tossing his helmet forward and back.

"If you shift fire for a safety margin, Van Meter,

before you see us in those gook trenchs, I'll run my rifle butt up your ass," Grant grumbled.

"Only find syrup."

Grant wanted not to smile, but he did, for his mens' sake. "Fix bayonets," Grant ordered.

Brannagh opened fire at the order.

Van watched the men of the third squad lead Charley's third platoon towards the crest. Shouts were heard. The third squad jumped rocks taller than track hurdles. They sidestepped bodies with deer footed grace. Eyes flashed lightening. Third squad's bayonets swept the crest like a steel flail, men screaming their heads off. The momentum of the attackers chased Chinamen from their fighting holes to disappear over the reverse slope. The tardy tasted icy steel. Lanced chests heaved and shivered, struggling for breath. Grant's men had gone mad, Van discerned. They chewed up the crest blasting away at departing Chinese, bayoneting every enemy soldier daring to tread the crimson landscape. The anger in their minds was triggering round after round into every gun hole. Bedlam was a peaceful place in contrast.

Grant tossed his head in unbelieving fascination. His replacements had the spring of mountain lions, the fangs of tigers. This new American Army, the army of the truce talks, was turning Chinese held hills into tombs. The shadow of the stalled peace negotiations on the will of his men to fight had passed. Grant's eyes glazed with pride.

The slaughter dried out any need for Brannagh to relieve himself. The death shrieks lingered in his ears. Were the dying thirsty? Brannagh reached for his canteen. It wasn't there. He saw the webbing of his cartridge belt smoldering, his canteen blown away, the handle of his entrenching tool chewed as if a beaver had partaken of dinner. He felt no wound; no broken skin, not even a tear in his field fatigues. His equipment was ruined but he wasn't touched. He wondered why.

"Deo Gratias," he prayed.

"There's no purpose in staying here," Grant said.

Singletary didn't cotton to the freshly dug shallow holes either, or giving time to the Chinese to fall back to check point 35.

"Van, send a runner to Cervera to bring him up," Sing ordered. "Move your squad forward fifty yards and dig in." Sing calculated the Chinese had a firing card on the knob and might let loose misery on his troops. There was concealment ahead to mount the machine guns. They might be able to cover the third platoon's advance from there.

"Hey, Grant," spoke Singletary, "wait for my second gun squad to come up, will you? We're moving Van's gun forward, until Cervera gets here with his gun and more ammo."

"How long," asked Grant?

"Does it matter if we run out of ammo on this gun? Five minutes," he grumbled.

La Vie felt as if he were swimming in a sea of anxiety as his long legs reciprocated toward Cervera's gun. "Sing said fifty yard, front of knob," La Vie muttered. "Move up, vite!" He pointed the way.

"Saddle up," called Cervera.

He gave Baiter's gun crew time to clear the weapon and close up the ammo and water cans.

"Double time, move!" Cervera ordered.

He trotted up the ridgeline with his dragon tail whirling behind.

"Third squad," Sergeant Grant called, "let's go!

We're the point!"

He pushed up out of his protective hole, jumped to his feet, and ran ahead.

Singletary watched the other riflemen push up in sequence and follow their squad leader at fifteen yard intervals, running in time with their sergeant. It was a cross country team, runners setting a pace calculated to get them to the finish line before their adversaries.

It was Grant's tactic. He was a ridgeline soldier. He would have his squad break free from incoming by running towards the objective. He never stayed his attack long enough to get pinned down. It was his strategy, after taking an objective, to move ahead fifty or more yards, clearing out stragglers and rear guard, while removing his men from zeroed in zones.

Grant went to the prone behind a small outcropping of stones. He waited for his men to deploy. He stared down from a low puckered crest on the ridgeline into a concave draw that slowly rose to another protruding point. The whole of the scene was weird and imposing. Although it was devoid of life, there must have been a time before soldiers mounted its ridges when it palpitated with energy and beauty so high up and alone and as far removed from village life in the valley as it was. But he saw no charm in this wilderness and momentary solitude. Somewhere there were hidden enemy troops. It would be a steep scramble for his skirmishers to go up to the rocky grass grown ledge.

He elected to flank, lest his squad should be laid for in ambush. He gazed at his objective, studying the best approach. The day was long on into the afternoon. There were meters to go.

"Pass it on," Grant whispered to his men either side of him. "Paisley and Crane will cover the draw from here. The rest of you go with me."

Paisley and Crane were the short and long of his squad, both as to size and time, but Grant felt confident about them. The smallish Paisley took naturally to the Browning Automatic Rifle, its length of nearly forty eight inches an ideal chin hold for him when at parade rest. It gave him a plausible air during his eight months among infantrymen who weren't prone to argue with a BAR man whose maximum effective rate of fire per minute with reasonable hits was 130 rounds. Crane's appearance at Charley was as if a Michaelangelo sculpture had been cast to embody the best traits, vitality and looks of the idealized infantryman. His blue eyes smiled. He always hung a happy grin below his Oregonian nose. Crane was easy of address, fond of company, but quiet in its presence. Grant figured it was the manner of Crane's forebearers. When England and the U.S. in 1825 covenanted to leave Oregon unused and unoccupied, Cranes squatted. They quietly ignored the policy. Indifferent to the denial of title on their lands from their government at Washington, they took actual possession near the river against all comers. Crane's folks came to stay. Fifty four forty or fight settled Crane's title question!

"Move out," called Grant.

He maneuvered his skirmishers toward the rock outcropping, thankful for the lull in fire from Chinese territory, appreciative for heavy thirty coverage. He constantly checked his deployment, alert to the objective, the bunching of his men, location of the units on his flanks. He advanced rapidly up the slow incline.

"To the knob's left, move," Grant hollered.

He kept it a precision parade, a close order drill. He moved his squad left of the knob in a skirmish line towards the final phase of the assault.

"Up the knob, move," he ordered.

Paisley and Crane waited to shoot. The shock of GIs coming up on the Chinese flank rather than their front seemed to have caught the knob's defenders by surprise. Their advantage was jeopardized. They took to running off the place like ducks taking wing. Paisley took up the fire. He felt the spirit of the third squad, and sustained a rate of sixty rounds per minute into the bugging out enemy. Paisley knew he was the key man now in this assault. His blood ran high from the killing. He stood up on the outcropping to shoot down at the Chinese. He brought down one, then another, a third, a fourth.

"Come on, you gooks," Paisley yelled. "Stand and fight."

"Get down, Paisley," Crane hollered!

"I can't see them from there," Paisley answered.

Grant saw his BAR position go up in a furnace of flame. He saw rock splinters pelt Paisley's body. It twisted up, his right leg sawed off. He fell, broken apart, all bloody.

Crane endured the rain of flesh. He endured the momentary blindness from particles of dust and dirt, then he pulled Paisley off and back slope, realizing the moisture on the body was blood. Crane's clearing vision saw a terrible sight. The helpless Paisey had a crushed skull.

"Shoot me," begged Paisley.

Crane wouldn't do it. He held Paisley's hands in his the few seconds death wasted finding this harvest. In reverie, Crane worried even his short acquaintance

with Paisley would become a dim remembrance in the
battle ahead. Crane vowed Paisley's memory would live
in any church he prayed.

Grant cursed the fate inflicted on Paisley. Had
Crane got it too, he worried? Suddenly, he felt an
impact as someone grabbed him around his waist. A
Chinaman was holding on for dear life. Grant didn't
know what to make of it. He swatted like hell, to no
avail.

Pocaski saw it. The assistant squad leader
jumped down the slope. He had his bayonet in hand.
He started after the clutching enemy, who kept twirling
around Grant like a horseshoe ringer.

"Tao zhong," jabbered the enemy.

Grant understood.

"Back off, Pocaski," Grant ordered, "he's
surrendering."

It took a moment to persuade the Chinese he
wasn't going to be bayonetted before he released his
armcuffs on Grant's waist. He ordered Pocaski to dig in
forward fifty yards and hold until the squad leader
returned.

"Where ya' going," inquired Pocaski?

"Taking this chink back to Paisley. The chink can
carry Paisley out," explained Grant.

Corporal Pocaski set up his firing line. He noted
the six of them were so low on ammo that they had
better fix bayonets. He figured Grant would fetch some
bandoliers from back there.

Singletary watched Grant aim a Chinese south,
carrying a grisly cargo across his shoulders from the
little spur where the BAR team had been positioned.
Sing recognized the surviving sinew as the remains of
Paisley. The new guy now carried the automatic

weapon.

Singletary and Grant viewed several hundred yards more that must be crossed under the sights of enemy guns. There was even a hundred yards between them and the ridgeline's break off, before the deep draw rose, leading directly into the face of dug in Chinese guns on the eastern half of the outpost.

"Hold your fire," Grant instructed Sing. "Pass it on."

Grant decided his squad could dash the hundred yards without cover, if the Chinese figured the lateness of the day had put the GI attack into a night defensive perimeter. "Third squad," Grant called, "double time move!"

His outfit was to repeat its peel off maneuver when Grant was the first to drive out, followed by his seven soldiers at fifteen yard intervals. He halted behind a small rise crowded with brush. He shuddered at a wicked drop into the long drawn out draw. A glance to his right revealed two enemy at ease twenty yards away, unconcerned. Grant raised his rifle horizontally above his head, arms extended, signalling enemy within his sight. As he signalled his squad, his eyes detected movement to his left - another Chinese light machine gun. Grant quickly spread his arms parallel to the ground, calling for a skirmish line. As quickly, he next extended his right arm sideward and upward to an angle of forty-five degrees above the horizontal, palm down. Then he lowered it to his side. His squad was to take cover.

Grant couldn't figure it. Nothing had yet happened to him. Why were the Chinese asleep at the switch? It must have been Paisley's doings, knocking off the bug outs, the sergeant concluded. He readied two grenades, popping fuses to his right, and to his left. Grant whirled his M1 to hand and loosened a clip in both directions. Simultaneously, the light machine guns belched until the shrieks of their gunners announced the detonations of the grenades.

Grant doubled his right fist and rapidly thrust it up and down vertically.

Third squad's riflemen swept up. A firing line was formed and brushed the ridgeline clear of enemy defenders. Grant had his GIs lay as close to the ground as belly buttons could wallow in the dirt, while peering across the wide divide at the bastion of the eastern side of the outpost. It was still a long way away. Grant reckoned a few hundred yards advance without massive artillery support would be on life's last thoroughfare. If there were a hell on earth, the third squad had been running a gauntlet towards it.

Brannagh mounted his weapon in a crater which gathering shadows might soon hide. The devil on the outpost was quiet, yet the gunner knew this was but a temporary failing.

CHAPTER NINE
KILLER FROM A DISTANCE

A study of the terrain indicated the moving of the third platoon across the long draw would expose it to automatic fire from the saddle in the middle of the outpost. Grant was told the third platoon in a 'V' was the better way to attack, with third squad on the left, second squad eighty yards to the right, the light machine guns in between and forty yards back with the others as reserve. They would place the other two rifle platoons either side, on high ground, with mortar men displacing in a defile. Grant would take advantage of natural coverage and Dog heavies under artillery.

"Fire," ordered Singletary in concert with the outgoing rounds.

He wanted his machine gun tracers sparkling like flashes in a charcoal fire. He heard the Chinese answer fire with fire power, increasing its intensity gradually. Suddenly, the Chinese response roared to a thunderous volume.

"It's getting pretty hot, Grant," hollered Pocaski! "Keep moving."

When the Chinese mortar rounds dropped into the draw, and walked toward the third squad, "Take cover," Grant shouted.

He began signalling the second squad to his right, but stopped. He hit the ground. He hadn't seen anyone where they should have been. Behind him, he saw the light machine guns and first squad had displaced. His squad seemed alone, abandoned. He crept back to the connecting radio man.

"Find out what happened to the second squad," Grant asked?

"Sergeant Grant," Gibbard related, "an air strike is coming in. Keep to cover."

As if knives thrown from the brow of overhead clouds, jets sliced through the smoke of the fire fight and fired blazing cannons into the face of the outpost.

Mad plunging fifty calibre casings bit into Brannagh's sand bags. In terrorized confusion, he grappled with Im Ta Song for possession of the gun hole's deepest level as bursts of deep thunder, sudden and loud, swelled auditory senses to near eruption.

With the ghost haunted sky free of its madness, Brannagh's heart throbbed more slowly and slid back out of his throat. He studied the crimson glow on the far hill after the F-84s had shaken their wings and turned the battle into a charnal house.

Brannagh's horror at his first sight of the airborne dread oblivion inflicted on the Chinese faded when he realized the third platoon had been confronted like deer in the hunting season. Chinese guns were still placing grazing fire across GI riflemen.

They weren't in a quiet place, Brannagh witnessed. Automatic weapon fire had rippled the advancing ranks with such intensity, that further advances would be through a snarling crossfire. Mortar shells fell thick, their barbs hotter than branding irons.

"How can anyone face such fire," asked Brannagh?

Im Ta Song hadn't an understanding.

Brannagh trembled and deplored his shortcomings. Had he left the third platoon uncovered and now trapped? He commenced firing, a release of emotion.

Grant saw it was time for the day to die in twilight gray. Damned if they hadn't chased Chinese for thousands of meters only to be pinned where birds dared not whistle. Damned if they weren't flat on terrain where Chinese bullets zinged low.

Grant knew his men's jangled nerves were already playing high C on the guitar strings of their synapses. They needed outside help. There was no moving up the hundred or so yards to the fortified objective, or back to the line of departure.

Brannagh stared into the starless gloom. He saw automatic weapon flashes freckle the dark. He and the second gun were firing too high. They had shifted fire to maintain the minimum clearance between the skirmishing troops and the center of the machine guns' cones of fire. Yet his eyes could see this safety margin was too high. The Chinese knew it.

"To hell with the gunner's rule," Brannagh exclaimed.

"Shoot GI in the ass," answered Im Ta Song.

Brannagh had followed the book. He had laid his machine gun on the target with the correct sight setting to hit the target, then set his rear sight. Then he had looked through the sight to note the point where his new line of aim might strike the ground. At that point he had set the safety limit. It was the rule, but Chinese filled the safety margin with unsafe weaponry.

Im Ta Song's eyes jerked from Brannagh to Van Meter, as if to suggest the recruit gunner get his order from the squad leader.

"I've got to shift fire," Brannagh said.

"Van no say to do," Im warned.

Brannagh saw a flicker of gun flashes. He lowered his aim. He fired a short blast, tracers lining the path of his aim. He adjusted, traversing and searching, turning loose a cluster of bursts. He had his target, but to make sure, crossed the enemy gun hole with the sign of a crucifix.

"What the hell are you doing," hollered Van Meter?

Brannagh didn't respond. He placed six counts where ever he had seen flashes. He walked his tracers down the slope, then across. Then he traversed and searched just above the assault area, lingering several bursts if he saw a communist's gun flash.

"Brannagh, shift fire," screamed Van Meter!

Van lept from his foxhole and charged into Brannagh's with the force of a charging bull.

"You're shooting into the third squad," Van yelled. "Get the hell off the gun. I'm busting your ass."

Van forcibly pushed Brannagh out from behind the gun, and took the gunner's position. He set the sight to the safety margin and commenced firing.

Singletary had noted the impact the down and deep shooting had had on Chinese return fire. Fire shouldn't be shifted, it should be doubled.

"Van," ordered Sing, "have Brannagh lower his fire again, back where it was."

"Cervera," Singletary called to his second gun squad leader, "shift fire, sight on the first gun's tracers."

"Yes, Sergeant."

Cervera adjusted his gunner's fire.

"Coming in," called the third squad leader.

"Cease fire," Singletary ordered.

Looking down, Brannagh saw Grant, a tall conifer with a rider on his right shoulder, carefully picking his way. There followed Crane. He, too, was attired with a GI casualty. Brannagh gave Grant, then Pocaski, a hand up. They gently laid their wounded down on the reverse slope, as if a drop might chase the slumber from their pained eyes. They waited in the darkening shadows to be certain that Doc Sugrue did his job. Heavy artillery shells started churning northerly again.

"Move the squad to positions on the firing line, Pocaski," Grant directed. "I've got something to say to Dog three."

"Alright," Pocaski acknowledged.

Grant gathered Dog's three stripers at the first gun's emplacement. They stood there like corn stalks. Grant looked down into the gun hole.

"Sing, that guy there is a killer from a distance."

Grant reached down to shake the hand of Private Brannagh.

"You're a killer from a distance," Grant repeated, "Your shooting saved my squad."

Van Meter kept quiet.

Grant looked again at the face of the squad's deliverer. He knew of no emotion so strong, so imperative of expression than that of appreciation to another for staying death's hand.

Grant was known to Van Meter as a soldier who wasn't afraid. It had been said that one who gained Grant's trust, had the respect of every rifle man in Charley Company, even through the line companies of the battalion. It was an honor higher than a medal.

"Get back on your gun, Red," Van ordered as he and the sergeants departed.

"Put our butts in slingee," whispered Im Ta Song.

"Why," asked the gunner? "It looks like Van won't bust me."

"Not in Sergee Van's slingee, but Sergee Grant's," Im said. "Grant knowee you run hills with gun likee chogie bearer. Grant knowee you do riskee," Im sputtered in spittal English."Won't be rifle squad crossee LD without youee on gun. Havee Van and squad follow Grant, not Singee. Put butts in slingee."

He hoped it wasn't so. Each rifle company had its own section of Dog's heavy thirties assigned to go out with it, as the third section did with Charley Company.

Im Ta Song set about rearranging the portable ramparts. He freed the last of Harville's sand bags from a web belt, filling it with gun hole soil, then fitting it to place as a craftsman fitted interlocking stones. He worried about what he could use for sandbags about his head when they took the outpost. It came to him. He vowed to disgorge the bags of their fundament, and refill them when up there. It was a hell of a time, he surmised, for a last ammo bearer's promotion to assistant gunner.

Brannagh threw dirt, while his mind worked over Grant's phraseology - 'killer from a distance'. It was seven months ago, Brannagh recalled, when the fingers of his hands were folded in seminary chapel prayer. Now they pulled a trigger and turned knobs to traverse and search for chinks to kill. Had he metamorphosed? Then, transformation from seminarian to soldier was done by natural agencies, changing him from the godly to the deadly. Surely the Holy Ghost had refuge in the breasts of his mongolian children, clothed in padded cotton and Confucian philosophy. Wasn't there more than one mansion in heaven? So there must be more than one road there! God, by any name, wouldn't deny His presence to any race that sought His sight, Brannagh meditated, unless all of China's soldiers were as atheistic as their communist leaders. The gunner was convinced, however, a one time follower of Confucianism was as likely as a one time follower of Christianity or Judaism to rediscover his beliefs in a foxhole under fire. Combat was war between believers, disbelievers sat safely in the chairs of universities.

Brannagh gave thought to his role as a killer. He wasn't a murderer, he reasoned. Didn't the principle of the defense of third persons free him from the appellation of murderer? Wasn't the Eighth Army a part of the United Nations effort in Korea to defend an invaded people? Next, didn't the Chinese rip into the U.N. defenders of the third party only because the original perpetrator was about to be captured? Wasn't killing justifiable when it was necessary as an emergency measure to avoid the imminent subjugation of the South Koreans by brutish and deadly force? He thought it was.

Another version of the facts arose in the meditative process. Were the Chinese defenders of a third party against U.N. aggressors invading North Korea? Brannagh recalled doubts had been cast on the propriety of crossing the 38th parallel after the apparent defeat of the North Koreans, but were overridden by the legal theory of hot pursuit; the political theory that the 38th parrallel wasn't more than a line of convenience drawn after the end of the war with Japan solely for the purpose of accepting Japanese surrenders. It wasn't a line of legal partition. It was nothing more than a line in the dirt drawn by the bully from Russia, daring anyone to cross at their peril. Mao's troops were the peril.

What was the morality of combat between two defenders of third parties? Whatever theologians might have argued on that point, it was clear to Brannagh that the Chinese on the outpost would have decimated Charley Company if Dog's machine guns hadn't become killer's from a distance. Whatever the morality of freeing souls from the bodies of enemy soldiers, it wasn't by a murderer, the gunner reasoned, it was by a military killer loyal to his outfit.

Brannagh broadened the application of Grant's phrase to mortar men, artillerymen, even quad-fifties and tankers, all killers from a distance; albeit, the distance from the enemy varied greatly to the proximity of the hot barrel of the M1917A1 machine gun to the enemy. Would the concept of justifiability apply to the governments in Washington, Peking and Moscow? Not with the same implications, Brannagh reasoned, as applied to soldiers.

Were then all politicians in these governments murderers? They were in Moscow, he deduced, when they knowingly planned the military invasion of South Korea for its forcible subjugation, or even for any other purpose that took the lives of the innocent. Murder was a willful, knowing, deliberate, premeditated act that killed or caused the killing of another human being.

Did the artificial division of Korea provide a legal basis for the north to invade? Brannagh was certain in his mind there was no substance to that argument. Korea stayed divided only because Stalin wanted it so. Stalin had no persuasive influence in the south. He would have had if the Imum Gun had taken Pusan before the Americans came! So, Brannagh concluded, the Russians and North Koreans were murderers, but not the United States and the United Nations, if the attack of the Eighth Army across the 38th parallel was legally justified? Did it happen only because General MacArthur, an extraordinarily competent field general deliberately moved the X corps, his anvil, before the pursuing Eighth Army, his hammer, could destroy the fleeing North Koreans, letting them escape? What if General MacArthur did this for a pretext to cross the 38th, conquer the north, and sit on a Manchurian pony, Brannagh cogitated?

These were mad thoughts; fluttering wildly, tumbling about a mind that sought explanations, yet explanations didn't come easily. Introspections that seemed so clear before Dad Brannagh's letters to Kumhwa, now were gray.

Brannagh instinctively ducked into his gun hole at the blast of a Chinese grenade down the perimeter. It wasn't very far away. He pushed at the shriveled Im Ta Song.

"Chinkee lookee. Want machine gun to shoot," Im Ta Song advised.

He noted the shining surprise on his gunner's face. It was a common reaction of recruits upon first realization that they were being probed by a patrol trying to discover the exact location of automatic weaponry.

Brannagh marvelled at the guts of infantrymen, Chinese and GI, that probed fighting positions by flipping grenades at suspects. They hoped a jumpy trigger finger might reveal its location to a forward observer. It was a hell of an occupation, prober that was, not observer, Brannagh concluded. He felt no honor that the probe was for machine guns.

Brannagh's instincts kept his head behind cover as the blasts of two more heavy concussion grenades rippled the air and propelled rocks off stone that sounded like cracking whips. Another three explosions followed, coming closer each time.

"Isn't anybody fighting," was his dismal murmur?

Somewhere on this sombre mountain, he sensed at least one GI must be glancing down. The gunner knew he wasn't the one. He worried that no one on the perimeter wanted to fire and reveal themselves.

Van Meter worked his way towards his gunner's hole.

"Coming up behind you," Van whispered.

He noted his men had their carbines at the ready. It was what he had trained them to do in defense of their position against a probe. They were to fire carbines and throw grenades only. Use of the heavy thirty might pin point their position. "Coming in," Van said. He stepped into the ever deepening fighting position.

"Just a probe," he said, "looking for you, Brannagh. Keep your head down. Use carbines, or they'll drop a load on us."

"Why are we just waiting," asked the gunner?

"We'er waiting for the right moment," Van assured. "Don't shoot unless some Chinese rips up here to bayonet you."

Van saw four large eyes, as if in a nest of owls.

"Sergeant Grant has a system," Van confided.

Brannagh worried that Grant's system meant the machine gun crew was the bait in which the fish hook bayonets of the Chinese would lodge. The gunner tried not to have such thoughts.

Brannagh pulled his head close to the sand bags for cover at the sounds of the unexpected eruptions and zings of GI fragmentation grenades about ten yards down, and across the perimeter line. When he saw white phosphorus grenades, either end of the fragmentation explosions, light the black desolation, he looked and saw Chinese bugging into a torrent of luminous wax and gun fire, and one at a time, from front to the fourth man, were hit.

"That's Grant's system," marvelled Van Meter.

Came a quiet after Van Meter's departure when Brannagh's cogitative processes returned to philosophical reflections. He reasoned that whatever the motives of General MacArthur, the law allowed pursuit of fleeing felons, their accomplices no less guilty than the perpetrators. Brannagh held the Chinese were murderers, having intervened with deadly force against an army justified, if only because of atrocities inflicted on bound and gagged captured GIs. China had plotted its murderous adventure. It had no right of sancturary as against the rights of every dead South Korean civilian and soldier and executed American.

Brannagh reasoned on another theory - that of conspiracy. The Chinese government knew that Russia was reequipping and relocating North Korean infantry and tank divisions in the Iron Triangle area, for China's army also reequipped and relocated divisions on North Korea's border. They did this with the purpose of promoting the original invasion. They did it in concert. When the North Koreans were finally put to flight, then the final act of the conspiracy was played in November! Indeed, the Chinese were murderers!

Brannagh questioned if stateside politicians were murderers or killers from a distance. The President had authority over MacArthur. The President and his Joint Chiefs of Staff might have kept the X corps southwest of the 38th parallel as the anvil while

the Eighth Army hammered the core of the North
Koreans. There would have been no threat left to chase
north. Neiher the President nor his Joint Chiefs did it.
They left unification to a majestic General flushed with
the success of Inchon, when the choice was political.
*****

Van Meter needed to do more than peer from his
foxhole across the saddle. He was giving considerable
thought to the day's heavy resistance compared with
just three months ago. He worried if there was any bit
of Korea ahead that would give him less of the
awestruck shudders than those he had undergone on
this attack.

What had happened to joy with the coming of
the truce talks, those dreamy wishes of home by Labor
Day? Were they gone forever? Was the regiment
launched upon a war of attrition since the discussions
dissolved?

The grim face of the outpost looked to him more
primevally savage in the darkness than in sunshine,
particularly when the thunder of distant howitzers
announced dancers going to rehersal on the outpost's
dark haunts. The overhanging crest of the objective
looked as if it might at any moment topple down from
the pounding. He saw rocks over there as big as low
round topped oblong hay stacks on every acre of the
outpost, a place that was one vast chaotic upheaval of
inorganic and organic matter wrought into fearful
shapes. Above him he saw clouds contriving to organize
dissidents, as if bidding them to avoid the glaring
searchlights of field illumination. It was to no avail.

He felt the wind's breath on his ears, and
wondered how a man from the fertile plain called Iowa
became a slave to these high haunts? It was his lot, the

squad leader figured, to work hard, to be infantry. Weren't both farming and soldiering dangerous occupations requiring hard work? Even in this year of Our Lord 1951, after many years of progress in farming mechanization, there still remained much hard work. He felt no less work was his in the infantry where mechanization of the water cooled heavy machine gun apparently ended its progress in 1917. Grandpa used the same machine gun against the Kaiser's soldiers that was Van's against Chinese troops.

Van Meter recalled that Grandpa had equipment back home in Lake Mills as old as the M1917A1 heavy gun. Back home grandpa wouldn't go into debt to buy modern machinery. Was that it with the United States Army and its M1917A1, Van inquired of his reasoning? If so it meant, like on grandpa's farm, Van hadn't the best equipment as either a farmer or soldier.

Maybe, he theorized, one didn't need to be the best equipped if one's equipment at hand was sufficient to do the job. It strained his imagination to conjure a heavy weapon better suited to fight roaring battles with massed men on the attack than the M1917A1, particularly in the hands of his new gunner despite almost busting him from the weapon. Some men might be born to farming, but Brannagh was born to sing the machine gun's anthem in battle better than any of the dread engines of war of the destroying Eighth Army, Van decided.

What of his own future? What if he got off the hills of Korea without being gored? He needed a plan, a long range plan showing the acreage of each crop he would put in each year, how he would prepare the land, cultivate and harvest! He felt excited. Time in a foxhole, pulling a full alert, went so much more quickly with a mind afire on farming; but slowly if the imagery of lithesome auburn haired Katie once again covorted in the nude in the hayloft!

His plan included the amount of the crop he might sell, the amount he might feed to the stock. He would try to avoid custom work. What would a general purpose, two plow tractor cost if he bought it this winter when he got back home? What if he went in jointly with a neighbor on a corn picker and ensilage cutter? The cost would be split between them. Grandpa still had his horse drawn sulky plow and spring tooth harrow, didn't he?

Van felt good about the financing. He had combat pay pyramiding like an endowment that would 'dow' up when he was discharged. Cash might bulge his wallet, coins jingle in his coveralls down at the cafe. He was to become a well monied man.

Van continued to eye the misshapen peaks on the outpost, his mind still in flights of fantasy. He conjured he had been one of the twenty-eight from the first battalion who were rotated the very day the battalion went on this attack. They were all standing on their own two feet, not riding a medic's litter. What went through the rotatees' minds when the outfit pulled out north and they rode south? Would they have been silent back at regiment, but talkative at Division HQ, then forgetful back in the Zone of the Interior? They had done their time! What a hell of a note thought Van, that one or some of them might have felt a twinge of guilt. He didn't know if he would feel any guilt back at Lake Mills cafe eating pecan pie and sipping hot coffee! He would feel fat, not guilty.

"Might I," Van asked the dread unknown on the outpost? Maybe Baiter was right about him, that Van was nothing but a clod kicker, too dumb to ride the truck's buckboards south. Van guessed he might have come back from the rear and up the hill to rejoin his squad. He would have had to, to prevent Baiter from taking over.

Van was dismayed that Fenton hadn't come up the hill. He must have had too much sickness in his mind after all, but he once had pride. Fenton was no coward. If gratitude existed in stateside civilians for the services of their combat soldiery, which Van figured was a remote probability, how would the civilians ever determine the quantity earned by the Fenton's of the Eighth Army? Maybe gratitude was a life term in a VA hospital's psychiatric ward?

CHAPTER TEN
BATTLE FOR THE OUTPOST

"Snap to it, Van Meter," growled Singletary!

Sing had his orders. He was bitter about the dirty detail. His section of heavy thirties had been ordered to attack with Able Company's riflemen, leaving behind the first section of heavy thirties to provide overhead cover. He knew it wasn't an unheard of tactic, but hell, his section had been on the attack all yesterday and last night with Charley Company; and now again received that honor! To what was it owed? It must be Van's new gunner, that was it! That damnable fool had been running his machine gun up and down hills like an Ohio State half back ran over the Michigan Wolverines. There wern't any All-American honors awarded on the long mountains of Korea, only casualty statistics. Sing was loathe to become one.

"Saddle up," Sing ordered. "We're moving out with Able Company's attack."

"Saddle up," Van called to this gun crew. "Pass it on."

"Get your squad ready, Cervera," Sing ordered. "We're moving out with Able Company's attack."

"Where the hell is the first section," bitched Baiter?

"Saddle up," spat the section sergeant!

Sing wanted no crap from anyone. He didn't like the order either. An uncharacteristic shudder suddenly wracked his body, his head spun. He bowed his heated face into the ground. He couldn't figure it. It was as if hidden hands had grabbed his shoulders to shake him silly. He pitched the shakes, then plucked bits of grass and dirt from his helmet beak. No one saw him, Sing figured. It was too dark before the dawn.

"Keep eye contact," Sing ordered, "and follow me."

"Move out," the section sergeant commanded.

Dog's third section was taking it stoically, Brannagh sensed. What else could they do but keep nose to neck so as not to go north all alone. Night marching on an unknown topography wasn't much to his liking, Brannagh thought, where there wasn't even a rugged path. His mind could see the face of the outpost, his eyes saw but a few feet in front of him, his feet grappled with the rocks, his olfactory sense inhaled wisps of sulphur the few hundred yards he stumbled before a halt and Singletary's chat with his squad leaders.

"Able will jump off under the cover of the guns of the first section," Sing told it. "We wait here until a platoon takes check point one, where the rocks look like tree stumps. We set up there to cover the final attack."

Van Meter stared into the lifting curtain of the long night but saw only images of hills that looked as shaved as Baldy Swinford's skull.

"Which stumps, Sing," inquired Van Meter?

"Straight ahead," answered Sing!

White phophorus came in to mark caves in which Chinese might escape from bombardment but not from a fluid inferno that peeled eyelids like potato chips. As if WP were a burst from a brilliant sun releasing billows of smoke as white as dove wings enfolding a beauteous red rose, Sing saw that it marked the target for circling F8os that banked away to form a line of flight to hit the designated vapors.

As the yellowish red phosphorus shone through

the smoke of the crimson fringed outpost, Singletary heard the Chinese mortar men retaliate. A round of their own white phosphorus fell between the line of departure and the attacking Able platoon. Sing noted an F80 was decoyed to redirect its fire. Under its drop, the field between the attacking GI platoon and Dog third section writhed and withered.

"Damn," Sing cursed, "whose side is the F80 on?" He watched horrified as the death fluid spread its searing liquid and billowing flames.

"Double time, move," Singletary ordered.

He pumped his arm up and down rapidly. He would get his section to the rock stump line as quickly as he could. In no-mans-land he preferred his chances against small arms and automatic weapons than against a friendly creamatory.

"Fire mission," he called to his displaced heavy thirties. "Right front! Across the lower trench line. First gun, take the right half. Second gun, fire the left half. One hundred! Traverse! Rapid fire! At my command." He paused to check readiness.

"Up," called Brannagh.

"Up," grunted Baiter.

"Fire," commanded Singletary.

The gunners watched their tracers hone home. They moved their guns two mills between bursts to distribute their bullets impacting each target.

Sing checked the movement of the squads of riflemen into the horizontal steelstorm. There wasn't a single straggler. They made good use of terrain. Their eyes honed in on the tracer line as if it were a highway center line guiding them to their objective. Riflemen moved forward with as relentless a perserverance as his drumming heavy thirties.

Able Company seemed to seethe with a peculiarly aggressive morale. Its infantrymen bristled as they attacked, bayonets fixed, to close with the Chinese by killing strokes - the long point and the short point of sharpened steel.

From a spur came automatic weapon fire ranging in, the lead squad of skirmishers taking casualties. They came to a temporary halt.

"Van," Sing ordered, "swing your gun to the spur."

Van ordered it, his gun's eruption of answering tracers giving the range to friendly mortars and suppressing counter fire. The weapon on the spur fell silent.

"Shift fire first gun," Singletary directed.

He followed the assault squad as it arose in near unison from opposite flanks, and ran straight for the spur. GIs death curses sprang from them with a vengeance that wanted to not leave an enemy alive. Casualties taken on the charge didn't seem to discourage the unscathed soldiers from weaving in and out of loose stone and rock outcroppings with quick steps and jumps. Their gunfire splattered across the spur. They closed with a roar. Within this mad and awful tumult, Singletary watched helmets and cotton caps churn.

"Cervera, shift fire onto the bugging gooks," Sing cried out.

Cervera pointed the directions. Baiter's gun hit three Chinese bugging from their foxholes and running up the face of the slope towards the main trench line. Able company was following, hurling forward to assault the crest under the protective air cover.

Brannagh was bewildered when turning toward

the roaring cascade created by the F80s, he saw a deep
diving aircraft firing its red rivets at him. He ducked
down, pulling Im Ta Song quite flat. Cautiously, their
raised eyes saw in the F80s wake, a decimated Able
company platoon.

"Saddle up," Singletary cried, "we're going to the
spur."

"Move out," ordered Singletary.

Grant hurried the relief to reach the spur under
the cover of pulverizing artillery fire. He noted that air
support was coming from Corsairs which dropped their
loads from a much more cautious distance than F80s.
One enemy at a time, he figured.

Brannagh gave thanks that Im Ta Song had
salvaged four sand bags, which were set in place to
shelter their heads. The gunner gripped the gun's
handle in a death like vise. Artillery had loosed an
intense bombardment. When it lifted, Charley
Company was to attack under cover of Dog's heavies.
The din was terrible. The ground trembled beneath
him.

"Jump off in five minutes," yelled Grant.

"Fire," yelled Singletary.

Van and Cervera had their Dog heavies opened
up above the heads of the rifles of Charley, who moved
up the crest against tenacious defenders lobbing
grenades down slope.

Singletary felt the battle for the outpost was a
test of human life blood during the havoc of sleeping
truce talks. It was a new war, a rock to rock, ridgeline to
crest warfare. It was combat on the hill tops. It was a
new era of siege surge! He felt sick about it!

Grant made his riflemen carry three or four
grenades, between one hundred and one hundred and

sixty rounds. His BAR teams were loaded with clips. His carbine men toted one hundred and twenty rounds. Light machine gun squads carried a maximum of ammo boxes.

He questioned whether many Chinese had bugged out from the air strikes. Spotters reported that Chinese, as numerous as ants, had fled. If so, who was dropping the grenades from the trench line? Grant had considerable reservations on the quality of the eyesight of the air force. His deployed riflemen snaked their way forward. The chopping of the earth into bits and chunks showed him the enemy were still on the castle-like redoubt.

Working nearer Chinese trenches, his rifleman crouched over broken ground, through craters, over ditches, towards the trenchline connecting caves and bunkers, firing at targets of opportunity, tossing in grenades.

Grant shivered when an eirie quiet fell over the darkly shadowed trenches; and the winds whispered from the caves. To him it sounded as if Chinamen were in prayer within, when suddenly they popped out of their holes like field mice escaping from a snake in the burrow. His hard breathing men plunged into the vacated holes screaming obscenities at the withdrawing enemy, firing at the bugouts, killing any slow to surrender. Some of his exhausted GIs had the urge to rest from the killing, one so strongly tempted, that he laid down to sleep among the deceased on the ghastly rock. Grant kicked butt.

He saw the end of the battle was further up the crest. It was a time for cold steel and hot hearts. He ordered his headstrong squad to yell defiance as it followed him. They engaged the last remnants of the

Chinese atop the last knob, routing them.

Brannagh walked up on the outpost of the dead. A mortal silence had fallen over it. He saw bone and sinew divided in two, bleeding bodies beneath the grim dust of the battle that shaded gristly remains from the burning sun. How many crushed and torn Chinese were there, he questioned? Scores, he estimated! Maybe six or eight score in deadly poses, severed forever from their five senses. It was a dreadful struggle, until the enemy fled in bloody disarray. Brannagh saw the Eighth Army as it must have been the first six months of 1951, and as it had again become in September - a deluge of destruction! It wasn't what he had anticipated. Over this somber mountain of spectral trenches he looked with pity. He had expected only a few of the enemy might have been killed. The rest should have bugged out or been taken prisoner. He saw the opposite. Blackened bodies crowded the trench line, sprawled in hideous lumps. Intestines still oozed. Bloody shreds of flesh appeared to have been ripped from cadavers by greedy wolves or rapacious lions. Torn skin puckered in volcanoes with innards poised as if lava were ready to pour forth. Mouths gaped widely, and lifeless eyes stared at palls of dark flies stuck to drying blood. While there might have been hope before the truce talks failure, for an end to such unseemly slaughter, Brannagh foresaw battle banners flying in a fiercely flaming sky.

CHAPTER ELEVEN
RESERVE

Brannagh couldn't believe that the first twelve hours of September 10 had been spent in combat, while the next twelve were to witness his section's return to reserve, like on a furlough. It would be a day he remembered. He ascribed it as his day of coming of age in a land of bloodshed among soldiers marshalled for the deadly toil of war. It pronounced him a combat infantryman, a man among fighting men nearly six months before his twenty first birthdate; the day when the great state of Michigan legally agreed that he and his beer drinking were finally tolerated.

Every bone in his body ached, even though coming off the hill put him in a convivial mood. His tour of the outpost's environs had lasted but three days as the calendar recorded it, but by the calculations of stress, he felt it had been three years. Each step southward was more and more relaxing. In front of him was hot food, hot showers and warm cots. Behind him was the debris of death.

It would be quite a switch, from dirt holes to tent flaps, from whistling shrapnel to barbershop quartets, from cheese and bacon rations to slabs of hot tender beef. Hot coffee would be as potent a trance producer as would be cold milk. Sleep would follow, Brannagh daydreamed! He wouldn't be late for supper or somnolence. He thought no more of the mortuary on the mount!

Singletary was thinking of nothing else. He felt bewildered at the order for the entire 35th regiment to pull off the outpost, and for Baker Company to hold hill 432. A bit late, he concluded. Sing figured the full regimental attack was launched to break through to the trapped third battalion, but he didn't understand why the 35th was now abandoning the outpost in favor of hill 432. He knew he wasn't a military genius, but whatever the military tactic in giving up the outpost was, it wasn't clear to him. It left the chinks with hills 1062, 717, 682 and 598, the high ground! Was it that the 25th Infantry Division had gone as far north in Kumhwa as the Eighth Army would ever go again, Sing asked himself? Did the blue gloom of the burned hills mark the boundaries of the future? He assumed it was so. The battalion had fought only because a sister battalion had been cut off, not because of a general order to attack. Proof was found in this withdrawal to the line at Kumhwa. Clearly the regiment had been ordered to pull back, and stand and hold a main line of resistance. The line had been drawn! This conclusion was inescapable, Singletary reasoned. It was a signal to the Chinese that the 25th Infantry's present battle line at Kumhwa was it, no more, no less!

So there it was, as Sing examined it, the tactics of the government and the Far East Command: to hold what we had. He realized his remaining time in Korea would be in trenches, a reversionary tactic to the First World War. Wasn't that the President's war?

It bothered Singletary that his thoughts were turning from his section's to his own personal survival. Was he becoming a mental, a worrier as had Fenton, anxious and baffled by the reality of an obviously conceded battle line set by ghostly politicians? Sing felt his breathing change. He needed to gulp booze to drown his anger and quiet his short intense breaths wheezing like an old dog's pant through a deviated septum. Sing's mind whirled. He felt dizzy. He worried he was folding his hand. Had he played too long? He'd drink to meaningless objectives like the outpost, the meaningless lost lives on it, and his lost faith in meaningful objectives.

*****

"The cook's a secret," Van Meter said.

Brannagh didn't ask why. He savored the flavorful hamburgers that must be putting roses back on his grimy cheeks and a glint in each eye that before had been staring hundreds of yards to his next target. The barrel bottom chef's culinary skills did more than equal justice to each of the five ground beef patties, the gunner acknowledged, that diminished his gustatory grumbling.

"Usually, any skilled cook was kept for the officers' mess, the best assigned back to battalion or regiment," Van Meter told it. "They never let a skilled cook slip by to a line company. We usually get trained cooks, not professionals."

"The guys a culinary artist," intoned Brannagh!

He was in infantry heaven. There was a hill between him and the front line. There were tents with cots again. He was to get a hot shower down by the river, and clean clothes. He looked forward to clothes not plastered to his body by sweat, grit, dirt and slime - soldiery cement. For the moment though, his mess kit bulged with the bounty of the hot field stove; his canteen cup oozed with hot black coffee. He was alive, eating, drinking and grinning as inanely as Baldy was. Brannagh saw his squad members had his lunatic look, too. They were a colony of drunken baboons at a fermented fig tree!

"HQ staff thinks line troops will eat rat with body heat restored," Van continued his lecture. "They figure combat soldiers think c-rations are steak after a diet of combat rations, so hot food is a delicacy no matter the skill of the cook. So why waste good cooks on cast iron guts? Only reason we got the fatted calf as our cook," said Van Meter between mastications, "was that Koenig only showed skill in cutting heifers' carcasses into serviceable cuts back in stateside messes. Didn't flash a hint he had even minimal cookery inclinations. When he put his beer belly near a stove, they worried he would flavor the soup with sweat dripping from his overhanging porch. Each mess officer shipped him out. Dog company is the end of the line," Van said.

"In more ways than cooking," answered Brannagh.

"Ever since Sergeant O'Hara's first meal, he put a muzzle on each of us canines," Van Meter related," so the word doesn't get back to S-1 about Koenig."

"Fat chance," Dreamer spewed. "Be no rear echelon who ever voluntar' to visit a line company. Cook safe with us!"

Brannagh looked with admiration at the becircled being encapsulated as if by a turf clump, who could burp loud as a tuba. Dreamer seemed to have no fear of the powers in the rear. Where could they send him worse than where he was? How could they ever check up on him if they did? The rear transcribed combat reports. They didn't dictate them. Brannagh witnessed the ammo bearer's shrug. The gunner didn't mind the burp of appreciation for cook Koenig's deliciously prepared hot food, but there was a decided olfactory dissatisfaction for Dreamer's subsequent punctuation from his other end!

*****

"Sergeant, when you think I visit mon frere, passer l' apres-midi," La Vie asked of Singletary?

La Vie worried about his brother's 9th regiment. He had word that the Second Infantry Division's 9th had taken high casualties on a hill to the east of Kumhwa. Rumor had given it an ominous name: Bloody Ridge!

"Tell you what, La Vie," answered the section sergeant, "Brannagh here is college educated. How about I have him figure out a way?"

Brannagh mentally measured the assignment as one calculated to get the Cajun away from disrupting Sing's ongoing boozing party and poker game. The gunner couldn't figure why the bushel chested sergeant first class still kept his cot in the first gun's squad tent, since Im Ta Song as an assistant gunner, wasn't subject to polishing Sing's brass anymore. All the other KATUSAs were in Cervera's tent. But then Sing made them tend to his needs here. Brannagh saw no democratic leanings in this conqueror, Singletary. He made house boys of his Korean soldiers. He had John ROK and Bill ROK use ammo box wood to fabricate his poker table and chairs, his dresser with drawers of metal ammo boxes, a chest of boxes reminiscent of Sing's back home hardware bins, and a peg board to hang field gear. Brannagh didn't have to guess why the cots were closely clustered in opposite rows either side of the tent towards its rear, with a double lantern on the front tent pole near the poker table. It was as if Singletary had made over the inside of the tent into a Las Vegas store house of rustic military antiques.

"Oui, Oui, mon sergeant," responded Brannagh!

He wished he had paid more attention in his French class, but then he never figured he would have any need for the French language in Korea.

"Merci. Coup de main." said La Vie.

"Coup de main," asked Brannagh, sounding 'coup' as if he were driving in it? He had at first thought he had heard 'coup de gras'.

"Helping hand," translated La Vie. "On the bayou, families and friends help each other."

La Vie felt his Charles De Galle smile was called for, to express his deepest satisfaction. It had been a great embarrassment, expressing himself to Sergeant O'Hara. At first, before studied boredom set in, the top kick acted impressed until he asked La Vie if he was a volunteer from France fighting for America like the Irish Brigade - Walsh's and Dillon's regiments - under Rochambleau at Yorketown did, defeating General Cornwallis? When La Vie told he was an American from Louisiana, he senses O'Hara's disdain that the bayou accent and its speaker were uneducated and unworthy.

"Le Bon Dieu will help us," La Vie said.

Brannagh hoped so, but the help of the catholic chaplain was a first step if he was to effect the brothers La Vie visitation. Perhaps a bit of Irish history might catch the ear of a Flynn descendant of the emerald isle's emigrants? That might be the best tactic to delay the hurrying padre after the day's Mass to the Most Holy Name of Mary, the gunner planned.

The beauty in the prayers of the Mass were never more joyful. His mind floated back in a vision to Sacred Heart Seminary, to the days when he played baseball on its green clad diamond, when he read Chaucer in its study hall, when the Junior class raided the Senior's dorm, when he had visitors on Sundays before vespers. He drank in the shade of the tree-lined campus' circular walkway, the spell of the class rooms, the magnificence of the choir at solemn high Mass. He hadn't known it was such a banquet of glory, but he hadn't known combat before. How bright ran his memories of the seminary now, he recollected, perhaps as bright as La Vie's, an amiable angel at prayer, thinking of his brother.

"Mass, she is over right now," spoke La Vie.

"Right," responded Brannagh.

He hurried from his place to tie down chaplain Flynn while he was still removing his vestments.

"Father," the word was pronounced 'feather' as Dad Brannagh's brogue spoke it, "our families have met before," said Brannagh.

The cleric's wind whipped reddened face expressed considerably more than quizzical doubt, Brannagh discerned, although nothing was said in reply. A removed cassock revealed a gaunt and muscular frame, fatigues streaked with sweat; his eyes showing questionable interest.

"You see, Father Flynn, our families met in Ireland over seven hundred years ago when the Flynn's kicked the tails of the Brannaghs."

"And you are a Brannagh," the smiling priest deduced! "I should kick your tail, again!"

The priest saw a smile as broad across the boy's freckled face, as that he was returning.

Brannagh knew he had caught the priest's attention. It was time to explain the purpose at hand - the La Vies' reunion.

Brannagh saw the squad's three quarter ton truck was reloading for the return trip. He came to the point.

"Padre, La Vie here has a brother in the 9th

regiment, of the 2d Division. No one will help them visit. Will you?"

"I will," answered Father Flynn, "but there's a lot of red tape I'll need to cut."

He knew the 9th had been in battle after ROK regiments had taken hill 983, but were driven off by the North Koreans. He had heard the North Koreans had tunnelled the entire ridgeline. It was a nearly vertical hill with concentrated fields of fire. Everytime the 9th went across its razor ridgeline, it was like walking the backbone of a raging bear. North Koreans popped out from camouflaged bunkers nestled like beaver mounds over grass.

He knew that reported casualties were high - someone said 2700 among the ROKs and the 9th Infantry to 15,000 for the North Koreans. It was a blood bath, he realized, but he felt he couldn't tell the La Vie lad of it, without knowledge of the well being of his brother. He wouldn't tell it had been meatgrinder combat with elements of both the ROKs and the 9th Infantry being fed piecemeal before regimental command belatedly awoke, and committed all its battalions at once. Father Flynn didn't want to presume the failure of leadership might cost a La Vie his life.

Brannagh handed Father Flynn written details of the La Vie's two surviving soldier sons. He and La Vie saluted a goodby.

*****

The mountains above this Kumhwa valley Brannagh viewed were as tall and with as many big rocks as those he'd climbed to secure the outpost, but now the trees were giving in to nature and changing clothes to dress in a multicolored autumn regalia. He saw loosened boulders had fallen like so many teeth

from six year old children either side of the narrowing
and climbing hollow. He saw a flash of red on a bird, a
very large black and white one with a crimson crown
and a sword for a bill poised to peck a tree trunk. As
quickly as it was glimpsed, it was gone. Did it disappear
on the far side? If it were a woodpecker, he reflected,
this was one of the few safe places near Kumhwa that
had enough trees unbroken by shells to encourage a
woodpecker's permanent residency, and a soldier's
momentary tent. Both he and the woodpecker were
more than crimson crowned, Brannagh reflected. They
were birds of a feather. The woodpecker was looking
for its next meal; Brannagh was killing time until
supper. The woodpecker kept a low profile behind a
tree, Brannagh behind a boulder. He had completed
the disassembly, cleaning and reassembly of the
component parts of each grouping of his M1917A1, as
Van Meter had instructed; but too quickly! The lectures
on military discipline were still boring on.

Now was time to get Im's explanation. They
were out of earshot, and sight. The landscape enfolded
them as if they were caterpillars hidden by lines and
shadings drawn by the western sun's paint brush.

"You grade Korean woman for marriage?"

"Havee yes," answered Im Ta Song to the moon
eyed inquisitor. Im Ta Song had to be slowed down.
Even though Brannagh's awareness of the meanings in
Im's use of GI words had improved. Im had a tendency
to rush GI sounds telling his own history outside of the
KATUSA. He said it was a family custom when a
woman was wooed to first give her a gift of flowers to
express interest, then by wrapping a couple of coins in
a leaf making a cross. The flowers and coins were
intended to represent spiritual and material values, but

with the expulsion of the Japanese from Korea in 1945, more women tended to place coins over flowers. Im told family custom allowed him to grade a woman's character, intelligence, beauty, purity and fertility as the highest among one hundred and eight different characteristics. Fortunately, Im left out a hundred and four, except a Korean man usually chose a woman for wife if her features matched his own.

"How many of the woman's characteristics did you grade," asked Brannagh, feeling an incredulous occidental?

"Hundree eight," answered the oriental.

"Back in Detroit it's a hundred and seven less," Brannagh exclaimed!

"Mostee want wife not knowee Trout!"

Brannagh was momentarily at a loss to pursue this conversation. He saw Im Ta Song's disc shaped face looked like an unfolded omelette that had sat too long in a hot, deep skillet. If the woman he selected had features that matched his, they would produce lollipop-head babies!

Im was wound up. He told he gave his woman's Papasan a Munchurian horse as a bride price, for his woman was a Kat maker on Cheju Island. Im's hand movements outline a top hat, "makee of horsee hair."

Brannagh visualized Abe Lincoln's stovepipe hat. Brannagh marvelled at the facile use of English that came from the relaxed Korean. Im's words had but a mere trace of accent tiptoeing from sound to sound, unlike his horrid pronunciations when responding to Singletary or Baiter.

"There was more. Kats were made on Cheju Island, held on the head by a black ribbon tied under the chin. Why Cheju? There were many horses there. If

not Kat maker, women worked as divers or concubines.
Im smiled slightly. Kat maker get much esteem, so
bride price a Manchurian horse; for divers, a Cheju
horse; for concubines, a saddle.

Brannagh dared not smile at the subtlety!
*****

His squad had its assigned zone behind the MLR
on a mountain's north face, and trenches to dig. It was
about as basic as an infantryman could get. Brannagh
worked the long handle. He realized the shovel fit. He
had dirt to remove, machine gun bunkers to complete,
trenches to dig in preparation of a blocking position.

"I don't mind digging Korea flat," he said to
Dreamer, "but who knows if there are live duds under
here?"

"Dirt squishy," said the mud splattered
Dreamer, "soft from rain, not rounds."

Brannagh wasn't so sure. More than one pine
had been chewed by other than a ten foot beaver. He
wondered if North Korea had beavers? A look down the
forward slope revealed but rounded gnomes in the
valley bedecked in GI gear, no sign of a lodge. No
self-respecting beaver would climb a long hill to fell a
tree. It was a shell that chopped it, more than one for
sure, he concluded. Baldy Swinford and Im Ta Song
were as unconcerned as was Dreamer, Brannagh noted.
So he dug. The zigzag trench was to run the slope at
least eight feet deep and three wide, which might take
three years the way Balcyzk, La Vie, Swinford, Davis
and the new guy, Glorio, were tickling earth. Brannagh
marveled at the muscle of Van Meter. The farmer knew
his tool's usage. So did Im. The two of them were up to
the rest of the squad, Brannagh realized.

Digging had been in progress about an hour

when Brannagh noticed the zigzag reached a depth of
four feet where he stood, three feet where Im Ta Song
was tossing earth to the forward side, but only two or so
feet where Dreamer dug. It had taken on the
appearance of a stair step, with Baldy Swinford
standing on the landing. He was huffing and puffing
like a steam shovel.

"Let's take ten, Van," demanded Baldy.

Van took note of the sweat oozing out of
Swinford's hood ornament. "Take ten," Van agreed.
"Smoke if you got them."

As if Van had turned on an electrical appliance,
Brannagh melted like toasted cheese onto the freshly
dug earth. "I'll never be able to use these fingers again,"
he said.

"Won't fondle nuttin' either," giggled Dreamer.

"Well, you can fondle da pick next," Swinford
said to Dreamer.

"Alrite," replied Dreamer, "I take the next turn
on the pick."

"Gunner," Dreamer said, "use less arm and back
when you dig. Use more body. Not get so sore."

Dreamer felt a surge of pride in knowing
something the gunner didn't. They both were still
private soldiers in the Army at the moment, but the
gunner was soon to get the ratings. Why hadn't
Brannagh moved him to assistant gunner, Dreamer
questioned? If he had, he was a sure bet for the rating
of private first class. First class! He had never before
gone first class!

"Breaks up," said Van. "Back to digging."

Dreamer took the pick to the landing, Brannagh
was a step down, then Im Ta Song, next Swinford.
Below them Blaczyk, La Vie, and recruit Glorio were

situated.

Van Meter placed Davis on guard at the bunker. The squad leader watched as his squad went at it pick and shovel. There were no slackers he could see, when suddenly he watched Dreamer turn a slow Virginia reel, twisting in slow motion, gasping and gagging, projectile vomiting a purplish oatmeal. Van saw Brannagh leap out of the vomit's way, but Im took a face full, and Swinford ran into Blaczyk like a bowling ball against the ten pin. Then the odor hit Van like a mule's kick.

"What have you done in your pants, Dreamer," hollered Van Meter.

He saw that Baldy's lumpy face had contorted. He was pinching his nose. Im Ta Song was on his knees, dirt washing the foulness off his face. Blaczyk and La Vie were on all fours crawling down the new trench line. Glorio backed away from the madmen. Brannagh had climbed the hill to the upwind. What ever they had all said about Dreamer's bodily odor did him an injustice, Van adjudged. No one else's innards were capable of producing such a pungency. Another sniff identified the decomposing incense. Dreamer had cut his pick into a putrefying cadaver of a Chinaman.

"Pull the pick out, Dreamer. Throw lots of dirt on him," Van ordered as he walked upwind. "Turn the trench at a right angle at the chink's feet until you dig past him. Then turn back again towards the reverse slope," Van instructed. "I need to see Sing. Finish up the undertaker bit, and get back to digging," he ordered.

"Hey, Sergeant," called Baldy, "I better go with you."

"Me, too," said Brannagh!

Both hoped Van Meter might elect their

company. He didn't!

*****

Master Sergeant O'Hara saw to the absence of all of the staff from Dog's command tent. No fox wanted witnesses while devouring rabbits, and three baby bunnies were following their daddy's white tail to O'Hara's burrow. He brought forth a quart of American bourbon, what with the difficulty of Koreans importing Ireland's 'uisce beatha'. He sensed Singletary was seeking numbing relief in the wet tranquilizer, Cervera sought giddiness, while Van Meter stayed forever sober. Top Kick expected it.

"Plan Overwhelming was to have been launched last week to take the Eighth Army to Pyongyang on the west and to Wonsan on the east," informed O'Hara to his three sitting sergeants, "but Ridgeway never gave approval because of the peace talks."

"Peace talks are over now," groaned Van Meter.

"We better hope the politicians get the truce talks back on track," answered O'Hara emphatically.

"You know something," Sing asserted.

"I know," O'Hara emphasized the words, "that there were so many GI casualties up on Bloody Ridge, it popped the eyeballs of the general staff. Still, preparations haven't stopped."

If so, thought Sing, why did division order the 35th regiment off the outpost after recapturing it? He was puzzled. He couldn't figure the brass out anymore. It had lost sight of short term military objectives. He drank to their stupidity. He couldn't drown out the words he had to speak.

"Sixty-one dead, two hundred and five wounded and thirty-eight missing over that outpost," said the disgusted Singletary.

211

"What's that," asked Cervera?

"Our casualties, not the gooks," Singletary slurred. "All because the brass couldn't see to put a squad on hill 432 to protect the MSR to the outpost."

O'Hara was glad for the topical change. He had it in mind, but preferred Singletary's introduction of the outpost. O'Hara baited his hook.

"Corporal Baiter," O'Hara said in lower tones, "blames Private Brannagh for Charley's casualties."

"Bullshit," snapped Van Meter. "Brannagh's gun was the one that freed Charley from being riddled."

"Baiter's told me," Cervera replied, "that Brannagh's gun hit some of Charley's men."

"Bullshit," shivered Van Meter! "But for Brannagh, Charley would still be on the outpost taking casualties," Van argued.

"Why are you after Baiter," Cervera challenged?

"He's a sick shithead," answered Van. "He's more a queer than straight. He's always sizing butt, looking for a sissy mujerado."

"What in hell is a mujerado," the flabbergasted O'Hara inquired?

"Some damned Pueblo Indian fairy," answered Van Meter. "Chiefs made this queer ride horses until his manhood shrunk, and he had no beard and his voice was a woman's. Then the chiefs serviced him."

"The chiefs were queers, too," the astonished O'Hara asked?

In all of his Ireland there wasn't a queer. There were fairies, of course, but they were formerly angels who stood aloof when the devil challenged God, Who punished them by banishment to Ireland pending good behavior.

"Must have been," Van accused. "There ain't

many of those chiefs left, but Baiter's taken their place. He's a distorted turd! Transfer him to the third battalion," Van mandated.

"Can't transfer but top three graders to the third battalion," O'Hara answered. "Baiter's a corporal."

"Don't promote him," Cervera debated. "I don't want to lose him. He's got time in grade."

O'Hara desired argument. He had them where he wanted, at each others throat over Brannagh and Baiter. O'Hara expected the gunners would fist fight to uphold the honor of each's squad leader. O'Hara bet on it.

"Enough of this," O'Hara interrupted! "The battalion's soon to move up to the MLR. We don't want bad blood. Forget it."

O'Hara assumed the anger in the faces of the squad leaders wouldn't allow forgetfulness over Baiter and Brannagh. As for Singletary, the booze numbness falling inside his head might keep him from interfering with a future fist fight. Singletary's mind was losing its sharpness to the bottle and the fear of the unknown bullet. O'Hara knew the signs. He had been there. Sing's courage was being starved by constant combat. It was traceable from frenzied actions when a replacement, to the studied moves when experienced, to caution as an old timer, to protruding skeletal nerves when contemplating death before rotation. O'Hara saw Brannagh as the frenzied; Baiter as the studied; Cervera and Van Meter as cautious; while Sing was falling to the trauma of psychological starvation and drowning it in liquor. It was this deprivation that would submerge the section sergeant, freeing squad leaders and gunners to enter rancorous factions enhanced by Baiter's native miserableness. It would be good versus evil, purity versus the putrid. O'Hara would make a fortune on it.

"Return to your men," O'Hara ordered. "No more crap. I'll forget it. Best for all of you, you forget it, too," he warned.

O'Hara was convinced he had to be ready in case the truce talking turds set aside this little war.

Every soldier in Singletary's gun section, even Dreamer, had taken a shower downstream from where the cooks drew water, but upstream from the laundry and truck wash.

Clean clothes were as welcome as Christmas gifts. Brannagh added to his private collection of clean socks. Despite Trout's argument to the contrary, the gunner saw a greater importance in changing his socks frequently than Trout's morning ritual of clean undershorts. It was an infantryman's feet that were objects of fashion, not his cylindrical column, the ex-seminarian argued to the wind. However, R & R returnees agreed with Trout, often emptying fluid from their bladders to test urinary tracts for burning sensations before a short arm inspection.

A comfort station was the five pipe urinals implanted in the loose stones of a soaking pit, with nearby hand washing facilities of gallon cans pierced by long sticks mounted on twin y-spits for ease of pouring warm water on soiled fingers. The army catered to the comfort of its line troops while they were in reserve, Brannagh agreed. The latrine pit, its eight seater constructed of the finest wood of ammo boxes, had cut holes handcrafted to fit the roundest bottom.

How elegant had become the relative simplicity of his squad tent. The tent's high poles spread canvas above him in two tit-peaks descending to the four corner poles. The four side walls of canvas were rolled up for ventilation. His cot was above ground level, his field gear neatly organized in readiness for rapid movement. His machine gun stood a lonely sentinel between cots of its gunner and assistant. He heard the two rows of cots groan at the return of their military occupiers. They all waited for the confirmation of rumor. A sobering Singletary was on his way.

Brannagh studied the orderly row of tents throughout the valley. Trucks were as well organized. Outside the cook's tent stood, systematically, cans for washing mess kits. The whole of the military mind was mathematical precision; they measured the country of Korea in a series of grid coordinates. He didn't. He saw grass hurting where hundreds of combat boots had walked. He saw needle-leaved trees. He saw a surviving broad leaf tree on a nearby hill. He saw a land surface of rugged terrain and steep slopes. There wasn't an order at all, save that of geological weathering. It was a land of A-frames and unhurry, except when soldiers walked.

"Hear the word," hollered the arriving Singletary. "It ain't no outpost this time. We're moving up to the MLR, the main line of resistance. That's where we're going to stay, truce talks or no truce talks. No more outposts!"

"We're heading for the trenches at 0500 hours," said Sing. "You should have listened to Grandpa's tales of the trenches back in his war to end wars. You can update him when you rotate."

Brannagh envisioned miles of communication trenches zigzagging from bunker to bunker, and back to the reverse slope. He would be a common laborer, not a carpenter's apprentice. It would be picks, shovels, sandbags and machine gun. Work all day, and pull guard at night crouching against dirt walls when Chinese sharpshooters squeezed off a round, or dropped a mortar shell to measure the distance. It would be barbed wire details, hanging c-ration cans with rocks from the wire, laying flares and trip mines, digging firing positions and gun holes, toting logs from the rear to build bunkers.

The forward slope would be his front line, yet his company's forward command post, aid station, latrines and supply dumps were on the reverse slope. He marvelled at the difference the ridgeline made. It's reverse slope was far more safe from flat trajectory incoming.

Some soldiers within the same company were always on the forward slope, others on the reverse. The pleasure of Dog Six or O'Hara, the top kick? So it was. Hadn't forward slope troops dug the back slope CP! With luck, however, a forward slope heavy weapons' soldier might not have to go out on patrol. None the less, if his heavy thirty weapon were needed, so went the gunner, assistant and first ammo bearer, most likely not with the advance element, but left at a drop off point to cover a withdrawal or disrupt an ambush. Safety in combat was a measurement on officers' slide rules.

Dreamer felt depressed. It saddened him to go up the hill. He admitted to gladness when he came off the outpost, even though Baker company and Dog's second section of machine guns were left behind on hill 432. It was wrong for him, he believed, to feel glad to leave war, while others went into it. It saddened him to think there were casualties, but gladdened him he wasn't among them. It also maddened him at the

Chinese for hurting GIs. Dreamer's depression deepened. He felt sad, glad and mad each time a GI was hit. He couldn't reconcile feeling glad he hadn't been hit, and sad for his buddy, mad at the enemy.

He recollected he had first tasted the bitter water of Korea when the Eighth Army set out an outpost line of resistance in front of lines Lincoln and No Name. He had heard the Chinese had half their army ready for a sixth phase offensive. Those Chinese ran over the ROKs on the east coast. Nearly 40,000 ROKs bugged out, leaving the 2nd Infantry Division firing day and night, slowing the attack headed for Wonju to Pusan.

Dreamer recalled the sergeants named their counterattack Detonate. The Chinese at first fought like mad ants, before the battalion started to take prisoners. He recollected they looked like the Chinese back in California, except so many of them were sick; probably of the shit stink, he surmised. They were surrendering in wholesale lots, little yellow men with wide pecan eyes, tennis shoes and cotton padded clothes. He concluded that May or June would be the last month of the Korean War. There couldn't be lots of enemy left, as so many of them were mouldering in the rice paddies and on the slopes of South Korea.

Brannagh had a hard time keeping facts out of his letters home. Should he write Dad the Korean War wasn't anywhere near its end? Now that he was a gunner all of a few weeks, would its revelation depress this family? Dad wouldn't see the placement of one's body in a position of sudden demise as any distinction. He might relate that death on an Asiatic battle field was devoid of meaning to a nation of Caucasians - at most eliciting a tisk tisk of puckering lips - about as deep an emotional expression Dad's adopted country espoused for any police action of little consequence.

Im Ta Song took cover in the caverns of his imagination. He contemplated not the front line, but the tall Tennesean from Cervera's squad; the weeping willow limbed Trout who was expounding on circumference differentials between Van Meter's weapon cleaning rod and Trout's rounded mass of erectile tissue when filled with arterial blood.

Was the historic personage of Kim Ch'ang-su reincarnated in Trout, Im questioned? In olden times, when the lecherous Kim was on trial for having caused the downfall of a young female teenager - only one among scores of other women of Seoul, Korea, he had fascinated - large numbers of women dressed in traditional long shawls which concealed everything but their eyes surged forth to reach the alleged scoundrel. They freed him! Im Ta Song proclaimed America had sent forth its own Kim Ch'ang-su in the form of the gangly Trout.

Why did megooks focus so on breeding, Im Ta Song queried? Why did they not establish shrines to ward off female spirits. Before, when Korean soldiers were deprived of their women, to avoid being haunted by dangerous recollections, they built a shrine to a local deity, its real purpose masking the presence of a phallus. Wasn't there civilization in Trout's village?

CHAPTER TWELVE
THE MAIN LINE OF RESISTANCE

Climbing Kumhwa's rough, steep and not conspicuously interesting path up the rocky mountain to the MLR, Brannagh concluded, was tantamount to trimming a ship. It caused him to adjust the weight of his equipment so he might maintain his footing at an angle best able to contravene gravity. Korea's paths were spiral staircases masked by fog.

He blinked when his eyes revealed the absolute absence of communication trenches running from the reverse slope through the ridgeline and down to the front line positions. Soldiers were running across the skyline like carnival targets in a shooting gallery. Had they death wishes, he pondered?

A crawl to the crest, a peek down the forward slope revealed a long horizontal procession of mushroom like fighting holes. They popped out of the convex surface around root tips of pine trees.

"To the bunker under the spruce tree, Brannagh," Van Meter instructed. He pointed to the machine gun's placement down slope.

"Davis," called Van Meter?

"Yo," came the reply.

"After Brannagh and Joe ROK get to their hole and set up, you follow them with the water can and ammo. Stay with them," Van ordered.

"Got it, Sergeant!"

"Baldy," called Van Meter?

"Yes, Sergeant."

"One after the other; first you, then Blacyzk, then La Vie, drop your ammo at the gun bunker, then dash left two bunkers. The three of you occupy that position. Dig in there, right," Van Meter checked.

"Right," came the chorus.

"Next," Van continued his instructions, "Glorio and Dreamer, one after the other, drop your ammo at the gun, then dash left one bunker. Both of you dig in there."

"Why Baldy get two for guard duty," Dreamer whined, "me got only the new meat?"

"I'll be with you," growled Van Meter.

Oh, good," sighed Private Glorio.

He came out of the Bronx, a barber's son, square jawed and clean shaven. He had pulled his helmet low over his black hair, and readied his sturdy body to bear the demands of a field soldier. His draftee intellect, however, kept composing an affidavit wherein he would swear to the unfairness of Truman's selective service. Especially now when he had to alternate guard duty on the front line with homo sapiens' most questionable member, namely Dreamer. In all of the Bronx, Manhattan, Queens or Staten Island he hadn't met anyone as bereft of human dignity as was Dreamer. Glorio wasn't sure that was the case in Brooklyn.

"Everyone ready," Van asked?

"Ready," came the chorus.

"Move out, Brannagh."

Van covered as his gunner shot up like a rocket, his tripod's fifty three pounds of weight held firmly by his right hand. He zigzagged the ten yards down slope like a chased rabbit.

Brannagh saw a pothole that the Wolfhounds had squared by corner posts on which rode ceiling beams crossed by pine logs covered with sequential layers of cardboard, ponchos, dirt, then sandbags. He lunged through the back aperture, landing on his hands and knees.

"You a bulldozer," asked the Wolfhound gunner?

"Brannagh, of Dog three, 35th," was the reply.

He had barely moved when Im Ta Song squirted in with the gun. As they waited while the Mike Company gunner took his weapon out of action, Davis jammed into the crowded position.

"It's all yours," smiled happy Wolfhounds.

Brannagh's eyes followed them as they dashed up the forward slope and disappeared. It was the way of armys. Soldiers never knew who served in their division, or regiment, or battalion, or company, often not even in their own platoon. They mostly knew their squad buddies.

Brannagh viewed a gun hole with a gun port as big as a dining room bay window, through which peering binoculars from north of no-man's land might peep for targets. He was in a bunker dug by the hopelessly lazy, or by a crew that had little expectancy of enemy visits, or by an outfit that was a true believer in a quick resumption of the truce talks. He felt differently. Whether or not the truce negotioations might revive from their suspended animation, there was standing north of the 38th parallel across Korea a continuous front line with no flanks to attack. He envisioned ceaseless fighting across it, as if a fuse was always sputtering, from west to east, and back again. From day to day and from place to place, he surmised, firefights would vary in intensity. It might be quiet at Kumhwa, but raging in the punchbowl. There would be a battle somewhere, for some seemingly useless geography, every day, and Kumhwa wouldn't be exempt. Every day could be a battle day.

Dreamer grunted as he slipped into the machine gun bunker. The ground trembled beneath him. He saw a column of sable smog rise into the air in front of the gun port.

Brannagh popped his jack-in-the-box head high through the opening when his breath broke from his mouth as his fatigue shirt pulled around his throat like a hangman's rope with a python's squeeze. He fell backwards on top of the prone Davis and Im Ta Song.

Dreamer heard the ripped air sing in its guttural voice, delivering triplets in rapid succession. Then the sudden bursts sank like any stone into the sea. Dreamer raised himself cautiously.

"Keep yor' head down, dummy," Dreamer croaked, spewing saliva. "Be incoming down the trench line. Gooks be walking the dog."

"Why did you do that, Dreamer," came Brannagh's exasperated question?

"Be seeing that you last one more day, dog face!"

Dreamer's pronunciation of dog seemed to carry at least three 'o's pulled long like taffy. Dreamer stared down, vulture like, at his prey.

"Be dead if you peek. Incoming what swooshes be yards away, but not shrapnel," he said. "Incoming what sound like a C-ration box pulled across grass-a whish," his sound was short and quick, "will get ya'."

Dreamer dramatized his point. He drew fingers as if they were knives across his throat. He persisted in several repetitions.

Brannagh felt such persistence was the ammo bearer's best military trait. He just didn't belong in the army, no matter why the Army took him, or put him in a line outfit. There were just too many able minded and able bodied men back on stateside campuses and playing professional sports. Still, as for Dreamer, he was persistent in his efforts to be a combat infantryman, if not a barrack's trooper. That was beyond him. He was intellectually, maybe even genetically, incapable of doing soldiery tasks by the book. Still, he tried. He kept trying. He was trying. Yet his persistence to be an infantryman equal to the rest of the men in the squad was admirable. Maybe he could teach a course on persistence. His eyes weren't wearing their vacancy signs. His fatigue shirt hung floppily, but his pants fitted tightly except for pockets bulging with personal items.

Dreamer cocked his thumb, his index finger a gun barrel this time pointing at Brannagh's forehead. "Shrapnel kill more dogfaces than bullets. Don't peek." he urged. "Hide in the hole."

Brannagh knew eloquence when he heard it, no matter the status of the orator.

"I won't peek anymore, Dreamer," Brannagh answered as if in submission. "Once was one too many."

Brannagh reached for Dreamer's hand, to shake it, but Dreamer didn't reciprocate with his own paw.

"With you to teach me line soldiering, I'll make it yet."

Brannagh meant the compliment. He knew enough about the literature on deprived children to know some of them, like Dreamer, might not seemed to have thrived in the deserts of institutions, but not all sparks had been doused. One could burst into flame if an opportunity for combustion happened along.

"Gooks be walking artillery up and down the MLR to drain their loads," Dreamer said to the mass of facial freckles he saw, his hand gesture tracing the elliptical path of a flat trajectory incoming round. "Artillery come in long and low, but mortars come in from on high then down like a rollercoaster," he said with another gesture taking the form of a high arc. "Stay undercov' if gooks pop mortars. Be a mean Santa Claus, com' down chimneys like a blowout."

Dreamer slipped his entrenching tool into his left hand, then ran from Brannagh's hole towards his own fighting hole to fall into his digger's transendentalism. He sensed the crapping by the gooks' dog was in abeyance. Now he would furrow his own defensive position before the dog walked again.

The gunner turned to stare across his field of fire, then up the distant ridgeline where the Chinese must be staring back. He didn't see movement, yet he sensed something if not over there, in himself. He sensed hate. He felt he had gone beyond hostility for the Chinese. There had been just a vestige of hope that the truce talks would resume, but that melted with the dog walking, as Dreamer described it.

Van Meter entered the machine gun bunker.

"Davis, Joe ROK," the squad sergeant ordered, "grab your entrenching tools and get up to Singletary's hole."

"Nikola Shibola," muttered Im Ta Song, as he went with Davis.

"We're not where great decisions of strategy will be played out, Sergeant Van Meter," Brannagh said, "but we are where tactics come to the fore. It's here where what ever we do, operational leadership against the Chinks falls upon Sergeant Singletary."

Van shook his head in agreement. He hadn't seen an officer on the forward slope since the section came up the hill. He didn't think them chicken, just smart. The Korean War had become something else to them. It was becoming something else to Singletary, too. His ideology was draining as fast as cow pee. All that patriotism he believed in from stateside, all the military discipline pounded into him was dwindling each setting sun.

Van Meter kept stewing the ingredients of the gunner's words. If Singletary was the section's key link in the chain of command, and if he kept milking hootch bottles, one of the squad leaders, Cervera or Van was going to have to take leadership. Could he and Cervera work together? Maybe, Maybe not.

Van yearned to rid himself of the unpleasant feelings he bore for arguing against Cervera and Baiter about Brannagh, and before the top kick, yet! Van felt he had been foolish by lashing out with dirty words, and unnecessarily hurtful.

Brannagh missed the meaning in Van's silence.

"I've read the object of military defense is --."

"You read too damn much," Van Meter raged.

Cervera crawled into the first gun bunker. He raised himself upon his knees to see all of the unsettled Van Meter. "What you yelling for, Van?"

"Yelling," inquired Van. "Am I yelling?"

"Whatever." Cervera wasn't looking for any more guff from his counterpart at this moment. "Singletary's sitting in his hole sipping booze from his canteen. He's tanked to the gills. Ain't of no use to no one."

Van Meter digested the information. If leadership was fired by spirit, Singletary was drowning his spark plugs in moonshine. There was another Fenton in the section, but Van worried if he could cover for him, too. He bore strong bonds of friendship with

Singletary. They had pulled through hard combat together; Sing the leader, Van following. They were wartime friends and that was not the same as peacetime friends. The emotional costs were too great if friendship was severed by shrapnel. Now, however, the time had come to organize the outfit, even if the section had a twisted up sergeant, a tired soldier, a very quiet leader. Van thought of the days ahead on the MLR. If Sing wasn't up to cracking backsides, his squad leaders were. Van figured it was his turn for personal responsibility.

"If we're to hold the MLR against the rest of the Chink army," Van Meter warned, "we had better dig as deep as the trench across the ocean floor, with as many twists and turns as the Burma road, with sleeping holes separate from gun holes. If we're hit like the outpost was," Van related, "then we fight. If the 25th Division isn't going to launch a regimental attack, or if the regiment isn't going to launch a battalion in attack, or the battalion isn't going to launch a company on an assault, or a company attack with a platoon, then it'll come down to squad actions with HMGs in support. We'll be caught up in isolated sieges. Sieges will mean life and death to us, but they aren't of any importance to the world," Van concluded.

"We're frigging ants," Cervera exclaimed!

Van declined to update the migrant labor boss that ants, except for a few princes which didn't live long, were females, whether they were gardeners, farmers, hunters or soldiers.

"We certainly have to be insect engineers," Van admitted.

Singletary staggered into the first gun hole. "Get your asses up the slope. Get my hole finished."

Singletary squatted near Brannagh, fakir style, tipsy as an officer. His sergeants exited, pushing aside a poncho hung to dangle from the roof sandbags to serve as a water repellant back door.

"First thing," Van whispered to Cervera, "is for each squad to dig a commo trench from the reverse slope to its gun hole."

"What about Sing's bunker," asked Cervera?

"I'll leave Davis on it but pull my Korean," Van said.

"I'll pull my gooks, too," Cervera agreed.
*****
Singletary's eyes were seeing the soot of combat on every gingko, fir and pine tree down the slow slope in front of the machine gun placement.

Singletary's reverie turned to the Chinese that had cut off the Blue battalion. He hadn't told his section about the radio intercept of the Chinese order: 'After we surround them be sure what your orders are and follow through.'

Sing shuddered over his rumination about hill 432. He reflected on the Chinese across no man's land. They would be digging tunnels and marching up reinforcements. They must be chattering in caves like chipmunks. This was a different enemy in September compared to last May. Now the Chinese were concentrating on small unit actions, which meant to Sing a high likelihood of close combat, with infiltration the Chinese preferred form of assault.

Everything had changed. What Sing had heard with his own ears and seen with his own eyes and incorporated in his own battle book was being rewritten by ghost writers. The new book was odd, even peculiar. It was overtaking his mind, contaminating it with despair. Hopelessness was crawling into his brain, questioning whether or not his men had the guts to fight infiltrators. He had neighborly Van Meter and wet-back Cervera, blister mouth Baiter and beatified Brannagh, zoophilic Trout and church supper Davis, even a gook as an assistant gunner. They were the section's top men, armed but dangerous, Sing concluded, only to his survival for rotation.

On looking across the valley, Singletary thought he saw O'Hara on a high peak, a dizzy height the convulsions of nature had roughly chipped from a savage and precipitous pinnacle. O'Hara was seated behind a heavy thirty as if posing for a photograph. He appeared to loom even larger, to Singletary's astonishment, before the image vanished behind dark scudding clouds.

Brannagh watched Singletary raise his canteen as if in salute to some distant phantom. When Sing spilled the last remnants of its pungent contents between his legs, he exhorted the devil with language that would make him blush.

Brannagh offered no words to delay his leader's departure. The flapping poncho door, however, waved a goodbye.

"How long till the truce," Brannagh sighed. His question floated on soft breezes across the vast valley brimming with sunlight, towards an unknown enemy on guard. It came to Brannagh that Chinese and Americans on front line guard duty might know why they sat behind formidable weapons, but none knew for how long. The gunner guessed. He was in Korea to stay for a long while. Dad's letter made it clear that if a truce line was to be settled, it would be within a football field of where his son was pulling guard duty. China might even settle for a wall!

Brannagh's reflections disquieted him. Were his trepidations becoming dominant as Dad foretold? Brannagh visualized the kitchen table's checkered red and white oil cloth decorated by Mom's glazed plates. There was always green for Dad, blue and yellow for the rest of the family. Mom wouldn't purchase any plates glazed orange. How often had Dad lectured on the hatred burning within him because of the partition of Ireland and the dominance of the Green Catholics by Orange Protestant Unionist politicians? No, there weren't any orange plates on the table. Green and orange lit Dad's short fuse quicker than mention of volunteering for the army. Yet the kitchen was Mom's favorite room, the breakfast nook her place for tea. It was her cozy, peaceful spot for chatting about the day's events. She had gathered all her favorite dishes and antique tins on the shelves above the nook's benches that she might rediscover the ephemeral beauty of each piece during reflective pauses in conversations.

Brannagh read his Dad's letter again.

"Here, on the one hand, we have the Holy Father himself calling for a Holy Unity of Protestants and Catholics in the war against the Communists, while on the other hand, the Americans signed the Japanese Peace treaty in San Francisco. All that will go into the war against the Reds in Korea, Danny, will be men like you and taxpayers dollars. All that will come out of the Korean War will be a wealthy Japan.

"The question is why the truce talks broke off? The Reds may have complained about the supposed violations of the neutral zone, but their real reason was Acheson's double cross. He had said the line of the truce would be the 38th parallel. When the Reds

realized they wouldn't be after getting back the land
north of the 38th, they broke off over the double cross.

"Back in January 1950 this same Acheson had
stated that America's defense perimeter didn't include
Korea. For a foreign secretary he suren't had
knowledge of the Russian-Japanese War of 1904.
Japan won and considered Korea the prize. The
Japanese viewed the Korean penisula as a thumb
strategically placed in the eye of China, Manchuria and
Russia.

"Let me tell ye, Danny. Korea isn't a
geographical thumb, but Chairman Mao's geologic
urinary tract held by Anglophile Acheson, emptying
onto American soldiers.

"My finanical support for the IRA reaped
dividends June last when the lads successfully
burglared British guns from a military barracks. These
guns are being placed in the hands of Irishmen who are
willing to use them to drive the British Army out of
Ulster. Danny, my lad, the men of the IRA need
professional military training!"

Dad wanted the Brannagh of Kumhwa to fight in
the orange and green conflict! Dad's son was in the
wrong army fighting the wrong foe.

Brannagh felt his pulse palpitate like a plunked
banjo.

*****

Lava flows during a geological past had
developed plateaus that were cut by streams leaving
vertical valley walls weathered by the winds of
centuries. Brannagh's night guard in these mountain's
meant observation of innumerable sloping ridgelines
that ran down from the peaks of the MLR like fingers
from a hand. The early days of fall had remained hot,

and evenings muggy. Yesterday's heavy thunderstorm was perculated by the day's sun to a misty tea. The gunner tried to fill his canteen cup with its vapors. Were the days of heat and high humidity preferable to the coming winter monsoon? Old timers told the gunner the winter monsoon came from the interior of Asia with the Chinese invasion. While the monsoon was dry and extremely cold except for a few winter snowfalls, the Chinese were padded and blazing. Look for the full moon and a Siberian high pressure cell. Look for a long winter of miserable weather that never once would interfere with the killing.

Twice in the night, near Brannagh's firing step in the newly dug, but uncompleted commo trench running from the first gun towards the 2nd gun position, he heard Chinese seeking the locations of heavy thirties. Twice in the night, the Chinese were fed small arms and grenades instead.

To Brannagh, these enemies were like mountain waters whirling toward a sea which came surging back to wash them away in an encircling fringe of foam, or were they bent grass that merely quivered in sheltered hollows? In the moonlight he could see single strands of the newly laid wire stretching across Charley Company's front that looked as if cacti were parading on them. Homesteaders, the gunner heard his squad leader tell, protected themselves against trespassing cattle with Glidden's invention, why not soldiers?

Brannagh saw someone suddenly jump up from a crevice, who let loose a long burst of lead towards the gun bunker, his burp gun sounding like Dreamer's belches scored by a musician. Before the night guard could raise his weapon, the enemy was gone. As suddenly as the firing had started, it had stopped.

There was an absolute silence of weaponry on the hill.

"Whatsamatter out there, Brannagh," a timorous Davis asked? Davis' dream of a lovely soprano in the tabernacle choir had been punctured.

Im Ta Song's eyes were boundless ocean spaces.

Brannagh moved to the bunker's entry, his eyes' radars scanning the slopes crevices for more Chinese.

"Get your weapons. Chinese are infiltrating."

From the night came the padded sound of shoe soles that moved toward Brannagh with strong motion, then a broad shadow glided across rocks from the second gun area. Brannagh saw nothing GI. Before he could squeeze off a round the wolf on the ridgeline plunged into his trench.

"Whats going on Brannagh," whined Davis from the bunker?

Brannagh gnashed his teeth when destruction, in silence, sprung with the hungry wolf at the night guard. His carbine parried the cold steel bayonet to his left. He crashed his right forearm to the mandible of the infiltrator. There was a resounding click. The enemy wheeled, then fled forward of the trench. Left behind was his overhanging odor of cooked rice and garlic.

Brannagh wanted to catch the ghost, break his every bone, then draw and quarter him. He couldn't even see his disappearing form in front of his bunker.

"Branee," whispered Im Ta Song from behind the bunker's poncho, "Chinkee come?"

"Yea," understated the night guard, "cover the gun port Im; Davis, whistle the line we had a chink infiltrator.

A white hot plume erupted on the roof of the gun bunker.

Brannagh gasped loudly as he sucked in air, sounding as if he had been choked. He rolled under the back overhang of his bunker. Phosphorus snowed into his trench, its searing sparklers hungering for his flesh.

Davis forgot about whistling an alert. It was obvious to him that Brannagh was hit. There was a gasp. Was he alive? Davis' quick glance behind the bunker witnessed a fallen body. Davis was shaken at the sight. He needed help.

"Joe ROK, Brannagh's hit. Cover the hole. I'll get Van Meter and the medic."

Brannagh was about to cover any burns with mud when he heard, then saw a fleeting figure scurrying away from him. He grabbed his carbine. His burst was deflected by the zigzag in the trench.

Davis forgot his weapon. He had nothing available to return fire. Somehow there was still a Chinese in the trench. Had Joe ROK got it too? He told Van Meter.

Van whistled the line alert.

Cervera moved into position to cover the commo trench that ran from the reverse slope toward the first gun. He alerted Baiter to move two men to the end of the unfinished commo trench to cover Van Meter's probe of Brannagh's gun position. They were to cut down anything moving in front of the first gun bunker.

Van Meter hurled a fragmentation grenade down the trench, it exploded, zinging fragments. To Brannagh it looked like a ball of fire erupting. He scrambled into the gun bunker.

"Someone's grenading us from the direction of Van's bunker. Tell them we're still in here, Davis," the gunner hollered at the form on the gun.

"Nikola shibola," Im Ta Song cursed. "Davis say

you hit. Davis go get help."

"Lord," replied Brannagh! "We're being hit by our own people."

"Nikola shibola!"

There was no spittal to wet whistling lips, and try as he did, he couldn't. He could yell. Button down on the phone, the gunner's verbal reverberations were heard back to battalion.

"Van Meter, cease firing! We're on your side!"

Brannagh and Im Ta Song hugged the rear sand bags, the gunner hollering, all the while on alert to kick any hot grenade into the bunker's deep grenade pit.

"Why didn't you whistle an alert," Van Meter challenged?

"No time. The shooting started first."

"Why did you fire at Davis?"

"I thought it was another chink."

"Were there Chinese?"

"One or two! One ripped off a burst. The other jumped me and I knocked him down, but he bugged out."

Cervera crept up the commo trench and Baiter followed. Brannagh was sure the odor of GIs must be as distinctive to the Chinese as theirs was to GIs. At least close combat had come down to a war of noses.

Van Meter told Brannagh's story. Baiter's funny bone was struck numb by the lunatics in the first gun squad. It was its leader and gunner who had turned a job to O'Hara on the Texan. Now he had an opportunity to blow his hole on a group of lames!

Baiter's hysterical laughing echoed the trench line.

*****

There was a regular routine evolving about the

work on the MLR. The real work was at sundown, as
Brannagh discovered, when Chinese became cat
burglars padding softly in its dark. It put no balm on
the gunners psychological wounds that the infiltration
was through the second gun squad's positions and not
his. It was his machine gun position that was hit.
Absent a captured or dead chink, Baiter's painting the
first gun squad with a yellow brush was sticking.

Rumor had it Singletary was bitching for not
having transferred Van Meter to the third battalion
when they needed top three graders to replace
casualties taken on the outpost. Worse, Sing had Baiter
in mind as first gun's squad leader. Fortunately Sing
would rotate before Van would.

Whatever Singletary's alleged representations,
the first gun's night guard had heard the burp gun's
voice, and believed, ostensibly, in their gunner. Yet
they dug trenches, repaired bunkers, and filled sand
bags at a pace not before a part of the lore of Dogs' third
section's first gun. Diligence on night guard became a
standard against which other units were measured.
Brannagh recognized the ammo bearer's diligence for
what it was. He could taste their uncertainty, even Van
Meter's. The squad leader was everywhere. He checked
shifts as often as Scrooge counted his money. Just
before dawn Van invariably woke those in repose, while
warning against the lighting of portable stoves to heat
water for shaves, or c-rations until sunup. A count
taken, he set out his order of the day for guard duty,
two of the squad never fogetting its frontage. The rest
of the men washed and shaved before heating
c-rations. Van was instituting the order of a new Red
Six, that his spirited fighters were to be bodily clean.
Drag butts would be transferred to the 27th

Wolfhounds, was the aside, but Van covered for Dreamer. Then came Van's daily orders: dig, fill sandbags, dig, carry logs from the valley up the reverse slope, dig, dig, dig, haul more logs, dig, fill sand bags, dig, clean weapons, check for lice, wash, night guard. It wasn't a wonder why his troops looked forward to their turn in the bunker on day guard. It was the only time they got any rest.

Van remodeled his gun positions. Silhouettes as high as toadstools were being reprofiled to hug their terrain. A dismal deep trench was scarring the mountain between positions, its depth rapidly heading for the desired eight feet. The commo trench from the forward bunkers snaked a crooked way to the reverse slope where the command sand bagged CP replicated a German pill box at the Normandy beachhead.

Brannagh had viewed the CPs many comforts. He sought to recall GI living conditions back at Regimental, Divisional or Corps HQs, compared to those his squad endured, but he had a different frame of reference then. Coming from stateside, everything he viewed in sequence was less appetizing then its predecessor. Now he stood at the end of a passenger train, its caboose, the least vestige of human comfort. He couldn't remember the life in the rear echelon. He hadn't eaten in its dining car.

Brannagh conjured his constitution was so onery it repelled lice. He never found any in his clothes, but it was a break from digging. Van Meter mandated a search, perhaps because he too felt the effect of a day's dig, even trained to it as he was by youthful shoveling of manure. At first, the trenches weren't deep. Everyone got backaches from bending down. It wasn't safe to stand upright. If one's helmet showed over the top, some fool Chinese would drive it back down. Digging was being a turtle in reverse, like digging on the Panama canal with leaden mosquitoes biting sandbags to shreds. It was the better part of the machine gunner's valor to prick hand blisters with alcohol sterilized sewing needles. So his sore back was rested while on a cootie hunt, where none of his pale bare chested buddies looked like soldiers. They looked to Brannagh more like skinny consumptives in a TB ward. When shells started bursting up the ridgeline towards the back slope circle, he and each pale foot bent down despite aches and scurried like albino rats to their holes. Each sensed they would get hit if time was up; but there just wasn't any need to advance the alarm.

When the dog stopped walking, Dreamer returned to his hunt. Lice loved the seams of his fatigues, so his fingernails bisected an innumerable herd; but cold weather outside meant more lice inside. Brannagh felt a twinge of sympathy for Glorio and Van Meter. There was so much louse powder between their skins and fatigues they had a ghostly appearance.

The gunner found other creatures of the night were attracted to the diggings. They were brother rats as big as rabbits and opportunistic as infiltrators. They nibbled on commo wire and phone lines, even on opened c-rations, unless spoiled; rats found it as hard to tell as did GIs! Once rats came to stay in the bunkers, they had as many battles overhead as armies exchanged artillery. They burrowed towards heat, their tunnels channeling rain water like a run to a water wheel. Wildly flailing, rats cascaded so often onto sleeping GI faces, that rifle butts swung until the interloper met a grisly death in a bunker that looked as if it had taken a direct hit. Rats, friendly or Chinese, were unwelcome.

Variations on Van's order of the day offered his squad the relief of upright digging on the reverse slope, putting down garbage pits and straddle crappers for the section.

While the evenings' lice circle gossiped, Glorio was the first seen by Brannagh to venture the fifty feet down slope to drop a note of welcome within the arrangement. Though privacy was afforded by shelter halfs either flank of the depositor, the dropping of Glorios fatigue pants and green shorts were visible to peering eyes aft, and cold updrafts fore! Glorio's squat was assumed just as the twilight's incoming awakened eruptions a hundred yards to his right. His pole vault from a sitting position failed to raise his pants above his knees. Brannagh stood transfixed watching Glorio come down, trip on his trousers, roll ten yards or more down slope, then log roll off a small cliff to disappear.

Van's unease was for Glorio. He laid sprawled on a rocky overhang. Van looked at a face as purple as the distant mountains. What was most stupefying was Glorio's clothing. His shirts buttons were torn loose and had released flaps that dangled dozens of garlic cloves sewn inside. Increduously, absent a DDT insecticide mixture to disinfest his clothing and body against Dreamer's boarders, Van concluded the unconscious GI had applied his own ancient Roman remedy. Van and the gunner lifted the ammo bearer on a litter up to Doc's aid station where Glorio came to. His thin neck stretched in aid of his curious eyes. He saw gloomy looking soldiers. When Van told Glorio he hadn't been hit, he emptied his lumpy fatigue pockets, garlic clove by garlic clove.

The wind sang a slow requiem, the withered moon had faded, yet Brannagh gave thanks to his Lord the sun of the east was giving discreet indication its waves of dawn were not long in coming. Last guard of the night had a joy when it ended with sunlight spanning no man's land and the slopes of the front line. The Chinese went their way into caves beneath stubble clad hills, while Brannagh went to another day's dig.

His eyes swept the slope's every grim wrinkle, where dark's crevices kept black secrets. Brannagh hadn't heard a sound from the barbed wire, but was there movement? Unlike every other soldier in the outfit on night guard, he alone had encountered an infiltrator, invisible to others' eyes. He determined not to embarrass himself and Van Meter again. He elected not to whistle an alert. If there were Chinese down below the wire they had to venture through concertina wire and bouncing betty's leg amputations. He would wait in silence, carbine at the ready, eyes glued.

Two Chinese stood tall, arms raised high. They didn't move any other part of their bodies. Brannagh was startled! They weren't infiltrating, but surrendering! What the hell should he do now? If he lifted his steel potted head too high, some hidden sniper might be waiting to swim a bullet through his thatch. He waved instead, encouraging the Chinese to proceed up the hill. They waved back, encouraging the GI to come to them. Their arms spoke as eloquently as did Glorio's, soundlessly informing their selected captor of their fear of the mine field between them and the trench line.

The gunner considered the silliness of the surrender: Chinese afraid to come up to the line, and him afraid to go down. It was an impasse. With dawn, these men were recruits for the army of the dead. Their own side would bury them.

Im Ta Song's illiteration on out-of-wedlock descendancy completed, he responded to his gunner's prodding. The ROK saw little sense in Brannagh's plan to descend the slope and march the enemy up. It was too dangerous. His gunner had Korean Won for a brain - both useless.

The morning's glow seemed to illuminate the arms of the surrendering enemies. Brannagh saw they were alone, unarmed, swaying. There was scant time left before the sun's radiance would cast their shadows long as target silhouettes. He whistled the line alert to a GI moving down slope in front of Dog's third section's first gun bunker to take two prisoners. Hold fire! Before an inquiry from Van Meter came, Brannagh gave the phone to an unintelligible Im Ta Song.

The gunner felt the burning eyes of Van's squad, of Cervera's. Singletary wasn't there, Brannagh was sure. The section chief was probably drunk. His body hadn't quit, what quit was his spirit. Yes, Sing's head would be in his reverse slope bunker, in mourning for the soldier he was. He had heard too many songs from haunting soldiers singing dirges.

Brannagh scanned carefully for mines. He crouched as he descended the slope, zigzagging the military way past barbed wire end poles and through concertina to take his prisoners. Silently, carbine in his right hand, he motioned to them to spread open their hip length cotton coats. Both lowered their arms and did so. There were no weapons, no grenades visible to their captor. He motioned them forward, to precede him up the finger. They wouldn't go, their expressive hands doubting they knew the correct path. Brannagh's heart nearly stilled. He hadn't marked the safe way down. His brain was as steel plated as his helmet.

"Lord God, have mercy on our souls," were the only words he wanted to say.

"Dumb shit's got the luck of the Irish," Baiter opined.

Brannagh, although quietly impressed with Van Meter's novel usage of barnyard phrases to excoriate the gunner's stupidity, felt the rise in him of the red blood of shame. He hadn't only jeopardized his own life, but exposed a glaring weakness in their defensive perimeter to any watching enemy.

On the reverse slope, Singletary commandeered the smiling orientals, scared them to fearful frowns with metallic clicks on an empty chamber of his 45 caliber pistol, and paraded them at gunpoint, newsreel style, to Dog's command post. Off the hill, O'Hara and Sing, with their captives tied and gagged, rode the chow truck from the base of the MLR back to batallion. S-2, Battalion's Intelligence, with a squad of armed MPs around the POWs, poured the sergeants drinks and promised medals.

*****

Now Brannagh knew Sing couldn't mean it when he said Van Meter was lazy, for there wasn't a season when the squad leader didn't work like a horse. Sing said it only because Van disagreed as to digging a warming bunker on the reverse slope. What was needed, Van argued, were sleeping holes on the trench line, across from each fighting bunker. On the reverse slope the troops would loll snug as cats. If the gooks broke through to the trench line, or infiltrated, most of the squad in a warming bunker would be cut off to the rear of their own trench line from their buddies on guard in the forward fighting positions!

"Do it," Singletary ordered, unpersuaded! He had the word and the word was made known.

Van Meter was downhearted. If only Sing's wound was physical, for it brought a long ride back to a rear echelon field hospital and acceptance. It was mere combat fatigue, however that might have happened: with the 35th's Red battalion at the Nam river in the Pusan perimeter; or crossing the Han river; or at the Ch'ongch'on river; or defending Seoul; or on hill 717; or riding on a tank of the 89th battalion; or firing the 21st AAA's quad fifties; or feeding a Van Fleet load from the tubes of the 35th mortar company or the howitzers of the 64th Field Artillery battalion. Was there anything else the doctors should know? They needed to know if Sing was faking it!

Van put his squad on the detail. There would be a warming bunker on the reverse slope as the word was wont, but a start on their own sleeping holes. Nothing wrong with planning the first gun's field layout to overcome the handicaps of rear echelon planners. Planners' practices rarely proved adaptable to front line survival. The rear never kept up with the times. The Chinese had changed. Van changed with them. Back home he adopted improved farm practices as soon as they had proved adaptable to Lake Mills, Iowa. In Kumhwa, he was adopting field practices the Chinese proved adaptable to Korea.

*****

"Don't be tellin me nuttin' about escape from gooks. They not be wantin' me," Dreamer was certain.

Brannagh was as certain that Singletary and Van Meter 'not be wantin' Dreamer either. They had him, however, courtesy of some asshole in classification and assignment. If assignment to infantry was tantamount to a sentence for being a high school dropout, then Dreamer was the epitome of the dispensable. The public tax supported army had to make up in training what the public tax supported primary and secondary educational system hadn't.

"It's three hours off the line, Dreamer," Brannagh said. Twin moons appeared where before black awnings had been drawn.

"Tree hours?"

"I go," Dreamer agreed.

There must be an unpublished manual, Brannagh deduced, privy to the officer corps, that extols a boring instructional methodology. Every training officer alive had the skill to turn a Virginia Mayo strip tease into the defrocking of an aged hag. A topic as important as evasion of or escape from capture based on the experiences of GIs who did so, was mouthed in rote like a string of rosary Hail Mary's by a recalcitrant penitent.

It was said the Chinese were unpredictable captors, often cruel, unconventional. A prisoner was guaranteed nothing. There was the prospect of a long, perhaps a lifelong imprisonment under extremely adverse conditions which might include torture, even execution, so evade and escape!

The gunner noted Glorio wasn't bored.

If the Chinese took a KATUSA prisoner, he was transferred to the North Korean Army as a volunteer.

Im Ta Song had heard this before. He wasn't a volunteer on the southern side. Damned if he would be a volunteer on the northern side either. He envisioned dying young on Kumhwa's hills, near the Hantan river, with a view of lovely 1062 northerly. Would its brown face then turn green, its blackened stones entwine with vines when his litter bearers passed its cliff paths?

Yes, the Chinese were more merciful that the North Koreans who had executed on the spot, but less often since Inchon.

Yes, a Chinese moved a GI to the rear for a tactical interrogation, then from regiment by night to the divisional cage. Seriously wounded might be carried, getting the same medical care as a wounded Chinese. Officers and enlisted men were separated but again interrogated. Another night's foot march was to Corps' cage. During the day POWs were kept in village huts. If there was incoming or an air strike, there was movement to the hills and chance for escape. It was at the Corps' cage where political indoctrination started. Interrogations went into military organization, equipment, personal and family matters, even civilian jobs in great detail. From Corps to the camps was an eight night march - a last chance for escape. The camps were closely guarded.

Yes, evasion was possible in holes, draws, debris, in rivers, or pretended death if the Chinese overran a position. Yes, a move to hide was possible immediately after capture if a soldier stalled for time, or faked a grieviously serious wound or a slight one, or faked madness.

The half of the third section that was present turned as one to look at Dreamer, envious of his innate nature.

The time for escape boiled in Brannagh's mind. As the Chinese moved at night, nights were the opportune time. Daytime escape was well limited to air or artillery strikes. The key to escape was anonymity.

Every single caucausian looked the same to mongolians! Brannagh had no rank to hide, only hair the color of a tiger lily, and freckles as wide as a Guernsey's spots.

Yes, a soldier might escape after recapture, if the soldier told the Chinese he had been released at the Corps' cage to rejoin his unit, but lost his release papers. The ruse was known to work.

Yes, winter weather was the most dangerous element to the escaping soldier. Skin surface exposed to the wind was likely to freeze. Perspiration was to avoided!

CHAPTER THIRTEEN
RECONNAISANCE

Singletary and Van Meter waited on the reverse slope with Grant as Brannagh hunched out of the commo trench.

"We depart at 1930 hours," Grant said. Grant rechecked his watch. It was 1730.

"I wish I could go with you, Grant," Sing pretended.

"Short timers should stay in their holes."

"I'll borrow Dog Six's binoculars," Sing mocked.

"Don't blink then, Sing," Grant joked. "It's quick up the valley, deploy, reconnoiter, then set up an ambush point on the return route."

Grant personally requested Brannagh's detail with a M1919A6 shouldered machine gun. Charley three's third squad needed firepower: an LMG, a BAR and automatic carbines. Dog's gunner was the only soldier Grant believed could carry the weapon in one hand, a can of ammo in the other and still have the energy and strength to lay down fire in an ambush.

Van Meter and Sing elected to let the heavy weapons specialist decide. He wasn't inclined to it, but declined to tell Grant so. Brannagh felt it was hardly his place to refuse. But for Grant, life in the battalion might have been sorting dirty fatigues in the laundry pool.

Brannagh felt the thrill of it in his throat. It was an obvious compliment. Yet it was an invitation to lessen his odds of taking a round. Why, after six seminary years of extra study to barely achieve entry at the lowest level of the upper ten percent of seminary scholars, or after years of practice to become the sixth man on its basketball team, should he now be declared the top Dog of a death dealing military speciality? He was throwing left jabs at death while parrying its right cross!

The rain was light before its clouds cleared, leaving behind a temperature in the mid-fifties. The searchlights beams quivered and gleamed on the moistened vegetation he passed on his way to the line of departure. Sandbagged bunkers were as quiet as were their masticating occupiers. Brannagh gazed over the slope at the dormant company's CP beneath the hillside's crest. He freed a sigh, but convinced himself it wasn't a last look.

Patrol Plan No. 46 was to reconnoiter at grid 705440, observe from northeast to northwest, determine enemy strength and disposition and capture prisoners. Its planner had a second thought: set up an ambush on the return route; return when ordered! So Brannagh wrapped his ammo box lid with strips torn from a Dreamer undershirt. The ammo box was encased with slices from a Dreamer towel. The natural darkness of the GI issue had been enhanced with Dreamer dirt. Masking tape held the cloth tight and subdued the handle, a key in subjecting the box to soundproofing. Each of the fifty tracers in a belt of ammo had been pulled from every fifth spot and replaced. All 250 rounds were M2 Ball cartridges.

"All of you have viewed the objective in daylight," Grant whispered. "All of you looked over the stone and dirt model I made from the aerial photos, so you know the route of advance and withdrawal to the ambush site, right?"

"Right."

Mostly, it looked to Brannagh as slopes bisected by streams with tiny patios, probably rice paddies stairstepping upwards like a library's circular steps.

"Third squad comes back with me," Grant emphasized, "walking or carried. This squad won't come back without all its men."

Grant practiced fundamentals. The certainty of help if any man in the squad became a casualty, bound his men as a unit, not individuals.

Brannagh stirred. "Adopt me," he requested? It satisfied him that Grant's smile was no less bright than Crane's, his BAR looking like a praying mantis, or Pocaski's and the rest of the guys. Even the medic, a grinning object of curiosity who looked like a period among exclamation points, was favorably inclined.

"Adoption granted," Grant ruled.

He paired his light machine gunner Brannagh with Kucharski's automatic carbine. Crane's BAR drew Demos' automatic weapon. Radioman Gibbard got Grant's M2. Pocaski, Gibbard, Aquilas, Corney and Wickstrand were assigned extra magazines for all the carbines. Odegard, the last of the black vikings, was paired to cover medic Sugrue. Grant moved his patrol forward to Charley Company's OP. A nod was given to the 64th Field's forward observer to commence the evening's usual harrassing fire mission when Grant moved down the finger, Gibbard on his backside, the rest of the men walking in an orderly column.

Nature, Brannagh viewed, with rare forethought formed steep and rugged walls that shot up several feet out of the creek bed before rolling up towards the higher crests. The low lying water way had been rain cut over time, not dug by an entrenching tool. He was thankful for the cover it provided in a clear night of good visibility. He saw the searchlight illuminated sky was clean to glow worm stars. It was a night he should be sleeping in a bunker, closing up his fart sack for warmth. Why then was he sweating? Fear must be running the bases around his ball diamond nerves, while scrub pines took the form of baseball bats ready to swing each time the patrol followed a twist or loop in the creek.

Only a half hour had passed, when he looked at his watch at the first check point. It seemed longer than that. Brannagh watched to the north as Grant radioed their location. He wasted no time. His patrol merely genuflected, and moved out.

A white flare a thousand yards to the east glimmered a 4th of July glare as it ultimately burned blue. The night flickered with purple orange spurts of rifle fire, and red flashes of tracers ricocheting into ghostly wavering lights. A real battle was maturing before ROK positions to the east, Brannagh deduced.

So far the warriors of Ch'in weren't patrolling the creek. Grant motioned his patrol from moist to drier terrain up a rise toward a saddle covered with brush between two bald tits. The artwork of wind and the 64th Field artillery had barbered the peaks bald. Their craggy neighbors were as nude. It was his check point two. He radioed, another genuflection was rendered, and his patrol moved on.

Brannagh's view of the shaved hills revealed blemishes darker than the black rocks on the slopes, one the size of a gloomy cave. He saw no light. He heard no sound but the breathing of his men, the crunch of loose rock under foot. He recalled the briefing made no mention of Chinese dug in in the area. The smell wasn't of garlic, but gohung and kimchee. Odd, he thought, then dismissed the olfactory evidence as the lingering odor of chogie bearers. At their hot noon meal, they boiled a fish head or two while waiting for the GIs to empty out the hot food containers.

The crossover, a brushy draw, brought the patrol to their objective, a dish shaped knoll with puffy points. Brannagh counted a score or more of hills beyond, one right after another, some high and steep with rocky pinacles piercing the sky.

Grant stopped and deployed, Brannagh to the right with his LMG, Crane's BAR to the left, riflemen interspersed between. Grant had Gibbard take the prone beside him. It was 2345 hours, Grant reported. There were many enemy on the hill to his right of the objective digging in on a finger running south. On his left, there was also much movement. How much? A company to the left, a company to the right. The patrol was between three hundred Chinese.

Brannagh watched the dark figures digging. A soldier in any army dug for his life. It was ironic that all foreigners on Korea's hills were modifying nature by digging pits for war, but down over the centuries the Korean's had left nature alone. They didn't build a network of roads or railways. Men at war built. Men at peace farmed. Men at war destroyed what was built. Men at peace rebuilt.

Grant figured it suicidal to cross further, either right or left, to capture prisoners, even one. The Chinese would be more likely to take ten GIs. He had seen all there was to be seen. He would pull back and set out his ambushers.

Brannagh sensed the relief of patrol veterans was as keen as his own.

Grant's patrol measured the distances in between. His column, as silently as it could crunch ground, moved back. He set Brannagh and ingot

Kucharski to cover their departure, tieing in with the last man. Grant charted a different passage for his crew, the other side of the blue gloom near where the gunner had whiffed kimchee.

Brannagh's nose had no doubt. It was the odor of Korea before it was bottled in honey buckets. He passed the word forward. He would check it out.

Grant deployed his patrol in firing positions, but sent Kurcharski and Wickstrand with Brannagh to probe the cave on the side of the hill.

Brannagh discovered dangling GI poncho's across a five foot entrance. He heard the unmistakeable sound of Korean words from within. He detected several voices. Signalling Grant of the discovery, the gunner raised his light machine gun to his hip and slowly worked his way, Kucharski and Wickstrand in tow, through a quartermaster's storage of dangling poncho doors toward sound. He burst through the last of the slickers. Kucharski and Wickstrand flanked him. He was glad all of the three topped six foot and were glowering mad men, intimidating occidentals! They captured fourteen prisoners, men and boys, and not a word was spoken. Brannagh's language of weaponry was universal. The Koreans raised hands. Quickly and thoroughly frisked by Brannagh, the Koreans were called to silence by fingers across Wickstrand's and Kucharski's lips, then moved in a tight cluster through the cave's entry. Brannagh doused the fires with their own boiled water and gohung. It sizzled like snakes. He pulled a pin from a grenade, with handle down inside a scooped hole, and covered it, leaving it under a mat.

Grant interspersed the Koreans between the men in his column, an adult and a boy between weaponry. He reported the patrol's find, receiving the order to return to the MLR with the catch of the day. Grant set a quiet but quicker pace. It was a hell of a result, he determined, to be sent out to recon and ambush Chinese, but return with fourteen North Koreans, half of which were little boys, maybe shoe shine boys! Damned if they wouldn't shine the patrol's boots back on the line before they did battalion's and regiment's. Some good might come of the mission after all, Grant surmised.

A boy started crying. His sobs resounded as loudly as the peals of the Liberty Bell. It was a call to ambush to every Chinese patrol working no man's land this never ending night, Brannagh groaned. Why in the name of all he held holy, hadn't his nose and curiousity shut off. He turned to scan for signs of Chinese, anticipating human waves. None came to view. He noticed his light machine gun wasn't loaded. Its ammo still sat snugly in the towel draped can. He realized he had attacked the Koreans in the cave without a round in his chamber. He sensed the urge to wet himself. He controlled it, and knelt down instead. Quickly opening the ammo can, his bayonet cut a thirty round slice from its belt. He hung the necklace of lead around his neck.

Grant clutched the boy, who wailed all the louder. Grant had little choice. He knocked the weeper out, then shoulder loaded the limp boy.

"Move out." Grant ordered, motioning to the Koreans to drag tail or lose it.

His orderly sheep procession followed its point. Carbines were at the ready. He placed Crane's BAR rearwards to backstop the light machine gun. He led the way to check point one without incident, but hesitated. As quickly as he slid his unconscious load to the cold earth, he passed on a warning. There were

Chinese in the creek. He radioed his situation to Charley's OP.

"Pocaski, stay here with Gibbard, Corney, Odegard, Demos and Crane. I'm going to flank the chinks in the stream. Cover us. If we flush the Chinese north, call in mortars. If any of our gooks act up, kill them."

Grant made the point vividly with a 45 pistol rotated from Korean head to Korean head. They understood.

"Brannagh, Aquilas, Wickstrand and Kurcharski will come with me. We'll swing wide south of the creek then come in from the east," Grant grunted.

Brannagh felt the weight of the ammo on his neck was heavier than the LMG he carried by handle. Maybe it was the points of the bullets against his neck chewing into flesh that made him so conscious of their presence. Maybe it was the stupidity of taking the stinking wailing gooks captives. He was startled by naming them gooks. He detested name calling and tried to refrain from it. How many fist fights had he in retaliation to fighting words? Too many, he acknowledged. It was stupid of him to capture a wailing Korean boy and end up in a fire fight with an ambush. Stupid, stupid, S-T-U-P-I-D, he confirmed! He shivered thinking that the white haired squad leader was disappointed.

Grant made his men simulate boomerangs. He doubled back behind the creek. He wanted the ambush of an ambush, GIs flexed like an arm. Grant and his men were the upper arm east of the enemy; Pocaski and his men the forearm north. Grant deployed his men. Brannagh was set to the south. The M2 carbines crept forward with Grant towards the creek. He stayed his men in place, but edged forward himself, then rolled left, his right arm throwing a grenade. When the living air was murdered by the blast, Aquilas, Wickstrand and Kurcharski were ordered to let loose lethal baseballs in sequence running southernly. Burp guns rippled the western slopes above them. Then the staccato chant of Crane's BAR threw plunging fire at the confused enemy. When a Chinese gunner with a drum magazine moved across the defilade to engage the automatic fire, Grant stitched the back of his neck. Another submachine. Grant smiled when his forearm played the angle and laid a long burst on the Chinese fighter, reinforced with volleys from Crane's BAR.

Brannagh waited with his light machine gun fully loaded for a target of opportunity. When another burp gun started to tattoo the check point, he let loose a long burst that searched the creek bed. There followed a silence, eerie as a Halloween midnight. Organized resistance ceased. He heard footsteps running south. He rotated his bypod to lay down neutralizing fire, but Grant stayed the shooting.

Pocaski's radio called in thundering mortar rounds that reworked the lay of the land between check point one and the MLR. He wanted no corner of that land to have a hostile left.

Grant regrouped in the creek bed. There were three dead Chinese in the shallow water.

"Lord, have mercy on their souls," Brannagh prayed.

Grant took umbrage. "You praying for gooks," he growled?

"For all of us. We're missing three Koreans," the gunner said to the granite face.

Grant counted. He was dismayed. "Did they

bug," he asked?

Doc Sugrue nodded negatively. "A chink burp gun caught them. Got the kid you carried, another kid and a man."

"Too bad."
*****

Baiter's tongue stung Brannagh like a wasp's. The scourge and whiplash of his invective was intended to bury the first gun's gunner in a cesspool of adverbs for blighting Dog Company's reputation by the taking of little boys as prisoners of war. Only when Grant passed the word that Counter Intelligence had complimented the patrol for its capture of a key North Korean spy ring did the stridency die down.

Every other one of Grant's soldiers aired themselves beneath the open sky on the reverse slope. Brannagh aired among them, a privilege for a returned patrol. A well placed round might have made devastating inroads into Charley three's and Dog three's table of organization, Brannagh reflected, taking a long look at Kucharski. His big brow had a half dozen trench lines. His small chin was nestled in his palms, while eight fingers of his hands walked his lower lip.

"Baiter's a pompous ass," Kucharski deduced. "Why don't cha' take him, Brannagh? O'Hara wants it!"

"O'Hara wants the money," Brannagh answered.

"I thought he was a right Joe," intoned Grant.

He was inclined to view the passage of the last war's veterans from line outfits like the closing of lighthouses along the Atlantic coast - dangerous. When Dog's top kick took over the weapons company it boded but good for Grant's rifle company.

"Didn't O'Hara bring you with him," he

inquired?

"We shipped over in the Marine Lynx. I met him aboard ship," the gunner related. "He didn't bring me with him, but now that he's here he's plotting another scam: a Baiter-Brannagh fight."

"Your top kick's a crook," Grant grumbled?

"A gambler, not like Singletary with all the cards on the table, but a back stage calculator. He schemed me on the ship. I ended up in the boxing ring with Joe Louis' unknown twin. Damned if I didn't find that O'Hara and Lieutenant Breezedale had conned the whole ship. They made a bundle."

The audience perked up. They wanted the story.

"What about the fight and O'Hara's scheme," asked Grant?

He purposely put doubt in his look. He found it hard to believe that O'Hara would plot on an enlisted man. The top kick had stormed and raved like a man demented about Dog Six's dishonor, Grant remembered, but that was a war ago. He placed his hands behind his bent knees to listen.

"I were on that ship. I seened the fight," said Crane. "Let me tell about it."

"We was all in the ship's hold around the boxing ring when Topkick O'Hara come out of a cabin with Red. I didn't know Red then. I only knowed he was the dumbest RA on the Marine Lynx to go and fight Stag. He had knocked crap out of five marines, then challenged any regular army soldier with guts enough to fight a draftee. This here Stag were a chocolate grizzly. He fought like a drunk lumber jack. Nothing hurt him. He had hardwood fists that sounded like axes when they landed. I had smarts enough to shut up.

"Anyhow, O'Hara sat Red down on his stool.

Paid him no mind. Went off to cover bets. Then this Lieutenant Breezedale come with Stag. He were the champ. Got a big hand from the draftees. They spread cash all over with O'Hara on Stag in two.

"It bothered me none when Breezedale held up ring ropes for Stag, not even when the Lieutenant tied his gloves and near as kissed ass. What surprised me was Breezedale were Red's second. O'Hara didn't say nothing!

"When Stag and Red was brought face to face in ring center for instructions, their seconds took off their fatigue shirts they used as robes. Red looked like a melting snowman in fatigue pants and combat boots. Stag were a Clydesdale stud!

"Just before the bell for the first round, I heard Breezedale tell Red there weren't no shame in hitting canvas."

Crane looked over to Brannagh. "Sorry, Red, RA or not, I looked to make some money on Stag. I can still see O'Hara stand up. He looked like a mortar tube about to fire. He took my bet.

"I didn't know if Red were madder at Breezedale for shoving him out of the corner at the bell or at Stag throwing a punch instead of touching gloves. I didn't believe my eyes. This here Red went to chopping inside Stag's guard like to take Stag out in one. He weren't no patsy. He laid all over Red, swarmed to the attack, but Red kept getting inside. Stag's shots was exploding like trip mines on Red's shoulders and arms. Red were throwing right crosses at a tooled steel chin. It were a hell of a round. Worth losing my money!

"Back in the corner, I heard Breezedale doing a Cain on Abel. 'You ain't got a chance Brannagh, if you don't stay outside and box', the Lieutenant told him.

Poor Red, he got the one officer aboard the ship that were as faithful as Benedict Arnold. If Red hadn't stayed inside, just one of Stag's punches to the kidneys would have knocked the piss out of him."

Crane cast another remorseful look at Brannagh. "I figured to double my money. I were hearing inside dope and O'Hara were willing.

"The second round were colossal. There was savages in that ring. They went toe to toe. Stag were swinging down from the high ground. Red were mauling Stag's ribs. They clenched. When Stag pushed off, he hollered: 'come on and fight, shithead'. Stag revved up. He were trying to decapitate, but Red stayed inside like a chest growth, getting in short shots. There he fought, face on Stag's chest. It must have seemed like he were inside a washing machine. Stag shoved him off again, hollering for the shithead to stay out and fight. Shithead were Stag's nickname for Red. Damned if Stag's best shot at the bell didn't miss!"

Crane took a swig of water from his canteen. He continued.

"Damned too, if Breezedale didn't start to look sick when Red's bloody nose, snot and all, dripped on Breezedale's tailored fatigues. Thought he'd puke. Instead, he told Red he couldn't win on points. Offered a hundred for a dive. Red were slurping his water bottle. He coughed it across Breezedale's crotch. It were then I knewed Breezedale would do something even dirtier. He wouldn't let the fight go the full third round. He'd throw the towel. Why not? Red burned like charcoal! I placed my last fin with O'Hara and the towel.

"At the bell, Stag lunged from his corner broad as a courthouse door. He'd came to brawl but Red's right could have dug a trench across the outpost. It caught Stag on the nose. It splurted like Old Faithful. It were unbelievable! Stag backed off. He raised his gloves, palms out. 'You a pro', he hollered. 'Won't fight no pro.' He quit. Breezedale didn't know what to do with the towel. Red just stood there bloody as a chopped chicken head."

Crane ended his narrative. "The crowd in the ship's hold were deadly still until O'Hara stood up and challenged Lieutenant Breezedale. '200 bucks, Lieutenant', O'Hara hollered. His palm looked the size of a church's collection plate. I was proud of O'Hara," said Crane.

"Thought Red said he schemed him," Grant injected.

Crane leaped to his feat. He grabbed Brannagh's right arm, pulling him to his feet, the arm raised in conquest. "The champ of the Marine Lynx," he extolled. "We'll knock Baiter on his ass, Champ." Crane took to shadow boxing.

Grant grunted and spat. He spoke challengingly, "O"Hara had money on you, Red."

"It seemed so and I thought it was so." Brannagh despaired.

"What changed your mind?" Grant wanted evidence.

"I saw Stag hurry the way of the officers. I followed him aft. There Stag was with Breezedale. I saw O'Hara join them. He had a roll that would have choked a Detroit city councilman," Brannagh sighed.

"They all shook hands on me," Brannagh moaned. "Now O'Hara's putting spite between Van and Cervera to get a Baiter-Brannagh fight."

Brannagh saw Grant's facial muscles change

from incredulity to angry redness. The gunner could only guess at the content of the rifle squad leader's mind.

CHAPTER FOURTEEN
D'ETRE TUE

Brannagh reflected on the language of LaVie's prayers during Mass. Was it French, Cajun or English?

"Hoc est enim Corpus Meum," prayed the priest in his sacerdotal robes - "For this is My Body."

Brannagh was impressed with the piety and devotion displayed by line troops receiving Holy Communion. Each opportunity to come off line, no matter the reason, was joyous. Yet, coming off the hill for Mass was special. Death was always with an infantryman. Communion put God there too. Many were the prayers to God to see them safely through until the happy day of a cease fire. Many were the prayers to God to motivate even the atheistic politicians, of their side and the other's, to meet and talk, and end this police action.

Dear God, Brannagh prayed, in the Holy Mass the mystery of the Eucharist is celebrated in the hands of your priest, where the Son is offered to His Father. Please accept Him as satisfaction for the sins of all the sons on either side of no-man's land, and end the wrath of our fathers.

Brannagh recognized Father Flynn's frequent sighs were more than the situation warranted. There was no other purpose for this meeting at Battalion HQ than to complete the visitationn arrangements for the brothers La Vie, Claude of the 25th Infantry Division; Jean of the 2d Infantry Division. This was the day for it: the light rains had ceased, the temperature was in the very comfortable sixties, and low rolling clouds were a blanket over the troubles of the MLR.

Yet Brannagh had the impression of an

emotionalism in the cleric that was impatient of restraint.

"I've written countless letters home to the loved ones of a soldier killed in action," the tired priest related. "I've talked to squads, platoons, even companies, expressing the grief they couldn't permit thenselves when a buddy fell." He paused. "I wept for them, but now I weep with you. Pfc. Jean La Vie, of the 2d Division 9th regiment was killed on September 15 on hill 894."

La Vie sat down on the Padre's jeep hood.

He appeared to be looking toward Brannagh. Was it for an explanation, the gunner wondered? He hadn't one. He had had only a hope to conclude the visitation plan. Of all the front line troops, Brannagh got some idea of the hideous nervous strain which now had fallen on the one soldier who had lost four brothers to combat. Claude La Vie deserved to be set free of it, but how?

The chaplain was unwontedly emotional. Tears were in his eyes. He wouldn't embellish the facts.

"When the 23rd regiment hadn't taken hills 931 and 851, the 9th was sent against hill 728 on September 14 to relieve the pressure. They had fire support from the 72nd tanks, but the North Koreans were sending over long range fire. Still, at 0200 hours they attacked within 600 or so meters of the crest before they formed a night perimeter. Next day, after hours of hard fighting, the 9th's second battalion took 894, despite heavy machine gun fire. Your brother was hit. They told me he pulled some of the wounded from an open area raked by North Korean fire, before he passed on."

Chaplain Flynn sat down on the Jeep's hood as mournful as the mournful brother.

"Your brother's regiment had the support of the
First French Battalion," the chaplain said. "It was their
chaplain that informed me 'La Vie vient d'etre tue - La
Vie was just killed.' "

Father Flynn's voice was soft; modulated in the
clerical fashion of empathy.

Brannagh didn't say anything. He watched the
last son of the La Vie's walk slowly away from the
consoling priest, as if the Cajun had had enough of
other's sympathy. Maybe he was looking for a few sea
shells for Jean's grave for when he was reinterred back
home. La Vie should feel better to know his brother
would be ferried stateside to be buried near the water
and banks that he had known as a boy, not in
Normandy with Theo La Vie, or at Brittany with Albert
La Vie, or with Pierre La Vie at Falais, but buried in the
bayous like his ancestors before him, a long litany of
Cajun Americans.

As if a stage master gave a cue, the reflection on
La Vie's ancestry told Brannagh that Claude was the
last of the La Vie line. None of his brothers had
fathered a child. Nor had Claude! There were no other
brothers left for the Army to expend, and no children of
these brothers. If the Army were to have a future
opportunity to recruit La Vies' to its ranks, then the
bow and arrow of the Kumhwa soldier should be
broken in favor of cupid's. Claude La Vie was a sole
suviving son, momentarily. Brannagh was determined
to reenlist the commiserating priest's efforts toward La
Vie's reassignment.

"La Vie is the sole surviving son, Padre, get him
home," he said.

"I'll get my friend from the Red Cross to come to
the front with me," the tearful, smiling priest replied.

"He'll help me get him home."

"Get him off the line now, chaplain," Brannagh pressed, his face a mask of command.

"It's not within my power."

"Pushing my Irish Catholic top kick to do it, is."

"He doesn't attend services," Father Flynn blurted.

"Maybe so, but his Irish Catholic conscience can't have escaped the Church's indoctrination in Ireland, of all places, or from you at the Company's forward CP," Brannagh asserted.

"Probably not," mused the priest.

Brannagh wanted more of a commitment, but his deuce-by was reving its coughing motor. He knew truckers were loathe to dally around after dark near the MLR. It was all a matter of perspective. Trucker's feared at a line company's HQ, but infantrymen on the reverse slope relaxed. Orientation was a funny phenomenon.

"I'll pray for you," Father Flynn said, "and for La Vie's safety. I'll do what I can."

Brannagh's worry was quieted. He saluted the religious officer, recognizing an oxymoron. He got the priest's blessing in return, his Lord's salutation.

The good Father was chagrined he hadn't told the red headed storehouse of Ireland's history, the yet unwritten history of the battle of Heartbreak Ridge, the piecemeal feeding of American battalions to the grist mill of concentrated North Korean fire power. The 2d Division's commander had planned but one regiment as his assault force against the ridge just north of Bloody Ridge. Battalion after battalion went up with no reinforcements as back-up. They took horribly heavy casualties. It was a heartbreaking order. The chaplain had a hope the change of commanding General's might bring the 2d Division more success and fewer casualties as October dawned. Perhaps he would quit an attack going after one hill after another, in favor of many attacks going on at once. If so, the North Koreans would have to disperse their automatic weapon and mortar fire. Where were the truce negotiators, the embarrassed priest questioned? He realized his theory on military tactics wasn't cannonical, but peace talks were.

Singletary twisted his facial muscles in disgust when the word came down that 43 points were required for rotation. It meant he would be in Korea until Christmas time. He felt dazed by the revelation. Worse, he felt a gripping tenseness since Lightning Six had come out to Charley Company's outpost. Front line appearances by big brass meant dog-face combat. Probably over on the right. Because the Cacti Raiders were placed under the Red battalion's operations control; but maybe to hill 440, with its four peaks jutting up along its ridgeline.

An attack out there was pointless, Sing conceded. It would isolate a unit several hundred yards in front of the MLR like the Blue battalion's was on the outpost. So he concluded the valley was the likely avenue of attack, towards 1062 itself, the big pyramid of the Iron Triangle, the high ground, the enemy's main observation post. Singletary figured on fighting the battle of hill 1062. He hadn't a doubt he would be killed there.

Sing felt his tenseness return. He was suspicious the spotter plane the Chinese brought down was up to more than the usual recon, because Lightning Six was forward after Charley Company's patrol rescued the flier, and had Dog's HMGs set it on fire. Secret stuff, Sing surmised, but he wasn't being suckered in. It all fitted. He would fight the battle of Sotong San. There was no other explanation. Didn't he foresee the planner's stupidity about hill 432? He did! The officer corps should listen to his ideas.

Singletary knew there was work for his men to do today and tomorrow. He whistled into his EE8.

"Van, Cervera, Brannagh come back here."

"Brannagh," Sing glowered, "you, Van and the first gun squad have been personally selected by O'Hara and me for a honor. You're on a tank infantry combat patrol in the morning."

The gunner regretted the extra duty his action had inflicted on the guns in the squad. By upsetting the two graders, the first gun was being sent to where sorrows were born. Brannagh's consternation over his troubles with Sergeants Singletary and O'Hara included a wariness of the top two sergeants. If he acted on the advice of O'Hara there would be a dive a day in the boxing ring. As he had also upset the tipsy Singletary, there would be a battle a day. It appeared the sergeant first class had no other duty but inexorably to send Van Meter's gun into combat. Brannagh felt it was worth remembering who had the power under military law to choose which of the troops stayed home, which not. There were specific versus general decisions Brannagh reasoned. He had paid too much attention to the killers from a distance, men who made the general decisions for armies to go to war, and less mind to the men who made the specific decisions, which squad went into combat. If O'Hara and Singletary were estranged from this one soldier, the commitment of the rest of the first gun squad was a barbarity.

He saw solemn squads, calm on the backs of tanks, riding on turbulent tracks northwardly. As impassive, half tracks bearing four fifty caliber machine guns made Brannagh conscious that the quad fifties of Battery C were there to stich distant rips in the changing hues across the golden landscape, out of the range of the gunner's heavy thirty.

Brannagh sensed the wind-slip off the turret was cooler than the morning air's fifty degrees; so cold weather wasn't much further in the future than the tanks were far from their objective. Scattered low clouds were fluffing, reflecting sun light, Brannagh saw.

The murmurous sound of increasing mortar rounds he heard, their broadening columns of churned earth and shrapnel forward five hundred yards from the LD, was a rebuke to these trespassers. Perhaps, mused Brannagh, the Chinese were irritated at another of the incessant tank platoon actions that rolled out for a quick gun fight with targets of opportunity before being rewound, as if on a yo-yo string and nothing more?

"Were they going to be surprised," he mumbled.

He remembered Grant had said that Patrol Plan 53A had a platoon of Charley's infantry, a platoon of five tanks from the 89th's C Company, and a section of quad fifties from the 21st AAA's C Company before O'Hara and Singletary had retouched its scope with Van Meter's squad. The patrol was to cross the LD at 0930 hours. By 1035 hours the quad fifties were to be positioned on the high ground at grids 643414 to support the infantry attacking the ridgeline northeast of the halftracks. The tanks were to move north towards the infantry objective, dismount the troops, and deploy on the low ground at grid 648413. The infantry was to maneuver towards the key terrain points at grid 648424. Their return to the MLR was upon order and cover of artillery placing a battery T.O.T. on grid 649422.

Brannagh figured the light observation plane overhead was the tankers' liaison. He was sure it would call in air support if enemy tanks were sighted. It was a comforting thought that relieved some anxiety born of rumors about Chinese tanks hidden behind hill 1062. He watched the quad fifties lumber into position. He felt the power of the tank beneath him. Would this same tank that bore them forward as living beings bear their dead back? He wished his mind wouldn't be so taciturn.

When the tanks fanned out, Van had his men dismount. He kept Grant's 3rd squad on the left and moved forward with them towards the bushy nail of the finger that ran with trees upward.

Brannagh caught movement among the scrub brush and trees. He saw Chinese wildly climbing the hill to the front right of Grant's men whose line of vision must have been curtailed by the rise of the long, narrow slope.

"Van, to our right two fingers, in the draw," Brannagh yelled. "Chinks going up the hill."

"Mount behind that lip, front right. Action," the squad leader ordered. "Grant, chinks to our right ahead," he yelled.

Brannagh, Im Ta Song and Davis, as one, mounted the guns behind the lip. Davis crawled off to the gun's left.

"Fire," Van ordered.

Brannagh threw his tracers at Chinamen

running up the hill towards a bunker line, and set ablaze the dry grass and colored leaves of fall. He watched the fire start eating on foliage in the tight pass. Then, as if an ancient animal was emerging from a fog, he saw the squat form of a long tongued monster peering back at him.

"Lord," he said! His fire ricocheted off a T-34 tank.

One after another Brannagh heard his tanks fire and impale the T-34 all across its width. He ducked as it exploded, its gasoline propelled chips flinging death in all directions.

"I'm hit," Davis cried. "I'm hit---medic," he hollered.

"Hit his lower ass," Sugrue hollered over.

"Fire into the smoke," Van ordered. Something in the hissing and sizzling of the tank's fire triggered a cautionary fear. "Get your heads down." He felt the earth beneath him suck in its stomach at the second explosion. He heard the flight of the tank's spun bits, then a quiet.

"Move out," Grant ordered. "Up the finger, to the trenches."

Van echeloned his squad to the right. He listened to the quad fifties tap dance their rounds above his advance, some bullets snorting on impact. He saw other bullets rebound like basketballs.

"Mount the gun in that shell hole forward and commence firing," Van ordered.

The third platoon had the bunker surrounded.

"Cease fire." Grant called. He covered the enemy who came out with their hands up.

"Pull out," Grant ordered, "time to go home."

Smoke was still drifting from the torn-up tanks.

Brannagh hadn't seen a Chinese tank before. He had heard the North Koreans had T-34's; perhaps these two burning ones were the same kind. Suddenly, a green tracer meteored from the tank's smoke towards the 89th tanks, exploding against a rock. He bit dirt, digging into it while the 89th's red and white hot rounds erupted into the smoky haze, hatcheting the daring Chinese anti tank gunners into silence.

Relief read like a road map on the faces of the first gun squad at the sight of Davis' limestone face. His legs were covered with aid packets that were snow capped but tinged with crimson under Autumn's sterile light. He lay on his stomach on a tank's back, his right ear on his elbow.

"Who took my water can?"

"Dreamer," the gunner replied.

"Going to be a first class private, for sure," Dreamer exclaimed!

"I'll be a while back in a stateside hospital," Davis said, "before I walk back to my insurance agency." He wasn't sure why he felt as he did, sick at heart, even empty, depressed. He might not be walking home but he was going home. By the time noon came, he knew he'd never see his squad buddies again.

CHAPTER FIFTEEN
WARMING BUNKER

"That's not the way I want to go home," Blaczyk said, "on a granite mountain. Emergency leave home to bury your mother is a tough detail, see. I'm sure ham-hock Revels will bug out in Kansas. He should hide in some wheatfield. Myself, I'd rather do time in Leavenworth and be right at home, then come back and go up this hill again, see."

Brannagh liked the A-frame ammo-bearer well enough, but had no need to be too close and ice-picked with an index finger, particularly when confined within the newly completed warming bunker. It was of CP quality, perhaps as reinforced as Singletary's solo bunker. It had ammo boxes for chairs. Spools from barbed wire rolls had been confiscated to support roughly fabricated tables. Lanterns hung from the ceiling logs, their brightly burning wicks providing writing and reading light.

"With Revels leaving, that moves Trout to be Baiter's assistant," Brannagh said. "Maybe if the truce talks start up again, Revels won't have to come back."

"Hey, look, Red," Glorio said, "the Army's like the government in New York City. Everything's garbage to them. There's kick-back money in garbage, so them what's got the sweetheart contracts pick up the garbage and split the loot. Revel's garbage to the rear. They'll send him back to this garbage dump."

"Revels got but 21 points, see," Blaczyk said. "Ain't no way the Army won't make him do 23 more, or them generals would hear from my union," he insisted.

Brannagh was coming to believe them. Dad's last letter related the liaison officers of the Commies

and the United Nations were meeting to discuss the
resumption of the truce negotiations. There was a
hitch, however. General Ridgeway wouldn't go back to
Kaesong as the site. He wanted a place named
Songhyon.

The lean, sparse frame of Trout tramped
through the elbow shaped warming bunker entry. Then
protruded the handsome profile of Watt. Side by side,
Brannagh viewed a twisted mulberry and a stately oak,
the Tennessean as homely as the Virginian was
handsome, Trout the apparent victim of alcoholic
epilepsy; Watt the depositee of all the right genes. They
sat on ammo boxes.

"It was about time my girl did this," Watt said.
"The hand of my lady always charmed me. At home I
always kissed and pressed her hand. I tried to get her to
uncover her hands, bat a finishing school woman
wouldn't. Just seeing her hand in my mind brings out
the lust in me. My mind was wearing out thinking
about her hand, so I wrote her for a glove. She sent it; I
can see her naked hand again."

"Thinking of wearing out reminds me of Charley
Boy back home," Trout said. "Charley Boy had a drive
even 28 years of insatiable sex in marriage couldn't
restrain to one woman. He told me he did it wild,
trembling over with excitement, even panting like a hot
hound dog. He nauseated his wife so that when she
found out he was doing her sister, too, she moved her
to Charley Boy's bed. Only change was he had two
women he was wearing out. When he thought they had
him wearied, danged if they didn't discover Charley
Boy was on their last sister, too. They moved her in.

"It was some bed Charley Boy had, humping
from woman to woman like kernels of roasted corn. I

saw that bed. As big as a pool table," Trout said.

He had his arms stretched as wide as possible. He looked from face to face, satisfied with the attention on them. He saw Watt had stopped kissing his white glove. It was slowly sinking between his thighs, a white swan sucked into a swamp.

"Now Charley Boy started casting his eye on the young widow down the road. He told the three sisters he couldn't help himself, his urges kept on increasing. His women tried to control his instinct, but Charley Boy just ate too much animal meat.

"Now this woman reveled in dirty songs and expressions, lustful attitudes and gestures. Charley Boy was beside himself when she put her arms and legs through the rope loops on her bed. She had unlimited desire. She was always in some sex crisis. She abandoned herself to Charley Boy."

Watt had recouped his white glove from its abyss.

"He must be the happiest man alive," Watt exclaimed!

"Good old Charley Boy," Trout said, "within a few days, lethal collapse!"

A round dropped next to the sand bagged roof. Others followed like a string of sheep. One crashed on the reverse slope nearby, rocking the ground beneath the warming bunker, its very earth seemingly flowing like jello.

Tobacco juice trickled out of the corners of Trout's mouth. He looked as hard as his eyes could squint. He squirted a well- aimed stream through his teeth and hit Watt's white glove.

Watt was giving as many horrible oaths as he was shedding tears, when at the elbow entry Brannagh saw a huge blue-gummed black soldier, bouncing on his toes, his fists doubled at the ends of long tree branches, his fatigues glued to stomach muscles that moved his shirt like a fast flowing stream over numerous small stones.

"Deuce-four down the Kumhwa road," Trout redirected.

"Ain't no more deuce-four," came the guttural reply.

"Stag?" asked the gunner, "from the Marine Lynx?"

"That's right, who you?"

"Brannagh!"

"The shithead what whipped me?"

"If you say so; more likely it was O'Hara and Breezedale."

"Ain't what it seemed," Stag mumbled?

"No? I saw you and them divvy the money on the ship."

"Ain't what it seemed. Ain't got nothing in common with them."

"O'Hara and Breezedale probably having a big laugh on me right now." Stag sucked his tobacco. "Breezedale's here."

Brannagh was surprised. His ears buzzed as they had after the fight with Stag. His eyes opened as if a flare had gone up and the time had changed, turning night into dawn.

"Breezedale in Dog Company," a piqued Brannagh asked?

"New platoon leader of the heavy thirties," Stag said.

"Why you all here?" Trout interrupted.

"Army busted up the 24th regiment. O'Hara sent

me to Sergeant Van Meter."

"You're in my squad then," Brannagh said. "I'm the gunner."

"Army's been going for bad on us, Red," Stag pointed to his chocolate coloring. "Even when every private soldier in the deuce-four was making something outa themselves, or trying to, the Army gave us Breezedales. If I got to fight them gooks, its gotta be right beside an officer who don't quit."

"I'll take him to Van," Glorio said.

He led Stag out. In all of New York, Glorio hadn't seen a man, black or white, whose body build would embarrass Charles Atlas'. Until he got Stag's biography in bull sessions, the first Negro in the third section bore watching as a probable hoodlum. Maybe Stag's only choice was going to the army and not jail, Glorio concluded. What bad luck to have a hoodlum in his bunker, and colored at that? The Army was going to the dogs, wasn't it? It clicked somewhere in his head that was where he was, too, and he a white man! Maybe there was more to it? He had it - garbage! Stag and Glorio, the whole of the enlisted man's infantry were garbage. America's most useless were black and white infantryman. Dump them in Korea. Who'd notice?

Brannagh watched as Trout and Watt sped away. They would tell of the integration of the thirty fifth regiment as if its Asiatic, Hispanics, and white descendants of every ethnic nationality on the European continent weren't already integrated.

There was Dad's letter to read.

"There is a belief in my construction gang that America's soldiers in Korea are being appallingly misused. We are all talking about the battle of Heartbreak Ridge. Its said the whole of Heartbreak

Ridge is ankle deep in rock dust; boulders broken into stones from tons of shells, bombs and napalm. The only way a soldier kept alive to fight was to dig caves, even tunnels. Its said the assault is a costly failure. I was relieved to read the battle for Heartbreak Ridge didn't involve your 35th regiment, yet I've prayed for the lads of the 23rd regiment.

"Van Fleet called the battle but one in a dim-out war; a school to season replacements. Some sort of corner needs to be turned by the Eighth Army and the IRA."

There it was again, Dad's not too subtle suggestion of a career for his son in Kumhwa, a fighter not for the politically partitioned Korea of the south, but for the politically partitioned Ireland of the north.

"Truman needs a victory on Heartbreak Ridge to save the Democrats. The Reds have built up their forces in Korea, but in America they say there are only three fully trained divisions, two of which are going to Europe where Truman believes the greatest Red Army danger exists; but there's no war there!

"Its said that Ridgeway doesn't want to resume the talks at Kaesong because, if he did, it would look like it was true that your side bombed it, Danny. So, if the Reds won't change the site, there won't be anymore talks. Ridgeway must think your side has won! If there isn't any more talks, sure, that would be proof that your side didn't want peace. The world would blame Americans, not the Reds.

"Its said that Truman then sent a state department diplomat and General Bradley to talk to Ridgeway. At least he's reported to have asked the Reds to suggest a new site between the front lines. We'll see!"
*****

Im Ta Song cleared his throat, and began his effort to divert attention from incoming.

"Koree ancient land. Comee from big lava, form Koema, flat, flat, flat." His hands moved back and forth to verify, somewhere in Korea, was flat land. "Big lava buildee cones." His hands then shaped a cone. "Havee Paektu-san." He pointed north, then, like a Hula dancer, swayed hands to demonstrate water flow. "Yalu river." He pointed north. 'Tumen river." He pointed east. "Now, air dry" He wiped his brow, as if from sweat. "Hot." He wrapped arms around himself and shivered. as if in Mongolia. "Soonee cold."

Brannagh was impressed with the continuing improvement in Im Ta Song's GI English. He was reasonably clear talking GI since he took over as assistant gunner.

All of the men up front expected the winter of 1951-1952 to be bitter.

Brannagh heard the shells bursting up the line, walking towards his gun hole. Dreamer was his guard. There was more than the usual chipping away at the mine fields and barbed wire that covered their finger and field of fire. He heard a whoosh come through the air, and a flash as quick as lightning fire dance out on the trench line. A deafening report castigated his ears. Sand bled, even from the bunker's skin.

"You OK Im?" Brannagh asked. He was. Both worried Dreamer went down. They took off, down the connecting trench, to the gun hole. Dreamer was no more dazed then usual. Brannagh whistled the EE8. "This is the first gun hole, Dog third section. We took a direct 82 millimeter hit. No casualties, little damage."

They listened as the enemy mortar crew worked its way eastwardly, stopping its excursion only when counterfire snapped a whip, when who should appear but Trout, face and lips animated, backside deposited on a sand bag when he took off on another back road tale.

"Willie Joe was the only man I know'd that had more cleavage than Susan Hayward," Trout said. "As a pup, he was weakly and dull, but he grew up playing the dulcimer. When he wasn't away playing, he was a silent and sullen whelp. Away, he kept making a play for the fiddle player. Fell in love with every damn male fiddle player in the county. Now the fiddlers were perturbed, but what could they do? Willie Joe was damn good on that dulcimer, and his tits were near as big as twin gook Paektu-san." Trout's vacant look was spooking Im, not Dreamer.

"As Willie Joe wasn't satisfied by the love he was getting, his breasts grew. He acted more and more the woman. He went to matching his bosoms with them that was endowed by nature the right way. Got so bad, he wouldn't play his dulcimer with the fiddler unless the fiddler brought him a delicate dessert. Soon after, Willie Joe became Wilma June. He said, I mean, she said she was always a woman. Just made out like she wasn't, so she'd not get knocked up by any fiddler's fiddling. Then she took to crocheting and embroidering and quilting and her music was a great as her mammalaries."

Dreamer liked this story. He turned himself around, his eyes on the dark form of Trout, not to the front.

"Then Wilma June did wrong. While the sheriff was playing his guitar to her dulcimer, Wilma June with her hair all up in a knot, went and kissed him, pulling his bon-bon in front of the people."

Trout paused. He heard nothing but deep breathing from his audience. "When the Sheriff's wife stripped searched Wilma June, she found her tits were rolls of bread, but Willie Joe's spear was all meat."

Dreamer laughed until his jaw jammed. Brannagh didn't.

"Me tell of Korea," Im Ta Song interjected. "My turnee."

The gunner noted Dreamer's position. "Turn around Dreamer. Keep your eyes forward."

"Namee Kumwha mean goldee frog," Im Ta Song's spoken whine was in his barely basic English. "Kingee Pujo old man, no son. He burnee calf to mountains and streams, wantee son. Riding horsee to Konyon, kingee see stone cry. King rollee over stone. Sawee small child, goldee, form of frogee. Kingee Pujo raisee as son, namee Kumhwa, goldee frog. He growee to Kingee. Long timee ago."

Dreamer had to tell Trout and the gunner he had a recently acquired scoop. Knowing the gunner had already jumped on him for eyes not forward, he'd talk out of the side of his mouth, like a movie star gangster. "Some guy be in Baker, got a letter from stateside asking him to desert to the gooks."

"His people must hate his guts?" Trout said.

"Wasn't his people," Dreamer said, turning away his eyes from the forward slope. "Be his pen pal. Folks put his name in the newspaper back home for a pen pal. Be getting letters from a Commie."

"The way the army works, some officer in Regimental S-2 will think that Baker troop is a pinko," Brannagh said.

"Third battalion's set up a system we're soon to start, too," Trout said, changing topics. "Everyday, each unit is to send one seventh of its men down the hill to shower, shave, get a hot meal and see a movie before they come back on line."

"Sounds like heaven." Brannagh said. It was an astoundingly satisfying revelation to get off line at least once a week and go south, not north. The gunner guessed regimental and battalion commanders wouldn't give their line troops a day of rest, if Divisional, Corps, and even the Eighth Army's generals hadn't so agreed. Obviously the truce talks were resuming.

"Grenade," screamed Dreamer!

Brannagh saw a C-ration can with a handle thump off the bunker's back wall. It richocetted between the four soldiers. Instinctively he and Im Ta Song kicked it toward the grenade hole.

Trout careened towards the sandbagged-elbow, to exit out of the bunker. He hurled himself behind its shelter.

Dreamer was chilled in place.

The hot grenade fell into the hole. Brannagh flipped a sandbag over it. His heart fluttered when the sandbag farted. The smell was like that of a dead rat. He sat still. God's and Buddha's goodness was on each of them.

The sound from outside the bunker's exit was like the thumping of a watermelon. It drummed again and again. Brannagh rotated off the safety of his M2 carbine. He slid himself into the sandbagged elbow. He stopped behind the giggling poncho covering the doorway, the barrel of his weapon inching the rain repellant sheet to his left as if drawing a curtain on a stage.

He looked into the trench line. A turtle form was

straddling a short log. The turtle's right arm rose like
an oil rig drill, dangled a moment in the air, then
cascaded downwards to elicit the thump. The gunner
saw no other movement up or down the trench line. He
moved towards the turtle, carbine at the ready. He saw
Trout, and beneath him, tortured torn flesh.

"Trout," the gunner said, "the chink's dead. Stop
hitting him."

The little log in the coffee brown uniform had
orbless sockets where once bright, black eyes must
have been. His face was gone. There was no discernible
nose. His flesh puckered like a carp's mouth.

Brannagh heard footsteps either side of Trout.
Familiar forms emerged from out of the dark; Van and
Stag from the west commo trench, Cervera and Baiter
from the east.

"Trout caught and killed a chink," Brannagh
said.

The ground suddenly danced beside him, dirt
jumping rope around Trout. Sod and rock rained from
cordite clouds rippled with flames.

"Darn, they're close," groaned the gunner. Two
more rounds released their thunderclaps and spikes
downstream. He watched Van and Stag melt into the
blackness. Cervera and Baiter pushed Trout ahead of
them. The gunner crawled back into his dugout, leaving
the carcass to incoming vultures. He began to shake,
his knees knocked. He saw his buddies shivered as fully
as he. Were they too contemplating legging it for the
reverse slope? He was sorely tried by a maddening
terror seizing his legs to run from the horrible din. He
curled into himself in fear at each shell burst, praying
that their lives be spared.

"Lord, have mercy on our souls!"

He saw Dreamer looked like a soldier except for his shrinking shoulders and haunted face. Tears were in his eyes. He was everlastingly shaking, his lips white and drawn. Even Im Ta Song looked to the gunner like a whipped puppy, the crescendo of eruptions above growing on his nerves.

Another scarlet tongue of flame suddenly shot up to his bunker's left, only ten yards away, and as suddenly died out, its sigh of steel a gasp. Up went another flare changing the time again. The rain of spears ended with the burnt out light. It wasn't his time, or the Korean farmer's, or the Californian orphan's to sing the tune to the shell's death song. This time the infiltrator groaned death's melody.

Dreamer's quivering from fright had turned to trembling in rage.

"That be it! Won't take no more from them gooks. Going to volunteer for the Raiders." He bit into each syllable. "Raiders be needing two men, rumor say; they not turn me down again," Dreamer said.

Brannagh heard the last phrase spoken with grief inflection, its words as if a turn down had been Dreamer's every experience.

"What do you mean, again," the doubting gunner asked?

"Before, asked Sarge Van in the warming bunker. He says they say no. Sarge Cervera and Baiter laugh," Dreamer said.

"Why don't you just stay with us, Dreamer," Brannagh said, "at least until your stripe and mine come down. Van said we'll both be PFC's by the end of the month. So stay," Brannagh implored.

Dreamer felt the tug of the words. He was wanted. He was already the first ammo bearer. Next he would make Private First Class. He was delighted. If only he had someone who cared to hear about it back home.

"Don't worry, I stay," Dreamer said proudly.
*****

"Don't need your gun out there tonight, Brannagh," Grant said, "but I'd feel a lot better if you'd gun on the heavy-thirty in the left bunker.

"Alright with you, Van," the gunner asked his leader?

"Okay! We'll switch crews," Van replied.

"We're going out to destroy bunkers just a couple of hundred yards away. The left gun has a direct bead on our route. What with that little knob, the right gun can't cover us in the defile, though it can up on the gook trench line.

Brannagh watched the patrol move out at 1900 hours. He was coming to know them. He recollected all of their names. Grant of course, and Crane with his BAR and smile, tailed by wolf-cub medic Sugrue. The quiet one, Aquilas, had the eyes of a shark. Gibbard bore his radio with his usual verbose irritation. Odegard wasn't taunting the medic, although the two of them had invented words that Satan would have enjoin by injunction in hell itself. Rifleman Corney had hoped to be a blue star commando back in supply services, but quickly adapted to the war paint of the MLR, face and hands blackened from the smoke of charcoal fires in the bunkers. Demos' face contrasted to Corney's, being lit up as if he were going on R&R. Kurcharski was eager to be back in the morning for delousing and fumigation, clean clothes and a movie.

Remembering the names of the guys in Dog Company, or in Charley Company wasn't easy. With

rotation and R&R, new replacements and returning
casualties, men were coming, men were going. Men hid
deep in holes, under helmets, in loose fitting fatigues,
in field jackets, under field caps, in sleeping bags, even
covered with grime. Winter clothes issue would devour
even more of recognizable mannerisms and limbs.
Brannagh knew who was in his squad, and in Charley
third platoon's third squad. They were melded, even
more so than his own section's 2d gun. He didn't
recollect many of the names of the other guys in Dog or
Charley. They, to the gunner, his squad, section and
Charley three-three were extras in a cast of thousands
of troops at war.

  There was a necessity for patrolling, but
Brannagh knew the rifle patrols went out cursing G-2
and S-2, Divisional and Regimental Staff Intelligence,
for having nothing else to do but draw patrol plans, like
57A, for infantry entertainment. The long weary hours
before crossing the line of departure were never as long
or as weary as the time expended after crossing the LD.
The time taken from going from checkpoint to
checkpoint, or setting up an ambush, or climbing a hill
to a Chinese trench line to blow-up bunkers might have
been intelligence's modus operandi, but dog foot
dangerous. Often a patrol went out at night to double
document what line troops had observed and whistle
phoned in - like a Chinese donkey carrying ammo, or a
forward digging party. There was dawning a realization
with line troops that the less they reported what was
seen in light wouldn't again need seeing in the dark.
This same dawning diminished sniping, when, by
happenstance, Pocaski forgot to shoot the 50 caliber
one day. He noted there was no reply. This he did tell
Grant. They sat on their gun. The Chineses did the

same. There was civility among line infantry whose
lives were already made miserable by artillery, mortars
and Korea's weather, for they entered their own
miniscule truce. None of this, of course had the rear
echelon known it, was acceptable. The rear was only
satisfied if the patrol brought back a warm mule
dropping, or the sniper exploded a pumpkin head, or
Grant's patrol blew Chinese bunkers to Manchuria.

The weather cooled considerably when the
overcast sky lost its distant red-eye. Sitting behind the
gun wasn't conducive to generation of bodily warmth,
the gunner decided, but admitted it was infinitely
preferable to lathering up a mist chugging up and down
hills to raise bodily heat. No sound rose to his ear. The
darkness was too quiet. Something must be up, he
thought. He concluded nothing was wrong. Yet the
atmosphere was tense. Van, Im Ta Song and Dreamer
were as muffled as if gagged. Were they all gripped by a
still hand? If they were uptight, it wasn't difficult for
the gunner to conjure the men on Grant's patrol felt it
was a nerve wracking ordeal.

The sounds of grenades sounded like Gregorian
chant, the punctuation of Chinese potato mashers
interspersed with GI fragmentation grenades. There
were fiendish monks down there chanting mournfully.
The grenade fight wasn't farther from Brannagh's
position than a football team's goal line. Where should
he fire?

"Wait till Grant tosses the WP. Traverse the
WP," Van directed!

It soon came, a blow torch blue flame that ate
the dark. Brannagh fed it lead, his ricochets sharply
cracking off the low ground. He traversed the upper
sweep, then searched.

"I'll have La Vie fire to the right. Maybe chase the Chineses towards your gun," Van said. "Keep traversing."

He whistled the EE8, then watched the flow of yellow tracers. It reminded him of the night pullman train passing the far side of his farm's patch of wood.

"Cease fire," Van ordered when grenading stopped.

Van Meter's brow was as wrinkled as the phone's wire was wound up. He listened intently to the details coming up from the patrol. The grenade fight had ended. Grant took no casualties, but killed two Chinese. Should he move up?

Red Six, himself, gave the go ahead.

"Grant's deployed," Van whispered to his 1st gun crew. "He's got Pocaski and Odegard on the point. They're moving up to the top of the small hill with the two bunkers."

It was quiet. The crew chewed worry as if it was chewing gum.

"Gibbard said Pocaski and Odegard went into the Chinese trench," Van Meter relayed to Brannagh.

The a'capello of a burp gun piped to Brannagh's ears. He saw that exploding grenade flashes rimmed the trench line, and heard burp guns flickering incessantly everywhere.

"At the trench line, Brannagh, La Vie, fire," Van ordered!

The two weapons of the first gun squad raked the trench line, ripping and tearing its parapets to shreds.

"Grant's moving up. Keep firing on the trench line. I'll tell you when to shift fire," Van said.

Van Meter waited for Gibbard's directions. He

was the mouth of Grant, not his eyes. Grant was a cat in the night, he saw everything. It would be the squad leader who came, saw and conquered, or came back on his shield.

Dog's gunners fed rounds to their ravenous weapons.

"Keep firing. Red Six has ordered the patrol to pull out. The chinks are firing a machine gun from the top of the hill,"

Van related. "La Vie, keep firing on the trench line. Keep the chinks pinned. Brannagh, engage that gook gun up there."

Van hadn't noticed he had slipped into the perjorative for the Chinese. It wasn't his way, but he was hot.

Brannagh shifted fire towards the flash. Bullets cracked in front of him, kicking up dirt, scattering vegetation and rocks which sounded like hailstones against his steel helmet. He took on the distant killer, a first burst measuring the distance to his enemy.

"Grant's patrol is down the hill. La Vie, shift fire on Brannagh's tracers," Van ordered.

A barrage of curtain fire joined on the small Chinese hill to break up any reply, when both guns lost sight of the flash.

"Cease fire," Van ordered.

The machine guns went quiet.

Brannagh listened to the 60 millimeter mortars hiss down on the enemy, exploding with sharp cracks. He saw the 81 millimeters burst with bright orange flashes, and artillery rumbled in bursts of red. It was a hellish rainbow covering Grant's men.

Van took Brannagh with him to the warming bunker. The word had it Grant was there with all his men, safe but not too sound.

"Chinks spot you," asked the gunner?

He saw Grant's mummified face was as red as a pepper.

"Damn Pocaski and Odegard got into the Chinese' trench, even into a bunker where they saw four gooks. Damn Chinese talked to them in Chinese, but did those assholes speak carbine? Hell no," he shouted. "They jumped out of the hole and came back to us. If I was in my boat in the gulf stream, I'd bait the water with their blood, then feed them to the sharks."

Pocaski's head ached. Odegard felt as if the other seventy-nine vikings were beating them with their oars, making him row the Longship all alone from Greenland to North America.

Neither could explain why he froze!

Brannagh had heard no infantryman ever understood the sudden loss of his trained tendency to kill an enemy in his front, or his resultant motionlessness. It was like falling into an iceberg's deep crevice and freezing blue, then just as suddenly, to thaw. Was it either end of a state of frenzy - a learned reluctance to kill a human being; a survival instinct to avoid being killed? Brannagh didn't know.

CHAPTER SIXTEEN
OBJECTIVE HILL 1062

The Red battalion had been on Kumhwa's front a third of Autumn. The squad leaders and gunners of Dog's third section, and every other ammo bearer, had passed out of the sunshine into the chill shadow of the warming bunker. Brannagh stopped to view the pitiless looking hills of the ROK troops on the east flank. Korea's abundant vegetation had cast its verdancy there when soldiers first climbed these hills, but Korea's stones, mellow and old now, predominated. The front side of the mountain was sliced by trenches. The reverse slope was studded with toadstool bunkers and ribbed with mammoth terraces on which ROKs and trucks crawled like lice in Dreamer's pants. The dull but constant roar of a fire fight ongoing in the distant trench line floated across the valley and rolled up their mountain to his ears, seemingly absorbed within them, like waves in a sea shell.

The soldiery of America, the troops of the United Nation's too for that matter, heard at all times and all seasons and with infinite humility of their superiority to the infantrymen of the Republic of Korea, the gunner knew. From these sources they also heard of the ROK's inferior character and minimal courage in the face of China's soldiers. A great catastrophe always followed, the ROKs bugging south to massive granite mountain leaves! The ROKs were held to be hapless troops, and nothing but fish heads to put in a honey pot.

If so, who were those little men in green crawling up the south side of the hill and flipping grenades over the crest at little men in brown who were responding in like kind? Brannagh couldn't leave the spot on which he stood. He had a panoramic view of a squad or more of Chinese assaulting a squad or more of ROKs. The gunner's pulse quickened. He hung back from Singletary's briefing and watched the battle unfold. It was great and grim, superb and defiant. It more than filled his eyes and imagination despite its minuscule proportions to the battle line across all of Korea. It wasn't an abstraction; it lived. It was an oasis of combat. At the very apex of the ridge Brannagh was watching, he saw a soldier on either side. The men from two countries did not see, but heard one another. Each misjudged the distance between them, perhaps but six feet, three feet either side of the razorback crest. Their grenades rolled harmlessly down the opposite slope. Then the grenades were gone. Silence must have been their signals. Both men rose from the prone and attacked up hill, weapons blazing, Brannagh saw.

An indescribable chill swept the gunner's nervous system. Upon that mountain's crest two soldiers stood face to face emptying burst after burst into one another, their line of antagonism drawn. Neither fell. Their weapons waxed fiercely until their ammo was expended, then they charged one another. The savage and upspringing ridge framed their desperate struggle. Enemies were seeking life or death. They seemed possessed of the notion that victory was in their hands, that each was extricating the most dangerous malignacy of the war. Arm in arm, each succumbed, falling for his country, as one.

Brannagh brushed away a tear. His eyes left the crest to follow its sweep into the wide, brownish, treeless valley below. Dark ominous forms of the 89th tanks marked the hollow. Was it their loud motors or the agonies of the dying that were floating on the winds? But for the abomination of stalled truce talks, the whole world would have raised monuments to the unknown South Korean and Chinese. The broken hearts of their weeping widows would be their remembrance. If there was eloquence in fighting and dying for one's country, Brannagh had seen it in two Asians.

*****

Brannagh watched the charcoal glow. He saw the sandbagged walls of the warming bunker were dangling pile jackets recently issued. The soft light of the lamps cast a mellow glow. Two thirds of the third section were assembled, seated on ammo boxes, or the bench.

Brannagh noted a green bean of a new guy was sitting in the northwest corner, next to coal digger Stag. Neither realized what lay beneath their bench, nor was Van, his gunner or La Vie about telling them that Brannagh had reburied a Chinese's shoe there. The shoe still had a foot in it, which, of course, was attached to a leg, the leg to a torso, the torso to a head. Rather than relocate and redig the monstrous bunker again, it was determined at the squad's coroner's inquest that the shoe be replanted, with its foot, leg, torso and head. Silence was sworn. Sandbag supports were erected, not as a tomb stone, but as legs for a comfy cozy for snoozing above he who was in everlasting repose below.

Brannagh saw that Singletary had a smile on his puffy face; he was chomping tobacco again, but his eyes hadn't that fierceness the gunner saw in September. Extreme hardness was always accompanied by extreme brittleness. Hadn't the section sergeant been tempered in the heat of battle last spring? Had he been plunged too soon into the cold water called the failed truce talks and cracked on the outpost? Brannagh concluded the stress of the failed talks and return to the front line was the process that annealed Sing's backbone and prolonged his cooling. His military world had changed from assault, to sit down, to defense. He couldn't be hurt or hit if he hid!

When Sing's right hand signalled for silence, he got it. Silence provided a backdrop for the section sergeant's sloshey chewing. Brannagh watched him load up to spit a slop at the slim cigar held between the thin fingers of the crewcut replacement. There was disappointment when the baptism was avoided, Sing splatting a butt can instead. It had been the section leader's way to establish dominance. He had lost his edge. Van felt a need to excuse his section sergeant. He leaned on Brannagh's ear to whisper.

"You should have seen Sing when I first got to Korea. Sing was all fire, real gung-ho. Since he's seen men killed for nothing after the outpost we took was lost, then retaken, only to be given back to the Chinks, it put his fire out."

"The word has it that thirty-six points will get me out of Korea. I got thirty-two," Singletary said.

The gunner was dismayed that the facial expression of the sergeant wasn't lit like one of the bunkers lamps, but conveyed a profound sadness.

"That's good news, Sergeant," said Van Meter.

"Is that right? Then what about this? Able of the 27th regiment has been sent to back up Charley Company. There's a hundred percent alert. HQ expects an all out Chinese attack soon."

This wasn't the word riding the rumor mill Brannagh expected to hear. Something big was going

on in the west. Dad had written about Heartbreak
Ridge in the east. The gunner saw faces profoundly sad.

"I Corps is still attacking," Sing related. "The
ROK 1st, the British Commonwealth Division, the 3rd
Division and the 27th regiment have moved up to the
Jamestown line, but the 1st cavalry ran into bunkers
like on Heartbreak Ridge. The gooks had trenches like
in the First World War, with all kinds of escape routes.
Air strikes and napalm was like lice on Dreamer. Last
night the gooks finally left hill 272, but the Cav ain't got
all of the Jamestown line. They got to push the gooks
back to the Yokkokchon river.

"Today, the ROK 2d to our right, the 24th
division and the ROK 6th jumped off for Kumsong."

"Ain't we in it," Baiter asked?

"Not yet!" Sing's deep voice trembled. "But ain't
no one attacking hill 1062. The generals are going to
fuse our carbon with their iron on that hill soon."

"When," asked Baiter?

His eyes were big. He had pulled attacks before.
He knew the climb up into 1062s clouds of death, each
laborious step on its steep sides was a step of death, a
step towards a scorching avanlance of molten lead. If
the 1st Cavalry discovered the Chinese had shifted from
a fluid defensive system to defense in depth; then they
intended to stay and defend in place. They would resist
to the end, rather than fall back and counterattack. The
battle for 1062 would be numbing moments of
enormous hardship.

"Soon," was all Singletary would say.

Brannagh could see worry run the lines on
Singletary's facial football field like ends out for the
quarterback's pass. He was right to worry. The ground
was shaking all across the MLR and Sing could sense it

in his bunker. His quiet world was collapsing around him. There was no one to cover for him, and he was tired. He continued.

"The 23rd regiment attacked at night on Heartbreak without artillery preparation and took half of it. In the morning, the French battalion moved up from the north; by noon the 23rd had the whole damn thing. Then they attacked hill 851. Sherman's from the 72nd tanks ran north up a valley and caught the chinks by surprise. The chinks were relieving the North Koreans. Our tanks shot the shit out of them gooks, no matter Chinese or North Korean. The 38th regiment then moved up to take hill 974. The 2d division's in position to take the whole damn thing now," he said.

Singletary recalled the outpost, and when the Chinese attacked in April and May. The images he saw were men that looked like andirons. They were combinations of straight and curved lines. Had he forged them? To Singletary, Watt looked like a jardiniere stand, Trout a fireplace shovel, Cervera an umbrella stand, and Brannagh a reading lamp.

"So our guys are attacking on our left and right," Sing said. "We ain't no neutrals. It's a hundred percent guard tonight; but be ready for the attack on 1062."

He lapsed into silence, turning his palms over like pancakes to study their lines, and his fingers, and his thumb, as if some horrible disease was rotting them.

The section remained silent. Each mind crawled like a cockroach over the indigestible words deposited by his section sergeant.

"Is that it, Sing," Baiter asked?

Sing's response was lethargic. "No, this new guy here is named Ptomaine. He's for Van's squad."

"It's Romaine," the replacement corrected.

Brannagh saw a recruit who had been picked off a vine; one who had walked off the manufacturing floor of shovel handles; but not one about to poison his buddies.

Singletary nodded as if he had noted the polite correction. He remembered to give the passwords.

"The sign for today is Big, the countersign is Bed."

Trout stirred. The wax covering his face didn't melt, but was cracking. The gunner figured the sign and countersign had stirred memories of some deviancy up in the hills, unlike its predecessors: Ice and Box, Foot and Locker; Service and Record. Simple words for simple troops.

Singletary didn't want to take time to listen to a Trout story. The mood wasn't right to hear about some hillbilly trying to clear up his clap by doing it with a cow. There was a new officer waiting to come in and lecture.

"Attention," ordered Singletary. The men rose as one to attention as a Lieutenant entered.

Brannagh contemplated the sound of Singletary's command. It more closely approached a pronunciation of 'trench-foot' than attention.

It was a strange looking Breezedale the gunner saw, now without a bushy moustache. Breezedale had a face as boyish as a sixth grader's, fragrant with after shave, a round face made even more prominent by the fullness of his cheeks. The Lieutenant looked like he hadn't reached puberty yet. He should have kept the moustache.

"At ease," Breezedale tooted. "Sit down!

Were they being made sport of, each soldier

pondered? What their ears heard and eyes saw was a platoon leader who twittered like a bird and jiggled like a kangaroo. Had the army sent Pierre the artiste to the platoon?

"Smoke if you have them," the officer said.

Breezedale enunciated each one sylable word as if he were singing them. It was the same psalm singing cadence Brannagh came to know on the troop ship. He gave a glance towards Stag who shrugged his shoulders, wrinkled his brow and opened his palms in a 'that's the way the man was'. It was graphic body language.

"We must learn the principles of the prevention of frostbite and immersion foot," Breezedale said. "I'm Second Lieutenant Samuel Breezedale, reassigned from what was the 24th regiment to Dog's heavy thirties."

As if the motor reflexes of the third section had been wired for simultaneous turns, Brannagh watched as heads pivoted toward Stag's ritualistic shrugging, emphasized by eyeballs bouncing around like the ball at movie sing alongs. Brannagh figured it was an explanation for the disbandment of the deuce four. The men in its ranks were commanded by nincompoops, a Breezedale who lacked experience, whose career had reached its peak at OCS, whose style provided images of ghastly days ahead.

Breezedale had hated every moment of his embarrassment of an assignment with negro soldiers. The shadow of their past was upon them; slaves, tenant farmers, ghetto criminals, unequal to the white man. Negroes were apathetic soldiers, full of foul words and gestures, uneducated, just plain lazy. Worst of all they were black. The most evil of their criminal soldiers had plotted against him to prevent his promotion. God was on his side, appointing him to save the honor of the Army by eradicating from its ranks its criminals.

"Blood circulation to the extremities is greatly retarded at low temperatures, even if not freezing and they become susceptible to frostbite or immersion foot. Amputations resulting from cold injuries can be reduced to negligible proportions by diligent rigorous application of prophylactic measures."

This time motor reflexes pivoted every head to Swinford's horrific expression of agony at the loss of his most treasured terminus. He was comforting it.

"When the weather is cold and wet, wear properly fitted shoepacs; the rubber foot and heavily oiled leather top will keep the feet dry."

Dreamer started a furious scratching under his right armpit, Brannagh saw, like a dog after a flea.

"In winter," Breezedale perculated, "do not fold your trousers into your boot tops to blouse them. In addition to restricting circulation, it prevents the evaporation of moisture from the foot through the top of the boot. Use the button tab on field trousers to snug the trouser leg around the ankle outside the boot. This is particularly important with shoepacs. All feet perspire, even in cold weather - - - -."

The Lieutenant was reading from a training memorandum, not lecturing, Brannagh was certain. The officer's eyes rarely scanned the assemblage.

Glorio farted, then violently flung his right arm up, folding it derrick-like to dig out a mite between his shoulder blades.

"- and in the case of the shoepac, the rubber foot and heavily oiled upper prevent the evaporation of moisture through the boot. Thus, the only means of escaping from the perspiration is through the open top.

Blocking the opening with tucked in trousers, tight rubber bands or wrapped laces prevent this evaporation. Without evaporation, socks and insoles will soon become damp even in dry weather. Do nothing to prevent maximum evaporation," Breezedale read.

Breezedale's eyes left his script and settled a scowl on Perkins, the gruff and rambunctious Cervera ammo bearer. The Lieutenant shifted his weight from one foot to the other, his eyes never quite able to focus on the cross-eyed enlisted man's he sought to wither.

Perkins snorted a nostril's mucus to the dirt floor of the bunker. His boot squished its moisture into the soil.

The Lieutenant wished he hadn't looked. He continued.

"Still air insulation in the uniform is obtained by wearing a windproof M-1943 field jacket with a hood and the cotton OD field trousers. The amount of insulation may be varied by different combinations of wool underwear, wool OD shirt, wool trousers, high neck sweater and pile jacket. Any combination of layers loses its value if the wind blows through it to dissipate the body heat. Porous, loose woven garments such as wool shirts and trousers, underwear and sweaters should always be worn as inner layers to insure maximum warmth. When so worn, their loose, thick weaves provide many air cells for absorbing and holding body heat."

Everyone hear Dreamer's lyrical puff. Brannagh wished the first ammo bearer was wearing those thick weaves now. When Mooshine Jones rotated the barrel of his carbine under his shirt as a backscratcher, and La Vie used his back as a washboard against the sand bags,

Brannagh knew the guys were on a lice and flea mission. It happened everytime a one note orator intoned vespers. The contagion was apt to spread like oleo.

"Clean clothing is warmer than dirty clothing as grease or dirt fill air cells and help conduct heat from the body."

Dreamer was the object of pivotal heads. Stag was unbuttoning his fly. His hand sunk into his pants, roving up and down its cloth to get at some prickly feeling, some insect in there that was armed with a bayonet and hunting.

Breezedale avoided turning his eyes towards the gyrations. He remembered his last embarrassment in the 24th regiment was at the hands of that dusky soldier.

Romaine, however, was fascinated with Stag's search.

"While sleeping, an individual should have as much insulation under him as over him. The water repellant case for the sleeping bag is windproof. Inside it the mountain sleeping bag or wool sleeping bag may be used for insulation. As this insulation is compressed by the weight of the body, additional insulation is required under the sleeper. Dry shelter halves, extra blankets, haversocks, field packs, web equipment, fiber ammunition or food containers, packboards, tree branches and bushes, or extra clothing may be placed under the sleeping bag or blankets. The more insulation, the warmer one sleeps. Use the inflatable sleeping pad when available."

Singletary was ticked. Bad enough he had to sit through the wearisome verbiage without turning around and enjoying the antics of the lice hunt, but the officer just added insult to injury, that needed addressing.

"The Lieutenant should know," Singletary said with soldierly deference, "that inflatable sleeping pads haven't gotten past division yet."

Breezedale wrinkled his face in pretended disbelief. He had a sleeping pad, although he had to repair the several holes he found in it after the deuce four; yet it was somewhat inflatable at the moment. Except for the studious presences of the three sergeants sitting fore, Breezedale noted the rest of the troops were scratching some odd parts of their bodies. The dirty faced one appeared to be popping insects, like grapes, into his mouth. Breezedale felt faint. He lost his place. He itched fiercely.

Stag winked to catch Brannagh's attention; to point towards a monstrous rodent promenading along the sandbags behind the Lieutenant.

The gunner passed the sign, then slipped his bayonet into his hand. He charged straight ahead as if to impale the lieutenant on a spit.

Horrified, Breezedale staggered backward, then spun himself like a top to the ground, falling flat on his back. He saw churning legs charge to the wall. He saw a startled rat falling on his face.

Breezedale's scream nearly woke the dead Chinese beneath Romaine. The officer struggled against the cold clammy feet on his face. He writhed like a python. "Oh, my God, oh my God," he screamed.

The gunner marvelled that Breezedale was capable of recalling his deity. The section marvelled that any being could tremble that violently, like a palm tree in a hurricane.

Brannagh seized the rat's tale. He swung it

against a log upright, smashing its head. The bloody gore was dropped at the feet of the stricken officer and gentleman.

Breezedale snapped to his feet. He stared at the dead critter, but inched away while rigging his nerves to recapture composure.

"That rat could have bitten me," he whispered.

"Yes, sir," Brannagh answered calmly.

"Dismissed," Breezedale said.

The troops watched quietly as the officer slinked away. The section was careful to cover the bunker's entry with blankets before they laughed themselves into pain. Stag's tale of a like happening over at the deuce four planted the idea for trapping and cultivating the furry creatures for future protection against another Breezedale front line lecture.

Breezedale was unable to conjure any other possible explanation. But for his twisting out of the bayonet's path, the red headed soldier would have struck him, not the rat. Red was clearly a criminal, but who could the Lieutenant tell? Certainly not O'Hara. He was already plotting with Stag. The Company Commander seemed uninterested in his command. Breezedale knew he, himself, had to inflict a punishment not in the military code.

*****

Blaczyk mumbled to himself while walking the commo trench up towards his line bunker. He hadn't any bed of lice free straw in his bunker, but he worried that funning that new officer wouldn't do an ammo bearer, his squad, or much less his section any good. An officer could order a PFC out to a listening post. No, Blaczyk confirmed, it wasn't any good funning an officer; even worse than funning the internal revenue.

Blaczyk expected retaliation.

He didn't want time in a self contained defensive point a hundred yards or so out front of the front, even if he wasn't expected to stand and fight. It was sick duty to give an early warning of enemy movement; then, when hit, to bug back to the MLR, so that 105s, 155s and mortars could fire for effect on a preregistered and coordinated pattern.

Trouble was, Blaczyk had heard, the Chinese were sly. They sent slick infiltrators to drop grenades in a soldier's pants. For sure, the perils of a listening post were as plentiful as Studebakers parked around South Bend's city hall. He wished he had had no part of the humiliation of the lieutenant.

*****

Stag was pulling the guard in Van Meter's bunker. He saw mountains on the Chinese side that were actually overhanging, which piled all the time against the sky, but which looked his way over a waste of shattered trees. Thinking on waste brought Breezedale to mind. He seemed always sneaking around, setting up a head start if the outfit bugged. It hadn't, though an outfit on Bloody Ridge had while under rapid fire. Rapid fire had a formidable effect on troops. Nervous self control alone stood between fighting and flight. Stag understood how a soldier might get worn down by the continued strain of combat, or he might be shattered by a single instance of shock. Imperceptible anxiety might wear out resolve. Noise from incoming might raise anxiety. Lack of sleep might fade tenacity. The shock of a surprise might snap the finely drawn thread of a soldier's will to resist, to fight. When a soldier in any army on any battlefield, petrified and awaiting doom, sensed apparent defeat or destruction from the missiles of death dealing weapons, his instinct for self preservation took over. He fled. Stag had it figured. No unit had a monopoly on flight, nor was it limited to either side of the MLR.

It was uncommonly quiet Stag noted, like a calm before a storm. Sergeant Singletary had said it clearly enough 'we ain't no neutrals'. Stag studied the isolated, cone shaped hill 1062 which sprang up sharply. Atop its crown and around its brow were long scars seemingly bidding defiance to the 35th regiment.

He felt wierd. His heart pumped faster, the expectation of death priming it. Down in the mines, death shoveled beside him. Up on that mountain he knew death was hiding, afraid to face him man to man. On second thought, death was as cowardly in the mines as on the hill. He worked the mines, but it was the big bosses who calculated the cost of safety, like officers did in the army. Stag's imagination didn't see any difference between them. What kept a high casualty rate or a mine disaster from being called murder if the bosses didn't take necessary safety measures; if officers committed troops piecemeal?

Stag's edginess drained. He figured his life had always been in the hands of bosses, now officers. He thought of Van Meter who took a colored soldier into his bunker without so much as a grunt. He thought of Brannagh who fought the good fight on the troop ship, yet believed he won a fixed fight. Stag thought of Momma. He would write her a letter. He would tell her of Kumhwa, where duty held his feet to the third section's first gun, where ever it went!

CHAPTER SEVENTEEN
OXIDIZING FIRE

Brannagh's guard witnessed nothing to his front. Chinese weren't even walking their dog. Seemed to him the Chinese weren't much interested in the 35th regiment what with their travails to the West and near Kumsong on the east. Rumor had it the 2d Division was again attacking over on Heartbreak; that the 14th regiment was coming over to Kumhwa. Sing must have it figured. Seemed to the gunner his section sergeant wasn't as tapped out as the section thought. There was life in Sing still. Too bad that the battle of 1062 was looming just when Singletary was getting to 36 points. Why didn't O'Hara pull the sergeant off line; La Vie, too? Well, Brannagh answered his own queries, this Sunday Father Flynn was bringing the Red Cross guy to meet La Vie. Perhaps the Cajun might get the hell out of here then.

The distant thunder of artillery and tuba mortars Brannagh heard were accompanied by piccolos of small arms fire. They were playing a deadly symphony over to the east. The ROKs must be moving, too. If the Chinese had their breath back after a summer of resupply, the ROKs would soon find out. On the west, the news he heard was the Chinese fought like hell to hold, pulling out only when casualties were high and ammo low; that they were falling back to prepared positions. Shades of the Eighth Army's lines in depth; both armies had adopted the strategy of siege warfare, the tactics of positional combat.

The gunner wondered if the Chinese rotated their unwounded. There were over a half billion of them the other side of the Yalu; on this side there must be nearly a million. Maybe the Chinese were relieved by divisions, while the Eighth Army rotated men. Which was the better system? A shiver ran the gunner's back. The U.S. Army had adopted America's factory system for rotation: replaceable parts. The Chinese must tend to replace the whole automobile. He shuddered.

Van Meter could only think of grandpa. No where in all of Iowa was there a thriftier, harder working and more independent farmer than he. He milked the cows, made the butter, looked after the marketing and did all the outdoor work too, that was, until Van could toddle. They deserved meals fit for field farmers, but ate frugally. It was in the army that Van reckoned he had all he wanted of fresh meat. Nor was grandpa induced to luxurious living. His small herd of cows dropped calves but once a year. If he sold high, he had to purchase high. If he sold cheap, he purchased cheap. He had to pay his bills whatever the market. He had a right to grumble when he hadn't anything in the bank at the close of the year. Frugality wasn't grandpa's motto, it was his way of life, Van remembered. Van figured grandpa would feel at home in this warming bunker, grey and spartan as it was. For primitive simplicity the place was worthy of him. The squad leader's ruminations changed course. On the morrow he was to have been the beneficiary of time off the line. He thought of the hot shower he would have had but for the 100% alert. If the Chinese hit at night or tomorrow, the joy of escaping the crust of Korea on his skin would be postponed. He would probably become caked with more soil. He might need an entrenching tool to cut through to skin. He already had lines that criss-crossed like railroad junctions where his web suspenders were worn at all times, combat pack attached or not, the regiment's signature. It was Singletary that mandated the hanging of hand grenades on the suspenders' upper loops.

Van unbuttoned his shirt to study the road across his stomach. He located Lake Mills in his bellybutton. He visualized the imprint of a county map. Here was Lake Harmon west of Scarville. Silver Lake was to the east of home. A little red vein ran eastwardly out of Lake Mills just north of Bristol, clear over to Northwood. It was Forest City he wanted to visit, just a little trip south. He'd heard some fine women lived there, not fast like the chicks in big Mason City. He had been there but once, when he reported for military service. Grandpa wouldn't let his grandson loose much. Much, questioned Van Meter? Not at all, he answered himself! Well, what of it? Wasn't the army keeping him on the hill away from a hot shower nearly the same thing: no trips at home nor a trip to the rear from the line. He buttoned his fatigue shirt.

Again, Van reflected, GIs were waiting for peace talks. The Chinese were as cautious as the GIs. No one was on a skyline. It wasn't a place for a Chinaman, absent a heavy overcast, or darkness, for Corsairs would stitch their cotton uniforms with leaden needles. Yet, the waiting gave the Chinese time to dig deeply underground. They might only have handtools, but they had moved mountains, as the 1st Cavalry had discovered.

No doubt hill 1062 was being mined with tunnels, bored through stone. The word from the 1st Cav told it that the Chinese had dormitories for ten men, with sleeping mats woven from local grasses, Van recalled. They were even using captured American equipment as iron boilers for cooking rice, GI helmets as wash pots. The Chinese even had blacksmiths readapting two ton truck parts for grinding soy beans for bean curd to go with their hot rice. Captured Chinese were hungry, Van remembered. Their officers had private quarters in those tunnels, with conference rooms yet. There were so many tunnels, it was apparent these officers could maneuver underground, reinforcements popping up where ever needed. If the 1st Cavalry Divison had been stymied by tunnel warfare, the 25th Division's 35th regiment would soon be chewing on the same wormy apple, the squad leader surmised.

*****

Singletary had worked his charcoal fire like a blacksmith's: a bed of hot coals covered by dampened and unburned charcoal holding its fire in a compact form. His bunker had lost its chill but had gained the essence of percolating coffee. He sat upon his snug bunk as if looking for Bill ROK in a black tie and white shirt to bring him a cup. He liked it there taking glances at news clippings. It mattered nothing that the New York Yankees had beaten the New York Giants in the World Series, four games to two. It mattered that his last great battle was ahead and he was a short timer. It mattered that outside his bunker entry there wasn't an oasis of peace, but a dun colored mountain fastness all up and down with scores of folds, covered with ashes, rubble and automatic weapons. He would have to climb and descend dozens of times before his section reached the ridgeline, then up, up, up, to the crest of 1062. He sensed he had played his last hand of poker. On the big hill he would be playing against rough spoken peasants with calloused hands and stubby fingers on the triggers of burp guns.

In the face of the bitter bite of battle, the fleeting odor of loyalty to army and country never mattered at all, Singletary reflected. It was the spirit in each squad, where a soldier was imbued with closeness and belonging, that he was hardend in the forge of combat discipline.

The section sergeant knew the best fire for perfect heating was one in which combustion of fuel was rapid enough that it used all the oxygen that was supplied. He was afraid he had been heated in an oxidizing fire, one that didn't use all the oxygen in the blast, one that left a black scale. He looked at his arms. He saw the black scale. He felt an awful strain. He let his coffee go on percolating. He slugged whiskey instead.

*****

Im Ta Song remembered when the hills were a luxuriant tender green with an edge of rugged boldness. There were tall twisted pines and rich lowland foliage. Distant mountains formed a border around his picturesque Korea, as exquisite as Yi Chaegwan's painting of a fisherman returning home. But Sotong San, hill 1062, although imposing, had lost its beauty to the weirdness of war. Im Ta Song feared over it.

The war was going to the trenches both armies had dug across the face of the country, he realized. The attack by the Americans in the west witnessed a Chinese retreat to fight at their next trench line, as had the Americans in April.

Im Ta Song believed that both the enemy and American units alike would bond to avoid their destruction. Van Meter would keep the 1st gun squad under cover. He always fought with unshakeable tenacity, yet with vigilant economy of the squad's blood. If there was survival after Sotong San, it depended upon the squad leader.

Im Ta Song saw a battle where artillery bracketed bunkers, air strikes lanced boils, but only the feverish flesh of soldiers felt the full fury of the traverse up the long slopes to hell. Rarely would a firefight settle a day's or night's battle. The crisis of combat would last until the dead and wounded were carried away and survivors relieved. Trench fever in the attack on Sotong San wouldn't be louse borne, Trench fever would be borne in incessant bombardments. Physical exhaustion would be added to combat shock.

Im Ta Song shook. He foresaw a collision where qualities of men's courage, dash and personal pride carried them forward, as if in brilliant intoxication, to meet the enemy. Had he the fervor to fight with Van Meter and Brannagh? Korea had nothing to give to them. They had their lives to give to Korea. Im Ta Song vowed no less.

CHAPTER EIGHTEEN
BREEZEDALE'S ORDERS

"Sergeant O'Hara," spoke Lieutenant Breezedale, "there's a recon patrol going out from Baker company at 1900 hours that needs a heavy thirty crew as a drop off. Send Brannagh's crew plus ammo bearer Stag." Breezedale would purge the criminal element working against him.

"Yes, Sir," O'Hara responded.

The top kick talked for effect when Corporal Miner was in the CP. O'Hara deduced the company clerk was relaying to Captain Busin the doings of the first sergeant. What usually saved O'Hara was his instinct for double cross. If Miner wanted to inform, O'Hara would see that Miner was aware of the faults of others, the strength of the Master Sergeant. This wasn't mere nervousness that Dog Six might get something on his top sergeant, it was maintaining iron control of events in the CP. O'Hara figured to say in private what he wouldn't say in the CP. This saved face for Busin who scheduled more time in his sleeping bunker, other CPs and back at battalion, than is his own forward command post. The Captain kept up his pretense of command. Busin's relationship was as a shareholder to corporate chairman of the Board, of absentee landowner to his land agent. The Captain had the grant of power over his heavy weapons company, but O'Hara exercised it. As O'Hara had iron control of the company, he was acutely aware of coincidence, of meaningful whispers, an acute sense of being undermined from outside, and Breezedale was responsible.

O'Hara's intuition sensed that Breezedale, by

specifying Brannagh and Stag for the patrol, was
playing a scurvy trick on the plot to get Brannagh to
fight Baiter. The top kick felt convinced Breezedale was
in league with the Captain and Corporal Miner. If the
first sergeant then sent out a gun crew from the second
section of heavies with Baker's recon patrol, as he
should, Captain Busin would have Miner as a witness to
support the Lieutenant's claim of disobedience of a
direct order.

O'Hara cocked his ears. He felt a flood of
consternation. Hadn't this same Breezedale conspired
with O'Hara and the referee to set up a double double
cross on the Stag-Brannagh fight? Then wasn't the
three way payoff stymied by the surprising but angry
appearance of Stag who threatened the three with an
endurance swim from somewhere in the Pacific Ocean
if Stag didn't get half? O'Hara felt the return of that
same gut queasiness he had on the troop ship. He was
convinced Breezedale had engineered a triple cross
aboard ship. Breezedale was setting the top kick up for
a fall from the CP to a machine gun section sergeant
slot, never mind Stag and Brannagh.

Breezedale heard O'Hara growl something
under his breath, but the officer devined little in
O'Hara's mumbles other than ill will for sending a
colored soldier out with the Irish Sergeant's favorite
Amercan mick - Brannagh! Breezedale tactfully
withdrew. He would not discuss the bug out
propensities of those people who came over to the 35th
regiment with him from the defunct deuce four. The
Lieutenant had an aversion to talk to O'Hara since the
troop ship frame up. O'Hara and Stag had descended to
fooling him when Stag took most of the loot in lieu of
castrating the officer and gentleman. Personnel's folly

had put them all together again, and Breezedale had his opportunity to put two of the three fools out in the rain. Who could question him if they got wet? There would come a time to chop O'Hara.

*****

Van and Cervera led their gun crews into the warming bunker where the word came down hard.

"Shit," groaned Dreamer. "Be all shit. Be covered with Chinese shit. Be shitted on by GI shit!"

"Nicola shibola," echoed Im Ta Song!

The Army had its way of passing down orders. Celestial Six, General Ridgeway, from Tokyo sent orders to Eighth Army's Scotch Six. He ordered Corps, Corps ordered Division, Division ordered Regiment, Regiment ordered Battalion, Battalion ordered Company, Company ordered its Platoon leader who ordered his section sergeant who ordered his squad leader whose enlisted men carried it out.

These dog face troops were the sole decisive arm of an army. Their power was based on human rather than planner's power. These front line men had learned to fight down fright, although they always had fear. Their confidence in themselves depended on their skills with their weapons, faith in Van Meter, trust in his squad members, assurance each would back the other. Squad discipline didn't imply an unthinking obedience; it implied the men's initiative and skill relentlessly preserverved for his squad's objective. It meant the over ruling of instinct, closing with the enemy. It meant the minimizing of reflection on the dangers to be faced.

Baiter wasn't about to minimize the presence of the deuce four drop out, or a Korean feeding the gun, or the first ammo bearer who should use the water can's content for washing himself, not cooling the gun barrel, to say nothing of the canary carrying the tripod. He was enjoying himself.

"Word is the gooks' activities have faded sharply on our front, that enemy regiments were pulled to defend Kumsong," Singletary said. "Ain't got nothing to worry about on this one. Baker's going out just to see if there's still gooks in front of the Red battalion."

"Then those mortar rounds on us must be short rounds from friendly fire," Van said. "Some friends!"

"Them gooks ain't all going to pull out, but enough of them must have," Sing responded. "We weren't hit by their expected attack. So we got to find them."

"You mean the first gun crew, and Baker company," Van retorted.

"Baker Company should be warned," Baiter taunted the assemblage, "that their backups are a gook, two porkholes and a coon."

He rose, his feet spreading his haunches wider than a bull's butt, his position a challenge.

"Coon's as much a coward as you, you yellow eyed, piss-sipper," Baiter said to Im Ta Song, keeping his eye on Brannagh. The hollow-eyed splinter of a KATUSA rose up, but Van slid in between the derrick from Texas, and the onion of the Orient. Brannagh and Dreamer rose up, too.

Baiter didn't quiver before the turbulent farmer or his three chumps, instead, he whistled a sucker right forward.

Van expected it. He slipped his head to his own right. He felt the force of whooshing air whip past his left ear as Baiter's fist bounded by. A push of the off-balanced 2d gunner turned his power to a whirlwind's exertion. Like a corkscrew, Baiter spun on his own axis, his animal shriek ringing in the ears of the bunker's rats as his back slapped onto the dirt floor. Van Meter quickly pinned Baiter's shoulders.

"There's pints of piss aplenty for you, Baiter, if you mess with my men," Van instructed.

Baiter seethed. He struggled, but the leverage and the power in the arms of the cow tit puller on his chest wasn't to be unseated. Van Meter let him up. Time would present an opportunity to scatter teeth.

*****

The 1st gun crew hadn't before seen the Baker Company front, nor known its men. There were familiar faces in Dog's Second Section of HMGs, but none volunteering to swap their line bunker for a drop off site somewhere in no-man's land. They didn't dare voice a gripe about dirty details if there was even a slight chance the new platoon leader might overhear; for Breezedale was a prick like that he was sticking to the Third section's gun crew.

There was a chill on the evening, Brannagh noted. Going out in the dark, he was glad for his new winter gear, particularly the inserts for the five fingered gloves. Others of the weapons men preferred the mittens with a trigger finger. With pile caps and parkas, the weather was nearly endurable, even on a patrol.

Several of the rises Brannagh saw to his front were almost bald; then a slope rose gently until interrupted by a series of rock outcroppings. He couldn't see a trench line for lack of light where sable sky and hill merged.

"You from Dog," a soldier asked?

The redness of lips on a face smoked with charcoal and squared by a fatigue cap stood out to the gunner like a lipstick advertisement.

"Yes," answered Brannagh.

"Follow my squad."

Preparatory details left a lot to be desired, the gunner was certain. It wasn't at all a Grant patrol with the most minimal detail studied beforehand.

"Move out," came the order.

Brannagh did, his heart leaping. He beckoned for his crew to follow. He saw Dreamer's eyes looked like two star worlds, glistening. The gunner couldn't figure whether Dreamer was delighted or fearful. There was no fear shown on the brown bark of Stag's face. Im Ta Song was as impassive as the land they walked on.

Like a snail leaving its tracing on a wall, Baker's patrol moved lightly through the wired landscape. They came clear of it; then went down to the lowest ground.

"Dog, come forward."

Brannagh brought his crew up. He saw wrinkled rolls of earth to his front, carved by wind and weather like sand dunes, that ran across his line of sight and stretched out in sleepy quietude. There could be a Chinese patrol in every crevice. The Baker leader pointed eastwardly, but Brannagh saw but blurred and indistinct features in the direction of his finger.

"Follow this defilade for thirty or so yards. There's pits there. That's the dropoff. Set up there, then watch that finger here," the squad leader said.

This time he pointed to rounded earth that went up a couple of hundred meters. Brannagh saw the small hill framed by the dirty sky. A cloud to the east was being drilled by a search light, lessening shadows. The squad leader was clear enough on his own objective. The gunner's was thirty yards over at limbo. Where was limbo?

"If there's a fire fight, I'll toss a phosphorus as

far in front of my skirmish line as I can. We're on recon, so we'll pull back. Keep us covered," the patrol leader directed. He hesitated, then spoke.

"Sorry you got the shaft," he said. "Second section said your new lieutenant's out for you and that colored guy. Frig that louie. Grant told me about you. You're okay," he said.

Brannagh didn't know whether to cheer or jeer. "We'll go set up. Give us two minutes," he said.

Whether or not the hole they were in was the pits, Brannagh cared less. It was about thirty yards removed. It afforded cover for the gun. He could see the finger clearly. He deployed Dreamer and Stag to the flanks. Im Ta Song would cover the rear. The gunner followed the movements of Baker's recon as it moved up the hill.

Stag was startled. He hoped it was a tree branch. It goosed him. He pulled out his bayonet to cut it away. Its feel was odd to his touch. He bend down to study its thickness, and he saw a hand sticking out of the dirt, its fingers stiffended into a claw. The rest of whatever was attached was buried somewhere within the mound of dirt. The ammo bearer pulled a magazine from his cartridge belt. He placed it in the pleading palm. A helping hand was always welcomed.

The gaunt grass rustled on the finger as Baker's men came trotting downslope, as if bugging.

"Ain't no Chinese up there," Baker leader said. "Ain't nothing up there but twelve empty bunkers that smell of Chinese. Hadn't been occupied for two of three days. We set the timer to blow in ten minutes. Lets get our tails out of here."

Brannagh hurried. He saw the faces of his crew that had looked weary and worn, now wore smirks. If this patrol was the measure of Breezedale's bite, then let the sorry son of a mustard plaster chew away.

The eruptions Brannagh heard from the Chinese's abandoned bunkers were thunderous, startling the reverse slope out of their sleep.

*****

Stein was delighted to be off the line. "Hell of a nice long ride back to division to hear the Rabbi," he said; "takes all day."

Brannagh had La Vie on another truck, their destination to battalion, where Father Flynn said the Mass for Catholic troops, and Chaplain Spurlock ministered to the protestants. The good priest was to have the Red Cross representative there to interview La Vie, hopefully to wrap up red tape to get him off the hill. It was a strange army they served. One could bug out off of line and get reassigned to some rear echelon job, but a guy like La Vie that wouldn't run from a cotton mouth snake, can't get back to the reverse slope.

The gunner chastised himself for bad mouthing. But for the grace of God, he hadn't yet fled. Not yet. If he did, he wished Dog Six and O'Hara might be as merciful as Charley Six. He didn't ship a man back for court martial. He reassigned him to the battalion laundry pool, leaving him there until he rotated. There was a bitter side to it though. No line troop spoke to the guy. He was an untouchable. He was shunned. It was silence in all its vicious eloquence, psychologically debilitating, but none the less merciful. No one back home ever knew, but one!

Thinking of back home, Brannagh recalled a few lines from Davis' letter. His leg wasn't amputated. There was a belief it would recover most of its vigor. He didn't mind a military limp what with all the stories he was telling the nurses about knocking out a T-34 with a machine gun. They were delighted to massage the muscles of such a humble hero. Wasn't bad at all in the hospital. What was bad was the docking of the troop ship in San Francisco, Davis had written.

"There must have been more than two thousand of us on the dock side of the ship looking for family, listening for the band. They weren't there. All that was on that broad pier was one middle aged couple, and a good looking woman, maybe twenty. We all watched from the ship's decks as a lone GI rushed off to greet the only caring people in the country, as if only they remembered we were returning from a war. Still, tears came to my eyes, I was so moved. It embarrassed me until I saw tears running down from other soldiers' eyes. Darn if the whole ship load of combat veterans wasn't crying."

"Mon ami happy for to go to church?"

"He is, indeed."

Brannagh saw a chubby civilian stood next to the robed priest.

"Danny Brannagh, my lad, and Claude La Vie," Father Flynn purred. "So glad you got here before Mass. I must depart immediately after. This is Mr. Woulfe of the Red Cross. He has good news for PFC La Vie."

"Oui," asked La Vie?

"Yes," answered the plumpish elf. "Your request has been granted. You will receive your orders by the end of October, and go home."

Brannagh watched him straddle step the way to his waiting jeep. He got in and was gone as quickly as gears could kick in.

Father didn't want to laugh. His cheeks puffed

like a bag pipe that ultimately might split under the pressure.

"Can you get La Vie off the line," the gunner asked?

"Lieutenant Breezedale promised to do so," the priest said, "when Dog receives its next replacement. That could be any time now."

"Our section sergeant believes we will attack hill 1062 soon. La Vie's replacement can't come any too soon," Brannagh said.

"La Vie will be in the CP before it happens. Lets give thanks for the life of one and pray for the repose of the souls of his four brothers," Father encouraged.

"I'll offer my Mass for them, too," the gunner replied.

La Vie was already on his knees before God with the Red battalion's troops. If smiles were wings his prayers of gratitude were flying to heaven.

*****

The sleeping bunker was taking on the qualities of a consecrated place of introspection, a sandbagged basilica, where Brannagh let his mind follow the road to a stateside paradise. Brannagh's contemplation of home brought Mom to mind, her hair as red as clouds catching the rays of a setting sun, eyes as blue as Great Lakes' water. She didn't write; she prayed for him. He wished she did both. And what of Brannagh's classmates at the seminary? Where were their letters, or just one? In Brannagh's heart there was the hurt of one forgotten.

He opened Dad's letter to read it.

"The United Nations and the Reds agreed to resume the truce talks the same day the Russian Communists exploded their third atom bomb, just a few days after President Truman approved a record military budget of nearly $57 billion. Of course, there was a tax hike, too. On the one hand the President wants a truce in Korea but prepares for war in Europe. If you are sent to Europe, Danny, maybe you can meet me in Ireland and go with me to see your sickly grandmother this November. Probably not, because the U.S. Army won't work that fast."

There was a decision to be made - between Dad and country, the gunner judged. Dad had rejected the credibility of the President and his minions, clear down to the generals of the Eighth Army. Truth among politicians was as scarce as a sunburn on New Year's Eve in Detroit, but why would combat commanders lie? Then the gunner thought of Breezedale, he of the twisted moods. He would lie like a pig laid in mud. Yet, what was attributable to Breezedale wasn't necessarily to the top brass. There was no one outside Van Meter's and Grant's squad's who had any degree of veracity when it came to the truth.

Dad's letter closed with more cogent thoughts.

"I'll be a business traveler in Ireland and the six counties this November, looking for information on the IRA'a active service units: A lad from Derry city founded Fianna Uladh while another group calls itself the Irish Republican Brotherhood. They are all opposed to the Ireland Act of 1949 which guaranteed that no part of the six counties would cease to be a part of the United Kingdom without the consent of the parliament of Northern Ireland. That is nothing other than a loyalist veto of a Irish nation. It must not stand. It will not stand. The future, with men properly equipped and trained, will not deny what the past already has."

What kind of business was Dad going to be about; what kind of information was he seeking, the gunner wondered? That crazy old man was going back to County Antrim to rejoin the IRA, Brannagh deduced.

*****

"Leopard Six calls it Operation Cacti," Singletary said.

Brannagh saw a dismal Section Sergeant. More ominous was the fear dripping from each of his words.

"Leopard Six calls it Operation Cacti," Sing repeated.

"Dog three has ordered the third section to attack with a platoon from Able Company."

Torturous maladies had kept Singletary from his men until the gnawing flame of duty made him convey the order of the brooding Lieutenant. The third section wasn't to relieve the second section of heavy thirties which was dug in with Baker Company, or the first section attached to Able. The third section was to attack with the first skirmishers. It was more than the dirty detail that Breezedale had inflicted on the 1st gun crew on the drop off, it was a diabolical detail. Sing remembered the tremulous look on O'Hara, the blanched face of Miner over Breezedale's order. It had been the way of Dog's sections to attack with their own riflemen to their checkpoint, then dig in to cover the leap frog unit. It wasn't the way of the tender cheeked officer.

"Shit," said Dreamer.

"That's garbage," added Glorio.

"Nicola Shibola," sang Im Ta Song.

Baiter was trembling. He shook his index finger at Brannagh. "You and that black rat done this," he said.

Stag stood, tall as an ancient city gate. He glowered like a burning sun. He held his bayonet.

"This black rat going to sever your head."

The shaking Baiter shivered, but grasped his own bayonet in hand, sweeping his arm in front of his chest.

The stunned silence was shattered by the click of Van Meter's weapon's safety.

"Either one of you don't put your scythes away now, third section's going to need two replacements," he said. Van held his weapon until both sheathed their bayonets. Van watched both continue to throw ponderous stares as they sat down.

Baiter felt unlike correcting Stag's misinterpretation.

Brannagh had another matter on his mind. "Breezedale said he would pull La Vie to the CP before the attack," the gunner blurted.

"I asked. Breezedale said no," answered Sing.

A gracious smile paved La Vie's face. The intervention of Brannagh was most welcomed, but he need not become a fanatic about it.

"I go."

The warming bunker was a shadowy maze of color and light in which the gunner sensed the presence of courage in La Vie.

CHAPTER NINETEEN
BATTLE ON HILL 440

Up the dark paths Brannagh and the 3d section strode toward the line of departure before dawn awoke the rear echelon from its long night's slumber. Stride by stride over hill's brows he trod slopes, passing through melting mists, toward the deep night shrouded jump off point behind second section's heavy thirties. But for the labored breathing of the climbing troops, the mountain seemed empty to him save for a gradual wind that crept by, pushing the mist into mystical forms that absorbed marching soldiers into its feathery whirls. He saw a faint gleam in the east which pierced the misty blueness, so morning's creamy splendor must be pouring its whiteness somewhere near the sea of Japan.

Singletary gave the word. While Able Company awaited day light Charley Company's recon patrol had been out the night at grid 692437 to the right of the largest tooth, hill 440, near check point 10. Grant had been ordered to stay put until the Cacti raiders relieved him. A ROK tank company would, on order, jump off from the MLR in the valley, to cut off some Chinese relief. Able third platoon would attack at 0835 hours, with third section's first gun on the right, the second gun on the left of the skirmish line, to dig in when hill 434 was seized. A second platoon of Able, with first section's heavy thirties, would leap frog and take the next check point. The final objective, Sing said, the big hill 440, was Able three's and Dog's third section. They would leap frog under cover of the first section's guns and win it.

The garbage sump was shell proof, if no direct

hit fell in, Glorio had noted. His encouragement of its occupation saw the first gun squad parked on their derrieres atop the waste of Baker Company.

"Garbage ain't so bad," Glorio lectured, "when you can hurry past it on the city streets and see the pretty girls with golden hair, or the old gray heads of the newspaper boys. Sitting around this pit is like my table at the deli, the clash and clang of the plates and pots, the crowds that knock your elbow and you spill hot coffee on your pants, the singing radio, the weeping drunk, the mocking hoodlums, the roar of the buses! I can even hear the cabbies cursing. Ah, life in New York is one long love, garbage and all!"

Grotesque, thought Brannagh, but he hadn't the mind for bantering or even loose criticism.

He too sat on garbage watching the crooked legs of riflemen scuttling toward their assembly positions. Did every rifleman have crooked legs? Probably. They were riders of sandbags; toters of back packs.

Downslope Brannagh saw witches fingers that looked like tree branches with mist dangling ornamentally. He felt a little breeze, as quiet as a brook. He heard the troops whispering for fear their sound might carry northward and startle the Chinese out of their caves, while he and the squad sat deep within the hole with its pyramidal borders, as crunched down as far as malleable flesh would allow. He saw the stars were fading into a vastness of gold. He heard the raging of hell from the objective, shells exploding above the check points from proximity fuses. He quivered. His heart chilled. Jump off was but a tick of the clock away, and time always double timed toward it.

Brannagh's eye caught Baiter's contorted body, bent double. He was in glee at the sight of first gun's hunchbacks.

"Look," the giggling Baiter hollered to the second gun squad, "ten maggots in an asshole."

The ground shook! To either side of the rapidly sober Baiter, a column of black earth and smoke rose into the air. Shrapnel had sung in every direction.

Brannagh hadn't heard the warning swish, but at the eruption balled his body. He cautiously raised his head, his eyes watching to see who arose. Baiter did. Riflemen, either side of the garbage pit, had taken hits. Medics were seen hurrying to tend to two wounded soldiers.

Lord, have mercy on them, all of us, the gunner prayed. He marvelled that, but for the sump, the first gun would have been between those two fellows, perhaps counted among the wounded in action, or worse killed in action. Lord, have mercy on them, he repeated. Deo gratias - thanks be to God, he added for the safety of the section.

Baiter jumped into first gun's trash bin where twenty tentacles caught his falling body before it hit the rubbish. They rejected him as junk. It was the first gun squads' turn for guffawing outrageously.

"Saddle up," ordered Singletary.

Brannagh had checked and rechecked his weapon, his first aid packet, his spare parts. Was his canteen full? Had he combat rations? Where was that damnable entrenching tool? He had it. It was as important a piece of gear as his helmet; both hid him from the enemy. It was a moment for prayer.

"Move out," Singletary ordered.

Brannagh heard the putt, putt of the mortars behind him. Sixty and Eighty-one millimeter tubes were belching rounds to destroy land mines and wire that might slow the infantry's advance. He saw the first molar on the long ridgeline was taking considerable artillery incoming, but it was so far away. He saw Able's platoon leader deploy his skirmishers, then heard Singletary order Van Meter's gun to the right of the skirmish line, Cervera's to the left. He saw Singletary go left with Cervera's crew the other side of the ridge. Each gun had a separate mission.

Brannagh worried more that he might fall off the nearly hand hold steep slope with its sudden perpendicular cuts, small cliffs of four or five feet drops, than get hit by Chinese emerging from cover below his feet. From the MLR, the check points looked an easy traverse, but on it, every inch of his way to check point 5 was a climb.

He heard the Chinese get busy just two hundred and fifty yards from the MLR. Their burp guns spat. Grenades, thick as mosquitoes in a swamp, flew toward the skirmishers.

"Action," called the 1st gun's leader.

Van Meter pointed to a position, slab and boulder strewn ten yards in front of him.

"Ready," Brannagh called.

"Fire at the grenades," Van ordered.

The flash of the spitting weapon lit the face of Brannagh. His tracers did their dance above the line of grenade explosions, yet the long traverse of arcing grenades continued. Brannagh sliced bullets through the Chinese's positions, but saw no silhouettes. Yet grenading by the Chinese picked up, but that of the GIs was slowing.

To his right, down a sharp incline, the corner of the gunner's eye caught movement. He turned to see.

Brannagh's shooting ceased. He slapped free the

cradle pintle clamp. His heart pounded a jazz beat.

"Swing right," he yelled.

He pushed Im Ta Song with such force Im rolled forward of their gun position. The gunner did a push up and lept in concert. He aimed due east. He ripped off a burst of six that stung stone ten yards away. He fired over the heads of La Vie, Glorio and Stag. Each clutched the earth at the craziness of the gunner.

"What you doing," Stag yelled?

"Chinese below," Brannagh warned.

He fired another burst that chewed into the cap of the drop-off. He saw two hands emerge, followed by a hatless Chinese, then followed by another. The gunner held his fire, but kept his weapon in their face. He held up his right hand with three fingers showing. Then flashed four, then five fingers on the hand, his face asking the silent question 'more', emphasized by the strong downward thrust of his index finger pointing towards the cave. His left finger never left the machine gun's trigger. The surrendering Chinese nodded a negative, then came up slope at the gunner's gesture. Van Meter took over, ordering Glorio to take the POWs back to the LD; for Stag to cook a grenade into the cave; to tickle its innards with his M 2 carbine. Stag found two dead Chinese there.

"Pull back," came Able three's command.

Van Meter was surprised, until he heard there was a method in the officer's madness: he wanted more grenades and an avalanche of incoming on those Chinese grenadiers.

Brannagh saw that the sump was full of Cevera's squad, with Baiter the largest glob of refuse situated in the safest corner next to Singletary. The gunner listened as the immense fire power immersed the area

from the MLR to the check points, its fury and violence
hurling stones through the air with an unknown
multiple the speed of fast balls. He saw the air was
filled with a pall of sulfite smoke, and earth was having
a fit. When the riflemen stood and readied their
weapons, the putt putt of the mortars turned on as if
their switch had been pulled. He heard a buzz, a
reciprocating whiz, increasing in volume. A spurt of
dirt spewed over his leg. It looked as if it was a slice of
whole wheat bread, so large was the shrapnel
embedded in the earth that had impaled his
entrenching shovel cover. It was hot to his touch. He
dimly wondered if his heart still beat.

"Saddle up," ordered Singletary. "Move out." He
watched from the garbage pit.

Van followed Able's men as they formed a
scything skirmish line under cover of Dog's second
section of heavy thirties' hammering at check point 5.
As the 3d section followed the skirmishers past the line
of grenadiers, Van saw a dreary, treeless, barren hill
ahead.

From the angry hill of check point 5 came a
heavy pouring of automatic fire. Brannagh fell on his
belly and like a worm, crawled forward towards the
cover of a shell hole. He dragged his tripod with him,
then watched as Im Ta Song turned on his back, the
weapon in his hands running the length of his torso,
while he fishtailed forward, but Dreamer casually
walked forward.

"Get down, Dreamer," warned the gunner.

Dreamer seemed oblivious to the hoarsely
whistling bullets. Brannagh used a ruse.

"Get down, Dreamer, or you won't make PFC."

The death chain which had the first ammo

bearer entangled, was broken. He got prone, then crept forward with the water can.

"Action," ordered Van Meter. "Fire on the checkpoint."

Brannagh ran lead across the horizontal trenches, while mortar rounds walked up into them. The firefight was momentarily vicious, grazing fire flying everywhere. He had his gun low on its tripod, the forward leg resting on a small puff of earth. When he squeezed off his bursts there was excessive vibration. He brushed the forward dirt feeling for loose stones. Instead he found the chest of a nearly buried Chinese. He fired another burst, the vibration seemingly giving breath back to a corpus delicto. He slid the tripod forward to straddle the dead. It steadied the gun. He picked up the close support of the advancing skirmishers, shifting fire at the safety point so that Able might take the check point in time for a lunch of cold combat rations.

Van had his squad mount its weapon on the right flank of the hill in a Chinese commo trench. He ordered his men to fire their entrenching tools like pistons. He saw shell holes everywhere. Bunkers were bashed in. Trenches had been blown down. Dead Chinese were mangled into grotesque poses. Van saw a morgue. Some had taken artillery hits, mortars took a number, but many had neat bullet holes. Broken weapons were scattered as aimlessly as their possessors were.

When Able Company jumped another squad through check point five's covering fire, Van ordered his squad of Dog's heavy thirties to toil. No return fire came in, the third section's guns going unchallenged. Van shut down when GIs ran the skyline like fools.

"Saddle up," Singletary was heard to say, "move out."

Sing's stay with the first section as it followed the skirmishers to check point 5, caught him up with his section when it dug in for overhead coverage of the leap froggers. It was his section's turn again to hop the heap towards hill 440. He elected not to go with them. He would stay with the first section at the second check point observing with binoculars. He would keep a close eye on them and keep Breezedale's radio channel warm.

Brannagh saw bearers return for the wounded Chinese, to carry them south. There wasn't time for Chinese dead. Rather than see the distorted discolored faces of the enemy's deceased, Brannagh loosened dirt from trench walls to cover as much of those mortal remains as was possible before the last push, up hill 440. Ammo, water, and supplies, brought forward by the chogie bearers, replenished each solider's depleted stores, and riflemen pocketed six to eight grenades, four bandoleers and water. There never was enough water. Brannagh felt nervous and restless.

As Able jumped off, Van's and Cervera's machine guns knocked rocks and stones from the trench lips, and any forehead that peeked to see the location of the advancing skirmishers. Riflemen fired as they advanced. Machine guns spoke above their heads. Tracers looked like hot fireflies pricking the sky where the Chinese trench wound like a snake upwards toward a formidable bunker.

Van saw a ring of fire from a monster dug out on the crest. The fire from there grew fiercer, plugging the tide of GIs. To move forward was a plunge into the teeth of barracuda. Van Meter had his gun throw in a heaving flood of rounds but the courageous hosts of the hill top hurled back a mad swell of automatic fire and grenades.

Across the sweeping ridgeline, Brannnagh witnessed a solitary hump backed soldier fling himself recklessly toward death on the crest. Leaping trenches, jumping boulders, this GI dashed with the nozzle of his flame thrower in hand to roast the heavy machine gun kicking GI butt in the horseshoe curve of the commo trench up to the bunker. Like a posed photograph for a Hollywood movie, the holder of the flame thrower stood at the enemy's gun hole amidst exploding grenades. He aimed his nozzle, then tried again and again to let its flame free. It trickled like a little kid taking a pee.

Brannagh's shooting erupted into a frenzy at the spectacle of the soldier ripping the flame thrower from his back in the attempt to escape down a defilade from a hail of lead and grenade fragments. Then he fell, plunging downward into a deep abyss. As if in salute, there was a momentary cease fire from both sides.

Brannagh heard Dreamer's scream. The gunner was astonished at the sight of the first ammo bearer running down the side of the check point. Dreamer was bugging out. He disappeared down the cut stone drop on the eastern slope of the ridgeline.

"La Vie," hollered Van. "Take over as first ammo bearer. Fire," he ordered his gunner.

There wasn't time to lament the loss of Dreamer. Brannagh's waves of tracers resumed the chafing of the crest bunker which swept the trench lines with its own lead in disdain. He saw a strange block of lumpy construction that lurched out at all who gave challenge on its windy, treeless pinnacle for mastery of the hill.

Strikingly dominating the ridgeline again was another humpback Soldier. Brannagh took a second look. The gait was the same as the last one. It was the same guy! He had risen from the dead. He was carrying the flame of hell on his back. His repeat presence woke up the skirmishers. His flashing torrent of liquid flames forced the enemy back from their gun holes, his shafts of fire sizzled some reddened frames and burning mats of straw. Brannagh watched him fling his flaming tool at the one he had left behind, then fall, rolling down the sharp slope like a prostrate log. The gunner felt the shock waves when the subdued flame thrower erupted like Vesuvius' shriek across the crest. GIs charged, loosening a hot hell on the objective.

Any Chinese who could bug out, Brannagh saw, was dashing down the long finger slanting away from his gun. He shifted his fire into their flight, slicing the fleers apart until there were but three who still chanced the accuracy of his fire. Each fell, rolling forward as did the prostrate flamethrower.

"Be not down there," said Dreamer.

It was as if a mouth had opened beneath the dispersed squads holes and spit out the filthy Dreamer like a peach pit. He was deeply sliced across his cheeks where grains of small stones had taken refuge.

"Be lost!" said Dreamer!

Too stunned by the shock of what he had written off as a bug out, Brannagh laid still behind his gun.

Van Meter composed himself.

"Who was lost," he asked?

"Flame thrower be lost. Not down there." Dreamer pointed downslope. "Didn't find him."

"You went down there to recover him?"

"Yea."

Van Meter quickly overcame his confusion. He had a hero on his hands, not a soldier who had fled in the face of the enemy. Dreamer wouldn't get a medal for it, medals were for few on the front line, but he would get his first ammo bearer job back.

"La Vie?"

"Mon Sergeant?"

"The water can to Dreamer, si vois plait."

"Oui," the impressed La Vie said.

"Move out," ordered Van Meter. "They want the section dug in on 440 along with first section. They expect the Chinese to counterattack. Love Company's on its way out to relieve us."

"When" asked Swinford?

"At 1730 hours; three hours from now," Van said.

Brannagh shuddered. He knew that arithmetical time changed to geometrical proportions on a newly conquered hill while waiting for a counterattack. It should come long before Love's relief.

He dug like a construction laborer. The horseshoe bend in the commo trench was cleared of its dead. Bloody stones were covered with dirt that was as lightly colored as the drab ocher brown of the the nearly gaunt hills. He saw the sun had moved west.

Brannagh's eyes studied his field of fire around the crest of the saw toothed peaks which lined the long ridgeline like a dinosaur's backbone. He saw a natural barricade which spiked his front fifty yards out. It looked to him like the blackened turret of a tank. He had Im Ta Song and Dreamer dig with fury. If he had to defend this dreadful precinct of the horseshoe bend on the crest, Brannagh would construct a battlement for all eternity.

His whole front was seething. The enemy was still popping away with mortars. Their fire was going long. Momentarily, it did no damage. Sooner, not later, a Chinese FO would adjust and fire for effect. Somewhere, Brannagh heard a machine gun sputtering. The last throes of a barrel burning out from overfiring. The gunner hoped it was a Chinese's. Suddenly, fire crackled to his left. Probably some nervous GI. There wasn't any return fire. He looked up and down the horseshoe bend. His was the only bunker that had been strongly rebuilt, the others were merely remodeled, but the commo trenches looked as if they had been replowed. He took comfort in a deep trench. He would take additional comfort in new logs, sandbags and rolls of barbed wire hung from pickets downslope, with trip flares, booby traps and mines. Would that a fourgass were rigged; its fifty-five gallon barrel of gasoline and napalm triggered by detonator and explosives, and roast to charcoal hamburgers a ten yard front of enemy. Chogie bearers were flooding the trenches, dropping off fragmentation grenades, boxes of ammo, bandoleers, combat rations. Brannagh had one refill his canteen. He had them drop off ten ammo cans before they moved up the trench line toward the burned out remnants of the fortified crest.

He heard a whistle behind the blackened hump just down slope. Then he saw them, enemy riflemen crawling to the tall rock, wiggling along depressions in the ravine riven land. It was their turn to try the hill.

A ghostly stomping rushed down the trench line behind the first gun's position; Brannagh turning. He grabbed his carbine to ward off the assumed infiltrators.

Im Ta Song recognized the frozen fearful faces

as those of the Chogie bearers just gone up the hill.

"No shoot, Chogie," he cried to Brannagh.

Brannagh watched a fleeing fold of sheep lashing at one another to beat their way away from the incoming blasts. They flew past, screaming. They would not be prey of the Chinese.

Dreamer screamed and bolted down the trench line, too.

"Nicola Shibola," muttered Im Ta Song!

The gunner blinked. Just when he had attributed a dauntlessness to the musty soldier, he had fled again. The gunner arched tracers into their red line of skirmishers. Brannagh walked his fire in bursts of six. Their exchange of bullets was becoming a noisy roar. Mortars were clobbering both sides. Yet above the din Brannagh could hear cries coming from serrated flesh.

"Medic, medic," someone, somewhere shouted.

"Litter bearer. Where are the litter bearers," came a voice?

"Bugged out," was a distant reply.

"Be moving," came the roaring voice.

Brannagh turned and saw Dreamer, his bayonet ladened carbine pointed at the backs of the chogie bearers.

"Be moving up," growled Dreamer.

He raised his weapon. He fired a burst to give emphasis to his command. His litter bearers went to their rounds as inscrutably as their captor.

The gunner was conscience stricken. Dreamer was a riddle without a single clue.

Brannagh kept up his fire. Chinese continued to answer. Grenades continued to send shreds and chips from rocks to render flesh. All around the perimeter

Brannagh felt the fighting instensify. Out front, Brannagh saw the big rock crawl and a buffalo gun peer from behind the turret like boulder. He flushed a morse code of bursts at it until the anti tank weapon keeled over like a dead vulture.

Dreamer's stomping in the trenches was as loud as a platoon, and Brannagh turned to see him pass by again.

"Be back soon," Dreamer said.

"I'll look for you," Brannagh answered.

Steel flew through the thunderous cordite cloud that engulfed Dreamer. His body, as if born on an ocean's tall wave, washed from the trench line. Brannagh saw him torn, his litter bearers fleeing, still with their wounded.

Brannagh gave his gun to Im Ta Song. The gunner rushed to the legless corpse and pulled Dreamer's torso into the trench. Without a thought, Brannagh lept from the trench to recover Dreamer's severed legs, returning them to the hot blood that spouted from Dreamer's thighs.

"Medic," Brannagh screamed. "Medic!"

Doc Block knew death. The long last heave of Dreamer's chest had been breathed. There was no pulse.

Close quarters fighting snuffed out the few Chinese attackers who made it through Baiter's and Im Ta Song's tracers, or the flakes of snowballing grenades. The attack was beaten off.

*****

Brannagh, Van Meter, Cervera and La Vie carried Dreamer home, the section following in a funeral procession. They walked past the binoculared Breezedale.

"Salute, Lieutenant," said Brannagh.

"He was just a private," the Lieutenant whined.

"The private's entitled," growled Van Meter.

*****

"Saddle up," said a drunk Singletary. "We're going out to 440 with Charley three and the Raiders. We'll relieve Love Company at 0700 hours."

Van Meter worried that the ever increasingly anxious section leader wouldn't make it out to the hill again, much less back. Sing had been through contradictory times crowned by a double jolt of combat; and he was a very short timer. He had lost his shield of invulnerability, Van realized.

Sing told them of the casualties. Able alone had taken sixteen casualties, two of them medics on 440. Love was hurt as well in repelling two counterattacks, and absorbing Chinese heavy mortar fire coming from the reverse of hills 448 and 598. Love's casualty count had reached twenty-six.

Van knew heavy mortar's continued the drilling leading to the high ground. He wondered if Sing could go. Return to the horseshoe bend on the crest would be a run through a punch press. No wonder that Singletary fretted. He had had too many close calls. The innundation of hill 400 under Chinese shelling was certain to present more than a few additional ones; just after the resumption of the truce talks, too. Van Meter worried about the Sergeant First Class. He had lost his self confidence. He sensed his luck had been topped, his war had lost its importance, his poker games had lost their players. His was a lone hand.

"It's another dirty detail," Blacyzk said. "The word had it the new shavetail again had volunteered Sing's section to battalion last night, after regiment had ordered the relief of Love's platoons."

"How do you know that," asked Brannagh?

"Miner was there. He drove Breezedale to Battalion. Miner told me," Blaczyk said.

It was abnormally quiet on the reverse slope. There were dancing lights on the eastern horizon.

"You smart asses funned that officer. He's sticking it to all of us," Blaczyk rumbled.

Brannagh felt uneasy. He sensed he was being watched by each guy. He tried to collect his thoughts. He didn't want to believe Breezedale was intent on mangling a whole section for chasing cooties and killing a rat. Wasn't it a joke?

Stag, too, was restless. It wasn't the distant rumbling on hill 440 that triggered his nervous system; it was his recollection of Breezedale's humor with the old deuce four.

"If I live to be a hundred, I'll never forget the sight of Breezedale up on the hill last September with the twenty fourth regiment. We had rigged white phosphorus, some Chinese concussion grenades, and gun powder together, waiting for him when he made his weekly visit to our night position. When he approached the crest, we tripped it. There was a fury of red, black, green, blue and purple clouds rolling in toward him all at once, like all hell was after him. He was smothered in its folds. He must have thought that he had gone to hell itself. Then came the most horrifying sound I ever heard, like that when the rat tap danced on his face. It was an inhuman shriek."

Stag gave his head a negative nodding.

"Breezedale was demented with anger. He swore to put us into hell. If you wonder where hell is, its 440."

Blaczyk was contorted into a jack knife, knees

doubled up under his chin, his chin on his knees, his arms roping his legs.

"You smart asses funned him, not me," he said.

"Five minutes," said Singletary.

"First gun, move out."

Brannagh saw Dreamer in every cave and crater toward 440. The gunner heard Dreamer rustling, murmuring, even speaking. The first ammo bearer never understood the usage of verbs. He spoke in the present tense. Brannagh cursed himself for his affrontery to Breezedale. Together, they had devoured an innocent.

A seventy-six cracked a round overhead, chipping plaque off the third tooth. Eight of the squad went prone. Romaine was as tall as a basketball center.

"Keep your head down, Recruit," Stag warned.

Romaine folded to his haunches. When a bullet cracked over his head he was as flat as a pancake.

"Ain't a man in the squad what's not pushing rocks with his nose when incoming comes. Just watch me, Recruit. I hit earth, you hit earth, got it," said Stag.

"Got it," Romaine answered.

He was glad for the attention. He felt as if few seemed to know he was there. The guys would laugh and joke in the warming bunker, but only the gunner and the squad leader had taken time to talk. If those two hadn't given him a feeling of welcome, he would have had no comfort. He wasn't even included in the joke on that jerk officer. Only Brannagh had so much as offered him a beer. Romaine wondered when his invisibility would end, when he would be treated like a combat infantryman? When his own veins would again run with pride like when he exchanged his football uniform for the army infantry's cross rifles? Hadn't he paraded town to accept the deification of a football star turned his Uncle's soldier? Bristling with a sharpshooter's metal, blue piping on his cap, hadn't he got back for the prom at the high scool, drank at roadhouses, and tore up and down the streets in his dad's Dodge? Hadn't he pretty cheerleaders all the hot days of his leave? He felt a soldier then. He wasn't anyone in this outfit.

"Move out," ordered Van Meter.

Brannagh saw that Love Company had strung barbed wire. The strands on the stakes were silhouetted like lattice windows, its stringing no mean detail. Chinese casualties were strewn about the wire around the horseshoe bend to the high point, like flat pavement stones. He saw a Chinaman laying on the reverse lip of the trench, groaning. Little wonder, thought the gunner, there wasn't much of a being remaining. His left arm was gone; its tourniquet had lost its purpose. His legs were mangled. His bloody face had an opened eye. His right hand formed a finger pistol against his temple. All the energy in the man pleaded for execution.

Brannagh couldn't do it.

"What's he want," asked Grant?

"Coup de gras," answered La Vie.

Old soldiers studied one another. The nod from the man of China to the man of America translated into a theme of chivalry. Grant sent him to a revoluntionary mansion.

The shells fell with rain drop frequency, as if the execution had rended clouds. The hillside turned into a blazing inferno. Brannagh's eyes caught more dirt than his entrenching tool. He remounted his gun in the horseshoe bend bunker he had left behind the day before yesterday. Its roof beams had sagged a bit, but would take a direct hit. He and Im Ta Song hurried their sand bagging of the forward aperture. Someone had opened it too widely. Brannagh heard two or three explosions in sequence, a ten or twenty second interval, then two or three more roared in. The time between rounds seemed to be lessening.

More mortars cracked the earth near him. Brannagh pulled his tripod back so the gun wasn't protruding through the aperture like a lightening rod if spotted by a Chinese forward observer.

The enemy barrage was incessant, the flashes of orange casting a Halloween tinge around him.

"Confiteor Dei omnipotenti - I confess to almighty God," was Brannagh's continuation of prayer.

He caught a movement in the trench. He looked and saw Romaine. He stood up on a firing step.

"Get down," yelled the gunner.

He swore he saw a smile as Romaine tumbled off into the trench.

Brannagh crawled quickly to the fallen ammo bearer. Stag rolled Romaine over. Doc saw a shrapnel hole in the forehead, neat, bloody.

"Wasn't of much use telling the recruit to keep his head down," said Stag in awe.

"What was his name," asked Block?

"Romaine," answered Brannagh.

Brannagh made the sign of the cross over Romaine.

"Was he Catholic," the Doc asked?

"Yea," answered Brannagh. "He went with me and La Vie to Mass, we talked of high school football, but La Vie and I got so busy with the Red Cross, we forgot about Romaine. I'm sorry that we didn't get to really know him."

A crushing explosion rocked the very floor of the trench. Stag dragged Romaine out of the trench into his position.

"Mama shouldn't get you home all mangled up like a prune," Stag said to Romaine.

Brannagh scurried like the rat in his MLR bunker did to get back to a safe hole.

"They're getting closer," he whispered to Im.

Im Ta Song acknowledged it. He felt he was being asphyxiated by the fumes from the constant shelling. He felt he was being made demented from concussion.

Brannagh figured the medics were tempting longevity. Both Sugrue and Block were traversing the horseshoe bend quick as crawling chipmunks. Their time at treatment kept them in a perpetual crawl or squat on haunches as low as frogs as they went from man to man.

A massive convulsion near the crest rolled a huge bolder down slope, and across the trench line, but Van's constantly whistling phone brought more anger than a near miss from a crushing stone.

"Look Lieutenant Breezedale, if you want a count of Chinese bodies, send up an accountant."

There was a long pause on the phone.

"I'm afraid, am I," Van responded in a bitter tone? "You're damned right I'm afraid, but I'm out here. Where the hell are you?"

A deafening roar echoed from the left side of the perimeter near the 2d gun squad. Some ears over there wouldn't hear another one, the gunner was sure. It was his worst day of war, this October 27 was. The Chinese were on the high ground, and Brannagh among the besieged. What a twist of tactics, he thought. He couldn't displace from these thoughts the recollection of Edgewater Park's shooting galleries. How many nickels that he had made from his Free Press paper route had he spent paying for turns behind the imitation machine gun that shot light flashes at enemy fighter planes? Well now, he knew what that airplane's pilot felt like. An awful load of Chinese firepower kept coming in. Van and Grant hung in there, keeping up whatever morale was left in targeted soldiers. Why the eyes of those squad leaders turned black while they chewed out a careless soldier was a mystery of leadership the gunner swore one day he would research - if he lived that long. He marvelled that the sound of ruptured shells sent out an echo of a hollow distant rumbling of a thunderstorm.

Corney was heard hollering for Doc Sugrue. The whole line listened as the rifleman extolled the miracle of the shrapnel that had sanded his back teeth smooth, the same as his incisors, without a trace of pain or blood. Corney's vulgar exclamations on St. Paul's dentist were cut off when he fainted.

The Chinese seemed to have 440 plotted to its square root. Brannagh felt that nature itself, however, wasn't up to getting him out of his steel pot when a rumble billowed clouds of debris that fell into the trench line around him and Charley Company.

Thirst was as rampant as the shelling. Refilling a canteen meant a crawl to the jerrican at Van Meter's hole. Brannagh saw Swinford chance it. He started his crawl just as a mortar round came in. He flew through the air towards the squad leader, then rolled over like a turtle. He pulled off his pack. It was in shreds. He flashed his half moon grin, got his water, and got the hell back to his hole.

The ground shivered again, this time rattling the machine gun's ammo belt. Im checked it.

Pocaski kept up the squeezing off of rounds as if he were back at a known distance rifle range. No way was he going to let the Chinese think there weren't fighting men on the buttoned up perimeter. Charley three three was there, Pocaski proclaimed.

The thunder of incoming swelled with no crescendo evident to Brannagh.

Blaczyk held his spoon in hand. Something had pulverized his last can of horded C-rations. He saw it splattered all over. He was giving thought to spooning off the butt of his carbine for chow, rather than wiping it clean.

The Chinese were obviously working on the violent relocation of hill 440, the gunner figured. He prayed for an end to the shelling. He knew if the shelling shifted or ceased, a counterattack would certainly follow.

A thunderclap at his head flung him as if he were a limp wrist against the far wall of the horseshoe bend. He stared at the silent swirling cloud mushrooming above him. He had entered its silent world. He saw Im Ta Song bleeding from his nose, but he was alive.

"I must be alive," Brannagh exclaimed!

He wondered where his words went. He hadn't heard himself talk. He couldn't hear whatever it was that Im Ta Song was saying. A glance at the gunner's field jacket saw red. He was splashed all over with gore. He moved his hands down his body, then back up. He couldn't find the wound. Nothing hurt but his ears. Someone had hit his ears with a sledge hammer. He felt them, but nothing leaked but his nose. Whose blood was it? He saw Gibbard's radio laid smashed up the line, Crane's BAR on the trench floor. The gunner saw the two men were shattered, seemingly impaled on the back wall of the commo trench. It was their blood, their flesh that covered him.

Brannagh saw his roof had disappeared, its sand bags bled. His machine gun was a twisted end-iron. Somehow he and Im Ta Song had escaped the deadly splinters of the 120 millimeter round that killed riflemen up the horseshoe bend, and wounded those down the angled line. The gunner gave thanks for the roof, for life. For the dead, he prayed for the repose of their souls.

The Chinese infantry came. They loomed across the barbed wire. Brannagh gave Crane's BAR life again.

Grant's defensive line poured out fire. Bullets and grenades raked the attackers. They went down in heaps, replaced by new forms looming in place of the front runners. They were stopped.

Van Meter answered Sing's call to come down the line. Van heard wounded crying, some for themselves, some for others.

"We being pulled out," said Singletary.

"Who's relieving," Van Meter wanted to know?

"No one. The brass don't want 440 no more, pass it on," Singletary instructed.

Van Meter hurried back up the trenches to do it when hundreds of anvils split and hissed as their steel hurled down the horseshoe bend at him, an unseen cascade. The quick flash of blue green light led the train of noise he heard. The ground began jerking him all around and about. He was thrown into a crater spooned the size of a farm pond. For two or three seconds he waited for the train's wheels to hit him, too.

Cautious helmets oozed out of fighting holes like newly hatched turtles out of sea sand. Doc Block crept on his hands and knees past Brannagh's gun hole.

Brannagh motioned for Im Ta Song to take the guard. The medic, with the gentleness of a surgeon, cut open Van Meter's field jacket, then Van's shirt and undershirt that freed puckered folds of bloody flesh. Brannagh saw his squad leader's clothes had the color of dark brown hay in flames; the first aid packet's whiteness had changed to the colors of autuum leaves. Van Meter had his hands pressing the bandage to his stomach, his fingers as red as roman candles fired the night of his nation's day of independence. Brannagh saw a snowy color stealing over Van's countenance even as Doc Block worked a vein to feed plasma beneath a pall of a sulfite cloud.

"Well, Brannagh," Van Meter coughed, "that must have been the heaviest round of the day."

The gunner saw Van's lips move, but sound wasn't visible. A look to Block for a repetition was useless. Brannagh realized he couldn't hear. His hand movements conveyed the malady of his sense of sound.

"Chinese must suspect something was up out here. They must suspect relief," he said.

Van Meter's voice grew fainter. Block lowered his head toward Van's. Doc had Brannagh do the same.

"Write my grandpa, Brannagh. Write he should use my insurance money for a tractor," Van sighed.

Brannagh saw lips in pantomime. He saw the fire in Van's eyes melt away; burning flesh turn to cold ash.

Medic Block found no pulse. He stopped the flow of plasma, but his own blood lept, his own pulse beat faster. In these gun pits all wild with wrath, he thought, soldiers who never met before, directed cannons and weapons to bruise, wound and kill one another. It was madness to fight for choice humpty backs to shoot from to kill one another. There was no end, for across the next valley rose a chain of other peaks clear through Manchuria. Was the well being of America more assured on any one high peak as opposed to another? What madness must occupy the minds of those who talk a truce resting on one peak or another.

Dreamer was dead. Romaine was dead. Van Meter was dead. Singletary was near the point of delirium. Brannagh was deaf. Block had read that war was a tree of bitterness grown from evil roots. He knew it was so!

Grant jostled the gunner from the wake.

"Pull out," he said, "Carry Van with you."

Brannagh tried to read lips, but couldn't with any certainty. The medic heard. he related signs that the gunner grasped at once.

Grant wanted an orderly withdrawal. He had his 3d squad cover the right side of the hill, while the Raiders put a squad over on the left. They were his covering force for the two platoons. He didn't need to goose anyone to pull out. He did, however, check that they brought their dead, equipment and ammo. Satisfied, he called in massive artillery and heavy mortar fire, coordinating its impact to follow on his heels. He kept a wall of shrapnel between his men and the pursuing Chinese.

Grant had an idea. He used the Raider's radio. He needed certain supplies at the first knob. His troops would hold, then bug back quickly, as if the first knob was their last stand. Instead, it was to be a fake. They would hesitate there, but come home. If the Chinese assaulted, he would give them his surprise.

Grant saw enemy on three of the four teeth of the ridge despite GI artillery murmuring in the dark. Their line of shadows could be seen through the blackening yonder, like phantoms from oblivion. They were pursuing more than the night. He smouldered that they thought the night was in their favor; that on the breast of the last tooth the remnants of the cowardly Americans they wanted would be overrun.

Grant faked his fight, but ran from the first check point, leaving four fifty pound charges of TNT. With the majesty of imperturbable infantry attacking the enemy's last strong point, Grant admired the Chinese that didn't hesitate to attack up the knob's slope. When they took the crest, Grant enfolded them forever in the power of unfurled destruction. All movement ceased on the long ridgeline.

CHAPTER TWENTY
OPERATION MESABI

Nothing was in Brannagh's intellect that wasn't first in his senses. He felt a breeze. He tasted a c-ration. He saw glimmering waves of power when a friendly round fell on the foe. He smelled the stench of its cordite, but his head hurt and ears so rang, he just couldn't hear its thunder.

Night guard had its perils even with all five senses acute to an infiltrator, but if he couldn't distinguish the shrill of a whistle, was he dangerous? He fretted about it. Perhaps the ringing would soon pass with an absence of explosive weaponry.

The sky was a pale grey with long thin clouds floating by like lines on note book paper, Brannagh saw. He felt utterly alone. Im Ta Song slept across the trench from him; a Dreamer unclaimed, would sleep where ever graves registration chanced; Romaine would rest in a shrine beneath a cemetery's blue shrouded trees; Van Meter in perfect ease would be near home's plowed fields.

Brannagh composed mental letters to their next of kin. For Van Meter's Grandpa, the gunner would write that Van was a heavy thirty machine gunner who closed and killed, though he didn't give a damn for killing the enemy. Grandpa should know that Van talked of home's red maple leaves; gold in the birches; noisy tractors passing by on the rutted farm roads, their dust falling on corn sleeping in rows. Van talked of the farm's weeping willows and the gorgeous gloom of its poplars. He talked of the tractor Grandpa needed. He wanted Grandpa to get it.

Brannagh felt but an atom in the whole of the

high black shadowed sky composing about lives whose flames were too soon snuffed. To Romaine's parents a letter might tell that their son's yearning to be an infantryman was that of the brave to serve his country. The Romaines should know he remembered their cheers when beneath the broken clouds of November a forward pass on fourth and fourteen in the last quarter came out of a furrow in the sky into his outstretched fingers as he crossed the goal line to win the state championship. The Romaines should know he remembered their cheers when he shipped out to Korea. He cherished those cheers above all else.

To whom might Dreamer's letter be addressed? He was one who came alone into the Army and rattled around like an empty nut. Brannagh remembered that in First Corinthiam God chose those the world considered absurd to shame the strong. Dreamer might have been born into a life of futility, but he never lost hope. He was good seed among thorns, whose eyes were closed and backs turned. Yet Dreamer had taken root among these rocks at Kumhwa. He did for others what they hadn't done for him. Nothing compared to the glory revealed by this First Class Private.

Those were the thoughts Brannagh yearned to transcribe if his hands weren't under his mind's mysterious freezer. Those were the words he let flow into the lonely dark and cold running river of forgotten recollections.

*****

"Hear the word," Singletary proclaimed to his gathered section in the warming bunker! "The good word has rotation points down to 35."

Sing's blond hair had lightened, not under the sun, but from stresses' agency. Brannagh took note of

Sing's irritability, his unfriendliness, his sullen withdrawal.

The gunner excused Sing. He was a short timer who would soon rotate. Of more concern than Singletary's personality was Sing's successor - coffee bean Cervera and his choices for squad leader. One of the squads would be under the iron rule of the Texan. He could skin a man from his own brain like an Indian did a scalp. The other squad should get Trout. The one was a sex fiend, the other a complete nut. Watt might want the job if he got control of Sing's money making. Blaczyk belonged to the UAW. He wouldn't take a squad without collective bargaining. Brannagh knew he was no squad leader. He was only a PFC and hard of hearing, but he didn't want to go off the hill. He felt his hearing was clearing up. If so, why was he trying to read Sing's lips?

Singletary moved his lips again. "Grant and three volunteers just came back off the four check points looking for three dead left behind by Love Company. They brought one back."

Brannagh was relying on Glorio's notes to clarify Sing's words. He read - 'Grant's volunteers recovered one Love KIA from 440.'

Glorio was fascinated by Grant, Charley's top rifle squad leader. If those guys left on 440 were known to be dead there was no obligation to collect them, Glorio figured. Why did Grant risk himself for the dead? It came to Glorio those dead guys weren't garbage to be tossed aside. Pride swelled in the New Yorker as he realized he was in an outfit that took care of its troops, bringing their dead back with them. Glorio excused Love. They had had their bowels riddled by Chinese confetti. They were punch drunk! Glorio shared their feeling. Weren't they all crushed in the dump called 440? It would be a dark faced day the spirit of Grant didn't bless this outfit, Glorio concluded.

Singletary continued. "We ain't going to get any more replacements on this hill." He ignored the groan. "We'll get four back in blocking on Monday after we're relieved by Blue."

If assholes smiled, Baiter's must be puckering, the first gun's gunner reflected as he saw delight recolor the war paint of the man's face. Something was up, or else the guy with the pederastic passion was going on R & R. Brannagh tugged at Glorio's sleeve. He wrote, 'going off the hill tomorrow - 3d battalion is relieving.'

The gunner tried to smile but three months of Kumhwa had left wounds for which he had no salve.

"Sing," Brannagh shouted. "Did La Vie's orders come down?" The gunner was unaware of his loudness. The sounds he mostly heard were the pitches from birds of prey continually ringing his door bell. His was a hearing loss from the extraordinarily loud reverberations of incoming having done a Gene Krupa on his eardrums. The whirring, whistling, roaring, hissing ringing in Brannagh's ears were Krupa's sidemen. Brannagh didn't understand the dismay on Sing's brooding kisser. So the gunner looked to Glorio for the explanation.

'Loud!!!' wrote Glorio, 'too loud. Every Chinese on 440 heard you.'

It was a revelation to Brannagh. He wasn't hearing well; now he talked in shouts. He was losing control of two of his senses.

"Tell him Breezedale said he didn't get no order on La Vie." Singletary hesitated, then continued, "but he got Operation Order 26, the battle for 1062. D-Day is Wednesday."

Brannagh looked from fearful face to fearful face. He discerned the words from Im Ta Song's lips were the usual. The rest of the faces were showering other priceless gems of a similar profane nature.

'No orders for La Vie, but orders to attack 1062,' Glorio wrote, 'after Halloween.'

Glorio wrung his hands. Cervera crossed himself, the gunner saw. He gave La Vie a look of pity.

"The 1st battalion is being attached to the 14th regiment." Sing said. "As soon as the 7th Infantry Division is in place, Leopard and the Wolfhounds go together."

Sing sensed the stark reality of the horror ahead on 1062. The 25th Division would take the hideous crest with Leopard's iron claws, but there would be a pile of broken bones and bodies on its slopes.

"The brass call it Operation Mesabi."

Brannagh saw Sing was shaking as he left the reverse slope bunker.

*****

Singletary lost his balance. He fell down on his bunker's matted floor. He was nervous, even jumpy. He hoped he could crawl to his cot, even if he couldn't sleep. Lord knew he felt low. He had a battle to do before he got off the hill. Yet the truce talks had resumed on October 25, the day Able and his Dog heavies took hill 440. The word was the delegates had agreed to the resumption of meetings of the subdelegates about the line of demarcation, but that the negotiators toyed with each other to see who would present the first proposal. Of course the U.N. did, but the Chinese took it home overnight. Next day while

Love and Mike Companies were beating off counterattacks on hill 440, the Chinese put forward a new proposal. Of course the U.N. took that home overnight. On the third day he lost Van, Dreamer, and the new kid; Grant lost Gibbard and Crane, but the damnable negotiators weren't arguing over land at Kumhwa that Dog had fought for over those days. The negotiators were arguing over land at Kaesong and a four kilometer demilitarized zone based on the MLR. Leopard Six never expected to hold hill 440.

Sing sensed another betrayal on hill 1062. He stared at nothingness. He wanted to sleep, but he was shaking instead. He worried the line of demarcation would remove the pressure, not on his men, but on the Chinese. If the U.N. negotiators didn't agree to the line on the MLR instead of the 38th parallel, then who wanted a truce, the Chinese or Americans? The Communists had tricked the United Nations for a soft reply.

*****

Cook Koenig watched his men stumble down the slope, their long distance stares bearing the aura of dim headlights. He rejoiced to have his own men around his chow line. His good cooking pumped up morale, but his own heart was heavy at seeing fewer from the third section's first gun at chow than had gone up to the MLR forty-one days before. The old earth might grow tender grass, but it was but a pillow for cold heads.

Koenig had the idea that the true solution of the Korean war was to get the negotiations out of the hands of the men who were the nominal, but not the real, meat cutters. Peking and Washington maintained dominance, acting not for the men in the field, but for the meat markets back home that were making money

from it.
*****

Cervera told his men now that it was under the command of the 14th regiment, the battalion was to move into blocking with its machine gun sections to ready weapons and positions, for the moment, in support.

Cervera sensed the power in the dispersed squads of GIs moving towards the assembly area, squad members apart at five yard intervals. He wasn't a single clothes pin on a long clothes line, but one of an organized blooded group acting together. Each member of his squad was under the eye and subtle influences of his squad buddies, known personally by those who would remember any wavering. His squad had its values! In a fire fight, his squad, the section and the platoon were important, were together. Each man yielded to the psychology of the squad which swept him on, which acted in unison. Each of third section's squads acted as a team. For in a fire fight Cervera had learned, these men needed the rock of unity to which they held fast, fighting to their front, supporting those on their flanks.

Cervera had heard the Battalion was the last command position. Its four companies were to meet the enemy head on and stop their attack, then hurl the enemy back in confusion begetting a conviction of inferiority from the break up of its units. When the enemy's parts didn't function, his hope of victory vanished. The wisest plans of Lightening Six, of Leopard Six and of Red Six, their most thorough preparations, their most brilliant guidance would avail nothing unless the line companies were ready, their platoons in place, their squads ready to fight. It was the

355

squad leader, Cervera realized, that led men towards sandbagged mausoleums. Squad leaders took their serpentine files up the hill into blocking positions where work was begun on improving them. Cervera felt he was ready to do his duty one last time.

He saw the tankers below were huffing. Damage sustained from Chinese box mines had increased. Sometimes two or three of them had been planted beneath a road but inserted from a side ditch. The Chinese were known to bore holes, dig out a small tunnel, then slide in the box mines which couldn't be seen from the road's surface. The Chinese even dug at sharp turns of the road, or at a culvert, or in a sandy wash out. A sandy spot was easy to camouflage. Even when engineers were sent out with infantry patrols to sweep the roads, too often their probing failed to penetrate deeply enough, or couldn't penetrate rocky, hard surfaces of some roads. Engineers were gutsy troops alright, Cervera agreed, but their mine detectors were ineffective where a mine was deep. If a detector's sensors were turned up sufficiently to pick up a mine, it also registered on every bit of foreign material in a road bed. If they dug each such time, delays were as effective as the mine field. Cervera praised these tankers and their engineers. Infantrymen needed tankers, and tankers needed the infantry.

*****

Blaczyk fretted about who his new squad leader would be. If he were Brannagh, there'd be no end to the misery, and the guy wasn't even in Kumhwa three weeks when he was made the gunner. Blaczyk hadn't wanted the gun. He didn't want the squad either. Both spots were lightning rods. All he ever wanted from this man's army was corporal stripes on an intact body and an honorable discharge. Yet Blaczyk fretted over Brannagh and Breezedale. There had been too many rusted fenders dumped on the 1st gun squad since the fool funning. Then, the Detroit guy was educated and tough, but stupid for jerking the lieutenant's bell; and stupid for taking the gun when his rotation was still months in the distance.

Blaczyk liked the nippy air of late October. It reminded him of the home he expected to see in February. Back in South Bend then, the street department would have Western Avenue cleared of deep snow. He saw himself dressed in full field gear - his parka over his field jacket, his helmet over his pile cap, his field trousers over his wool trousers, mittens on, full field pack supporting his duck down sleeping bag, shoe pac over his ski socks, his web belting holding his canteen, first aid packet and entrenching tool, his carbine at right shoulder slung, his right hand holding its strap, his left hand carrying an ammo box - walking into Studebaker's to reclaim his job. The grandson of Polish immigrants smiled. A solo parade was the epitomy of patriotism. Maybe he would rotate in February.

*****

It was a reunion of sorts. At least Harrison came from the disbanded deuce four. Otherwise, Stag realized they were on the opposite sides of emancipation. Stag's ancestors were in West Virginia when it was still a part of Virginia and had stayed there as tenant farmers, then into the coal mines. Harrison on the other hand was from Chicago where his daddy jumped the train before the railroad bulls ran him off. Harrison had come up pretty tough until the army selected him for its service. He told it's officers didn't want anything but his butt; its enlisted men, his money. So he just got so that he did little else than gamble while on army time.

"Shit," Harrison exclaimed with extended hissing!

He was pleased he wasn't the only pepper in this section of salt.

"Shit," he repeated, "a deuce-four troop. You from Dog or How," he asked?

"How," answered Stag.

"Yeah, well, I was in Mike Company. I tried to get in the honor guard back to corps but some shithead sitting around like he always do, shipped my ass back to a line outfit," Harrison said. "No telling them nothing."

Stag saw a nervous troop. Couldn't guess what he had done back at Corps but he was up front without a smile, expecting to get killed.

"Ain't civil back at Dog CP," Harrison said. "Some little gold bar was getting into it with the top kick. I mean they was standing one another off."

"What ya saying," asked Stag?

"Some shit about orders for a frenchy."

"Tell me," Stag said.

Stag felt exasperation. The new guy wouldn't know about La Vie's sole surviving son status: that he had been waiting for orders to go home, that if those orders didn't come, La Vie would have to fight the battle of 1062. There wasn't a line GI who begrudged the luck of a buddy being pulled off the hill before an attack. Stag needed to know for La Vie's sake, for the sake of the squad.

"Ain't meaning to tell no tales, but that old sergeant was saying something about that officer losing frenchy's orders."

Harrison felt the tension. "Ain't meaning to snitch," he said.

"It's all right," Stag answered, "that Louie was my platoon leader in the deuce four, before we were sent to Dog. He treats men low down. Doing me a favor if you recollect when he put those orders in his pocket."

Harrison wanted to do any favor for Stag. The man was as big as Soldier's Field.

"The top said something about last Wednesday," Harrison said.

Stag knew that was the day before the first assault against hill 440. He looked a while at the broad nose of Harrison, a nose flared and flat, before Stag spoke.

"Ain't trying to keep you quiet, Harrison, but keep this between you and me," he asked.

Harrison detected the deep disturbance beneath the quiet words. He knew he wasn't about to mess around with the John Henry he was talking to.

"I will," Harrison so much as swore.

Stag's soul was shot through with flame. What part had O'Hara? Stag realized he was in a white man's army, just as he came out of the white man's economy back in West Virginia, where the union got the Negro work in the mines. His unit was his union now. Mess with anyone in his squad and you were messing with him, too. Stag knew Breezedale saw Negro soldiers as military slaves, but hopefully not O'Hara. He had worked himself up the ranks; but if he sat back knowing what Breezedale did - ?

*****

"Captain," asked Brannagh?

He, Stag and La Vie saluted smartly as they

359

stepped past O'Hara into the Company HQ tent.

"He is PFC La Vie," Brannagh said, pointing to Vie. "This is Private Stag. I'm PFC Brannagh."

"I remember you," Busin answered. "You quit leadership school." Busin returned the salutes.

Brannagh looked to Stag for a summary of the Captain's words. He was chagrined at the interpretation.

"I'm sorry, Captain, but my ears ring with fire sirens. I can't hear everything yet, but we're here for La Vie."

"What about him," Busin asked. "At ease," he ordered.

Brannagh read Stag's lips, then took military ease.

"The orders for PFC La Vie to go home as a sole surviving son are here," Brannagh said, bluffing that he had seen what Harrison had only heard about. "Sergeant O'Hara has them."

Brannagh figured O'Hara was listening to every word. He knew O'Hara would produce the orders to embarrass Breezedale. Harrison had said they were at each others throats over them.

"What the hell are you talking about," asked Busin?

Stag didn't translate to Brannagh, instead he raised the tent's separation flap and exposed an eavesdropping O'Hara.

"Sergeant," Stag asked humbly, "you got them La Vie papers?"

Busin was pissed off. He hadn't a knowledge of any sole surviving son, much less orders to rotate him.

"Sergeant O'Hara," Busin commanded strongly as of old, "bring me those papers."

"Yes, Sir," O'Hara answered in a subdued tone.

O'Hara had them. They had been folded several times, their creases a tic-tac-toe pattern of dirt; their white paper a yellowish gray.

"Got these from Lieutenant Breezedale this morning, Sir," O'Hara said.

He handed the lonely sheet of parchment appearing material to the company commander.

"This is dated October 24," a surprised Busin stated.

"Yes, Sir," O'Hara answered.

He was surprised that Busin didn't ask any more questions. O'Hara worried Dog Six might use this incident as a lever to wedge his way back into command. Obviously, the Captain wasn't. As obvious, the Captain wasn't going to move against Breezedale either. If Miner had been snitching to the Captain on Breezedale and the top kick, as O'Hara was certain he was doing, either Busin didn't care or hadn't what he wanted. Well, he wouldn't get what he wanted from O'Hara.

Captain Busin sat very still. He looked a long pull at Brannagh, at Stag; another at La Vie.

"Collect your gear, PFC La Vie. Corporal Miner will drive you to battalion in thirty minutes," Dog Six said.

" 'tenshun," ordered O'Hara.

Everyone saluted everyone. Brannagh and Stag were ordered back to their unit.

Busin stared into the golden light seemingly melting La Vie as he rode away. It was a warrior Busin was sending home. What had become of the one he was?

*****

The replacement wasn't happy about assignment to Dog's third section, not happy at all. Whenever a top kick and platoon leader shout over command, Brownlee knew right off he was in a eight-ball outfit, but transfers were for buses, not soldiers.

The plumpish Private balled up in the trench line on the blocking position where pines breathed scent, and rumbles of guns stirred the distant air. His innocent face played the feelings on his nerves as he laid out what he heard.

"The top kick said he wanted to pull a guy named Singletary back to the C.P. and replace him with some Mexican. He said the two gunners would take the squads."

"Like hell, the officer said," Brownlee related. "That officer said he wanted Singletary and the Mexican where they were. That's an order, he said."

The men of the first gun squad weren't certain of the outcome. They kept looking for the toad like recruit to continue, but he shrugged his shoulders not knowing more.

Brannagh contemplated a while after reading Glorio's notes about Baiter's promotion to sergeant and squad leader. Temporary hearing loss had its blessing. He hadn't made out a harsh word spoken since Saturday. Reading that Baiter had his squad was a dirty detail. If only the Texas turd wasn't spoiling for everyone's hide.

Why not seek a transfer to Grant's squad, the gunner pondered? He wouldn't long be disabled by ear ringing. The sounds of outgoing were faintly there, or was it just a higher note of the band playing a piccolo in his cochlea? He remembered when he first met

Sergeant Grant. He was smiling from the prone, his whitish gray hair in a crew cut, with lips puckered fish-like on a sun weathered face. He looked like the creatures he netted off Florida's coast.

The gunner longed to serve with Grant, in his squad, with the epitomy of riflemen; the first up the hill firing clip after clip into Chinese positions; the first to overrun the trench line; the first to drive a bayonet's cold steel through a thunderstruck enemy; the first to rally their squad on the objective; the first to mourn at the tolling of his men's lives by death's grasp; but now, the one who saw no warrior in a hard of hearing gunner unfit to run with a patrol. Brannagh felt down low in his mind's spark, for with his auditory sense was going his spirit. He felt under the spell of a wasting sickness that tortured him. If his genius was firing the heavy machine gun at the enemy, it was offset by the trail of casualties he left behind him: Harville, Davis, Dreamer, Romaine, Van Meter. For them, this descendant of the Brannagh's of Detroit was ready to be consumed in the dark world of Sotong San.
*****

Baiter felt the pride of being a sergeant, a squad leader, heir apparent to the suffering Singletary's section. There wasn't competition from the chili-pot Cervera, a transporter of indentured migrants, a twister of fair hourly wages, a trickster of the bonus he kept for himself when his field hands wouldn't wait out the season's end, set and reset by the big labor boss in kickback with Cervera. By the time it took Baiter to unload a moving van of furniture after a Dallas to Austin trip, he would unload the details of the life of the miserable Mexican into the theatrical intellect of Breezedale. Baiter felt the pride of a sergeant, proud to take his 1st gun squad into battle.

There was but one obstacle, Baiter realized. It was his inherited gunner, who was needed for Mesabi, hard of hearing or not. Baiter figured on finding a way to rid his squad of his only contender for leadership, but it would have to wait after the battle of 1062. It wasn't safe to have an Indian tracking his every step looking for colt meat.

*****

The veins to O'Hara's heart were pulsating, for Captain Busin, himself, laid out the elements of Operation Mesabi. He told his officers and sergeants that their men were going up against well entrenched Chinese with a division in reserve; that the Chinese were capable of offensive action but indications were such that they planned a determined defense along the line they held. The 14th regiment was to lead the attack and seize objectives Desoto, Pontiac and Olds on line Duluth and assist the Turks on Objective Packard. Busin pointed to hills bearing names of Detroit's motorized products. The Turks were to tie in on the 14th regiment's flank on Packard while seizing Ford, Dodge, Stutz and Fiat, too. Busin wasn't sure why an Italian automobile made the list of American objectives, but as a descendant of a son of Italy who dropped the Italian "netti" from Busin, its inclusion was a good omen. He said the Wolfhounds on the left flank were to seize Objectives Reo, Buick and Auburn on Line Duluth. The 7th regiment of the 3rd Division would be blocking for the 14th regiment. D-day was November 1st. H-hour was 0615 hours. The 35th regiment, initially, was being held as division reserve, with its first battalion reverting to 35th's control on D-day at 0700 hours, but was to remain in place as a

blocking force for the 14th. On order, all battalions
were to be prepared to attack and destroy anywhere in
the zone. On further orders on D-Day plus 1, the 3d
battalion was to be prepared to relieve elements of the
27th regiment on Objective Reo and defend in zone.
The first battalion had an additional order. On D-day,
prior to darkness and a Chinese counterattack, together
with Company A of the 89th tanks and a platoon of the
Heavy Mortars, it was to tie in with the 14th as
directed. Air panels were to be displayed for easy
recognition by friendly aircraft. Busin said the battalion
was to be in place by noon, tomorrow, October 31st.
Assembly was 0600 hours. They were headed west to
grid 635405, away from grid 705435, towards the
smaller valley that divided the southern base of the
Kumhwa triangular MLR. He told them it was a quicker
route to 1062.

O'Hara sighed. he had wrathfully flogged Jimmy
Busin, but there he stood, a soldier, calm of voice, eyes
afire. Busin didn't know whether the Communists had
come back to conclude an agreement or just to
continue talking? If the Chinese were talking to end the
fighting, no purpose would be served in further
sustained fighting and heavy casualties. If not, it was
less costly to attack than allow the Communists time to
replenish their battered forces.

Busin told it that Scotch Six's plan was for an
advance into the Iron Triangle from Kumhwa on the
west and beyond Kumsong on the east. He wanted hill
1062, the high ground north of the Kumhwa railroad
and a firm screen along a new defensive line called
Duluth, south of the village of Pyonggang and north.
After seizing the dominating terrain, he wanted a push
to the northeast along the road to Tongchon, while the

ROKs moved forward along the east coastal road to Tongchon and linked up with the GIs just south of the town. The objectives were to cut off the North Korean Peoples forces caught between the double envelopment and to set up a new defensive line. The clock would be started on the first battalion when Red Six snaked squads down hill to the waiting two and a half ton trucks. Able Company would be on the road by 0645, then Charley. Dog and Baker would follow. Before noon Charley Company with Dog heavies would relieve George of the 14th's second battalion. By 1400 hours, full responsibility was to be assumed.

*****

Back home it was Halloweeen, where witches and goblins were roaming Detroit's streets for goodies or deviltry. The whole of the world of the supernatural was astir for the dead might return. It was unlucky not to give presents to the masked children at one's door or suffer the evil of grave ghosts and pagan pranksters. Mom Brannagh said the people of Tubercurry, Ireland, prepared for the return of the dead by putting out tobacco and porridge on the table, setting seats for them around the fire. Her ancient Roman Catholic Church, however, tried to funnel such superstitions into a feast for all the saints when Pope Gregory IV fixed its celebration in A.D. 835 on November 1, delaying to the next day the feast of All Souls. It hadn't worked. The ancient festival of Samhain, the first day of winter, retained its eve of active spirits.

So it was at Kumhwa! The gunner's grief evoked visions of martyrs who had fought so diligently for a truce that their lives were sown as its seeds: Van Meter of Iowa, Dreamer of California, Romaine of Pennsylvania, Crane of Oregon, Gibbard of New Jersey.

The rear echelon planners were sending the troops forward before morning's first light to pay further on the price due for a truce.

If a tree fell in a forest unpopulated by a single human being was there sound? Brannagh hadn't even sensed the reverberations of any crunching outgoing rounds falling on the Chinese. He hadn't lost his sense of touch, he realized, as the morning's cold had been received. Yet there was a grand silence as if Kumhwa had reverted to a sweeping desert where not even a breeze stirred, nor a sound of rock groaned, or a slipping avalanche emitted its low rumble. If there were vibrations of sonorous bodies afoot, they had stolen past him.

Glorio wrote the word that Operation Mesabi had been postponed twenty-four hours. He didn't know the reason why.

Brannagh accepted it with a dim mysterious discomfort. A letter from Dad was in his pocket.

He opened it with a grave heart.

"I tell you Danny, the British have more troops fighting at the Suez canal than in Korea. Whatever the bulldog wants for his absentee landlords he seizes. There's obviously no profit for Britain's nobility in Korea so there's a limit to the number of poor lads they'll expend on those distant hills.

"There's a limit to American's patience too. All your high thoughts and deeds, Danny, haven't found common ground here. You've been too long on lofty clouds. A vast majority of Americans recently polled have agreed that Korea was an utterly useless war. In just your three months at Kumhwa, all during the time of the supposed truce talks, there were 22,000 American casualties.

"I'll be in Dublin within a fortnight, Danny. I've had friends obtain an interview with certain men of the IRA's GHQ staff to conclude your commission. Your combat record will attract men to campaign with you in the north. You are a lad of faith. The IRA movement is centered on faith. You, Danny, will be a key to abolition of the partition of the north of Ireland from its south, while Americans care not to do so in Korea."

Dad's American, like the Minstrel Boy, to Ireland's war needed to go.

Im Ta Song was as silent as his gunner. He feared he lacked the words of help. Position and power were in those letters; filial piety of son to father in the reader. It was an onerous burden, the assistant gunner surmised from the gunner's facial travail.

Not less was the prison to which Im Ta Song felt headed under his guard Baiter. Koreans weren't of skills sufficient, the sergeant decreed, to man a crew served weapon; only capable of bearing ammo at best. There would be a change after 1062.

Im Ta Song expected a career of broom and shovel, and from time to time, laundry boy; until his rebellion resulted in a hanging from a persimon tree. His rebellion was inevitable, he realized, without the buffer of a Brannagh. Although this KATUSA had paid his initiation fee to Dog's machine guns, he had never, but for Van Meter and Brannagh, been accorded a niche in the section's order. Im Ta Song vowed the doors of Baiter's prison wouldn't hold him. Im felt a sorrow as fathomless as that of the gunner, plunging him into the same sea of disquiet.

Glorio only saw blue in the sky, and green on the earth. He didn't smell any garbage. He was impervious to the near freezing temperature and the smoke twists

spreading from bunkers and squad tents; and to light
bite of a frosty wind. The sun was where it was
supposed to straggle. So was he when he heard Mesabi
was postponed for another 72 hours. He scribbled a
note on it to Brannagh, who felt the decision wrong. He
was tired of the jerking.

O'Hara had the word that delay was ordered by
Celestial Six. The truce hadn't been wrapped up, but
the planned offensive might take considerable
casualties and new territory would have to be
abandoned if it was satisfactorily concluded. It was
hollow news to O'Hara, for Busin had blown a cold
blast on his top kick. He was to lead the third section to
1062 if the order changed.

Baiter took hard to command. He would have no
idleness. He resumed training. He emphasized
practical infantry work for the new recruits. He ran a
multiplicity of squad problems and small unit tactics.
He delighted in his gun crew's repetitious drills. He
seethed that none, not even his Negroes could cut a
time in gun drills even close to Brannagh and Im Ta
Song.

Cervera whistled. "Singletary is on this rotation
quota. He's on his way to regiment. Men with 32 or
more points are with him. O'Hara will lead his section
into Mesabi. Sloppy so longs weren't expected, a
handshake was," Cervera said. he crossed himself. "I'm
the acting section sergeant and squad leader."

Cervera knew he had been slighted by being
made an 'acting' section sergeant, not the real thing. He
was a lowly Hispanic in America. His grandparents
may have fled the Mexican Civil War's thorny problem
of Huerta's blood drenched hands in 1913 to the safety
of California, but residency since never elevated his

family to anglo status. He was certain that O'Hara hadn't imposed this slight, for he hadn't shown the vaguest inclination to reprove his machismo on Korea's battlefields. All O'Hara wanted was 'rifa', to rule, not war, Cervera reasoned. This slight had to be that of the false and faithless Breezedale. Why had the army given that madman such sharp weapons? Cervera felt his safe passage through Chinese controlled territory was lessened, but he vowed to do his job.

Cervera told about the west coast where Chinese brought greetings via a reinforced division supported by more than a dozen tanks against the British Commonwealth Division that had penetrated the Commonwealth's MLR. The 7th Cavalry regiment was also hit by an undetermined size chink force supported by four tanks, yet its MLR was holding. The engagements poured over into daylight, but fighting was slowing to small arms and artillery.

Breezedale was pleased at the apparent attention he found at the lecture. The third section wasn't scratching, guffawing or farting. It had obviously been humbled under his leadership. O'Hara would be the next felon to weep. Breezedale would have his shame extinguished, his honor finally restored, if it took the withering of the entire section. If these criminals weren't reformed, he would make them wish they were dead. He pitched his opening words high.

"Intelligence's analysis of enemy documents had determined their non combat casualties from suicide and self injury were alarmingly serious."

Glorio questioned any alarm. Every damn chunk of Chinese garbage could do themselves in as far as he cared. They sure as hell hadn't done so on hill 440. He expected a surviving Chinese or two would be on hill

1062. He translated his thoughts to notes for his gunner to read - 'Breeze said mass gook suicides.'

Brannagh's gray chill revery defrosted. He conjectured, if suicide was rampant among the enemy, it must have had its birth in maddening bombardments like that of hill 440. He felt a twinge of sympathy for the Chinese. They had always suffered under ponderous incoming, while GIs, only since September.

He knew the enemy was recreating the First World War's Western front across their positions, to have it fortified with Russian artillery so deeply dug in, it wasn't to be moved out and up to support its attacking infantry. Theirs was a fourteen mile deep salient being engineered for nuclear attack. Their weaponry of November could contain a regimental size attack. By year's end their fire power would match that of the Eighthh Army. November was crucial.

"What were the principal causes of the enemy's strength decreases," Breezedale asked rhetorically? "They have a feudal army, whose officers treat the men unreasonably by abuse and beatings and bodily maltreatment."

Trout's were the first eyes uplifted, followed in sequence like blossoming flowers, the blue, brown, gray and black eyes of the old timers. Whose officers? Trout figured it had never crossed Breezedale's mind that he was reading his biography.

"As a result, many enemy soldiers have committed suicide or deserted. Furthermore, the fact that personnel in the lower ranks have rebelled on several occcasions may lead to even greater calamities among their forces," Breezedale read.

Stag loosened his sphincter muscle. Trout freed the snort of a sea elephant.

Baiter's burning eyes were as piss-holes in lake ice at Stag. If the electricity in their beams could have been harnessed, Kumhwa might have lights.

Breezedale took careful note of the continued support of Baiter, the inaction of Cervera. The Lieutenant studied the red-headed soldier. He saw a spiritless fugitive. The Platoon leader would rectify the leadership of this section soon, if Mesabi didn't. As soon as he could transfer Cervera to the laundry pool, it would be Baiter, Blaczyk and Watt. Trout, Stag and Brannagh would walk the night hours on patrols where their fates would be unveiled. No officer should be subjected to these flutterings of flatulence, the Lieutenant swore. Those men were jealous of their superior's ability and efficiency.

Glorio scribbled his observations: 'the talking garbage said Chinese rebelled over brass' shit dropped on troops. Stag and Trout broke wind like zephyrs.'

Brannagh smiled. The squad wasn't finished yet! Even O'Hara had been heard from in Sing's behalf. Was his taking the third section for Mesabi more of the same? Was Captain Busin back?

The Lieutenant paused to read through his notes. They indicated the enemy Corps Communist Party Commissioner recommended the strenghtening of unity between officers and troops; the elimination of wrongs by encouraging and awarding personnel who had good conduct; that officers should be democratic; and that officers should be in the field with their attacking or defending troops, living as the troops did. Breezedale saw no purpose in its presentation. He elected to conclude his seminar.

"The enemy has a serious problem. So much so he has gone out of his way to issue winter clothing to his enlisted men in October, while higher ranks are still waiting," he said.

Breezedale paused for effect before dismissal.

"Dismissed," he said.

No one called the section to attention. No one but Baiter stood up.

"Trench-shun," Baiter ordered.

None but the replacements, Blaczyk and Watt came to attention. Brannagh watched as the officer, clothed warmer than a polar bear with binoculars, departed.

CHAPTER TWENTY ONE
DIVISION REAR

"Here's the word," said Cervera, crossing himself with the Sign of the Cross. "Celestial Six's negotiators at Panmunjon couldn't budge the Communist's from their 4 kilometer demilitarized zone based solely on the battle line. This means Kaesong would remain in the enemy's hands. On November 4th, rumor has it that Ridgway concluded a settlement that will be based on the line of demarcation at hand. He's postponed Mesabi without a date. The 35th is ordered to rotate units on the MLR, each battalion on line for two weeks, followed by a week in reserve. The Blue battalion will go on line the 7th of November, with Red relieving on November 14. Glorio, write Brannagh a note. Breezedale ordered the gunner back to the rear for a medical check. He goes at 0800."

Brannagh reread the note. Cervera nodded confirmation. What was it with the Lieutenant? Whatever! Brannagh felt good about time away from Baiter.

Riding the buckboards of the jolting deuce-by must be shaking every soldier's words to stutters, Brannagh concluded by the rippling cheeks he saw. He was glad of it. He wasn't up to discerning even intelligble talk. He let his mind whirl. He envisioned the ghost of Breezedale. Was this order to the mobile hospital meant to demean one without a visible wound as a malingerer? Was it?

The maddened trucker had the mind to bump butts off the boards the entire route, Brannagh complained. Were they but piss ants? Brannagh leaned as the truck turned onto a corrugated gravel road and

roared toward a village. Suddenly the rig jerked to a
shuddering stop. Brannagh rolled forward until he hit
the wooden rails at the cab, helmetless. Other guys
were piled on in a cord. He untangled from the
writhing mess. He felt he had been hurled like a sock
with holes that had covered its last foot. He rose
unseadily. He stared. The front right axle had broken.

Someone would have to check out a village up
the road. There was discussion aplenty, but a review of
the situation left a nagging fear they would end up in an
ambush. Brannagh agreed to scout it out. The gunner
shouldered his carbine and set out on foot.

Chung Hyung Chul was worried. Chung sat on
his wax paper floor meditating on an approaching
American. He knew he was but a chunk of Korea, a
squat boulder rolled down from the mountain, and
born here, but he had learned to farm the mountain's
side. Now he saw a tall soldier coming up the road.
Hadn't Chung's four decades of life felt the weight of
this terrible century: from the Japanese, from the Imun
Gun Communists, the Megooks from America, the
Chinese Red Communists, and South Korean
Hangooks?

When the Megooks first came last October, so
fast did their war columns pass by, they only waived to
his daughter, Myo. When fell the winter of war and
dreadful cold and the maurauding Chinese came over
the narrow mountain trails, they scattered Megooks
and Hangooks like leaves before a whirlwind. His wife
had died after their only son was seized to serve in the
Imun Gun and her huge jars with the family's winter
supply of pickled kim-che were stolen. He had now
only Myo, and a Megook was coming to make her his
Kisaeng. His eyes took on an artificial light, his mind

was sensing a fuzziness from his mak-gul-li. Was it health or illness he sought in this sour but strong wine?

Brannagh focused on the thatched hut beside the road down the valley. Most of the rest of the village's huts were remnants of mud walls, reinforced with corn stalks. This one had a roof. Its door was open. He looked in. The rooms were very small, the size of a city jail cell. There weren't any furnishings, just mats, but the floor was warm. Someone had been there. Brannagh smelled the wine's odor. He entered, looking. In the back room, he saw three holes, two covered by clay lids, the third open. It emitted smoke. There was a moment of puzzlement. If this were a latrine, some Korean's backside would be barbequed. It was a kitchen. There were bowls for rice no doubt; a stone water jar; cooking pots for rice or boiling water and making soup. The three holes were a ground floor stove with its fire built beneath the floor, its flues running under the raised floors in the other two rooms. There was no waste of heat. The fire wasn't out, but the papasan was.

Brannagh noted back yard honey pots set down into a dug out hollow, their fetid feces masked from sight by wooden lids, but not the wind which whirled the incense into the air.

He saw one lid move. He was inclined to get out of there and back to the truck. If it were a trick commode full of guerrillas and not turds, he had an obligation to drop a grenade. If it wasn't, he would be covered with the odor of sanctity: that certain smell that permeated monks after a forty day non stop stay in their cells. He pulled the grenade's pin, put the pin in his pocket while he held the grenade's handle in place. With his left, he gently lifted the honey pot's wooden lid.

As startled as if a cobra struck at his face,
Brannagh fell backwards. He held onto the grenade. A
girl was in there! The gunner returned the pin to place,
and the grenade to his pack belt loop. He lifted the lid
again and pulled the nearly asphyxiated child from
inside the rancid pot. She did again the same for her
papasan. The gunner poured water freely over them
and himself. Lord, he reflected, armies have done these
peasants wrong. Wet as a sewer rag, he grabbed his
weapon to return to the truck. There were no guerillas
in this area.

Chung and Myo watched the soldier go away.
Chung could think of no other place to hide. He
remembered when the Japanese soldiers lined them all
up to shout Banzai when he was taken to work in their
machine shop. He remembered when the Imun Gun
seized his only son. He recalled it was the Chinese who
stole his bullock. He feared the Megooks were coming
as Fire Bandits. In the old days of the Japanese
occupation of Korea, Koreans in the underground first
fought the Japanese invaders, then resorted to
pillaging, rape and arson, as fire bandits. Chung feared
the firehead soldier's departure would lead the other
soldiers to return. Chung knew he was a simple man.
Before, he attributed his troubles to ghostly actions, as
taught by his ancient animistic religion. He changed his
beliefs when the world around his village became a
place of horror, filled with real assailants. He made his
daughter gather her things. They would flee to refuge in
a cave in the hills. He sighed. His crop had reached
harvest, but his spirit was plowed under.
*****

His was a difficult walk through tents of the

mobile hospital. Brannagh saw others on stretchers
and cots in long rows that never seemed to end. Some
GIs were flat as shirt irons. Others were rigged for
trapeezes with pulleys, levers and ropes levitating limbs
to various heights. A few troops were sitting, staring at
their chameleon bandages, in awe that their circulating
blood was taking a detour. Brannagh heard mumbling
from the cots. He saw an unceasing activity. Some of
the men, log-like, were carried elsewhere. Their beds
were reclaimed by newer arrivals. A soldier had a pretty
nurse holding his hand. It was the first American
woman the gunner had seen since July. Other nurses
appeared, all as beautiful, all as eager to hold GI hands
like sweethearts on a front porch swing. Their
tenderness and smiles elevated memories, and morale.

Brannagh felt unworthy of the place. He walked;
every muscle in his body was intact; he had no visible
wounds. He felt ashamed. He felt the eyes of the
seriously wounded were upon him, the eyes of brave
men on a mental case.

Brannagh felt humiliation for having a body free
from apparent blemish. He wore guilt. Hadn't he been
the cause of Harville's wound. Hadn't his spoof of
Breezedale put his squad on 440? Though he hadn't
fired the rounds that took Dreamer, Romaine and Van
Meter, wasn't there a law of accessory? Or was it
mischance? He was in the depths of emotional hurt.
He'd no answers.

A medic did a deal of talking in the face of his
patient. The gunner watched his lips flap like parade
ground flags. There was sound that competed with the
noise within his ears! For the first time since hill 440 it
was other than a whimsical shriek.

Brannagh smiled. A note was given him,

redirecting him to Division's EENT unit.

"I hear your sound," the gunner said. "Its been close to two weeks since I've could distinguish syllables."

He knew then he wouldn't be permanently hard of hearing. Although the doctor looked like an oboe, and his tone was pitched high like Breezedale's, the gunner heard, and word's were distinguishable.

He couldn't wait to return to his unit! He reflected on that. Baiter didn't want him; Breezedale either! Brannagh acknowledged he had too easily agreed to go to the rear, to bug, even if it had an honorable face. The wounded in the hospital must have sensed he had bugged. He felt emptied, worthless.

He suffered an instrument poked into both ears into which the medical man peeked. Brannagh could decipher most of the writing on the medical record -'ear drums perforated, tinitus bilateral, reprofile. Recuperate a few days at division. Return to line unit.' It was succinct enough.

The opulence of Divisional HQ put the gunner in mind of a visiting circus setting up amidst the county fairgrounds. It was a big midway of clean fatigues and spitshined boots. He looked for a ferris wheel, for the racing horses. He saw a marvel of logistics, a self sufficient mobile town that stayed in place as long as the infantry held the MLR. It was an amazing community of officers, accountants, typists, physicians, cooks, quartermasters, truckers, all with innumerable tents and huts with abundant stoves, and generator powered electric lights. It was a behind the line spectacle Brannagh must have viewed when he first arrived in Korea, but couldn't recall, not even an iota of the colorful quarters. The several sandbagged air raid shelters were evidence that roustabouts, probably infantrymen, were called in to protect a field division's bureaucrats from the ravages of bedcheck Charley's occasional bomb.

Brannagh felt the country bumpkin in a big city. His eye saw ornate furnishings and accommodations he had forgotten at Kumhwa; his nose detected the odor of sweet frying bacon; he walked on gravel paths towards the division's personnel tent. If only he could sip coffee at the cook's tent, or taste some frying bacon covered with eggs over easy. The whole place had a tantalizing irresistibility about it - yet there were drawbacks. Rear echelon types had longer time to pull in Korea to rotate. It might well be worth it, he thought.

"PFC Brannagh," he reported. "I don't hear real well at the moment but I read notes."

He saluted the soldier behind the desk, but saw no return. He saw a neatly dressed smiling corporal rise and extend his hand. Brannagh returned both. He took the seat offered. He watched the corporal write out some words. He read them - 'I've read your record. We're both from Detroit - my brother Joe Moran attends Sacred Heart.'

The gunner instantly saw the close resemblance. Joe was a dynamo on the basketball court, a forward to Brannagh's guard position. They had combined for so many fast breaks that the opposition often dropped a defensive man to the free throw line to stymie a quick two points.

"I last saw Joe in January when I quit and joined the army. He's still there," Brannagh asked?

The corporal returned an affirmative nod. He wrote - 'I got drafted. Enough that one Moran's here.'

Brannagh visualized La Vie in Moran's chair, his

brothers in graves across the world of America's wars.

"Yea, one's enough," the gunner answered.

Moran's squad tent had a comfort that Brannagh had deemed impossible for anyone other than Singletary. There were little houseboys everywhere doing the chores an infantryman takes for granted - cleaning weapons and equipment. Those little mice-like boys were making beds, folding clothes, doing all the things a well-to-do family hired a housemaid for. Even basic training in Camp Breckenridge's wooden barracks didn't have the down home comfort of division's HQ troops.

"Have a beer," Moran offered.

Brannagh saw him lift a towel from a tub filled with can's chilled by chunked ice. It was getting cold in Korea, and ice aplenty would be available in the polluted pools and paddies if a GI elected its use, but Moran's was manufactured. The gunner marveled at it. Brannagh was as surprised at the plentitude of full beer cans as he was at the ice. There had to be a couple of dozen cans. It was a horde to delight the languishing heart of the machine gunner. He remembered his manners. He gave thanks to his benefactor, put a smile in the can's lid with the ever trusty P-38, and chug-a-lugged its contents.

Moran was impressed. He offered another, glad that the friend of his brother was so thankful for such a slight luxury.

"I'll drink your beer dry if you keep being the nice guy," Brannagh said.

Moran's gestures had invited the gunner to do just that, so he was surprised at the reluctance. He wished for Brannagh to drink up. A note to that effect, confirmed the wish.

The gunner nodded a no, his face displaying the same reluctance. He explained.

"It must have taken you two months to save up such a horde. I wouldn't feel right."

Now Moran was perplexed. He drafted a reply - 'no horde. We get all the beer we can drink.' He handed it to the gunner. Then he showed him several other deposits of cold beer; even a half dozen jugs of the hard stuff.

The gunner took a long look at the big browed, small chinned accountant whose heart was so kind he hadn't realized there was a negative in the plethora of distilled spirits at headquarters. He simply hadn't been forward, where regiment's supply was halved; battalions' quartered; line troops recipients of but a trickle down of seven cans a man per week! Brannagh wouldn't insult his host. He thanked him, and set about diminisment of the brewer's art. After all, Corporal Moran had nothing to do with the maldistribution of America's scarce resources.

He was dreaming he heard a tenor somewhere singing the "Ode to Joy," an organ picking up the melody and accompaniment. His blurred eyes focused on the long greenish canvas spread above his head. He saw a baby-faced boy in baggy GI fatigues smiling down on him, a cherub type that sat around the throne of God. The singing was so moving, Brannagh sensed he must be back in the seminary chapel. His soul glowed. He was enraptured. He hadn't died! He hurt too much to have died. He just had partied too long. He was waking from a drunk.

Brannagh saw troops around a pock-faced short soldier barely bigger than the houseboy he hugged. Everyone seemed excited. The gunner heard the noise of the sideshow, but not discernible voices, which was considerable auditory improvement since before his drinking orgy. Beer obviously had medicinal qualities, he reflected, never before realized. A paper should be presented to the medical societies on its curative properties. A couple more such orgies should do the trick. He pledged himself to the orgies, not the research papers.

"Corporal," Brannagh asked Moran, "what's going on with that stumpy troop and his kid?"

Moran's note had but one word - 'rotation'.

"How many points?" asked the gunner.

Moran's manuscript indicated - 'thirty'.

"Thirty," shouted the still befuddled gunner. "What ya' mean thirty? Cervera's got more than thirty. He's still on the hill! What the shit's going on?"

Moran was startled. His guest's voice was thundering. He saw a twisted visage, the shape of terror, a demon. He saw Brannagh fix his bayonet.

"I'll kill that little turd. He's messed with Cervera's points. No little shit of a rear echelon bastard's going to go home when men here before him are left on the line."

Grappling with the raving lunatic turned maniac, typists, accountants, auditors, and supply sergeants forced the raging animal to the tent's wooden floor where half a dozen soldiers fought for their lives to restrain him. A medic with a syringe full of horse tranquilizer drove a knife-like needle deeply within an arm bulging with contorted muscles. It took minutes for effect.

CHAPTER TWENTY TWO
LAUNDRY POOL

Brannagh wished he recalled the trip. For the life of him, he couldn't remember how or when he had gotten back to Dog Company's CP. His snowpacs were brand new and fitted. His pack was heavy, full of beer. He was shaven. His clothes were new, even his longjohns. He smelled of some kind of fragrance. Was it his, Breezedale's or O'Hara's? The top kick looked to be a dispirited slug.

The gunner was certain now of beer's curative powers. He heard the loathesome lieutenant's hissing, scalding words letting out a volley of curses, saying something about injuring five soldiers and two little Korean boys; something about tearing up a division tent; something about being an embarrassment to Dog's reputation; something about assignment to the laundry pool where he belonged.

Brannagh concentrated on the last blast. "Laundry pool? I'm going back to the 1st gun," he said.

"No," Breezedale responded. "You've been reprofiled on your ears. You're not fit for the machine gun."

If he had been directed to hell by St. Peter, he wouldn't have been stung nearly as hard as being declared unfit by the coward likes of the lieutenant. Exile of a front line soldier to the laundry pool was tantamount to shunning.

*****

Cloudy winter was sneaking up the hills of Kumhwa with the stealth of Chinese infiltrators. The days were running a shorter race. Brannagh could hear the winds dance with inclement moods. He saw brooks had drawn over their pools crystalline quilts against the night. His laundry tent was winged with white sweat that after morning's thaw dripped into rhinoceros' horns.

The hills Brannagh saw weren't much different than those on the right flank, mostly nose warts either side of narrow valleys. Devils with cloven hooves wandered those heights from each side of no man's land. Each cut or point of rock was covered by weaponry forward; but reverse slopes had a calm complacency with sandbagged CPs ever enlarging into hotel suites. Nature's beauty had been so altered by contending armies, galleries wasted no exhibit time on photographs of Kumhwa's fantastic forms. The gunner didn't think he was seeing anything of elegance, only a scene reminiscent of poop in a mess kit.

The gunner worked at sorting soiled clothes within a tent's brownish walls. He saw in the tent's mirror rusted eyes and pallid cheeks. He saw a drooping brow. Who was it in that mirror? He trembled. He felt alone, isolated. Worse he had been forgotten. There was no mystery about it. His every action since August was a road sign of ineptitude. What ever he might have done on the right lane of his highway of combat, the left was strewn with wreakage. He felt his emotional gastank had been pierced by rejection. He was out of gas!

There was a time he saw his government acting in the best interests of its citizen soldiery. Dad had drowned that belief. There was a time he thought his enlistment was to join a twentieth century crusade against atheistic communism, but nary a letter from a fellow seminarian came. Van Meter had shown him a soldier might fight the enemy for military advantage without hatred; all the while his brass' military objectives were haphazard tosses of the dice for truce talk puffery. Brannagh felt his fate fluctuated in negotiator's positions solid as fishnets. Hadn't Dad questioned his courage? Hadn't Breezedale buried the gunner's raving conscience in a solitary sepulchre? His gun squad was in Baiter's hands, in the control of a man who had a way with oppression.

The gunner tried to conceal his anger. It had become a contagion of spirit, of soul, of mind.

"Get your fat ass from here," Stag said. "You letting that Breezedale fix this fight, too. You letting down the squad."

Brannagh saw the black god of the mines had come to his grave, not in a white shroud, but with a wild step.

"That frigging drinker of honey pot slop double crossed both of us, you pale skinned fart," Stag said. "Breezedale lied on the fight. I didn't expect no trouble from you. My cut was a month's pay after the fight. I should'a known when O'Hara covered that bet. I knowed when you fought like a milky Joe Louis. I knew I'd been had. Noways was I getting a decision from all them white folks there. So I quit, said you a pro, so Breeze and O'Hara make big bucks! I forced a hell of a cut from 'em." Stag grabbed his breath. "We're going up the hill today. Don't let Breezedale make you double cross your squad."

Being cussed out was just what he needed. "What a friend you are, Stag! You said the right thing!"

*****

The frost had come but Brannagh heated the fire in his heart. He marched the distance from the battalion laundry pool to Dog's CP. He saw tents'

chimneys were smoking, their curling towers writing
an unknown language in the wind. He heard shouts of
GIs and clamorous trucks splashing white mud out of
their tires' way. He enjoyed the noise from crunched
soil's thin crust under foot. Brownish hills appeared to
have gray streaks from frost's fingers like old men
combed their own long hairs across balding domes.

"Lieutenant," Brannagh said while saluting, "I
want to go back up to my squad."

His throat rumbled the words throughout the
CP. He saw the surprise on Breezedale's face.

"Like hell you will," answered the Lieutenant.

"I must go," Brannagh roared, wishing he hadn't
saluted.

"Like hell you will," repeated Breezedale, "that's
an order."

He hadn't gotten rid of this criminal on line, but
he had humiliated him. Breezedale was convinced of a
treachery.

"Shove your order up your ass, Lieutenant,"
O'Hara cursed, "with La Vie's and the 3d section's on
440. If they don't fit, shove your binoculars for
packing." O'Hara turned to Brannagh. "Go back up to
your unit, Brannagh. The Lieutenant will never find
you there. It's on the forward slope."

The gunner saw Breezedale surprisingly back
off, though he acted perfectly normal in his
emotionality, his conduct of himself. O'Hara, on the
other hand, was ablaze.

Breezedale's suspicions were fact. He had been
sold out. One criminal was helping another escape.

Brannagh set out at route march. He noticed
Captain Busin beside the CP tent, so a salute was
snapped which the Captain returned without a word

spoken. Brannagh noted no movement by Busin into the CP; rather Busin watched him as he made the long climb over the road to the cut path up to the commo trench.

*****

Swinford and Blaczyk got the hell out of Brannagh's and Im Ta Song's way. When the gunner cocked that big thumb to take a hike, both got their gear on the road, bumping the recruits, rather than messing with the bunker of Glorio, Stag and Harrison.

Swinford had a reason to go for it. With Baiter in the machine gun hole, Swinford had to force himself to make sharp cut backs on his tool manipulation time, what with guarding his butt from possible predations. With the cold weather here, winter clothes and duck down fart sacks added protective layers against the squad leader's night crawling.

Blaczyk puffed a bit when these scabs crossed Baiter's picket line, but his squad leader wasn't there to back him up. Blaczyk wasn't about to issue any union demands. Baiter might have made him the assistant gunner, but not a shop steward. Let the leader do the bargaining. Blaczyk would go tell.

Brannagh viewed hills to his front riven this way and that, with bloody surprises on each one of them. It was a place for a quiet retreat with few roads. He saw many streams, with an air an artist might paint however shadowy made by November's somber clouds after slaying sunshine.

Im Ta Song stared at Baiter's outcast. Even the lieutenant's verdict failed to crush the gunner. He had thrown off his cruel cross. Again he had the good heart. His eyes were quick and bright, strong as an ox, straight as his rifle. Im Ta Song felt the need to build a road idol to represent the evil Baiter, spitting at it to curse the man. Im decided he would scratch an inscription on a stone - the place of Baiter - with the intention of casting a spell on the dangerous American. Im Ta Song wished to counteract Baiter's expected retribution.

The whirl of heavy GI clothing and the thumping stride of a horse in the trench could be heard by Brannagh clear inside the gun hole, but he waited for Baiter's furious roar before coming out. The gunner wore only his winter undershirt and field trousers. He clenched his fists the size of oars against Baiter's carbine, at the ready.

"If that gook don't come out, I'll kick his ass out," Baiter said.

Brannagh saw lightening blazing from Baiter's eyes, his voice a thundering animosity.

"You go in that bunker, the only ass you'll feel is yours with a machine gun stuck in it," Brannagh replied.

He spoke as softly as an april shower. He saw that the squad had come out of their bunkers like chipmunks standing near their holes, surveying the doings. He saw Stag rotate off his carbine's safety. "You put your weapon agin' the trench wall, Bait," Stag commanded.

Harrison and Glorio leveled their weapons on their squad leader to emphasize Stag's directive.

Baiter downed his weapon, but thought of an angle.

"We'll fight down the reverse slope. Just you and me," Baiter said to Brannagh.

"And me," Stag said. "There ain't going be no frog sticking. Ain't going to be nothing but fist thumping. Just you, Brannagh, and me down there. Ain't going to be no body else, you hear," Stag said to the squad!

Stag marched the two in front of him like POWs until they reached a flat space down the hill a ways. He would referee the fight O'Hara would kill to promote.

Baiter stripped to his undershirt. He was amused at Brannagh's challenge. The guy was a looser. He lived in fear. He had flaked out after Van Meter and Dreamer were killed. It wasn't his hearing, it was his courage that left him, Baiter confirmed. Brannagh was at fault the section was up on 440 twice. Yea, Brannagh was at fault.

Brannagh waited as quietly as the iceberg that approached the unsinkable Titanic. He didn't want any pre-fight demonstration. He didn't want his hot temper to be the dominant element in his fight tactics.

Baiter sounded to Stag as a hungry hound savoring a fresh killed possum. Sweat was beading his forehead, never mind the chill air. Stag figured no one could see them. The back slope landscape was as brown as a hickory nut. Pines and firs bowed slightly; the wind whispered a hush. Bent weeds watched, but no one else, Stag affirmed.

Stag's motion to start was timed by Baiter's sucker punch. He disdained the touching hands in favor of plowing a mouthful of tombstone teeth behind the fat lips of the pretended gunner.

Stag watched Brannagh bend away from the earthquake's sudden jolt, its right cross plowing Brannagh's left ear. The gunner answered with his own right hook to Baiter's rocky forehead. Neither fighter was hurt, Stag saw. Both went to the attack. The squad leader fired synchronized lefts and rights from close range against targets of opportunity. The gunner's defense slipped a right and blocked a left. He moved inside, hitting Baiter's chest, an uppercut missing his chin. They were head to head. Neither would clinch. Neither lost his timing. They were exchanging shots that thumped flesh like a doctor's mallet testing a knee's reflexes. The guard of both men warded off direct shots to the head, their arms and fists deflecting well aimed punches to the chin. They butted in unison, retaliating with bloody fists on each other's cuts. Stag heard the gunner grunt like a cannon's roar. The squad leader spat at him. They surged in anger, both rolling with the exchange. Brannagh glared at Baiter who careened a right high to Brannagh's temple, answered by the gunner's short shot on Baiter's chin. Stag saw Baiter fall onto a knee, but get up immediately. Then Brannagh returned to the attack, tossing a hard right hook caught by Baiter's left shoulder.

Stag saw Baiter spit again. His jeering laughter seemed to belie the numbness in his paralyzed deltoids, but he was unable to raise his left. Stag hollered for a break, but Baiter and Brannagh wanted no bells, no breaks, no rounds in this fight, just fists.

Baiter saw the right come in. He knew he was hurt. He looked at his left. It dangled like a dead cottonhead snake from a clothesline. He knew he was wide open. He pushed his right in the gunner's face.

Brannagh wanted to beat the shit out of Baiter, to place more than one spear in his steer hide. the gunner fired a burst of six rights followed by a hard hook to Baiter's left rib cage, another to his right.

Stag saw a methodical mauling of the new sergeant by a storm of knuckles that relieved anger as they churned Baiter's clay insensible. The gunner would rob the squad leader of his health; would leave him a broken wreck; would cleave off his vicious mouth.

"You'll kill the turd, Gunner. You'll do Leavenworth time, Gunner," warned Stag.

It was of little mind to the West Virginian that the bigot died. It was a powerful concern the gunner didn't do prison time for it.

Brannagh stepped away. He saw Baiter struggling for equilibrium, but he wouldn't let himself fall. There was a twinge of admiration for the squad leader; he could fight! Some other place under different circumstances without a Stag for a referee, the result might have been different, Brannagh surmised.

Baiter felt the shame sweep his aching body like a hot shower. His left arm was still numb. He showed his crimson teeth at Brannagh like an old beaten cur might at the new young stud; until night's frown gave him cover for an ambush.

*****

Brannagh felt the strife had passed from his troubled mind. He enjoyed the chilly night's free wind that licked his fevered face. He had come out of the depths. He savored the voices of Kumhwa, its nature, the sigh of its winds, the whispering pines of its slopes, its air in a silvery shiver, its bleak world at momentary rest, until death came out of the trenchlines. He heard the high incoming fall like solitary snowballs walking Dreamer's dog across the bunker line. Their strange beat rippled earth, leaving twisted shreds in their stream. The Chinese were still over there! Brannagh didn't care!

*****

Korea, when invaded, usually had more

volunteer sorcerers than volunteer combat soldiers to
defend it, Im Ta Song reflected. Baiter's exorcism called
for more than the inscribed road side tablet, Im Ta
Song determined. He would end once and for all his
fear of that foreign barbarian, his depradations on the
dignity of at least one soldierly Korean.

The KATUSA recalled history's story of an
American incursion in 1871 against the Kwangsong
heights where Korean soldiers fought with mud and
clay lumps thrown to temporarily blind their attackers
in order to close and fight with bayonets. The
Americans conquered, but were moved to eulogize the
defenders as soldiers imbued with a firm warrior spirit
unknown to the western world. Im Ta Song felt imbued
with the same warrior spirit. He prepared for
Baiter-Oh: one who took everything for himself.
*****

The Stag's owned their home and farm a quarter
of a century after emancipation. Stag thought of his
father, a deacon, the conductor of prayer meetings.
Papa Stag was the fourth generation to attend their
Baptist Church, his son, the fifth. Papa was a moral
man, a man of temperance. Papa even beat the debt of
the depression.

Momma Stag lived and worked to feed her
children, Stag recollected. She was a self-taught nurse;
a natural gardener whose touch made seedling sweet
potatoes grow. When Mama died, she didn't leave
much of herself behind to bury, but her last words
"walk in the straight path," were followed by her son.
Until now! Mama and Papa hadn't twice suffered a
Breezedale, a lord over primitives; a deamon brooding.
Stag would explain the man to Papa by 2 Samuel XII,
14-17, as a David who ordered Uriah to the forefront of

the hottest battle, that he might be smitten and die. The Uriah's were the first gun squad, and Breezedale the David of the Korean war.

"The things David had done displeased the Lord," Stag muttered. "I will raise up evil against him out of his own house, for he did it secretly."

*****

The silence from the rear CP was an unaccountable wonder on the wintry day. Blaczyk watched spell bound for the appearance of his squad leader, the commo trench capturing more of his vision than the frosty bumps on his forward slope. Im Ta Song sat astride a sand bag with the stillness of a sleeper. Stag's survey to his front and down slope saw not a rock colored the same as yesterday. He made himself a seat on the topmost log of the warming bunker.

Brannagh was distracted, his mind in awe at the silent beauty of 1062 spotlighted by a single ray of the sun. He marvelled at its pillar effect which might be sufficient to melt its chosen place of frozen earth, but insufficient to offset the wind's stinging, icey edge. There were winds at all times now, too rapid to be warmed by heavenly fire. These winds were but the babies of the winter. Their elders were growing in Siberia, awaiting passage south. The ground was hardening with the onset of the cold, despite a few rains. Snow wasn't far off, the gunner thought, nor were frozen canteens. He had put antifreeze in place of water to cool the machine gun, checking the packing on the barrel for water tightness. October had brought its clear dry weather from the Siberian continent and soon the Kumhwa wasteland would be covered by snow clad hills. Tales of last winter still lingered in the gunner's memory. The troops suffered terrible privations, both sides, particularly in bitterly cold sleet storms. The cold was intense, the snow deep. The wind howled as it bit through fatigues during the short days and long icy nights on the bare hills, while a soldier lay on frozen ground. The sudden shock of Korea's winter demoralized many outfits that tried to stand and fight the invading Chinese of November last; Korea was an earthly place with an unearthly weather.

*****

Squinty eyed Captain Busin brought the word to the MLR that there was a tentative agreement to a line to separate the battling armies. Busin gave the word to Grant of Charley Company, which spread from there like contagion on tamales, and undermined Cervera's acting leadership. If he wasn't to be promoted, he hoped the Captain might have his order to get off the hill on rotation, but he didn't. Cervera had expected Baiter back, but he wasn't. Cervera even expected that Breezedale would have whistled the phone to keep his acting section sergeant and only squad leader in the know. He hadn't. Cervera cursed them all as worse than growers back in California.

Brannagh sensed a bad day. Dog Six, himself, had finally come out to the forward positions, seeking out Grant, the top soldier. The gunner didn't know what Busin might want, but Grant and Busin were World War II infantry veterans that knew war. The hatred between Captain Busin and Master Sergeant O'Hara, must still be knife sharp and deadly, so the gunner wasn't expecting the top kick alongside the fire plug officer, nor Breezedale for obvious reasons, but why not Baiter?

The gunner and Im Ta Song were joined by Stag. They stared at the back of their company commander moving through the commo trench back slope. The three soldiers looked at one another when the Captain passed from sight. The looks exchanged were of puzzlement. Not a word had been spoken but questions were flying in the air.

"I'll go to Grant and ask," Brannagh said.

"Don't know," Grant answered diffidently.

"Don't know, or won't say," the gunner persisted?

"Either," Grant answered without animation.
*****

O'Hara looked as if he was encrusted by Cromwellian chains and on his way to penal servitude in the British West Indies in 1652 A.D. He stood on a sand bag in the warming bunker, his eyes set with a stern visage, his awful stare plunging on the 3d section.

Brannagh saw the heroic form wore a helmet with two blue rockers newly painted. Behind him was the little abstract of a company commander. Both grimaced as if their bowels were full of wrath.

"Hear the word, ye slathering dolts," O'Hara said.

He spit tobacco on Sergeant Revel's new Shoe Pacs which the water balloon had just gotten upon his return from Granite Mountain leave.

"Hear the word," O'Hara repeated. "That vagabond of a fruit picker Cervera is to roll up his fart sack and rotate to some stateside pickle picking field. He's to be a double rocker sergeant and act as Santa Claus in olive drab," O'Hara pointed to Revels, "will take Cervera's scalpeen and squad."

Cervera gave a murmur of approval.

"At ease, ye blaggards," O'Hara said. "I'll be the one to kick backbone straight up into the skulls of the third section from now on."

Other murmurs didn't turn to approval. O'Hara looked toward Captain Busin. O'Hara nodded his head in obeisance, yet he envisioned the image of the captain as one of Father Christmas' elves.

"Everybody knows Trout would try the vow of chastity of St. Patrick himself," O'Hara said, "so he goes to the first gun squad as its new sergeant. He's slicker than Satan. He'll lay a trap on purity Brannagh."

O'Hara had the laugh of a soul free at last from military sin, once again nodding humbly to the waif who wore railroad tracks on his helmet.

Brannagh's mood was warming that all but a few wrong stains on the section had been bleached. He waited anxiously for the last drops to splash.

Captain Busin jumped up on a three sandbag platform. He was uncommonly emotional for an officer.

"Lieutenant Breezedale has returned to the valley in quiet submission to head the Battalion's task force," Busin paused for dramatic effect - "on the washing of long johns. The wolf of these dark mountains deserved more. Baiter's in the motor pool." Busin continued. "The platoon's new Second Lieutenant will report within several days, or as soon as Sergeant Grant's field commission and transfer clears paper work."

"Attention," O'Hara shouted.

Im Ta Song bowed in respect. Stag gave thanks to Mama, for he had stayed on the straight way. The gunner felt a spark of the divine. Cervera kept crossing himself the long way down the back slope to the rotation jeep.

*****

Conversion to Dad's adherence that his son violently overthrow the arrogant British in the north of Ireland gave evidence of a considerable emotional disturbance. Brannagh reread Dad's letter.

"I buried my mother next to my father in the green grave yard with white celtic crosses around St. Patrick church in Loughguile. My tears were more for my own shame.

"Twenty-seven years had passed since I ducked from Orangemen's contempt and oppression. Yes, I ducked! I never fought in the IRA against those who caused Ireland unfathomable woe! I told myself I had left to find work, for twelve acres in Loughguile without other work was long term famine calculated to cause Catholics to emigrate. Didn't I have a mother and sister to support? Over a quarter of a century I buried my misery in tall tales of IRA heroics. I felt expiation of my sin was bound to your ordination, Danny.

"When you crossed me I sought another way. I sought for your service to Ireland in the IRA. GHQ in Dublin was willing; the lad's in Belfast weren't. They called me - Yank!

"It was a burning word, a word of indignation and revenge. My conscience was deeply wounded. I had been banished from the house of my fathers. It was an imperishable word, yet it opened my eyes. I saw my inconsistency, perfidy and venality to my own son who did for his country what I hadn't done for mine. Forgive me Danny for my words, deeds and actions. I pray for you. Your loving Dad!"

Brannagh heard a solemnic croon, a gaudete, a hosanna in the wild winds of Kumhwa despite the clashing cymbals of incoming mortar rounds. He had, at last, been freed from geneologic treason. Dad, too, in the evening of his life, Brannagh sighed, was out of the laundry pool. Dad had overcome the tyranny of his troubled repressions over leaving a land where liberty was a temporary sufferance, where faith was tantamount to work proscription, where politics and social mores were the objects of annihilation. Dad hadn't bugged out, he just got his ass out of a land where the British had exhausted the strength of the natives by unnatural contentions; successively robbing the Irish of their own leaders, their laws, their commerce and their land, their prosperity and national dignity.

The green grave of Loughguile had closed up on Dad's wounds. He had left Ireland, but he'd never forgotten it. Ireland forgot him. Dad would get better, Brannagh figured, as Dad had freed himself from his mental chains and flung them away. By the triumph of his reason, Dad had gained a victory such as no IRA active service unit could have achieved by ambush. The son shared in his Dad's recovery.

CHAPTER TWENTY THREE
DIM OUT WAR

The increasing intensity of the incoming ended cogitation of the letter's messages. Flat trajectory rounds were as plentiful as the usual mortars, and that was unusual! Brannagh whistled an alert that it was an umbrella of lead covering a Chinese infantry assault, with suppressing fire to pin him within his fighting hole. He pulled the tab of a full belt of ammo into the weapon's feedway, then its bolt fully to the rear and released, twice.

It was more than a probe. He saw a line coming up across his field of fire. These Chinese were tossing grenades ahead of them into the barbed wire to explode booby traps and trip mines that the blanket coverage of mortars might have missed. Damned if they weren't intending a break through. He whistled for a fire command.

"Fire mission," answered O'Hara. "Right to left front. Chinese extending from chopped tree right to Charley's finger right. Two Hundred. 1st gun, right one third. 2nd gun, left two thirds. Traverse. Rapid. Fire."

Brannagh's machine gun stuttered its staccato chatter into ranks of padded quilted jackets colored the mustard on hot dogs below fur caps. The gunner flinched when a mortar round hit his roof, its great burst of red vomiting chunks of sand bags and greasy black smoke. Other Chinese 82 millimeters went up with sharp cracks and orange flashes, and hurled whining steel slivers in all directions. He saw a ghostly light that illuminated the fire fight area giving Grant's riflemen targets of opportunity. Their crackling rifles were taking a toll.

O'Hara had his guns keep up their talk in controlled unison. He allowed no swiveling. Fields of fire had been laid. Target charts drawn. The Chinese must cross his furrows of death plowed by coordinated fire against a line that didn't sleep. He called for friendly fire to lob Willie Peter's white phosphorus on Chinese soldiers who had cast no shadows this November night. O'Hara exposed them to heat, and sizzling pieces ate through their quilted cotton into flesh, clinging with the burning of a cigarette fire. Close support of attackers and defenders brought down immense firepower, a deluge of destruction from the bunker line down through the barbed wire.

Brannagh heard the piercing bugle call, a rapid run of notes that was repeated three times. He saw Chinese withdrawing, yet bullets were splattering against his bunker. Some enemy had the 1st gun in his sights.

"Cease fire," ordered O'Hara.

Brannagh's bunker took a burst across its front, from the gunner's right to his left. At least two of the rounds danced on the back of the sandbags freeing their dirt to spill through puckered burlap simulating a mans leg wound. Somewhere to the gunner's right was a Chinaman with a death wish - Brannagh's! He perceived edginess, his trigger finger twitching belligerently. He studied the slope for any movement among the gnarled twisted wreckage of dead, dying and wounded enemy to his front. Brannagh's edginess stimulated his adrenalin. Some where on that dark slope was a slithering snake. He saw it move, a roundish gnome. The gunner emptied a fiery pattern of tracer bullets into him. He ceased firing.

The gun hole phone whistled.

"What's up," asked O'Hara?

"A sniper was!" Brannagh emphasized was.

"Well, cease fire."

"Right, Sarge."

"O'Hara passed the word on Chinese tactics. He called them new. Their pattern now was to attack with infantry coming in on the heels of intense artillery and mortar fire. It had worked for them. Some friendly forces had been caught inside their warming bunkers, unable to get out under the heavy incoming, back to their fighting holes. Damned if the Chinese hadn't some local successes before reserves could respond and run them off.

Brannagh said a prayerful thanks to Van Meter in heavenly Iowa for his foresight or digging sleeping holes near to the fighting holes.

*****

Blaczyk had a need to talk about the changes in section leadership. He didn't want the end of the dirty stick. He worried he had been too friendly with the outgroup.

"Miner told me," Blaczyk said, "that Dog Six has it all on paper we was getting the shaft from Breezedale for funning him"

Blaczyk's face was the color of a dirty seagull's, the gunner saw, and the morning's wind was as weary as the men who fought and pulled an all night hundred percent alert.

"Dog Six knew about everything that shit head Louie was up too," Blaczyk continued. "Six was mad at O'Hara for sitting on it - Six was even mad at himself, for taking O'Hara's guff. The CO said O'Hara was right that Busin got O'Hara's medal and commission, but not the captain's two purple hearts before VE day came, or

the one Busin took last April. Busin said he had been a
man until O'Hara came and bummed him out. Busin
took the blame for that, but not O'Hara's sitting on his
ass while the paranoid Breezedale tried to kill off an
entire section."

Blaczyk sucked air before continuing. He looked
at the important people in Trout's sleeping hole.
Besides Trout, there was Brannagh, Stag, Swinford and
Glorio there. Blaczyk saw three fabricated bunks
within, made from barbed wire poles as bedposts and
bedsides woven with commo wire for springs, covered
with c-ration cardboard, blankets and winter duck
down sleeping bags. Trout laid on his lower bunk,
Brannagh opposite. Im Ta Song had the top bunk, but
he was pulling guard, the only one of the old timers not
present. The rest of the guys sat on emptied wooden
ammo boxes warming hands above the charcoal fire.
Blaczyk jumped when the poncho at the bunker's elbow
entry popped. He was sensitive to feelings about him,
but he had no where else to go until rotation came with
its Christmas gift of 29 points. Then he and Trout
might drink to the new year of 1952 on a troop ship
home. Blaczyk wanted to belong.

"O'Hara said something about being as low as a
serpent's ass for not shooting the 3d section's satan,"
Blaczyk said. "O'Hara admitted to pushing a fist fight,
like eating meat on Friday, but not a hanging of troops
on Chinese clothes line," Blaczyk emphasized. "O'Hara,
to prove himself, offered to take a bust one stripe and
lead the third section. Done, the Captain said."

"What about Baiter," inquired Trout?

"Dog Six had him bag and baggage in Miner's
jeep with new cut orders back to the regimental motor
pool. Miner heard the CO say something to Baiter

about sticking his genitals into a hot truck muffler."

Stag rubbed some of his Joe Louis pomade from his hair onto his carbine's firing mechanism. It was a better lubricant than army graphite. It never froze during the cold nights. Then he worked his weapon's mechanism over the charcoal fire. He wasn't much pleased with the cold weather. Most every shift on night guard, he nearly staggered into shock when he freed himself from his sleeping sack into the cold. On guard he moved so his sweat didn't freeze; kept his ear flaps down to avoid frostbite; and kept dry socks next to his belly for a warm change. Best thing, he wore that vest, not against the cold, but shrapnel, since he was told it worked. He took their word for it. He wore it most every hour of a day's twenty four.

"Say Trout," Stag said, "how it feel to be a single rocker?"

Trout was pleased to be asked. He laid on his back as if to study the weaving of the commo wire in the bunk above. Yep, Trout would show he was different than Baiter.

"It's the mastery of one man over others," he said.

He caught a lot of attention. He wanted it. Until he said it most of his old timers, as line time characterized them, were off in their own imaginations wandering the streets back home somewhere in the zone of the interior.

"What you mean," Swinford asked?

It wasn't often he asked anything. Swinford was just there, not wise, nor courageous; but a pud puller who was most always tugging, forever wearing the grin of a drunken monkey.

"Well, like Abner had over others," Trout said.

"You see Abner would'a made a good sergeant. The sound of chastisement flipped his blade. Everytime he was chewed out by our teacher, Abner got it up. I can still see old lady Wilkins' eyeballs get as big as bull nuts when Abner's pole spread his overalls like the big top at the traveling circus. It got that Abner acted ornery with old Wilkins just for chastisement, but she done learned to soft talk him.

"One day when the school principal wanted old Wilkins do chores what ain't no task of a teacher, she sic Abner on him with a note Ab had done bad and needed chastisement. You can imagine the principal's surprise when he near lost an eye.

"Now that good old boy principal knewed he had a secret weapon of irresistible force when next the township trustee wanted to cut the school's budget. Yep, that's right," Trout said to his attentive troops, "Abner sat beside the principal the whole while the yelling went on. That damn principal got to worrying that Abner's muscle might have volcanoed too often to carry up the revised budget to the trustee's desk. Needn't to have worried. Abner carried it like a crow's nest atop a tall mast. I'm here to tell you," Trout continued, "there ain't no dummies back to my county. That good old trustee's nigh on as smart as Wilkins and the principal; what that he took Abner with him to the hearing before the state legislature. Now that's big time hollering, and Abner rose to it.

"That there Abner had a powerful influence on the state governor. He ain't said a mean word all the legislative session for fear of an impaling by Abner's fancy. Yep, Abner had a mastery of one man over others. Would have made a good sergeant."
*****

Grant knew that rumor, but hoped any moment Scotch Six or Lightning Six would drop the truce on them and the war would be over. Grant expected it, despite hearing intelligence tell that all indications pointed to a gook attack in the 35th regiment's zone during the coming cold front. The freeze was moving from the west to the east, with winds from the northwest at twenty-five knots per hour with gusts up to forty knots. It would freeze the river that the Chinese might walk on water. He had agreed to take a recon patrol with a drop-off squad to reconnoiter at grid 671423. He would depart the LD at 1825 hours.

"I need a M1919A6 gunner. Do you know where a good man might be found," Grant asked?

Brannagh did, and O'Hara agreed. He felt the soon to be commissioned Grant and his gunner were two of a kind. O'Hara remembered he had been as dauntless once. Maybe there would be another time?

Since Thanksgiving's sleet, the bitter cold had left icy trails in the shadows of the valley. Every landmark appeared a mutant variant of the original, so Grant marked his way with stones loosened from earth's tentacles. Everything was frozen over, increasing his frontage where Chinese might set up ambushes. Where there had been wetlands, Grant saw ice skating rinks that were penetrated by reeds and bushes. Grant knew the defender had a definite advantage in winter by disappearing under cover to wait the moment the patrol cracked ice or were silhouetted against a frosty background.

Brannagh began to realize what war in the Arctic circle would be like. The cold of November was worse than the humidity of August. Had he worn enough clothes even with the parka over his bullet proof vest?

Would his sweat freeze? If he removed his gloves, would his hand freeze to the machine gun? He had heard GIs pissed on their weapons' firing mechanisms to free them from ice, chancing the loss of more than a testicle. He used Stag's pomade instead.

"Drop off squad, here," Grant pointed.

Brannagh set up his M1919A6 to cover in the direction Grant faded. The gunner gave passing thought to his immobility, that his sweaty ski socks might freeze. He readied his weapon instead. He checked to see that the riflemen had set up their posts.

The night had absorbed the forms of Grant's third squad within its sable folds. A bitter wind haughtily stole heat from the gunner's body like an invisible burglar. Did the cold numb his mental processes? Had his mind frozen?

Grant moved cautiously up the valley floor, keeping his men close to the slope on its east side. He observed bunkers up above him. He led his skirmishers upwards, but found only unoccupied holes, some caved in. Grant moved his patrol down into the demolished village, checking huts; then crossed the frozen stream to proceed down its west side. Near Steward's hill, Grant and his men recrossed the ice, rechecking the village. Nothing was on.

Grant took the tail to cover the patrol's return to its blocking squad, when he saw Chinese far behind him to his left.

"Double time to the drop off," he said. "I'll cover."

He picked out a hole to set up. He'd wait but a minute, fire a burst, toss a grenade, then bug. He saw some Chinese beat him to the grenade. Grant fell silent. He simulated death, his blood freezing pinkish on his tattered face. He felt a hand on his limp wrist, not for his pulse, but for his watch. Some one took his watch, his gloves and his rifle, then moved away. He heard other Chinese moving up and down constantly, he hoped more for warmth then to engage his patrol. He watched as his blood coagulated on his right hand, then froze a dark brown. Cold was seeping to his toes, inching up his feet. If he didn't get out soon he would be an icicle.

The echoes of the grenades ran down the valley like so many runners in a track meet, but without Grant in the race, Brannagh heard. He peered to see into the low level of illumination to detect the scarecrow jangle of bones that carried the squad leader's cranium. It was a nerve wracking wait.

"I'm going out," said the assistant squad leader.

"No, me," commanded Brannagh. "I owe Grant. I can carry him back if he's hit."

Brannagh's pull on Pocaski's field jacket forced him to ground, as Brannagh pushed off into the dark.

He remembered how he had acted since August, as a revengeful soul that wouldn't forget the insults of Dad; as an insolent soul that had insulted a delusional Breezedale; as an angry soul that had raged at a wrathful Baiter. Brannagh confessed his obviously perilous sins had brought about deadly repercussions as if insult, insolence and anger were offended gods impersonating storms. Brannagh's crusade hadn't been testimony against atheistic communism, but rather that of Satan. What better atonement than to risk his life for Grant's.

Brannagh entered winter's tunnel, treading the frost bound soil northwardly. Hard packed stones cut like glass into his shoe pacs. The absence of trees as windbreaks freed the breeze's teeth. Charred hulks of trees he saw reminded him there had been life and warmth once, before artillery and the cold came so suddenly. Explosions had also loosened, but not pulverized, great chunks of solidly frozen earth. The winter freeze up had even turned the streams of water into routes of approach. Somewhere in night's deep gloom ahead Brannagh's frozen trance searched for Grant.

As thick as pebbles on a beach, Brannagh viewed a flying cloud of Chinese swaying as they trotted toward him. He slipped into a crater, snuggling beside dark boulders. As the murmuring unit passed, their draft was as cold as a sullen blast of the wintry wind. Were they after Pocaski's patrol? He corrected the question by inserting Grant's name for Pocaski's.

At the tail of the night winging Chinese column, he crept forward as hushed as if he were nature's snail probing for a Chinese drop-off squad. He saw something forward cowering in a dim spectral hole. With the soul of a mourner, Brannagh crept toward the figure, bayonet at the ready to divide sinew from bone. Yet, cautiously he pushed up to silently envelope the prostrate form, covering its mouth to prevent an outcry. The cold figure was still, without motion, like the pile of rocks that long ago had rolled down from the mountain. It was Grant. His lips seemed unmoved, as if frozen together, yet a ghostly mist slipped from his nostrils. Brannagh placed his gloves on Grant's clawish fingers, too long exposed to the elements. A feel of the sergeant's fatigues revealed to Brannagh that Grant's sweat had stiffened in his clothes under the night cold. Frostbite was as likely a grim reaper as were Grant's untreated wounds. The gunner lifted Grant as if he were a tripod, and draped the numbed body like a scarf around the neck. Brannagh moved the same direction as had the Chinese unit, confident of an absence of land mines, or on the other hand, that the ground encasing the mines had frozen above them as hard as steel. Wherever the enemy had gone, Brannagh heard nor saw any signs of their return. He hoped they were running their patrol to the west, that he might get Grant back to the drop off point toward the east. Brannagh strode forward into the silent night angling northeast-east.

Sharp blasts rang out on his front right. Bullets pupped, pupped, cracking angrily. Pocaski had found the Chinese, or the enemy Pocaski, Brannagh concluded. He heard only small arms, no mortars or artillery, which must mean Pocaski wasn't calling in supporting fire, to keep open the chance of returning. Brannagh kept his movement going towards the left flank, away from the fire fight. He reasoned the twelve men with Pocaski, without artillery or mortar cover, couldn't long hold off a platoon of Chinese. Brannagh figured his and Grant's survival was to the east, then north to the drop off before Pocaski was forced to pull back. For the moment the volume of fire from Pocaski's patrol was as heavy as a Miami thunderstorm's rain. It danced madly up toward the Chinese, who were answering with concussion grenades sounding to the gunner as second bass voices.

Brannagh worried his own numbing agony from slipping on icey rocks, the pain in his knees from falling on them, would so slow him down that he'd not reach the drop off before Pocaski pulled out. Brannagh sensed he was alone in Korea, his fingers unfeeling, his nose a white glob with big snouts, his sweat but an invitation to the terrific cold to use the moisture to congeal his clothes to his flesh.

He saw an uncanny radiance above him. He felt privy to a vision of the archangel Michael, until the flare's hiss registered on his mind. He knew it was a warning. Artillery would follow. Pocaski's patrol was pulling back, so too might be the little dwarfs in padded cotton uniforms. Brannagh hustled towards black rocks to wedge himself and Grant between bolders. The hills in front appeared to be gemmed, those behind covered with bed sheets. Brannagh laid as inertly as did the bolders and Grant in the gloom. The gunner listened. He heard the icy whistle of incoming despite the ear flaps of his cap. Four sixty millimeter mortar rounds hissed, then exploded with sharp cracks; followed by four soft shuffling wooshes of 81 millimeter mortar rounds that crunched the frigid ground to icicle shrapnel.

Brannagh saw coffee brown Chinese rise from their firing slots, then disappear west behind a fold of ground. Were they pulling out? What happened to the mortar fire? Why wasn't there artillery? Brannagh felt confused. He wondered if his own mind was frozen. His nerves were shot, he figured. He expected hell to rage around him, but it wasn't. What did it signify? He visualized the thoughts in his mind were dog sleds, one of which was being mushed by Van Meter who was pointing to the south side of the ice berg in Brannagh's intellect. It came to him! Pocaski was still at the drop off, waiting. He had fired mortars to fake the Chinese out. He would hold fire but a while more, before his hurt heart let loose the high pitched chug a lug up overhead with wooshing vacuums and thunderous bursting crashes.

Brannagh put Grant back on his shoulders asking his pardon that his bearer might be the first to die, if he couldn't get him back to his patrol.
*****

Grant refocused his eyes to rid them from a desolate scene: he was floating on an iceberg in the Artic ocean trying to light a charcoal fire in an ammo cannister to warm up a canteen of coffee. His orientation revealed an olive drab tent full of cots on which lay prone troops under blankets and sleeping bags. He was sitting on a cot. He felt a parka that was draped across his shoulders. He sensed a radiant heat coming from a wood fire stove in the middle of the tent, but his gauzed hands that held his canteen cup didn't sense any warmth in the metal despite the steam wafting from the hot coffee. He noticed the pressure bandage on his left shoulder, and felt the tugging at his right calf. He saw Doc Sugrue changing a bandage.

"Pocaski came and got me," asked Grant?

"Brannagh, it was," Sugrue told him.
*****

Trout read aloud the order from Scotch Six:

"Counterattacks to regain key terrain lost to enemy assault will be the only offensive action taken unless otherwise directed by this headquarters. Every effort will be made to prevent unnecessary casualties."
*****

"Havee true?"

"Seems so," Trout answered. "Last year it was MacArthur what said there weren't Chinese in Korea and our troops would be back home by Christmas. Still we got them Chinese by the balls now, so it seems so."

Trout stabbed a finger at his adam's apple to push it out of his throat. He did't want to choke up over

a truce. He sought out the blue, wintry eyes of
Brannagh.

"You're always thinking, Gunner," Trout said.
"What you think?"

Brannagh's eyes turned away. He looked afar at
the saw toothed rocks of hill 440 which ran the east
horizon like a devil's barricade. He saw gaunt hills of
bloody stones. Above the masses of stone, he saw
disturbed and ragged clouds that tore across a feeble
sun and held an illusion of strength and a secret of
terror. He saw a fortress with a forbidding demeanor.
He saw a habitation for the dead.

Brannagh felt as if he were mortally cold. He
shivered. He heard the scraggy black branches that
rattled in the wind. He sighed, and cleared his throat.
Turning his eyes, Brannagh caught a wary gaze in Im
Ta Song's deeply set sight pits; in Trout's purple brown
eyes were reflected the follies of this unsure military
world.

"My thoughts," the gunner replied, "are in this
Christmas song:

Kumhwa night, lonely night; Naught is calm, set
gun sight.

Round yon table in Panmunjon; men would not
war abandon.

Sleep in the truce's spell, not when the Chinese
shell."

Sleep under commies' dire, fight when their
infantry fire."